PRAISE FOR *TH*

"A beautifully written historical r̶ Joy Callaway has impeccably researched the life of Dorothy Draper from her days as 'Greenbrier' debutante to her return as the hotel's decorator. Five Stars!"

—CARLETON VARNEY, PRESIDENT OF DOROTHY DRAPER
& COMPANY, INC., FOR *THE GRAND DESIGN*

"A backstage peek into the life of one of America's most famed designers—and most glittering hotels—*The Grand Design* is a spellbinding tale of a woman's quest to escape the confines of upper crust society and make her own way in the world. Joy Callaway effortlessly captures the essence of Dorothy Draper, a woman who was determined to live life on her own terms—and changed the field of interior design forever in the process. With vivid characters, illuminating prose, and perfect pacing, this novel is as captivating and confident as the heroine at its center. Callaway shines as a master storyteller."

—KRISTY WOODSON HARVEY, *NEW YORK TIMES*
BESTSELLING AUTHOR OF *THE WEDDING VEIL*

"Joy Callaway's *The Grand Design* is a sumptuous look at the complicated life of famous interior designer Dorothy Draper. A woman before her time, Dorothy finds herself unable to lead a life that fits into society's narrow expectations. Callaway masterfully brings this complex and fascinating character to life, while doing equal justice to the remarkable setting: the world-famous Greenbrier resort. A compelling read, not to be missed!"

—AIMIE K. RUNYAN, BESTSELLING AUTHOR OF
THE SCHOOL FOR GERMAN BRIDES

"Full of luscious details of fashion and luxury, *The Grand Design* also explores the tension between duty and longing. This book will transport you!"

—KELLY O'CONNOR MCNEES, AUTHOR OF *THE LOST SUMMER OF LOUISA MAY ALCOTT* AND *UNDISCOVERED COUNTRY*

"I absolutely loved *The Grand Design*. Callaway expertly brings the famous setting to life. I could feel the fabrics and smell the wood polish as I was reading. Her portrayal of designer Dorothy Draper is fascinating and intriguing and offers a genuine lens into a segment of society rich with intrigue, nuance and plenty of drama. This is historical fiction at its finest."

—ELYSSA FRIEDLAND, AUTHOR OF *LAST SUMMER AT THE GOLDEN HOTEL*

"Rich in historic detail with exquisite atmospheric elements, Callaway creates a dazzling, intimate portrait of a woman navigating the parties, politics, and power dynamics of society's smart set—who dared to dream for a life beyond the traditional expectations imposed upon her."

—LOUISE CLAIRE JOHNSON, AUTHOR OF *BEHIND THE RED DOOR*

"Meticulously researched and passionately imagined, this tale of genius decorator Dorothy Draper and her most storied design has it all: high society, hot desire, grit, glamour, star-crossed love and political intrigue. *The Grand Design* will make you want to pack your bags and go!"

—JULIA CLAIBORNE JOHNSON, AUTHOR OF *BETTER LUCK NEXT TIME* AND *BE FRANK WITH ME*

"*The Grand Design* by Joy Callaway is the best sort of historical fiction— it's a novel that truly takes you to another time and place, grounding you completely in the world of Dorothy Draper. Immersive and lush, Callaway imagines the life of Dorothy Draper at two crucial times in

"There is something so intimate and personal about Callaway's love for her eponymous Greenbrier resort that when met with her competent blend of research and well-crafted fictional speculation will delight aficionados of Marie Benedict and Allison Pataki. Callaway fashions her prose with the same flourish, span and vision as Draper foresaw a revolution of interior artistry. A consummate wordsmith, Callaway's fictional love letter is not only written for a woman who defied the structure of her gender and time period, but also to a place that incites as much magic in the reader as it clearly does its author. *The Grand Design* made me homesick for a place I have never been."

—RACHEL MCMILLAN, AUTHOR OF *THE LONDON RESTORATION* AND *THE MOZART CODE* her life, and readers will love exploring the famed Greenbrier resort, whose name is inextricably tied to Dorothy Draper, as much as they love learning about the woman herself."

—BRENDA JANOWITZ, AUTHOR OF *THE LIZ TAYLOR RING*

"Joy Callaway gracefully transports readers to the early glamour of the landmark Greenbrier resort, introducing the brash, young Dorothy Draper, ill-suited for the bleak confines of high society. The story follows her into the future as a renowned decorator, hired to restore the hotel. As she leaves her infamous mark, both The Greenbrier and Dorothy boldly come to life, filling the page with color and reflections on heartbreak and passion. Clandestine undertakings and encounters with historical figures who've frequented the resort are delightful surprises, crafted and researched meticulously. But it is Dorothy herself, and a timeless love story that ultimately deliver an ending that will leave readers eager to visit The Greenbrier for themselves, feeling they've stepped from dreary Kansas into Oz."

—KIMBERLY BROCK, AUTHOR OF *THE LOST BOOK OF ELEANOR DARE*

"Sparkling and atmospheric, Joy Callaway's *The Grand Design* brings the world and heart of legendary decorator Dorothy Draper to luminous life. Richly-detailed and deeply-romantic, the novel is a poignant portrait of a fascinating and fiercely independent woman at the crossroads of her career who revisits two great romances from her past to find her way forward: one, an Italian racecar driver—the other, a once-grand resort that stole her heart with equal intensity in the fraught days of her youth. A master of building immersive settings and compelling characters, Joy Callaway has done more than merely open the door to the glamorous world of The Greenbrier and its expansive history and famous guests—she has welcomed readers deep within its walls where they will quickly make themselves at home and—like Dorothy herself—wish to linger under its spell, long after the last page."

—ERIKA MONTGOMERY, AUTHOR OF *A SUMMER TO REMEMBER*

The
GRAND
DESIGN

ALSO BY JOY CALLAWAY

The Fifth Avenue Artists Society
Secret Sisters

The
GRAND
DESIGN

A Novel of Dorothy Draper

JOY CALLAWAY

HARPER MUSE

The Grand Design

Copyright © 2022 Joy Callaway

Published by Harper Muse, an imprint of HarperCollins Focus LLC.

Library of Congress Cataloging-in-Publication Data

Names: Callaway, Joy, author.
Title: The Grand Design : a novel of Dorothy Draper / Joy Callaway.
Description: [Nashville] : Harper Muse, [2022] | Summary: "The Grand Design, set at The Greenbrier in White Sulphur Springs, West Virginia, in both 1908 and 1946, tells the story famed interior designer Dorothy Draper and how the historic retreat and the love she found there as a young woman influenced her bold shift from illustrious New York socialite to world-renowned decorator"-- Provided by publisher.
Identifiers: LCCN 2021054589 (print) | LCCN 2021054590 (ebook) | ISBN 9781400234370 (paperback) | ISBN 9781400234387 (epub) | ISBN 9781400234394
Subjects: LCSH: Draper, Dorothy, 1889-1969 Fiction. | Greenbrier (White Sulphur Springs, W. Va.)--Fiction. | Resorts--West Virginia--White Sulphur Springs--Fiction. | LCGFT: Biographical fiction. | Novels.
Classification: LCC PS3603.A4455 G74 2022 (print) | LCC PS3603.A4455 (ebook) | DDC 813/.6--dc23/eng/20211119
LC record available at https://lccn.loc.gov/2021054589
LC ebook record available at https://lccn.loc.gov/2021054590

Printed in the United States of America

22 23 24 25 26 LSC 5 4 3 2 1

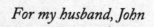

For my husband, John

"You don't sell a commodity.
You sell joy, gaiety, excitement.
You aim at people's hearts,
not their minds."

—DOROTHY DRAPER

One

I'd been lured to the dining room as prey. I eyed the roast chicken in front of me and had pity on the poor fowl whose end was drizzled in sage butter and decorated with dainty carrots and pearl onions. I, too, was draped in finery for my final presentation—a Charles Worth ensemble of yellow-green silk with metallic gold floral brocade and beaded tassels at the back to accentuate my sleek figure. *Sleek* was the polite way of saying much too tall and imposing, but no one—especially our seamstress—dared say so to a Tuckerman.

I wasn't the only one being prepared for a swift devouring. The dining room was filled with silk and chiffon served atop a platter of tradition and romance. I eyed one of the stately Corinthian pillars behind me and followed the rows of them down the length of the enormous dining hall, imagining how many women they'd seen sacrificed in their shadows. There were more than a thousand people here for the Greenbrier's Centennial Celebration, and the room was bustling with waiters and Vanderbilts and Du Ponts and Beckleys and Stevenses and Hendersons and Alexanders and Julliards and Kanes, and likely a few European ministers thrown in for variety, though even their presence wouldn't stop the incestuous matchmaking ritual that had been established among these proper families.

"They've arrived, Dorothy," Anzonella muttered, tapping my leg with hers. I didn't want to look up but did so reflexively as Warren Abercrombie III and his father glided into the room behind the kindly looking maître d' who, judging by his cheery smile, had no idea he was leading a wolf and his reluctant son to a table full of sheep. I wished that our au pair, Mademoiselle, had been swifter with my hair, that we'd been able to come down for dinner earlier so our table would be occupied by now. We always arrived late, however, and though it was almost a guarantee that the Kane girls would be even more delayed than we—there were five of them, after all—we were nearly always left with four or five unoccupied seats.

"Star, please keep an open mind this season," Father whispered across the circular table, not much caring that the Kanes, our neighbors back home in Tuxedo Park, New York, were hearing every word.

"I will not," I said. "And you know why, Father. He's one of my dearest friends, practically like a brother. Not to mention nearly four inches shorter than I."

Mother's swan-like neck turned just slightly, her eyes daring me to say another word. I could feel everyone's attention on me as Warren approached, as though I would suddenly begin to swoon after five seasons of our fathers' attempted pairing. Each year our families hoped we would see each other anew and fall in love, that we'd see how perfectly matched we were, how safe we would be in each other's arms. It wasn't that he was boring or irritating or ugly or poor. In fact, he was quite charming and handsome, a true gentleman, but I couldn't consider him despite the joy it would grant our parents. My heart would never be his, and standing next to him made me feel Amazonian, not to mention he wouldn't free me. Women in our set weren't actually married; we were commodities merged and traded, pawns exchanged for a European title or a monopoly of the railroads. Marrying a man in this circle would trap me in a penitentiary masquerading as something else: the Tuxedo Park village or a Fifth Avenue mansion or a Southern estate. I'd already been ensnared by the former two my whole life. Every time I thought of it, I wanted to walk into the woods that surrounded the Greenbrier and never come back. Unlike at home or in the city, I was barely chaperoned here and there weren't any gates, only the unoccupied wild of the Allegheny Mountains and whatever adventures were to be found beyond. I could find another town. I could become someone else, someone lauded for living in the color and eccentricity that defied dreary societal expectations. I'd always thought, deep inside, that I was intended for more than the life of an heiress wife. What that life was, I didn't quite know. I was hardly allowed to breathe without being instructed on its proper execution, let alone dream. Of course, running away was only a fantasy. The reality was that I would never do it, despite craving liberty. The prospect of starvation or murder was slightly worse than imprisonment.

Rose, the youngest of the Kanes, was the only one still watching Warren. Her already rosy cheeks deepened to a blush as she realized the maître d' was planning to seat the young Mr.

Abercrombie directly across from her and next to me. I wished I'd been situated between my father and my brother, Roger, but I had a feeling our circumstances were prearranged. It hadn't always been like this. As a child I'd felt free and thought my parents wanted me to feel that way always. They'd never minded that I tore my dresses playing and didn't give a fig for equestrian sport and had an imagination that made formal schooling nearly impossible. All of that changed when I was presented. Suddenly, there were rules and expectations and approved men. I knew they thought it their duty to find me a secure match, a guarantee that I would remain settled where I'd always been. Perhaps they supposed I could somehow find happiness despite it all as they had. But surely they knew their love was an anomaly, a happy coincidence that united the iron fortune of the Tuckermans with the shipping fortune of the Minturns.

"Miss Tuckerman." Warren's voice was almost a sigh, and I met his gaze as he appeared over my shoulder. He looked handsome for a man whose breeding had only awarded him an unfortunate five feet five inches, his dinner suit impeccably tailored just like every other man's in the room. His blond hair had been trimmed short and he'd grown a mustache since I'd last seen him.

"Good evening, Warren. It's lovely to see you again," I said, smiling for the both of us. It wasn't his fault that our parents couldn't concede our lack of romance. He didn't favor me either. He took his seat and turned his attention to my parents and our neighbors.

The elder Mr. Abercrombie peered around his son. "Hello, Miss Dorothy."

Father caught my eye and scowled as though I was intending

to ignore the greeting. Mr. Abercrombie—always "Ren" to Father—had been his childhood best friend. They'd lived next door to each other for a few years in Manhattan before Mr. Abercrombie's father, a railroad man, moved them to South Carolina following the Civil War, chasing an opportunity to reconstruct the battered Southern tracks.

"Mrs. Abercrombie is quite reluctant to miss the occasion to see you and sends her love," he continued.

"I'm sorry to miss her as well," I said politely.

Warren said under his breath, "She was going to attend but thought she'd simply stay home and wait for me to return with you as my bride." A waiter deposited his plate in front of him. I laughed, and the corners of his mouth twitched up in a smile.

"Did you bring an ample amount of ether with which to drug your intended?" I asked.

"Of course not!" He turned to me, feigning horror. "Chloroform is rumored to be much more suitable."

"I appreciate the consideration," I said. "On a more serious note, Warren, what are we to do about our fathers? I know you're just as keen to swear your life to me as I am to you."

He shrugged. "Wait until they give up?"

"That could be years," I whispered. "Five more at least. They're not quite desperate enough. Promise yours won't wear you down."

Warren grinned. "Let's grasp a spirit of optimism, shall we? This season will be the last," he said. "You forget that I'm older than you by two years. I'm nearly twenty-one, and my parents married at twenty-two. I have a feeling they'll soon think time is running out and cut us loose."

"I'll be happy to hope," I said.

I cut into my chicken and turned my attention to the bustle of the room. Charley and Ellen Bonaparte were at the table beside us, their hands clasped under the table. It was well-known that they'd met at the Greenbrier, the proposal offered on the edge of the Lovers' Leap trail surrounded by blooming rhododendrons. I hoped for such love. I wanted the passion I'd only read about in novels. I wanted to believe it could happen to me, but then I remembered the sharp sting of rejection, the way my two flirtations had ended—one lost to a girl six inches shorter, the other lost to the discovery that the man was a fortune hunter. Love could still ensnare. Freedom was my higher aspiration. But if both came calling, I'd welcome them with open arms.

I shifted my attention back to the table in time to hear Rose ask Warren about his family's summer travels. The Abercrombies always traveled far into the fall, the mosquitos in Sumter too thick to bear. In contrast, we would make this our last stop before home. We'd been to Europe in early May through June, followed by Newport in July, and now the Greenbrier. The Kanes had just joined. Being quite loyal to Tuxedo Park, they departed for a sojourn to the Greenbrier only because it was nearly required. Since what seemed like the beginning of time, if a family was absent from the Greenbrier, they were absent from society—and it was especially important to be seen on an occasion such as the Centennial, particularly when one's daughters were out and looking for suitable prospects.

Anzonella tipped her head at one of the Du Pont cousins at a table across from ours. "Do you suppose I should stand him up for our lovers' walk or embrace the pairing for the month and then feign a change of heart when I return home?" she asked, then took a bite of a carrot. I was about to ask her when he'd proposed the idea when the maître d' interrupted our dinner once again, this time bowing low between my father and Mr. Kane.

"Former Italian finance minister Mr. Pietro Vacchelli is just in on the late arrival at the station. I wondered if it would be much of an imposition to seat him and his nephew here?" Both men grunted in agreement as they always did when something was in fact an imposition. Gentlemen wouldn't dare concede that they were put off by the intrusion of an outsider.

"Very well. I thank you," he said and was gone at once.

"An Italian minister? Here? It will be a bit awkward, will it not?" Warren asked. "There's been quite a bit of talk about Italy possibly breaking from the Triple Alliance because of its strained relations with Austria-Hungary. Now that the Entente Cordiale has been formed, perhaps the country is courting allegiance elsewhere? Of course, if there were ever to be a European conflict, our great nation would side with the Entente Cordiale, so—" He looked around at the older men, whose silence said volumes. Political discussion was appropriate only when discussing pleasant things. Ill words were best forfeited to silence. I had no idea what he was talking about anyway.

"He's a *former* minister," Mother said, leaping into the conversation without thought. She had always been this way—riding her horse astride, wearing elaborate jeweled costumes when the occasion called for drab, speaking her mind when most did not. One would assume that Mother was an unconventional woman altogether, but Father's sensibilities still held her mostly to tradition. "I doubt he's come to the Greenbrier to discuss Italian-American relations."

"Or has he?" Edith interjected from her position next to Mother. She was the oldest Kane and always interested in some sort of dramatic happenings. "Suppose he's come to the Greenbrier to win us to their side? Won't Mr. Taft be here this season?"

She stopped talking and stared over my head, letting the chatter and the faraway sounds of Chopin's Piano Concerto no. 1 drift over us. Though it wasn't polite to turn away from the table, I did anyway and immediately understood the reason for her silence.

"Good evening, all. I am Pietro Vacchelli." The minister, a bulky man with sparse white hair and a full beard, shook hands with the men while his nephew, who unceremoniously folded himself into the seat beside Warren, captured the attention of the ladies. It could hardly be helped. His face was chiseled, his eyes were crystal blue, and though his ebony hair was much too long for the fashion of the season and his mustache was barely a shadow, the overall effect was a rugged sort of look.

"Thank you for accommodating us in the middle of your dinner," the minister's nephew said to Warren. His accent was thick, but his command of English was clear.

"Of course, sir," Warren said. "I'm Warren Abercrombie. And your name?"

"Oh!" The minister exclaimed, nearly toppling his water glass. "This is my . . . my . . ."

"I'm Fiorenzo Rossi, Enzo, Mr. Vacchelli's nephew," he said. His uncle seemed relieved at his interjection. Edith, sitting all the way across the table, quickly introduced herself, and as we went around the table making introductions, it seemed that Mr. Rossi was barely taking note.

"Are you enjoying America, Minister?" my father asked Mr. Vacchelli as he buttered a roll. Father's eyes met mine and I knew what he was thinking. It wouldn't do to have my attention shift from Warren to anyone else, especially an unknown entity, an Italian of possible paltry breeding. I nearly laughed at his concern, though the idea of running away to Italy did have its appeal. But Anzonella was one of the most sought-after women in New York. She'd received the best of her parents—her mother's high forehead and blue eyes, her father's fair complexion. If she couldn't command Mr. Rossi's attention, one of her remarkably pretty sisters would. All four of them had their eye on the mysterious Mr. Rossi.

Mr. Rossi leaned over to Mr. Vacchelli and said something in Italian. I couldn't understand any of it, and that irritated me. Mademoiselle had made sure that I was fluent in French but had given the other languages little to no mind. Perhaps it was my fault. I'd refused to spend more than two years studying at Brearley. I hated the way my classmates mastered the courses with ease while I'd struggled. Then again, I wasn't one to learn through books. I thrived in creativity, in thought, instead, and Mademoiselle, unlike my instructors at Brearley, had always understood that. Instead of giving me a set of facts to memorize, she'd asked questions and encouraged me to consider, to ponder an answer until I came upon the correct one.

Mr. Vacchelli replied to Mr. Rossi and he barely smiled, punctuating one dimple in his left cheek.

"I apologize, Mr. Tuckerman. Yes, I'm enjoying America very much, although we have only been here a week and have spent it all on a train. It's Enzo's fault, if I'm being honest," Mr. Vacchelli said with a grin.

"Yes, I suppose that's right," Mr. Rossi said. "If I hadn't taken to the very vulgar profession of auto racing—which, I must point out, was Uncle's doing, as he introduced me to the sport through his friend Pierre de Caters—we'd have been here a month ago. However, I would have missed my last race. It was quite a rush."

I imagined it was. I couldn't fathom how wonderful it must feel not only to drive an auto at such a tremendous speed, but to have the independence to engage in such a glamorous yet improper profession.

"Did you win?" Father asked, though his tone professed he didn't much care.

"I'm afraid not. It was my first time driving for Lancia and I found the engine lacking, if I'm honest," he said.

This interested me. "A Lancia, you say? My uncle just had one imported," I said. I'd thought the purchase quite an extravagance. He already had two Benzes—one of which I'd almost crashed taking a turn around his circular drive. Mr. Rossi didn't seem to hear me, instead gesturing for his uncle to pass the bread plate.

"I was there when the autos set out from Times Square in February," Rose sputtered. "It was so exciting." Mr. Kane's eyebrows rose. His youngest daughter's presence at the start of the New York to Paris round-the-world race was clearly news to him.

"I'm sure it was. Auto racing is a thrill in every sense," Mr. Rossi said. "It must have been especially exciting for the Italian driver, Antonio Scarfoglio, who had never driven an auto before." I wanted to comment that he seemed jealous he hadn't been chosen. "I specialize in shorter, faster distances. I often drive for Fiat. I must say that the autos driven during that race weren't necessarily the finest. Zust is clearly satisfactory, but I prefer the smoothness of Fiat."

Mr. Vacchelli coughed. "No one else is quite as passionate about the sport, Nephew," he said.

Warren said, "Perhaps, but it's still rather interesting. The world race was on the front page of all the papers here for months. It made me want to take up the sport myself."

I nearly laughed. I doubted he'd ever done anything remotely dangerous in his life.

Mr. Abercrombie cleared his throat. "I'm afraid you don't have the time," he said. "What with your studies and brokering land for the rail and helping your mother keep up our little cottage and grounds."

The Abercrombies' little cottage was a sprawling thirty-bedroom Federal-style estate designed by Richard Morris Hunt.

"What are your aspirations when you're not racing?" Mr. Abercrombie asked. "What sort of business do you involve yourself in?" The questions irritated me, as they were clear attempts to dilute Mr. Rossi's worth.

"I believe he said he's a professional," I said. "I would assume most of his time is spent perfecting his form." The statement bordered rude, but nothing irked me more than when our kind rubbed our high breeding in the faces of normal folk.

"Actually, I hope to be a businessman someday when I'm through with racing," Mr. Rossi said. "I've studied extensively in Rome."

"He's very proficient with languages," Mr. Vacchelli said. "French, German, English, and Portuguese so far."

Mr. Rossi busied himself with cutting a slice of tomato.

"I'm sure that comes in handy on the race circuit," Father said.

"It does," Mr. Rossi said. "I've been fortunate to meet some interesting men."

"And any young women?" Anzonella asked. "I like speed.

Perhaps I will take up racing too." Mr. Rossi glanced at her as if she'd misspoken but didn't bother to ask if she was earnest. She was.

Mr. Kane asked, "Did you arrive in New York City, Mr. Rossi, Mr. Vacchelli? It's quite a place, and at times I dearly miss having a home there, though not enough to leave the heaven of our Tuxedo Park for months at a time. Tuxedo is only forty miles northeast of Manhattan besides. Close enough to pop down to the city and back in a day." He would expunge any talk of auto racing from the conversation before his daughters fainted from swooning.

The truth was that Mr. Kane found city life completely unnecessary and a home away an added expense. On the other hand, my father adored our city house on East Sixty-Ninth. My grandfather had been a city man through and through, an industrialist of the highest rank, and my father's fondest memories were at his house on Madison Avenue.

"We came in at New York but didn't spend much time there," Mr. Rossi replied. "We live in Rome, and New York seemed a bit similar with the noise and crowded streets. Our destination was here. There was much talk about the Greenbrier from a friend of my uncle's back in Italy. On several occasions he urged us to visit and claimed that it was the most spectacular place in all the country—that the mountain views and blooming wildflowers served as the perfect backdrop to a resort of extraordinary elegance and glamour. Uncle decided when he retired, we must go."

I took a sip of my wine and turned to Anzonella, who was staring, enthralled, as Mr. Rossi cut a small bite of chicken.

"It is magnificent indeed," Warren said. "Nowhere in America will you find such lovely landscape, such lovely company, or such lovely women." He lowered his voice at the last statement and Mr. Rossi laughed under his breath.

"I am impressed," he said. "I've never seen anything so large seem so intimate . . . if that makes any sense?" I knew exactly what he meant. As beautiful as it was, the Greenbrier could seem positively stifling at times. All the families of families who had been seated here a century ago knew every rumor and embarrassment and joy of everyone else's heritage.

"Intimacy can hardly be helped regardless of space," I said. "We're the country's oldest families and probably all related in some way or another, so I imagine walking in here feels eerily like disrupting a private wedding. To tell you the truth, I wish it wasn't that way."

"I always hope for a bit of fresh air," Warren said, grinning. "It would be good for my prospects. I don't suppose you've brought along any sisters or cousins?"

Father wouldn't stand for our bemoaning tradition. "This resort was built before our country's Civil War. There are finer structures across our great nation, that is certain, but I doubt another resort has seen the history this one has. Do you know, Mr. Rossi, that the two opposing generals, Grant and Lee, vacationed here after the war? And this dining room itself held the wounded of both sides at points during the conflict."

"I can sense it," Mr. Rossi said candidly. "There's enough chatter about it overseas that the importance of the Greenbrier is clear."

Satisfied with his diversion, Father simply tipped his head and went back to his conversation with Mr. Kane. I loathed occasions like this, when our fathers felt threatened by those lacking an early American pedigree. It was embarrassing.

"Don't mind him," I said, low enough that Father couldn't hear me. "And there's no need to pretend that you're awed by our country's history when Italians boast nearly three thousand years."

"It's of no matter. I enjoy hearing about it," Mr. Rossi said. "Those plants in the urns, what are they?" He gestured to the blooming pink and purple flowers around the room.

"Mountain rhododendron, I suppose," Warren replied. "Is that right, Miss Tuckerman?" He glanced at me.

"Yes," I said. "Thank goodness they didn't settle for palms in a room this drab. It's much too reminiscent of a clubhouse . . . or perhaps a funeral parlor."

I'd always disliked the way our parents' generation decorated. Rich leathers and mahogany dressers and ferns and plaster pillars and frowning statues were all so unfriendly and cold. I suppose that's how we all were, really—stiff and beautiful.

Mr. Rossi laughed. "Your dead must enjoy quite beautiful surroundings," he said. "What would make this room more enjoyable for you, Miss Tuckerman? Would you prefer the walls done in pink?"

I stared at him, feeling my cheeks flush. The proper thing to do would have been to ignore him. To pick up my fork and take a bite of my now-cold chicken and strike up a conversation with Warren or Anzonella. Then I noticed the corners of his lips starting to twitch into a smile. Humor like this, like mine, was all but absent in proper society. It either went completely unnoticed or was passed off by most as brash or rude. Sparring with him was a challenge I couldn't refuse—despite knowing how much I'd horrify Father.

"Yes. I would," I said truthfully. I'd envisioned the room

differently more times than I could count. "Or kelly green or robin's-egg blue or coral, with the ceiling matching. The pillars could remain white. They'd disappear that way. And I'd line the windows with chintz, the print as large and bold as I could find." I was speaking dramatically on purpose, but I wasn't lying. I'd watched Mother decorate our homes—home after Tuxedo Park home—and I knew what I liked. Color made Mother feel alive, and it made me feel happy too.

"The owner of this lovely resort—the C&O Railroad, is it?—is truly blessed in the fact that you're a debutante and not the man charged with outfitting this magnificent room," he said. The table quieted toward the end of his sentence, and then Father let out a mighty laugh.

"Star has always had an eye for the dramatic," he said. "She's won it fairly—her mother is fond of outfitting our homes uniquely."

I wished he'd stop calling me Star. It sounded narcissistic to outsiders, as if Father was hoping I'd become famous, a possibility that was positively horrifying to any proper Tuxedo Parkian. Fame didn't sound quite so terrible to me. If I was ever to scandalize society by gracing the papers and the lips of people worldwide, I'd be confident, but certainly not vain. And I'd definitely not be called Star.

"And our homes are always lovely," Mother said. "I use what I have. Grandfather's antiques and Mr. Tuckerman's crystal decanters and color, yes, when it's appropriate." Though Mother was known for pushing the envelope with her costumes, her decorating styles were always classic with a touch of daring. She enjoyed rattling our Tuxedo Park traditions but didn't desire to break free from them as I did. I'd insisted my room at home be papered in wide royal blue and white stripes with curtains of the same trimmed in lemon-yellow fringe. Mother had only agreed because my quarters were out of guests' sight.

Mrs. Kane said, "Your homes are always breathtaking, Susan. The envy of our little neighborhood."

"They are," Father said, "but you should see Star's room. I have no doubt if she were the owner of this grand place, it would be decorated in such a manner that the naked eye could hardly stand it. The old fellows would go running back to Newport and Jekyll as quick as the trains would run."

I dabbed my napkin to my lips, blotting a drop of wine. "Who's to say that wouldn't be precisely my plan?" I asked. "If you can't abide cheer, you don't belong here." I winked at Father, pretending I didn't feel Mr. Rossi's eyes on my face. Most people likely thought me silly and ignorant when I spoke this way—perhaps Mr. Rossi did as well. But then again, he was an automobile driver, not an heir to some vast fortune, required to dissolve into expectation. There was a chance he didn't care at all for formal intellectual discourse and furnishings and wealth.

"I'd trust you with my home, Dorothy," Anzonella said. Predictably, she supported me regardless of my harebrained spoutings, and I loved her immeasurably for it.

"I pray your husband has the fortune of glass eyes, Miss Kane, in order to behold Miss Tuckerman's creation," Mr. Rossi said. His face didn't suggest humor in the slightest. Only the sparkle in his eyes gave away his wit. The whole table quieted—the society equivalent of a scolding for unsatisfactory behavior—but he didn't seem to notice. Perhaps he didn't care. I hoped that was the case.

The waiter took my plate and deposited a steaming bowl of

bread pudding in front of me as I placed the white linen napkin back on my lap and looked at Mr. Rossi around a stunned Warren.

"And I pray your future wife has glass eyes *and* sealed ears, in order to behold you, Mr. Rossi. In fact," I said, turning toward the entrance to the dining room, "if you'll just depart out that door and down the lawn, you'll find your perfect match atop the springhouse. She's rather lovely and immensely fond of old dullness since she's gray and unfeeling herself. I do hope you'll be happy together. Her name is Hebe."

I took a dainty sip of wine and heard Mother sigh. Warren cleared his throat. Clearly this exchange was making everyone uncomfortable. I loved it.

"Hebe you say?" Mr. Rossi asked, tipping his spoon unbecomingly my direction. He was visibly trying not to smile now. I could see the edges of his lips lifting and felt laughter bubble in my throat. "I suppose if Heracles won't mind sharing, I'd be agreeable. I'd look the picture of youth forever. Just please . . . please don't tell her about your ambitions with the resort, or else I'm certain my intended will go tumbling from her perch and shatter from the horror of it."

"This dessert is divine," Mother started.

Mr. Abercrombie spoke at the same time. "We've just returned from Athens and have had the opportunity to see many depictions of the lovely goddess, haven't we, Son?" He turned to Warren expecting a response, but my friend simply took a sip of his coffee and looked at me.

"Yes," he said finally, with the irritating cool of a gentleman, as though my exchange with Mr. Rossi hadn't happened at all. Every man at the Greenbrier behaved this way, and at once I wanted to do something scandalous—stand and scream, pitch my wine into Mr. Rossi's face, unpin my hair—just to see if I could rattle out a true reaction. Whoever responded would capture my attention, though I had a feeling no one save Mr. Rossi would, and heaven knows Father wouldn't consider him suitable.

"What do you think of the coffee, Miss Tuckerman?" Warren asked. "Isn't it divine?"

Two

Mademoiselle had begged me to wear the gold gown to the ball tonight. It was the safe choice, the choice that would match the rest of the angelic gowns traipsing the ballroom, the choice that would merit nods instead of whispers as I walked the treadmill on Warren's reluctant arm. But dinner had left me in a rebellious frame of mind, so I'd refused, choosing a turquoise ensemble with a narrow fit and draping train heavy with gold beads and glass ornaments. For as much as Mademoiselle loathed the gown, Mother loved it. She'd chosen the designer—Jeanne Hallée—the design, and the color, insisting turquoise complemented my skin tone and would make me stand out.

"Are you ready?" Warren asked, materializing at my side.

The parlor was crushed with my contemporaries desperately hoping to pair up before the opening notes of the treadmill processional lest they be forced to enter the ballroom unaccompanied and watch the introductory parade of their peers from the balcony seats designated for the elderly. Ever since we'd been presented five years ago, neither Warren nor I had had to experience the unease of looking for a match. It went without saying that we'd walk in together. That was one thing we actually agreed on—that our pairing was a convenience at the start of the nightly ball.

"I suppose," I said. "And you?"

Warren laughed, his gray eyes glistening in the lamplight. His smile was contagious, and I smiled in turn.

"What is it?" I asked. "Is there chocolate in my teeth? I didn't check after the bread pudding at dinner."

"No," he said, still laughing. "It just occurred to me that if we're not careful, this could be us on our wedding day. Me asking you if you're ready and you resignedly saying, 'I suppose.' As you mentioned, our fathers have ensnared us in quite a lengthy game of matchmaking, haven't they? Despite our protesting, I'm still extending my arm to you and you're taking it." Both of us sobered, the roar of the treadmill commotion eclipsing what would've been an uncomfortable silence.

"We know what we are to each other and what we're not," I said. "No amount of coercing will ever change that, I'm certain of it." I realized he was looking up at me. I suddenly wished for the absurd heeled shoes colonial men used to wear. I felt like Goliath to Warren's David. "It seems to me we'd simply rather be on the arm of a friend than hunt the parlor for a someone who's equally ill-matched."

"Yes. That's exactly—"

"My!" Anzonella careened into me. "Have you ever seen such a ruckus?" Violet Battenburg lace ornamented her lithe body, her gloved hand coiled around Mr. Harold Vanderbilt's arm. Apparently, she'd declined Mr. Du Pont after all. "Mike, look at them," she said, referring to her escort, who had always been "Mike" regardless of the fact that *Michael* was not in his name at all.

She tipped her head at a crowd of women gathered in the corner. It was quite peculiar, the throng including all of the Phinizy sisters, Miss Ellen Yuille, Miss Irma Jones, Edith Kane, and both Prather sisters—I could have sworn Margaret Allis was attached to William Van Culm, but what did I know? Ordinarily, the women were determined to scour the room alone, each lady for herself, in order to locate the last poor gentleman without a lady attached to his arm, but this time they were talking with each other while subtly trying to edge closer to whatever was in the middle.

"What in the world?" Warren asked.

"Surely they're squabbling over a box of diamonds," I said.

"One would think," Anzonella said, "but no. It's Mr. Rossi. Rumor has it he's handsome, foreign, and a driver of fast Italian cars."

I laughed.

"Fresh meat," Mike commented smugly. "I'm only glad Willie's not here or he'd be just as pathetic as the women." Willie was Mike's older brother. It was rumored he'd driven his first auto at the age of seven and had been transfixed ever since. "I can see him now, begging Mr. Rossi to race the Vanderbilt cup. Personally, I've never seen the appeal in autos or auto races."

Warren rolled his eyes.

"His allure will fade once they realize his worth is a fraction of theirs. He's Mr. Vacchelli's nephew, not even an heir to whatever scrabble his uncle has. And the way he spoke to Dorothy at dinner was appalling. He has no manners."

"I suppose you could be right," Anzonella said. Despite her words, her own cheeks were flushing. "Completely untrained . . . unlike the two of you." She collected herself and nodded at our escorts. Mr. Rossi was mysterious, and regardless of his likely being no one's eventual fiancé, he was interesting. At least, he would be until one of our fathers dug around enough to unearth his background and means. It happened at least once every season: a handsome newcomer would emerge on the scene, disrupting everyone's natural pairing, and when affection became too obvious for a father to bear, he would put an end to it by revealing that the suitor was a bastard or a fortune hunter or, worse yet, a divorcé. The intrigue was always exciting.

"Don't be too critical of Mr. Rossi on account of me," I said. "I was just as improper as he was, and to be quite honest, I enjoyed our little spat." I wondered what it was like for people outside of society. Did they still consider money and rank as important as character, or was love as effortless as finding someone who made your breath catch? I had to believe it was the latter, that in another life I could simply climb into Mr. Rossi's fast car and let him whisk me away to Italy.

"I've won!" Miss Bolling Phinizy squealed, holding a short straw up in the air. The women dispersed and the object of our conversation appeared. He was sitting in the leather chair next to the fire, his fist clutching an assortment of kindling.

"Did he just have the women draw straws for his arm?" Warren asked, disbelief and horror marked on his typically youthful face.

"It appears so, yes," I said, perplexed as he set the kindling down on a hideously dreary carved mahogany table and stood, barely smiling at Bolling as she took his arm. It didn't even appear that he was disappointed, just bored, as though this was some sort of routine charade. In contrast, Bolling smiled triumphantly and began to gush at him while her eyes searched the room for jealous glances. As far as I could tell, he hadn't said a word to her.

His eyes met mine. I could feel my cheeks burn. I hadn't intended to stare. I refused to be interested in a man who so blatantly thought himself a catch, and now he would assume I was just like the rest of the women here at the Greenbrier, desperate to feel the solidity of his arm under my hand, to stare into his piercing blue gaze, to marvel at the way his wavy black hair hung half in his eyes, just asking to be swept back against his forehead.

"Perhaps he should inquire of Thornton Lewis about drawing up flights for the horse show next week, since he's apparently so versed in games of chance," Mike said.

Anzonella laughed. "Jealousy doesn't suit either of you," she said, absentmindedly tucking a stray ebony strand back into her loose coiffure. Her hair had been coiled and drawn to the top of her head with a pin of fresh rhododendron. The strings in the ballroom were tuning, their familiar hum a natural cue to get in order with your partner for the treadmill.

"Remember last year?" I said, laughing. "All of you were in a tizzy over that woman Eleanor Balsam, who turned out not to be the French shipping heiress she claimed but a native of White Sulphur Springs keen to find her way down the aisle with one of you."

Warren had been her favorite and he'd been in love. We had all disregarded it as a fleeting infatuation at the time, and he would never admit the truth now, but looking back it was clear that Eleanor had stolen his heart. As soon as we processed in together, he'd find her and occupy her dance card for as long as she'd allow. His father had been furious, constantly apologizing to me about his lack of loyalty, though I'd appreciated the diversion.

"She had the gall to write me," Warren said, avoiding our eyes by appraising the vine stenciling bordering the ceiling. "She apologized and wanted me to call on her this summer."

"And will you?" Anzonella asked, shifting behind us to take Mike's arm.

"You know he won't," I said.

It was one thing to be of unfavorable breeding. That could be overcome given the right circumstance. But poverty could not. It was too difficult to determine whether a person was in love or in love with wealth. Fortune hunting could take a toll on a family, and almost no one was in love quite enough to live in squalor.

I glanced back at Anzonella and in the process caught Mr. Rossi's eye again. He now occupied the very last position with Bolling at the end of the coiling line. Before I could look away, he plucked a floral vase from the fireplace mantel and held the pink rose motif against the white wall, appraising it. Bolling looked at him as though he'd gone mad. I knew he was attempting to make me laugh, to revel in our private joke, but I turned away, unwilling to encourage a man with unbridled arrogance. In any case, I hadn't really been teasing about the Greenbrier's stuffy decor. Floral wall coverings and color would look magnificent. It would make this place sing of romance and softness and unbidden wilderness, reflecting the Greenbrier's natural state rather than the traditional structure society had imposed on it.

The French doors opened to reveal the same old scene— the ballroom illuminated by the old brass chandelier, white lampshades shielding the electric lights, and a crush of parents and grandparents gathered around the perimeter and up top in the balcony. Festive wide red linen streamers swooped from the ceiling to the corners of the windows, I suppose to match the crimson posters announcing General Watts's exhibition mile at the Centennial Horse Show next week. It could have been made lovelier with large bouquets and a trellis entry. But, of course, decorating was a far cry from my role as guest.

"Welcome to the Beckley ball," Mr. Beckley announced as the piano concluded a piece by Chopin. "We're honored to host this celebration in honor of Mr. and Mrs. John Simmonds, who are celebrating their twentieth wedding anniversary today. Please let the treadmill begin!"

I'd paraded in my first treadmill five years ago, marking me forever a Greenbrier debutante. The experience had been much different than my presentation to society at Sherry's in New York. Unlike at Sherry's, where my look and manner and fashion had been immediately praised, everyone here had gawked at me, scrutinizing my white sequined dress, which I had selected intentionally to stand out. Proper debutantes at the Greenbrier wore lace. The way I walked, the way I smiled, the manner in which I held Warren's arm mattered immensely. I'd known quite well all of it would be reported in papers from Virginia to New York the next day, and because I dared to be slightly different, the reporters deemed me splendid. I had been featured in all the stories. It had been satisfying indeed.

"Here we go, darling," Warren said as the line moved forward.

I laughed under my breath at his endearment, only half a joke. "Do you suppose we should just say we're engaged for the duration to avoid this absurd ritual?" Engaged and married couples weren't expected to parade in. Only those of us available for purchase were to be presented like choice livestock at a farmer's auction.

"Of course not," he said. "How else will my future wife catch sight of me? I can't be eclipsed by a sea of the elderly."

I could practically feel Anzonella fluffing her skirt behind me. She was the belle of the treadmill, always a favorite in the columns for her innocent smile—that, and she always looked like a pixie. She was petite, nearly half a foot shorter than I, and if I hadn't been fast friends with her before I realized I'd grow to what seemed like twice her height, I surely would have avoided her.

Martha Phinizy and Mr. Francis Kendall glided through the doorway into the ballroom, and Warren and I followed. The applause was stagnant as it always was, no one wanting to show favoritism, even though favorites always emerged throughout the season. I stepped with care, Warren's stride exactly in line with my own. Our parents were together, parallel to the chandelier. Warren turned toward them, but I tipped my face the other way, toward the orchestra, trying to avoid the joy in my father's eyes. Instead, I watched Bolling and Mr. Rossi enter the room, and heard a hush fall over the steady applause. It wasn't typical for a new guest to walk the treadmill, nor was it necessarily considered proper, and it went without saying that Mr. Phinizy wouldn't take too well to one of his daughters promenading on the arm of a man who wasn't an established guest of the Greenbrier.

"He's Italian," I heard an elderly woman shout to her husband as Warren and I disentangled at the end of the ballroom and dissolved into the crowd to find our friends.

"Good luck tonight, Dorothy," Warren said, grinning before he wandered over to find Mr. Bonaparte and Mr. Davis.

"I wish," I said under my breath, but Warren had already gone.

"It'll be Taft or Canada for me." Mr. Kane was talking loudly from the gathering of our fathers in the corner behind me. The election again. It was always about the election with the men these days, and I found the talk silly. There was no one to debate. Of course, everyone was for Taft. He was one of us. So was President Roosevelt, whose family was absent the Greenbrier for the first time in as long as I could remember in order to give Mr. Taft the attention he was due.

"Canada." My father laughed. "You're a Kane. Both of our families were here on the *Mayflower*. Canada isn't an option."

"Don't you suppose a change of power from time to time might be a blessed occasion for a country?" Mr. Vacchelli's question was what our fathers had all been waiting for. Absent womanly presence in their circle for a moment, they could discuss politics. And they'd finally found someone to disagree with.

I was watching Mr. Rossi. I realized it too late, the moment he twirled Bolling around at the end of the promenade and faced me. His eyes met mine, but he didn't smile, and I immediately began to walk toward Anzonella and Martha and Edith gathered under the chandelier to escape both the uncomfortable responses to Mr. Vacchelli's retort and Mr. Rossi's advance toward the train wreck of a conversation.

"I'm supposed to tell Bolling she's not to dance with Mr. Rossi," Martha said as I reached my friends. "Father is horrified, but of course she won't listen. She won five dances and I guarantee she fully intends to hold him to his promises."

"I wouldn't listen to your father either," Edith said, her gaze drifting to the politicians in the far-left corner, now including Mr. Rossi. She adjusted her wreath of bluebonnets and fiddled with her dance card, reminding me I'd forgotten to retrieve mine from Warren.

"Whatever possessed you all to play his little game?" I asked. So many ladies clamoring for his arm before he'd had as much as a conversation with any of them struck me as absurd. I was taken by him, too, but we had actually spoken. Why hadn't he asked me? I glanced around, immediately knowing. I was surrounded by beauty much greater than my own. My earlier daydream felt silly. No one would ever whisk me away to love and freedom. Forty years from now, I'd be right here, beaten into submission by the master that was society, chained to duty and expectation.

"Oh. It wasn't *his* game," Martha said. "Bolling begged him to do it, to make it fair. He was quite a poor sport about it. In fact, he kept insisting that he choose a partner on his own." Martha laughed. "Edith told him he really shouldn't be walking the treadmill in the first place. So he agreed."

"I don't understand," I said. "He's handsome, sure, but—"

"He's handsome, sure?" Anzonella practically laughed out loud. "Look at him and then look at Mike." I did just that, searching the ballroom for Mike, who was intermittently holding up his dance card and staring at Anzonella as though to figure how to occupy her all night. He was handsome, his brown eyes and square jaw the picture of masculinity, but his looks were completely eclipsed by Mr. Rossi's. "Before Mr. Rossi arrived, my arm would've been resting on the prize, but now it'll be Bolling's name in all the papers."

"The attention does have its rewards, I suppose," I said.

I'd never been one for the sort of publicity that determined my worth by the man whose arm I held. I enjoyed attention I won myself.

Martha snorted.

"I think it's his lips," she said.

"And his accent and his surety and his hair." Bolling walked up to us, her already rosy cheeks burned nearly red. "He races automobiles."

The opening notes of Strauss's "Voices of Spring" interrupted the hum of the room. Father would be pleased. He and Mother waltzed beautifully to the traditional piece, so unlike the Argentine tango that as of late had found its way to our ballroom on occasion. The new style of dancing dismayed the older set—most couldn't figure the steps—though it was terribly fun. I didn't much care what was played tonight so long as I'd be able to make my way to the refreshment table in the parlor by the fourth piece. The Greenbrier's lemon ice was my favorite and I liked watching the dancing from the sidelines. The spectacle was beautiful to the eye of an outsider, everyone decorated in color and flowers and gaiety. From the parlor, no one could see the silent feuds and jealousies.

Henry McVickar, a fellow Tuxedo Parkian, winked at me and held out his hand to my friend. "Anzonella . . . Miss Kane, could I have the pleasure of this dance?" She took it, much to the chagrin of Mike, who was too late making his way from his position against the windows to thwart Henry's advance. "I do hope you'll save me a waltz toward the end, Miss Tuckerman. You don't know how much I missed my neighbors during my time in Europe."

The crowd around the perimeter of the ballroom thinned, the majority of my peers taking space on the dance floor. I reached for the rhododendron in my hair, thinking that perhaps I should feign illness tomorrow. It was boring, watching the same couples, most of whom were only old friends. The sense of mystery and romance was all but absent, and even though lasting love was at times born from years of familiarity, that wasn't the sort I hoped for. I wanted surprise, something different, something worthy of an Elinor Glyn novel, someone that would take me places I'd never seen with people I'd never known.

"Shall we?" Mike appeared at my shoulder, his eyebrows knitted as he appraised Henry and Anzonella laughing as they twirled round their siblings.

"I suppose," I said, taking his hand. His grip was soft, limp even, and though he was still considered one of the most eligible bachelors at the Greenbrier, I couldn't see the appeal.

"Miss Tuckerman." The voice was low, coming from behind me, and I turned in Mike's arms in time to see Mr. Rossi pull Bolling against him. Something inside me hitched at the sight of the way he held her, though his dark eyes were locked on mine. "The sixth dance," he said. "The sixth dance will be mine?" I suppose it was phrased as a question, but he'd meant it as a statement. Before I could think to laugh at him, Mike whisked me away.

By the time the band struck up the fifth Strauss waltz, I was standing in the parlor enjoying a lemon ice. I leaned against the wall, wishing I could slump instead. My feet pinched in my kid leather oxfords. Everyone was sweating. The staff had opened the windows hoping for a breeze, but their efforts had done nothing but encourage the stifling warm air inside.

Bolling, who moments ago had been in Mr. Rossi's arms, was now sitting down on a tufted settee with her grandmother. The crown of her blonde hair was saturated. She took a handkerchief from one of the attendants dressed in the Greenbrier's smart white livery and dabbed her forehead.

"These are quite good." Mr. Rossi's voice startled me, and I turned to find him smiling.

"They must be. You haven't appeared this happy since your arrival." I immediately wished I could take back my words, and hastily spooned a bit of ice in my mouth to prevent more disastrous sentiments from emerging.

"I haven't been and neither have you," he said, gracefully settling the embarrassing insinuation that I'd been watching him all night with his own. "Whatever is the matter with you? It's not the wall color again, is it?"

I laughed. "Of course it is. I prefer color to drabness and hinge my satisfaction on the shade of the walls." I began to turn away, but his hand brushed my arm.

"I know you're being humorous. What is it truly? Why aren't you blissfully cheerful?"

I sighed.

"It's not that I'm unhappy. I suppose I'm only bored," I said, breaking from his eyes to watch the final steps of the waltz. "This place is beautiful, but it's the same thing year after year. I fear I'll spend my whole life doing nothing but the same things with the same set, abiding by the same rules."

"Oh," he said simply.

I wondered if I'd said too much.

"As difficult as it is to imagine boredom in the midst of these characters in this grand place, I suppose I understand. Perhaps you feel you're trapped?"

The crystal was frigid in my hand and I set it down on the linen tablecloth in front of us.

"Yes," I said. "What is it like to be free? You know. It seems you've taken hold of it."

Mr. Rossi laughed.

"At the start, it feels like you've just taken your first breath," he said. "It feels like you're weightless, like you'll never have to go back to the life you left behind."

"And you never regret leaving? Do you suppose you'll ever have to return?" I asked, well aware that, knowing nothing of his past, I was asking for me.

"I'm uncertain," he said. His face was serious again, his eyes settling on mine with a disconcerting weight. He bowed and held out his hand as Harry Lincoln's "A Southern Dream" began.

"It's the sixth song. May I have the pleasure, Miss Tuckerman?"

I took his hand without answering or thinking. He led me onto the dance floor and pulled me against his chest. I could feel the heat of his body, his gaze on my face, and the disapproving stares of my parents, but I didn't care. I knew well that I'd feigned indifference on purpose. Disinterest was the only way to avoid feeling put off when he hadn't asked me to accompany him on the treadmill and spent most of the evening in Bolling's arms. He moved gracefully, his posture straight, but his face tipped down toward mine. I glanced over his shoulder, watching my friends watching us.

"Miss Tuckerman," he said. "Are you looking for Mr. Abercrombie?"

"No," I said, meeting his eyes. "I'm looking at you." His lips quirked up in a smile and I could feel my cheeks redden as I held his gaze. "Won't Bolling, Miss Phinizy, won't she be offended that I'm occupying you?"

He didn't flinch at all.

"No," he said. "Well, perhaps, but if she is, I don't mind. I'm not taken with her in the slightest. I'm not spoken for at all." His eyebrows lifted as though he'd asked me a question, and I grinned, finding his manner of speaking altogether confusing and endearing.

"But you'd like to be, at least for the rest of the season," I said. "A man doesn't come waltzing into the Greenbrier and hold a contest for his escort in order to avoid being attached."

"That contest was silly. It wasn't my idea. I only wanted one woman to accompany me, but when I came into the room, I found her otherwise occupied," he said.

Butterflies riddled my stomach, but I wasn't naive enough to suppose he was speaking of me when the Kane girls had shared our dinner table. I laughed and felt his arm tighten around my waist. A few more inches and his lips would be on my forehead. I wanted to lean into him, to feel the thrill of standing that close, but I didn't. He was used to risk, accustomed to breaking the rules, and as much as I felt like being daring, I couldn't. I was a china doll tucked away in a cabinet.

"You could approach her again, you know."

"I have," he said quietly.

He blinked, and I realized then that we'd been missing the steps, going round nearly in circles as we talked. "I know she's not promised, but I can't tell if her heart belongs to someone else. I don't have the courage to ask. She's not like the rest."

I swallowed, hesitating. He spun me around, leading us back into the throng of dancers, and I knew then that if it was me, he would've been content in our unguided dancing, waiting to hear what I had to say.

"Ask her again," I said. "It's the only way to know. There are too many parents attempting to force arrangements. For instance, I love Warren as a—"

"You've been very kind," he said abruptly, just as the final notes sounded. "I'm sorry to have taken you away from your Mr. Abercrombie."

He let me go and paced toward the parlor. I tried to follow, needing to tell him that my love for Warren was as for a brother, but by the time I got to the parlor, he was gone.

"Is everything all right?" Anzonella was beside me, her face flushed from dancing.

"Yes," I said, eycing the discarded ice glasses still sitting side by side. I was confused. The night had stolen my sensibilities, Mr. Rossi's as well. Even if I had been the object of his attention—which was unlikely—he wasn't suitable even though he was handsome. I wondered if I'd actually have the courage to run away from my family, from comfort, from society if I had the chance. "Perfectly as it should be."

Three

The Greenbrier Resort
White Sulphur Springs, West Virginia
October 30, 1946

I could feel the ghosts. The phenomenon presented itself the
moment I stepped off the train, and the sensation grew stronger
as the coach took us up the drive to the new hotel. It wasn't the
same as before and yet it was. Thirty-eight years past, thirty-
eight years of dreams and love and disappointment and loss, and
in a moment, only a moment, the Greenbrier erased it all.

I stood in the lobby alone, shivering. I wondered if I should
have allowed Lee to accompany me. He could have fetched some
kindling. Then again, I could bear a little chill. I didn't need
Lee's assistance. This first look was mine alone. It had to be. It
couldn't be riddled with excited talk and hurry, with Lee's new-
fangled ideas. I owed it to the ghosts to listen to them, to stay
quiet and remember, and I owed it to myself.

This new hotel, this larger Greenbrier, which had replaced
the old hotel in order to accommodate year-round guests, wasn't

new anymore. It was thirty-three years old, but to me it was foreign. It didn't feel the same as the Greenbrier I knew, and yet I knew the ghosts were all here. Where else would they be?

The lobby was cavernous, occupying the entire first floor, really, though the architect had tried to break it into sections by adding arched doorways. Mr. Small had been kind enough to light the electric lamps before my arrival, but the glow didn't much help, nor did the mismatched antique tables and armchairs strewn here and there. I suppose they'd tried to make the entry comfortable for family and friends and soldiers well enough to move about, but despite the hotel's past, very little elegance remained. As far as I could tell, the Greenbrier hadn't received the news that the war was over. It was still Ashford General Hospital.

I stepped toward the windows, drawn to the heavy brocaded curtains. I pinched the fabric and let it go, watching the dust glitter in the sunshine. These trappings remained despite the hotel's transformation, but they did little to warm the room. The wood floors, the towering cracked plaster ceilings, the dreary mahogany mantels, the trim, the dark molding, the furniture. It all would need to be changed.

They'd warned me of a surgery at the far end, tucked away in the corner of the never-ending lobby. If I squinted down the corridor of arches, I could see the glint of the metal tables. I shivered. I didn't like thinking about the wars—either of them. The whole thing was horrifying and dreary. There had been so many deaths, so many dismemberments of limb and mind, and between the occasions of men going off to war, the world had fallen.

My former husband, Dan, had thought me frivolous when I

spoke of ignoring the first war. I'd tidied and decorated and entertained in our small apartment until both of us were exhausted,
hoping to divert the thought of my dear friends being sent off
to fight. If I let on that I was worried, he'd simply kiss me and
rub my pregnant belly and tell me that it was my duty to pray
and foster hope for peace, volunteer if I felt compelled. I didn't
do any of it. Instead I avoided the papers and pretended it wasn't
happening while his next wife left school to serve as a radio oper-
ator. Perhaps, ultimately, that's why he thought he was better
off without me. I lived in the clouds and he could not. That's
what I'd thought at the beginning, right after he left. He lived
in the muck. He loved studying disease and eventually became
obsessed with finding a polio cure for his patient and dear friend,
Frank Roosevelt, all the while worrying a solution wouldn't come
quickly enough. It had been all-absorbing, this first love of his,
and he'd chosen it over me. He asked for a divorce the day he
returned from an eighteen-month stint studying in Zurich with
Carl Jung in the wake of the stock market crash. He'd matter-
of-factly told me he was leaving, without room for discussion,
and moved out the same day. *"We've grown apart. I don't love
you anymore. I haven't the time for a wife right now."* I hated that
I could still recall his tone, his exact words. I'd tried to forget
them for seventeen years. He hadn't asked how I was faring or
if I minded terribly that my first two large ventures—the lobby
of the Carlyle Hotel and the Piping Rock Project—were lost to
the crash. He showed no interest in how I felt about the horror
of a divorcée label. He'd only cared about himself, about his own
importance and growing fame. Funny, looking back, how his star
began to fade in the wake of divorce while mine began to glow.

I started toward the operating tables, making my way under

the first arch. I would have to face the surgery eventually. I gasped, stopping to appraise a dingy brass chandelier hanging from the white ceiling of the plain ballroom. I could feel the memories, the ghosts, swirling around me. This was where they lived, where they still came every evening, and they weren't happy about its condition. I could sense it. This was hardly a ballroom, and the balls had been the lifeblood of this place forever. Since the old hotel was gone, it was here that the spirits of Henry Clay, Martin Van Buren, John Tyler, Alva Vanderbilt, and all the others convened every night to dance, to feel the thrill of love.

My free hand dropped to my waist. I could still feel the way he'd held me. It had been thirty-eight years and still his memory struck me. I wondered. Was he among the ghosts here?

Clearing my throat, I set my mind to the task at hand. I didn't enjoy thinking back and I hadn't been hired to reminisce. I'd been hired to transform this place into a resort again. It would take much ingenuity. It would take much time. I'd decorated mansions and the Drake and the Hampshire House and the Carlyle Hotel and the 50,000-square-foot Palácio Quitandinha Resort in Rio de Janeiro, but this project was my most challenging yet. To a lesser designer—to a woman like my ex-husband's wife, I liked to think—this would be an intimidation of such a grand scale that it couldn't be done. But I was the famed Dorothy Draper. This resort, the Greenbrier, would be my masterpiece. *So long as you're paid.* The thought jarred me. No one, especially my staff, knew how close I was to bankruptcy. The Versailles Restaurant closed in the wake of the owners' insolvency without a single check to us, and the owner of the Palácio Quitandinha dragged out the construction of the hotel, and consequently the project, over four years. He stopped paying me the final year. The uppers at the C&O Railroad, the owner of the Greenbrier, had promptly paid my retainer, buying the company more time. How much time, I wasn't entirely sure—six months at best. Contrary to everyone's belief, the pockets of an iron heiress weren't infinitely deep, especially when those pockets had been relieved of nearly forty thousand dollars of personal funds to cover more than a year's worth of work by the finest artists and visionaries one could employ. The Quitandinha had been slated to be my masterpiece too. The splash of my efforts there was supposed to ripple for years, but save a few small mentions of its opening, the papers' attention was on the war ending, not on a glitzy resort in faraway Brazil.

Now, only a year later, that hotel was closed, its owner penniless. This project could not turn out the same. If Dorothy Draper & Company declared bankruptcy, twenty-one careers would be lost, my reputation would be ruined, and in the process of liquidating everything I owned—the apartments, my new Packard, my jewelry—I would be forced to return to Tuxedo Park. As much as I tried to ignore it, I could already hear the gossip—that everyone had been right, that despite the feathers in my hat, a society girl had no business making a career. If I lost it all, if I wasn't *the* Dorothy Draper anymore, who would I be? Not a mother, not a wife, not a society darling. In one way or another I'd failed at all of those things. The Greenbrier would be my masterpiece. It had to be.

"Could I call up the elevator for you?" Bob Bowman, president of the C&O Railroad, appeared at the far end of the corridor, his voice echoing. He extracted his gold pocket watch from his simple gray suit and opened it, then snapped it shut again. "Or perhaps you'd like to retire to your cottage? I could escort you there, of course, and we could walk through the rest in the morning."

"I may be older than I once was, Mr. Bowman, but I'm still quite spry. Please call the elevator, but don't feel the need to accompany me. I can do it alone," I said. I could see the metal tables out of the corner of my eye as I passed but focused on Mr. Bowman instead. Perhaps I could have Lee and the others remove the surgery before I returned. Mr. Bowman smiled and shook his head.

"We knew you were the right woman for the job, Mrs. Draper," he said. I recalled my phone conversation with his boss, the chairman of the C&O, Robert Young. *"We're prepared to offer you $120,000. My wife, Anita, says you're the crème de la crème. I need every who's who back at the Greenbrier, and I think you can help me with that. It was $3.3 million to buy it back. I need it restored and brightened, and the C&O has committed $4.2 million to make it happen. From what I understand, there's no one else. Your work, your connections are what I need. You'll do it, won't you, Mrs. Draper?"* I'd pretended to think it over, but the money was more than I'd ever been offered—more than anyone in my industry had ever been offered—and the allure of being at the Greenbrier again was great. In that instant, I could see the sweep of green from the porch, the green that stretched as far as I could fathom, and was homesick for it.

"And we know how you love the Greenbrier too," Mr. Bowman went on, bringing me back to the conversation.

"I'm the only one who could do this effectively," I said, knowing well how prickly I sounded. Arrogance was good for business, regardless of how humble one really felt. "Mr. Young was right to call. The war has left this resort in shambles and

I'm afraid leaving it this way much longer would upset many people."

Mr. Bowman chuckled and pulled the elevator gate back for me to enter.

"I must admit we have a passionate group of people who are eager to vacation here again," he said. "Almost every day I receive a telegram or letter to that effect." He glanced around, and then his eyes found mine.

"You know very well I'm not only speaking of those sorts," I said. He looked at me, his head cocked to the side, and then he nodded. I knew he believed in spirits. On the way from the train station he'd muttered something about not particularly enjoying it here, feeling like he was never quite alone.

"I know," he said, his gaze sobering. "I know."

I didn't know if I could do this job. It was the first time I'd had the thought in nearly twenty years of decorating. Even facing my first commercial project, the Carlyle lobby, at the green age of thirty-eight, having no real clue what I was doing, I'd been sure it would be a masterpiece. Even when asked to design the Quitandinha before the structure was even in existence, I'd known it would dazzle. Not so here. My confidence fell away upon viewing the upper guest rooms. They were horrid, all bleach white with metal beds, metal chairs, and metal desks. The only sense of comfort came from the few oriental rugs scattered here and there, and even they were stained with years of meals upset by fragile table legs. There were a few pieces of satisfactory furniture, mostly in each floor's sitting room. Everything else would have to be replaced. In a sense, it was exciting. There would be no opinion but my own, and Mr. Young had made sure my budget was sizable. But I could not ignore the memory of the old hotel and what it had been. This project could be no less; in fact, it had to eclipse the simple glamour of the beloved old place.

I pulled my kid leather gloves down my arms and let Mr. Bowman fit my brown plaid jacket over my indigo suit.

"I'm sorry to say the winter has snuck in a bit early," Mr. Bowman said. He pulled the door open at the end of the corridor, and the crisp fall air chilled me through.

"It feels nice," I lied, wishing it were summer. "I'm quite used to the New York chill, after all."

"I suppose you're right," he said.

I hardly heard him as we stepped over the threshold. He offered his arm and I took it, barely registering that I'd just accepted a gesture I typically refused. I was strong enough to escort myself. The lawn stretched in front of me, the same wide wash of wild that had greeted me each summer morning when I was young. I could still feel the possibility of freedom, of sunlight on my face. I'd started each day by looking out the windows of our suite or the Colonnade House onto this exact view. Besides the new hotel, everything was exactly as I remembered.

"Of course, you'll recall that the old structure stood here," Mr. Bowman said as we made our way down the last steps. "This north entrance opens onto the same view from the old front porch. You're probably familiar with it."

I stopped abruptly, disturbed by the fact that nothing at all remained, that I was likely standing in the former location of the lobby, my boots deep in grass.

"Are you all right, Mrs. Draper?"

I glanced at him, strangely stunned to hear my married name. I hadn't gone by Tuckerman in thirty-four years, but standing here, watching the last leaves flutter and fall on the lawn, on the old familiar cottages, and on Hebe atop the springhouse, I forgot who I'd become. I was an older woman now—three years from sixty—a divorcée, a mother, a grandmother, an entrepreneur.

"Yes," I said.

"The car will be here shortly, and we'll get you settled at the Avlon Hotel. It's my understanding that Mr. Lee Carter is already there. I'm sure you're keen to get him up to speed."

"The Avlon? Whyever would we stay there?"

Mr. Bowman cleared his throat.

"Certainly you're not suggesting you'd like to stay here. You've seen the state of this place, Mrs. Draper. It's no place for a woman of your prominence."

I eyed him, pausing before I swept my hand across the tableau.

"And what of the cottages? They've all been made into reha-bilitation centers too?"

From our position I could see Spring Row and, through the trees, the Colonnade. I wondered if Lovers' Lane still existed, or if it had long since been eclipsed by grasses and weeds. Grand romance had faded under the threat of peril. In wartime, love didn't have opportunity to bloom. Instead, it was plucked as a bud and dropped into a vase in hopes it would someday root. But in recent years, many didn't. Those swift courthouse marriages before a man went to war often ended before they'd begun—cut short by a death, a loss of interest, a change of heart. I was more than familiar with the latter two.

"No, ma'am, but they're still not suitable. They were quarters, you know. For our officers during the first part of the war. This place was made a camp for Germans and Italians, a fanciful prison if you will, to encourage the enemy to treat our men with the same respect."

"I'm aware, and I know what an internment camp is, Mr. Bowman. But if I'm responsible for the transformation of this great place," I said, waving an arm back to the hotel, "I must stay here, on the resort grounds—to feel what it was and what it must be."

A blue Packard careened around the side of the hotel, stopping abruptly in front of us. A young man emerged in familiar kelly-green livery and a cloud of cigarette smoke, immediately stamping the source of the vapor on the gravel drive. Reflexively, I unhooked my arm from Mr. Bowman's to retrieve my own cigarettes from my pocketbook. I hadn't had a smoke since this morning, and I could feel my nerves beginning to jitter. I unsnapped the thin silver Tiffany case and extracted one, lifting it to my lips.

"Tom here says the only suitable outfitted cottage is Hawley House," Mr. Bowman said, referring to the man in the livery. "It's just up the hill." He gestured to my left.

As Mr. Bowman spoke, Tom rushed to my side and lit a match. I squinted into the distance. I'd never heard of Hawley House.

"That's right," Tom said as I inhaled. "But I'm afraid it's the only cottage, and Mr. Carter will need accommodations too. It's a three-bedroom home, but manners are at stake. I know he's only your business manager, but—"

"Oh, don't be silly," I said. "It's not 1900, and three bedrooms will certainly be enough for the two of us."

Tom unloaded my boxes as I sat on the porch. The cottage mimicked the others I'd known, though the place was much larger than most except for the Colonnade and the President's Cottage. I glanced down the expanse of whitewashed wood-planked porch surrounding the whole cottage and then lifted my eyes to the view. Through the wash of red and orange and yellow leaves, I could see the hotel. From here, I could imagine it was the old Greenbrier. I could imagine that I was young again. I'd made a mess of it—and a triumph too—the years following our last summer here. In a way, despite how much time had passed, I was back in that same position. Tuxedo Park chains awaited me if I didn't figure a way to freedom. I'd done it once. I'd broken away and claimed my life. I'd do it again.

"Would you like me to unpack your trunks, Mrs. Draper?"

Tom appeared in the doorway, his gloved hands folded across his chest. He smiled, and I detected a glint in his eyes. Surely that sort of reputation didn't precede me. Regardless of its truth, I was a lady of fine breeding.

"No," I said, rising from the rocking chair. Tom hastened to my side and latched onto my forearm. I yanked it away, forgetting myself.

"Apologies," he said. "It's only that it rained yesterday, and the porch is wet and—"

"I'm not an invalid," I said, avoiding his gaze. I marched past him into the cottage's sitting room. It was clear that the quarters had been made a residence for men. The overstuffed chairs looked comfortable but tattered, the once-grand hunter paisley print faded by the sun and the wear of frequent bodies. Tiny brass electric lamps were scattered about, one on a bulky buffet that blocked the adjacent window and another on an oblong tea table situated frighteningly close to the fireplace.

"Your room is just down the hall to the right. Mr. Carter's is, unfortunately, right across the way. I hope it won't cause too much trouble. I'm sure the C&O would be happy to keep him situated at the Avlon if the configuration is not suitable," Tom said.

I stopped in the dark hallway, eyeing a painting of Henry Clay greeting a crowd of guests in a relatively obscure rendering of the old Greenbrier's ballroom. The room was adorned in rich finery, something similar to Caroline Astor's place, and entirely unlike the simplicity I recalled.

"We need to work closely, so that will be fine," I said, not bothering to elaborate.

"Very well," he said. "I'll have your supper brought up in a few hours' time. Cook has been summoned from White Sulphur, and I imagine she'll follow the original schedule. Swedish meatballs with fresh mushroom sauce and a hot cloverleaf roll. Is that suitable to your taste?"

My stomach rumbled at the mention of food. I'd had only a bit of cream and a peach for breakfast, nothing for lunch. In my earlier days, I would have been famished by noon, but now I found myself with less and less of an appetite.

"That'll do nicely," I said.

Tom nodded in a quick farewell and then departed, leaving me alone. I sighed and let my shoulders slump, relieving the pinch of weathered bones. The cottage was a bit too cold, and I wished I had asked Tom to light a bit of coal in the hearth. Then again, I shouldn't have had to ask. The old hotel's employees would be turning over in their graves if they could see this bleak show of hospitality.

I flipped the switch in my room, and a horrid square ceiling light of heavy glass and aluminum beamed over the metal bed fitted with a patchwork quilt and my travel case. An unsightly overstuffed striped chair was situated between two narrow windows along the other side of the room, and a dainty mahogany writing desk outfitted with a short stool finished the room on the opposite wall. The stool made me smile. It was one of the old sort with the top that shifted and screeched under a person's weight, the sort Dan once picked up from an antique shop in Brooklyn. He'd thought it perfect for my first office, that it would match my great-grandfather Oliver Wolcott's writing desk. Of course, I'd hoped for something more comfortable—a tufted leather armchair, perhaps—but I'd endured the stool for the sake of Dan's fleeting enthusiasm. He was uncharacteristically thrilled that day, both of us riding the rush of the papers and our friends heralding my ingenuity. I'd recently completed what reporters called the Upside-Down House—a moniker we'd won by extending the ground floor of our old carriage house to the back of the lot and installing gardens on the roof of the extension. Though friends had been asking my advice for years, it was Dan who encouraged me to go into business in the wake of the Upside-Down House's acclaim. I opened my first company, the Architectural Clearing House, a matchmaking service of sorts between my society and architect friends. Four years later, his excitement was gone and so was he. Perhaps he'd encouraged my endeavors so I wouldn't have time to miss him, to realize he was never home.

I reached for the brass clasps on my Halliburton trunk and flipped it open. Home. The yards of beautiful English chintz welcomed me, and I pulled the fabric out along with my pins. It would fit perfectly over the armchair. Slipcovers always worked wonders on hideous upholstery.

Below the chintz was my comfort, my mother's quilt—a simple crisp white perfect for any color scheme—and strapped to the inside top of my case were my prints. I leaned over the headboard, snatched the hunting scene from the coveted place above the pillows, and shoved it under the bed. William Bliss Baker's *Woodland Brook* would replace it nicely. It was my favorite fall painting, a work that reminded me so much of home, of New York, and of the scene that greeted me every fall. The painting had been a wedding gift to Dan and me from my parents, intended to remind us of the day we got married in September of 1912, and the day we met a year before at an outdoor party at the Tuxedo Park clubhouse. By the time we met I'd given up on ever marrying. I'd thought my heart hardened to it. Even at the party we barely spoke, though I had taken note of the man wearing the simple gray suit in the sea of tuxedos, the man everyone excused from the rules because he wasn't one of us, because he was a physician. When he called on me the next day, I was surprised but decided to take a chance. He was an outsider, after all, but well-respected, and outsiders always interested me. Five months later, we were engaged with plans to live in the city. It wasn't a heart-pounding romance, but we were a good match, I'd never have to live in Tuxedo Park again, and I loved him.

I hung the painting above the bed and straightened it before reaching back into my trunk. Next were the photos—Diana and Nelson's wedding, George in his army uniform, ten-year-old

Penny standing outside of our old Sutton Hall apartment in New York.

Diana and George didn't speak to me much. I'd tried, but it was clear they didn't understand who I'd become after the humiliation of divorce. They had been old enough—sixteen and fourteen respectively—to overhear the lies society whispered about me: that Dan's leaving was my fault, that I hadn't doted on him enough, that I wasn't his intellectual equal, that my decorating distracted, that I didn't prioritize family, that I'd never loved him. My children believed some of them, as did so many of my childhood friends and society peers. Perhaps it was easy to suppose your mother wasn't who she claimed when you rarely spent time with her. Like the rest of their contemporaries, they attended boarding school when they were of age and summered at Grandmother and Grandfather's. Even so, Diana and George were my children, and I'd never forget the sounds of their laughter with Nanny upstairs or the way their chubby arms had reached to hug me at the end of each day. Penny's photograph went on the writing desk, a reminder to write each day. She was a kind soul, kinder than I'd ever been. She'd inherited it from someone else, perhaps Dan's mother or mine. Either way, I was grateful. She'd remained beside me, not bothered by the rumors or the armor I wore to protect myself from them. Then again, Penny wouldn't abandon anyone. Even Dan's sister, Ruth, was her fast friend first and her aunt second.

With the room situated to my liking, I extracted my notebook from my leather purse and made my way back to the sitting room. I chose the tufted leather couch across from the fireplace and settled in, kicking off my low-boy Naturalizers and lying down on the padded arm. Even for a space as large as the Greenbrier, I needed a theme. It couldn't be just anything. It had to be special. It had to welcome guests back with both fresh air and memories.

I heard the door open and then shut. I thought to sit up, to open my eyes, to be proper. It could be Tom back with another question. Then again, he would have knocked.

At once I felt those lips. The whisper of Lee's mouth on the hollow of my neck. I tilted my head toward the backrest, inviting his touch as his kisses swept down my shoulder, as his fingers drew my jacket away from my skin.

"Hello, DD," he muttered. I felt my breath catch. But then his lips lifted from my shoulder and I felt him pull away. "I brought you something."

I opened my eyes and found his face. Every time I looked at him, I was confronted by his youth, by the twenty years I'd lived that he hadn't. But he wasn't a child, and he'd been the one to initiate this change. I never would have—but then, I hadn't balked when he kissed me after only six months in my employ as my business manager. He wasn't the first. Perhaps that was why. I had a horrible habit of hiring men I found attractive, and with Dan gone, nothing held me back except for my own sense of workplace etiquette, which was simple enough. If everyone was working hard, they could do as they liked.

"I thought you should have some flowers. I know how much you enjoy them."

He was holding them behind his back, and when he drew them around to hand them to me, I paled. I could feel it, the blood draining from my face. A rhododendron bloom—the white-pink of my summers, the loveliness of Lovers' Lane—and a single pale pink rose.

"Impossible," I whispered. "It's October."

"You like them," he said, a smile stretching across his face. He was immaculately clean-shaven, just the way I preferred him, and his hazel eyes danced with my approval. I didn't know why he wanted me, why he'd agreed to this. We would never marry, he knew that. There would be no children together, no home, no future, and in a matter of months or years, this would end. Perhaps that was the draw.

"Yes, I do."

He chuckled and set them gently on the tea table in front of me, crawling down to my feet. His fingers kneaded the sore tendons through the thin hose, but I couldn't take my eyes off the small bouquet, my mind fixed on a scene from long ago.

"They were growing in the lobby at the hotel and I asked if I might have a sprig or two for my boss," he said. "I know we're working, but I'm glad we have this time together." We had arranged this rendezvous on purpose. I hadn't invited Bella or Mabel down to help with my dressing or my letters, so Lee and I could be alone. I liked Lee, probably more than any man since Dan. He had the irresistible combination of intelligence, vibrance, and good looks, and everyone deserved romance from time to time. Though I'd thought of how I might feel returning to the Greenbrier before I invited him a few months back, I hadn't anticipated my longing for the past. I made a habit of living for the present and thought my youth long behind me.

"They're perfect," I said softly. I sat up and stopped his hands. It was too much—the rhododendron, the ghosts, the memories—and I couldn't focus on Lee. Not at all. "I'm afraid I'm too tired tonight."

Four

OCTOBER 31, 1946

N ot like that," I snapped.

Lee looked at me sharply. I sighed and let my hand drop
to the back of his, still gripping the pencil. It wasn't his fault that I
was like this. I had dreamed vividly last night, and for a moment,
before I truly woke, I thought I was back in my family's suite at
the old hotel. It was jarring to realize that though I was here I was
older, much older, and he was gone. They all were, really. I hadn't
seen Anzonella for years. Our drifting wasn't intentional, but with
her parents' passing, the talk of my divorce, and the horror of my
decision to have a career, neither of us returned to Tuxedo Park
much. I'd forever lost touch with some of the others, such as
Bolling and Helen and the friends outside of our small community, when I departed the old Greenbrier for the last time.

"You didn't sleep well." Lee abandoned the pad of paper and
reached over to tuck the bedclothes around me. The sheets were
too thin, so was the quilt, and even though Tom had been kind

enough to turn on the gas heat, I was freezing. Lee, in contrast, wore only his flannel pajama bottoms, lounging otherwise
unadorned at the foot of my bed. Perhaps I was only old.

The dream played in my mind once more. I could feel the
echo of my heart fluttering, the whisper of his breath on my ear.
"Romance and rhododendron," he said right before I awoke. Feeling
the way I'd felt thirty-eight years ago unsettled me. I didn't feel
it even with Dan, though I had loved him immensely, or with
any of my lovers, though I couldn't pretend I opened myself up
enough for attachment to any of them. In truth, though time
had numbed the sting of heartache, I never got over him.

"I slept well enough," I said. "It's only that this romance-and-
rhododendron theme has to be perfect. I can see it so clearly and
I need it executed just as I see it."

My chief designer, Glenn, would come down from the city
next week after I had ample time to dream up the strategy and
fix everything. He was the only one I could count on to see
my vision correctly. I'd known I needed him on my staff the
moment I saw his drawings. He'd just resigned his teaching at
the Fashion Institute of Technology and was selling his art in
an alley near my apartment. Glenn was an artist. Lee was not,
though he wanted to be. He was only my lover masquerading as a
business manager. It wasn't that he was bad at his position. He'd
graduated from Yale at the top of his class. His father, a current
Tuxedo Parkian, had trained him to manage the family's estate
for years—a role he'd likely take on full-time eventually—but to
me, my company was my company. No one could tell me what
to do with it.

I eyed the small bouquet Lee had given me last night. It was
sitting on my bedside table in a vase much too small for the large

blooms, the only vase in the cottage. The whole resort would have to be redone. Not only the walls and the furnishings, but the little trappings as well—the liveries, the matchboxes, the hand towels, the vases. Everything was out of sorts—disproportionate, drab, and tired. It was the same as every project, really, and I thrived in the midst of shabbiness and disorder. I remembered Sutton Place, the tenement homes I'd transformed for our friends the Phipps a decade ago into the most sought-after addresses in New York. They had been run-down, rodent-infested places that even the most desperate of tenants refused. It had taken time and thought and thousands of gallons of paint, but when I was finished, the brownstones boasted a shiny black facade with dead-white trim, and each door was cloaked in an eye-grabbing brilliant shade. Transformations like that were the most satisfying, and I was always rewarded mightily by the press. The Greenbrier would be no different.

Lee groaned and lifted himself off the bed. He crossed the small room and opened the simple linen curtains to let the early morning light through. There was a maple outside my window, the brilliant scarlet leaves looking almost painted.

I plucked the pencil from the notepad next to me and scribbled "scarlet and sunshine" on it. All my colors would be formed by the Greenbrier's wilderness. That was part of the romance, after all.

"Try to be patient with me," he said finally, turning his back to the morning glow. "I only want to give it a try, to understand you. I'll get it right."

"I know you will," I said.

I smiled at him and he grinned back. He assumed I was confident in his creative abilities. It was good for him to believe so. But what I really knew was that he would work until he did exactly as I asked, even if that meant conceding the design work to Glenn and me. That was Lee's strength.

"So, this morning. Another walk-through with the architects, and then you and I take to planning for when the rest of the team comes to do the concepts and design development?"

I nodded, thinking of how many reams of drafting paper Glenn would end up going through by the time he sketched all of the room designs to perfect scale.

"Yes," I said. "While I'm planning and dreaming, I'd appreciate you getting me the pricing and writing to the jobbers. I'll need Handman and Cinquinni. Linker and Wexler, too, and likely Buck if I decide on a mural."

He pursed his lips but didn't bother to disagree with me. Deep down he knew he was a businessman, not a creative, but everyone contracted a whimsical virus working for me. I suppose my passion was catching, but I didn't enjoy it. Especially when their virus blossomed into a full-blown disease and encouraged betrayal. I still wasn't over two of my former assistants trying to break away and steal my clients.

"I'll need you to be your best with our figures on this project, Lee. I rely on you," I said, hoping to salve his disappointment.

"I know," he said. "We'll need to be very careful. Especially until we're paid and cushioned correctly. Because, as you know, DD, the current state of things is—"

"The place is enormous, and I plan to outfit every inch of it in splendor like no one has ever seen," I interrupted, hoping to get back to dreaming instead of discussing the state of our accounts. It would only depress me, stifle me. "They're giving us $4.2 million to play with. The Greenbrier will be my magnum opus."

"It will, but even a budget of that size will go fast if you insist on buying things like that $450,000 antique Persian carpet you had shipped in for the Quitandinha. Ten items of that expense and we'll be over budget. We'll be dipping into your commission, your pockets again," he said.

I pushed my way out of bed, irritated by his scolding, and Lee took my hand to help me up.

"Darling, it's just us here," he whispered. He turned me around, grasping my face in his palms. He leaned down, and his lips met my forehead. I stepped back.

"No . . . I . . . He . . . ," I said. A strange sensation filled the pit of my stomach. It felt like guilt, and suddenly I didn't want him here. I didn't want anyone here, even my memories. *The past is the past*, I thought to myself. *Be in the present. Look forward to the future.* These words had become my motto of sorts after my last season here, and they'd served me well.

"You're not implying that he's here with us, are you?" Lee's eyes were sympathetic, waiting for me to tell him that I wasn't crazy. I shook my head. I'd lied to him about the man in my dream, the reason behind my vision. I'd had to. And the first person I'd thought of was Martin Van Buren. "And the theme? Surely you're not going to tell Mr. Bowman about President Van Buren haunting your dreams."

"Of course I am," I said, still avoiding the fact that Martin Van Buren was only a stand-in, a man who'd played such a role in the history of this place that mentioning a dream of him here was hardly surprising. Mr. Bowman didn't need to know the truth— that the theme was personal. President Van Buren would surely agree that it was fitting, as I did, and the idea that he'd visited me in a dream would inspire everyone involved. "You're under the assumption that Mr. Bowman believes as you do, when in fact, he understands it too: the Greenbrier must be refreshed but preserved. It must be a place that embodies the future, replacing the drabness of the old hotel's stuffy furnishings with expectations of optimistic whimsy while retaining the luxurious feel of the past. The glamour of that era is no better told than by Van Buren himself."

Lee reached behind me and plucked the notepad from the quilt.

"Very well, Mrs. Draper." I glanced at the disappointing sketch before me. Lee's rhododendrons were only sprigs, not the lush, vibrant blooms I knew them to be, that I'd draw later, but I knew how hard he was trying to please me, to understand me. The thought gave me pause. Perhaps I should have let him go already, replaced him with someone new despite my feelings for him. It wasn't fair to keep him on when I knew we would eventually end. At times I rationalized us by thinking of Dan—his new wife was twenty years his junior as well. But continuing with Lee, marrying Lee, would also mean my forced reentry to Tuxedo Park society. He had mentioned countless times that he wanted to settle there. Though I wanted their respect and connections, I absolutely wouldn't live by their rules. I sighed. Regardless, I didn't have the energy to train right now, and I knew Lee wouldn't lead us into bankruptcy and ruin. I needed familiarity and romance to inspire me, and Lee was one of the best business minds I'd ever known. Even so, doubt crept in with weariness as I stared at Lee's sketch. Perhaps all was already lost. Perhaps this job was too big.

I shook my head, hoping to shift my thinking. The Will-to-Be-Dreary was a real thing, an enemy. Dan had spoken of it often, deeming it the single obstacle to healing and success—worse than disease, worse than the wrong treatment, worse than the wrong medication. I'd taken it to heart. Dan had feared seeing it in Frank—he'd feared the nation seeing it in their leader—but Franklin Delano Roosevelt had never given a fig for dreariness. Until his final breath, he'd been an optimist. Dan said that, and not the medical treatment he'd prescribed, was why the man conquered polio for so long. I needed Frank's cheery resolve today and I would have it.

"Let's start the morning over, Lee," I said. He was sitting on my bed, sketching again. This time, the blooms were erupting together, just as I'd imagined, just as I'd seen in my youth. "That's better."

Glenn and I would still redo it all, but Lee's rendering wasn't altogether terrible this time. He outlined the final blossom and I sat down beside him, my fingers seeking the pencil. "Go on and dress. I'll finish the leaves." They'd be a shamrock color, the shade they appeared in the sunlight. He left me. In a matter of moments, I was drawing the final spine on the last leaf.

I stared at the drawing, at the cluster of blooms that looked so familiar, and was filled with peace.

"You didn't have to remind me," I said to the empty room. "I've never forgotten."

I closed the notebook and tucked it into my leather briefcase propped beside the bedside table. I glanced over my shoulder and saw the looming gleam of the Greenbrier through the maple and smiled. Hope replaced all the doubts, silenced all the negatives. This project wouldn't be a failure. It couldn't be. I wouldn't allow it.

Five

I made it up to our suite well before my parents. Mademoiselle and Roger had retired hours ago, and the rooms were silent. I stood in the foyer, staring through to the drawing room at the gold brocade curtains drawn across the windows for the night. They were replicas of the curtains in the Colonnade House—our usual resort quarters for the summer, an old cottage situated on one of five rows of cottages built by industrialists from all over the country before the hotel—but these were thinner. You could tell by the amount of moonshine streaming through them to the knotty pine floor. The staff had tried to make the hotel luxurious enough for us, that was clear, though I knew Father still wasn't over the Greers claiming their home for the summer after all these years away.

"Hotel lodging is for the new blood," I'd heard him tell Mother when he received the letter from Mr. Greer. *"And the Colonnade is easily the most beautiful of the quarters. What will everyone say*

now that we've been banished to a four-room suite at the hotel? Do you even suppose we'll fit? Perhaps I should try to buy the Colonnade from old Nicholas." But then Mademoiselle had ushered Roger into the drawing room for his good-night kisses, interrupting Father's complaints.

The routine here was the same, nearly to the minute, as it was at home. When I was younger, bedtime was always eight thirty sharp, and after, Mademoiselle would drift around the Colonnade fluffing pillows and drawing drapes. I knew she'd done the same tonight with Roger. Mademoiselle's sole goal in life seemed to be to make sure we were never confused by disorder. *"A haphazard schedule makes for a flustered child."* I disagreed. A person used to living in perfect order was always thrown by change. That was clear every season at the Greenbrier, when uncommon guests rattled familiarity. In this moment, feeling my heart still drumming from dancing with Mr. Rossi, I knew I'd been made a creature of routine as well. Perhaps he would help me shake loose from the order and familiarity. Perhaps, if I let him, if he wanted to, he could show me a world of things I'd never known. I'd only been to Rome once, on summer tour with my family when I was eleven, but I could still taste the macaroni au gratin and feel the wonder and weight of the history. Was he from Tuscany? Or perhaps he woke up every day looking at the Mediterranean. I'd even heard that it wasn't scandalous in the slightest for Italian women to take a dip in a sleeveless swimming costume. I wondered if I would have the nerve.

I pulled my shoes from my feet, letting the coolness of the wood floor sink into my aching arches. Loping into the drawing room and onto the ancient oriental rug, I let my hands drift across the furnishings—the leather armchair, the mahogany table, and the maroon tufted couch. Funeral parlor decor. The same sort found at the Tuxedo Park clubhouse.

My eyes were heavy, and I thought to retire directly, but my mind wouldn't stop swirling. I could still feel Mr. Rossi's hands on my waist, hear the tone of his voice when it seemed he would confess being drawn to me. How strange and wonderful it had all been. Of course, I didn't believe it, but it was nice to think for a moment that the idea of my love for Warren tormented him.

Mr. Rossi wasn't here only for holiday. No one was. Everyone had some sort of agenda, and I wanted to know what Mr. Rossi's was, how I fit in that plan. He'd sought me out for a dance when he could have approached dozens of other women. Perhaps he sought financial gain. That was the least offensive possibility. We weren't the wealthiest family at the Greenbrier, but perhaps in comparison to the Kanes or Phinizys, an alliance with us was a surer way to secure wealth. My parents' estate would be split only two ways, between Roger and me, instead of five or six. At least that's how Grover Hartford had figured it. The charming, handsome outsider from California, a distant cousin of Ogden Mills, who claimed he was a partial heir to Mr. Mills's thoroughbred racing fortune, had swept me off my feet at Mary Cunningham's coming out and then called on me at our city house for the next two days. The second day, he began to speak of engagement. Though not directly, he made it clear that he was actually penniless, that Mr. Mills hadn't a clue he was in the city, and that he assumed I had a handsome inheritance, as Father had only two children. He embarrassed me terribly. I asked him to leave and he obliged, admitting he didn't really feel for me. I'd been a pawn. Afterward, I sent word to all of my friends that he was a snake, and never saw him again.

I lifted the silver pitcher from the cherry tea table next to the windows and poured a glass of water. I'd been interested in Grover, but I wasn't in love with him. Would my response have been different if he held my heart? Would I mind being a fortune hunter's wife if I loved him? I laughed under my breath. Why bother thinking on the question? The thought was ridiculous and irrelevant. Mr. Rossi had probably been speaking of someone else. Pulling the blinds aside, I looked down at the drive. I could make out a few figures silhouetted by the moonlight and the electric lamps along the path to the cottages. Couples held hands, while others walked alone, and clusters of young girls practically skipped, enlivened by the thrill of dancing with a man. I knew there were others out there in the dark, the few who dared slip away while the ball was still in full swing. It was a discreet practice, but I'd heard rumors of the kisses stolen in the woods among rhododendron groves. Mr. Rossi's face appeared in my mind, followed by Anzonella's comment about his lips. Had his departure from me been a ruse to rendezvous with someone else? I tried to recall if I'd seen Bolling before I left, but I couldn't. I'd had one last dance with Warren and decided, in the midst of the final steps, that I'd have to safeguard Warren's future wife from Mr. Rossi, for if she happened to fall into his arms during a ball, she'd be lost to Warren at once.

"Star, I am embarrassed and appalled."

The slap of the heavy carved door into the wall punctuated Father's statement as he and Mother appeared in the doorway. I eyed the closed bedroom doors around the edge of the semicircular room, thinking I should remind him that Roger and Mademoiselle were sleeping. Instead, I tugged the drapes closed again and waited, not bothering to guess what he was upset about.

"Paul, please. It's a ball and she's a lady. It would have been rude to refuse."

Behind my father, Mother rolled her eyes and started to remove the teardrop diamonds from her ears. She yawned and waved at me before disappearing into her bedroom. Father walked toward me, glaring.

"You're much too impulsive. Perhaps allowing you to come home from studying at Brearley was a mistake. Ever since, you have acted as though there are no rules, no order." Father's voice was raised and his face was flushed.

"I came home from Brearley six years ago, Father. And to my knowledge, I've not soiled the Tuckerman name," I said.

"Do you know who his father is? He's hardly one of us." He snatched the crystal scotch decanter from the tray beside me and poured a tall glass.

"I know full well that Mr. Abercrombie is Warren's father, and that he doesn't live in Tuxedo Park," I said.

Father's glass clacked hard against the table.

"Don't be flip. You know I'm not speaking of Warren and Ren," Father snapped. "That Italian auto driver. Vacchelli told us that his father is a *silver* miner. He's a disgrace, parading around the ballroom acting as though he belongs, like he's some sort of royalty. And his uncle is just as offensive. He's here either to attach himself to a great fortune or to interject himself into American politics. Does he suppose that putting his nephew up to seducing our daughters will win him to our side?"

Father had barely taken a breath. This was how he always was when angry, and I didn't have the nerve to interrupt him. It was like throwing kindling on a blazing fire. I wouldn't dare let on that I'd enjoyed my time with Mr. Rossi.

"The way you let him hold you, Star. It was much too intimate for my liking. And you should have seen the way poor Warren looked. He was tormented," he said. The sentiments reminded me of Mr. Rossi's face in the last moments of our dance, and before I could help it, I smiled. Perhaps he thought something of me after all. "Did I say something humorous?"

I straightened my mouth into a more acceptable smirk and sank down onto the sofa. My dress, once a sweltering swathe of fabric during the ball, was now frigid as my body cooled.

"Don't be so concerned for Warren, Father. He's not taken with me. We're not taken with each other. As much as you and Mr. Abercrombie wish it were so, it's not."

Father took a sip of his scotch and stared at the windows as though he could pretend to be distracted by the dull curtains.

"I danced with Mr. Rossi once. If he's seducing anyone, I think it would be safe to assume it's Bolling." I sighed. "And I would think his partner would need to be a bit closer to the commander in chief to get anywhere politically. Surely he and his uncle have been made aware that the Tafts will arrive tomorrow. Shouldn't we wait to see whether he attaches himself to Helen before assuming that Mr. Vacchelli is angling for the Italian advantage? How do you suppose that would occur anyway? A courtship and marriage and wooing of the wife's family and connections would be quite an undertaking. It's not as if he's Prince Adalbert."

"I don't want you dancing with him again." Father drained the last of his scotch. "Perhaps Bolling was his dance partner, but his eyes followed you all night."

I nodded, hoping my cheeks didn't give away any inkling of the way I felt.

"You'll realize soon enough that Warren should be your intended. Don't let the romance of a stranger and the Greenbrier lead you astray."

Anger flared. "Do you suppose me so easily ensnared, Father?" I stood as he did. "I've never swooned before and I'm not enticed by anyone unless I choose to be. Warren and I aren't like you and Mother. We're not pretending to be disinterested because we're unsure of the other's feelings. We simply aren't a fit."

"You'll not dance with Mr. Rossi again," Father repeated. He turned away from me and retreated toward his bedroom next to Mother's. I stared up at the high ceiling, examining the brass chandelier decorated in molded grapes and acorns and crystals, knowing I couldn't agree. "Remember. We're an important family with important connections. It would behoove you to be cautious. I'll not be made a fool. He may try to weasel his way into our families, our government, our businesses, but he will never catch my daughter in his trap. You are intended for a good life—a peaceful, comfortable course with a man of honor who loves you—and it is my duty to see to it that you're properly settled. Those Italians are up to something, and the Tuckerman family will not be a part of it. Do you understand me?"

His words reverberated in my ears as he slammed the bedroom door. The plaster walls seemed to close in. I'd read once that European royals felt trapped, that in spite of their advantage, they were in chains, prisoners in their palaces. I felt that often. How many seasons would I stand here among the same trappings, every disappointing conversation with my father reminding me of the last and of the one to come, the only way out a ring from Warren and a false promise of love from me. That would be a jail too. I couldn't bear being with these people any longer. I couldn't stand the sameness. Something had to change.

Reflexively I swept the drapes back, tying the sashes in bows against the window frames. I pushed the leather chair into the foyer and strode into my room for the floral settee at the bottom of the poster bed. The maroon sofa could stay, but it had to be reset parallel with the settee. There was a spare set of sheets in the trunk under my bed. I'd seen the maids extracting them once. I pulled out the white flat sheet, tossed it onto the settee, and dragged the couch into the drawing room, not minding if the loud screeching woke the whole suite and the rooms beneath. When the settee was situated, I doubled the sheet and flung it over the top of the drab, old, dark mahogany table. Suddenly everything seemed brighter, different, but the room needed something else. I recalled the Jasper Francis Cropsey painting in the hallway outside of our suite. It was a lovely landscape of the Hudson with colorful fall leaves and a breathtaking sunset. It could hang on the wall next to the portrait of President Van Buren and contribute quite well to the new room. But I'd have to find something to replace it.

I heard the steady Westminster chime coming from the breakfast room and wandered down the dark hallway beside Roger's closed door. The clock was made of cherry—I still couldn't figure everyone's obsession with polished wood—and the face was a strange octagon shape. No one would miss it, especially me. I plucked it from the wall and a small compartment below the clock edged open. Clicking it shut, I carried the clock down the hallway and out the door.

The Greenbrier was always quiet after the ball, everyone immediately retiring, but it was especially quiet tonight. No one wanted to greet the Tafts with bloodshot eyes. It was rumored that they would arrive on the ten o'clock train tomorrow. It was quite funny that anyone cared when the Tafts were arriving at all. True, we hoped Mr. Taft would be our next president, but their family had been friends with our families for generations. The ceremony of it all was strange—like Queen Victoria trying to woo Prince Albert after they'd been married for years.

I hoisted the painting down from the wall, hoping no one would materialize from the stairwell at the end of the hall. I hurriedly lifted the clock to hang in its place and then snatched the painting. My hands were sweating. Though my friends seemed to think otherwise—I suppose they assumed my boldness by the way I spoke—I was rarely daring. This was my first time overriding the Greenbrier's designer. Whoever that person was should be replaced anyway.

I tried the door, but the knob wouldn't turn. I tried again and again before realizing that I'd forgotten to turn the latch before I stepped out. No one would hear if I knocked. I'd have to go down to the lobby and hope one of the bellmen was still working.

No one was at the reception desk. Of course. I tried the bell again, dinging the brass clacker as if it was an emergency, but the shrill noise only echoed through the expansive room. I scrunched my toes against the oriental rug and tapped my fingers on the marble countertop. Sleeping on one of the settees wouldn't be an option; my feet would dangle, and heaven forbid someone find me drooling or snoring. I turned around and looked at the lobby, the sight of which, regardless of my feelings about my romantic pairing, had been welcome each year.

I plodded down the aisle between the pillars toward the wide whitewashed front door. Out the windows, I could see the lawn stretching before me, golden in the gas lamplight, the paths down to the cottages and the springhouse deserted. The crickets chirped their soothing song loud enough that I could hear it through the panes. I watched the lightning bugs twinkle in the dark, beckoning me away from the lobby to the wild beauty of a summer night in White Sulphur Springs.

There wasn't anyone on the porch either. I looked around, expecting someone to stop me, to wonder why I wasn't in bed. At once, I felt free. No one knew I was here, traipsing barefoot around the Greenbrier. I leaned against one of the porch columns and unpinned my hair, shaking the loose coils free. Tonight, I was going to walk unbidden, as though I weren't a Tuckerman or a marriage prospect, only a girl wandering alone through the most beautiful nature I had ever seen. The last time I'd done something like this, I was young, maybe ten. Mademoiselle had lost sight of me and I went down to the creek bed behind our house in Tuxedo Park. I'd walked atop the rocks nearly to the Alexanders' house, and by the time she found me, my white dress was brown and torn. Mademoiselle had scolded me, but Mother only laughed. That was before I found out that I could only go so far, that Tuxedo Park wasn't unending forest, but a community enclosed by a gate.

I smiled as I made my way down the steps. There were no fences here and no one awake to stop me. If I wanted to walk clear to California, I could, but tonight I was content where I was. The air was rich with the sweet smell of phlox and wildflowers. I breathed deep and followed the path down to the springhouse. Though the original springhouse had been destroyed during the Civil War, the new house with a vibrant green dome and white columns still housed the ancient healing spring that initiated our gatherings at the Greenbrier. I thought it was magical. A generation ago and generations before that, everyone came for the springhouse. They took the water three times each day, sure that the minerals and sulfur were the antidote to any ailment. It was still a healing exercise—my parents drank glasses each day—but the practice didn't occur so frequently now, mostly because there wasn't time. Tomorrow would begin a week of Centennial festivities to end the season—elegant dinners, lawn fetes, luncheons al fresco, the horse show, and the Hunt Ball. A ceremonial tasting would mark the start of the celebrations, but otherwise, the spring would be mostly forgotten.

The water was bubbling below me as I gripped the metal pump handle. Perhaps a sip would settle my restlessness. I lifted and pushed down a few times until water streamed from the nozzle. Absent a proper glass, I leaned over the well for a drink. Some of the water pooled in my mouth while the majority of the stream soaked the front of my gown, plastering the turquoise silk to my skin.

"Whatever are you doing, Miss Tuckerman?"

I jolted back from the spring to find Mr. Rossi behind me. He was leaning against one of the columns, grinning, as if he'd been there all along.

"I should ask you the same thing, Mr. Rossi," I said. My heart was still pounding from being startled and my words came out in a series of breaths. "How long have you been standing there?"

"Enzo, please," he said, walking toward me. "Just a moment. I was only visiting my fiancée."

He smiled, gesturing toward Hebe atop the dome. "You're soaked. Here. Have my jacket." He shrugged it off and placed it over my shoulders without waiting for my consent.

"Th-thank you," I said, my teeth clacking despite the warmth of the night. He remained close, inches in front of me, not moving back as a proper gentleman would. "But I shouldn't. My father doesn't know I'm here, and if he found—"

"I didn't say I was giving it to you, Miss Tuckerman," Enzo said, "and your father is sleeping, much like my uncle." I swallowed and threaded my arms through the sleeves. The jacket smelled like him, like lavender and sandalwood. I'd barely noticed anything but his touch when we'd danced, but the scent was unmistakable.

"Why aren't you?" I asked. "Sleeping, I mean." He smiled and looked away, his gaze drifting over my head in the direction of the cottages called Baltimore Row.

"Miss Phinizy asked me to walk her home," he said. My stomach dropped.

"Oh." I started to shrug out of his jacket, but his hand clutched the lapel and drew it back around me.

"That was hours ago, of course," he said, almost whispering. "I suppose she wanted me to linger, but I didn't. I didn't want to go home either." His eyes were on my face, but I kept my gaze on the spring, knowing if I looked at him I'd betray myself. I didn't want him to know that he affected me, that any part of me thought anything of him at all. "So I went walking. It's beautiful country here, the stars and the moon and the fireflies. I haven't seen fireflies in years, since I was on holiday in Tuscany with Uncle."

"They're brighter here than almost anywhere," I said, watching them flicker around us. I looked at him and he grinned.

"I'm sorry." He cleared his throat. "I'm sorry for departing our dance so abruptly. I didn't grow up this way. I'm not entirely used to veiling my emotions."

"It's quite all right," I said. I couldn't be made to look like I was fawning over him like the others, especially if even a hint of my father's speculation was correct. "Clearly, I'm not either, and I've been taught to stifle them from the moment I was born. I should've been politer at the onset. I was one of the only ladies you'd been introduced to, and it was unkind of me to neglect to seek you out for a dance myself. And, before I forget, I must clarify that I am not pining for Warren. We're just friends, though our fathers wish we were more."

His eyes crinkled and he smiled.

"I'll be sure to save you a dance at the Hunt Ball," I went on. "Although between Miss Phinizy and Miss Anzonella Kane and, of course, Miss Helen Taft, who will arrive tomorrow, I doubt you'll have much room on your dance card for me."

He reached for me but seemed to think better of taking me in his arms. Instead he clutched my hand and drew me closer.

"You know very well that I wasn't disturbed by your lack of manners, Miss Tuckerman. I clearly don't abide by the rules myself. It's that . . . you're enchanting. I haven't been able to stop thinking of you. Even tonight as I was walking around I kept looking up at the windows of the Greenbrier hoping for a glimpse, and then there you were, walking across the lawn. I thought I was seeing things, but I knew it was you, even with your hair unbound." His fingers combed through a strand, but in spite of the urge to fall against him, to let him kiss me, I stepped back.

"Why?" I asked. "Out of all the women here, why me? I'm not the most beautiful or the most charming. I'm not the most—"

"Please stop," he said, closing the divide between us once again. "From the moment I saw you, Miss Tuckerman, I—"

"Call me Dorothy," I said. Even though I doubted his words, I wanted so badly to believe them.

"Dorothy," he said. He leaned down. I could feel his breath on my neck, the whisper of his lips on my ear. "When I race, when I'm about to win, when everything is going right, I feel something—a surge and then a steadiness, a knowing." His hands drifted to my cheeks, his eyes meeting mine. He was different. He wasn't like the rest. Exactly what I'd always wanted. "*Voglio passareil resto della mia vita con te.* You might think I'm mad, but we're going to marry, you and I. We have the same spirit—a wildness and gentleness at the same time, a spirit that doesn't belong where we began, a spirit that knows it was made for more than circling the pen." I stared at him, unable to speak. My stomach swam with nerves, with wanting him to kiss me. "And someday we'll come back here and remember this, the way we started."

At once something shifted. My father's voice echoed in my mind, followed by the memories of being overlooked for someone more beautiful, of being conned for my fortune. Enzo couldn't feel this way about me this quickly, even if I did. It wasn't possible. Perhaps a man could fall in love with Anzonella or even Bolling in a night, but not with me. Despite my pretty face, I had never been dainty. My friend Helen's cousin Christopher had made that tremendously clear when, after two weeks of flirting and even a kiss, he transferred his affection to Lydia Stuart, a girl half a foot shorter than I.

I stepped away from Enzo, immediately slinging the jacket from my shoulders and pressing it to his chest.

"You're right. I think you're mad. Positively insane. And I'm certainly not going to marry you. I know nothing about you."

I snapped the words, forcing laughter at the end as though the thought that he could care for me so quickly was ridiculous. He simply knew that I was restless, desperate for adventure, desperate to be different, and that made me an easy target. "Do you suppose I'm the weak one? That my friends are smarter than I am? You chose the tall girl, the one who seemed most likely to fall for your overtures, but I'll tell you now that I don't believe you."

Enzo's eyes were stony, his jaw set.

"You must," he said quietly. "I know it seems impossible, but my parents were the same way, drawn to each other in the span of a night. I've always thought it ridiculous until now, but Mother swore I'd know immediately when I found you." His fingers drifted across mine and I paced away from him, up the steps of the springhouse.

"Why? Why do you need me to believe you? So you can win influence for your country, or so you can marry into a wealthy family? Everyone sees right through you, you know."

I immediately wished I could take it back. Tears welled in my eyes and I turned and started toward the Greenbrier. I wanted him to come after me, to argue with me, to tell me I was wrong, but there was only silence and then the sound of his footsteps disappearing as he walked the other way.

Six

One would have thought that Queen Victoria herself had come to the Greenbrier. Waiters in pure-snow liveries and bellmen in grass green and guests in linen and cotton finery scurried around the property, back and forth from the hotel to the springhouse. The Tafts were on the front lawn. They hadn't yet made it to their accommodations at the President's Cottage, swarmed by well-wishers the moment they arrived off the train.

I closed the copy of *Anne of Green Gables* that I'd swiped from the library and set it on my lap, unable to concentrate on anything but the commotion. In half an hour we were all supposed to gather round the springhouse for a ceremonial taste to kick off the final Centennial celebration, the end of the season. A crowd wrapped the perimeter of the well, the Phinizys already there. I couldn't figure if they were attempting to gain an advantageous position next to the guests of honor or simply wanted to be the first served and the first to leave. I couldn't get over the Tafts being made a spectacle. Mr. and Mrs. Taft had been just like the rest of the families here until recently. In fact, Father had been at the famous bobsledding party where the couple met.

"Do you suppose we should walk down?" Anzonella appeared at my side, sinking onto the stone steps.

"No." I sighed.

Father was probably already there, and I didn't want to run into him. I'd finally managed to find a bellman at twelve thirty in the morning, and although I didn't think I'd woken Father, I wasn't in the mood to engage his anger if someone besides Enzo had seen me out of my room in the early morning.

Charles Taft was sitting in the grass now, a ten-year-old's admission that he was stuck. A shrill whistle startled everyone's bustling for a moment, and Helen reached down and plucked the blade of grass from between her brother's thumbs. She was a few years younger than I, but she had always had an unusually grown-up personality—a mingling of her father's sternness and ambition and her mother's gregarious social manner. Her older brother, Robert, was an interesting sort and a literal genius, but the absolute worst to converse with if you were at all witty. He was away apprenticing at a law firm this season. Otherwise he too would be a commodity, both old men and young women clamoring to bid him welcome.

"Can you believe our fathers? What in the world has possessed them?" Anzonella tipped her head at the lawn. As the crowd shifted they came into view, standing next to Mr. Taft as though they were his guards.

"Of course I can. They're not men to be shown up, and—" The words died on my lips as Enzo appeared in my periphery by way of his accommodations on Paradise Row. The Bridgers family, who owned the cottage Enzo and Mr. Vacchelli occupied, was away this season, mourning the loss of their patriarch, who'd passed away only a month ago.

"Our fathers aren't men to be shown up," I started again, hoping to dispel the way Enzo's appearance rattled me. Mr. Vacchelli was at Enzo's side, but no one would notice him. Enzo was smiling, wearing a fitted linen suit in café au lait, his straw boater tucked under his arm, the breeze tousling his hair. My gaze flitted to Helen, hoping she wouldn't notice, but her eyes were already on him.

"My goodness," Anzonella whispered. "Did you see that?"

"What?" I asked, feigning indifference, running my hands down my cotton voile skirt, striped white, lemon, and sky. *"We're going to marry, you and I."* Enzo's voice sounded in my mind. I couldn't forget the way he'd looked in the moonlight. It was almost too much to bear, but I pushed it away. He'd meant none of it. If he had, he would have come after me, despite my cruelty, to tell me I was wrong. He would have known that in my heart I wanted to believe him.

"Well, for one, Helen Taft is practically ogling Mr. Rossi and he her, and Irma, Margaret Allis, and Bolling have all turned completely away from the Tafts to greet Mr. Rossi." She laughed. "He's handsome to be sure, but to be so enraptured . . . Dorothy, why aren't you throwing yourself in the running? He held you quite closely last night." I rolled my eyes and adjusted my wide-brimmed hat trimmed with a gargantuan silk cabbage rose, hoping my face wasn't as flushed as it felt. The only mercy was in the fact that no one had witnessed our conversation last night. As far as anyone knew, we'd only danced once, and I was far from his favorite.

"I don't throw myself at anyone," I said. "Most certainly not at a man so aware of his charm."

"Oh. I wouldn't blame him for that." Warren appeared behind me, wearing a costume nearly identical to Enzo's. He took a sip of his iced tea and swung down next to us, practically causing the elderly Mr. Jones to fall over him on his way down the steps. "And I wouldn't say I blame him for using his charm. If want for attention and influence is a sin, we'd all be guilty, would we not?"

"But he's playing on the feelings of these poor women," Anzonella said, as though his swagger didn't make her swoon at all. She lifted a hand to the lawn. Some of the crowd and our fathers had dispersed to the springhouse.

"Poor women? Bolling and Helen? You're speaking in jest, aren't you? You know how much they love to flirt too," Warren said. "Last year, Eleanor was—"

Warren stopped short, his face paling with her name.

"If you still feel for her, you should find her," I said, abruptly wondering if I'd spoken out of turn. If Warren was engaged, who would I walk the treadmill with? Last year, when he was clearly enamored, I wondered the same, dreading the possibility of facing the pairing alone. I forced the thoughts away. I couldn't be selfish. Not when it came to his heart. It wasn't as though I would ever love him, but I did appreciate him, and we were friends. "No matter her status, she still must be the woman you loved and—"

"She lied to me," he whispered, standing. "Would the two of you do me the honor of escorting me to the springhouse?" He forced a grin and crooked his elbows out for us to hold.

On the lawn I noticed Bolling and Helen doing the same, both drawing much closer to Enzo than Anzonella and I were to Warren. We walked down the steps and onto the path, converging with the other group. I was suddenly aware of my height, second only to Enzo.

"How lucky we are!" Warren said, nodding at Enzo. Enzo's eyes flicked to mine before settling on Warren. He tipped his head, barely mustering a smile. Why was he feigning misery? It angered me, the way he acted as though I'd hurt him. If I had, if my accusations were false, he should have told me. It could have been me by his side. My stomach flipped in spite of my irritation. I didn't want Helen or Bolling or Anzonella or Edith or Irma touching him at all. I could feel his hands on my face and wanted to sling away from Warren, clutch Enzo's lapels, and shake him until he told me the truth. Did he want me or my father's influence? Would he really take me back to Italy with him? But I would do none of it. Tuckermans weren't wrong, and I would stand by what I'd said. Also, he was escorting Helen Taft.

Mr. Dulaney, the owner of the Greenbrier, motioned to the line of waiters idling with crystal goblets. "Without further ado, the spring waters will be poured. As you drink it, remember our forefathers, whose lives have been renewed and healed by the White Sulphur Spring." Though we were in the back of the crush, I could hear the rhythmic creak of the pump and then the gurgle of water. The guests whooped and cheered as everyone pushed forward.

"The waters are truly magical," I heard Bolling say to Enzo. "There's something cleansing and lovely about taking them in. I'm thrilled for you to try it."

"I've had it already," he said. I could barely make out his reply amid the chatter. "It's putrid. I don't care to have it again, even if it does lend to health."

"There you are." Mother appeared, pushing her way through the crowd. She grasped my arm and lunged for Helen's. As she yanked me forward, my arm brushed Enzo's and I twitched away. "We're to take the water with the Tafts," she said. "Excuse us, Warren, Bolling, Anzonella." She eyed Enzo but didn't address him.

"With respect, Mrs. Tuckerman, I've promised Mr. Rossi that I'd show him the way of the Greenbrier, and I doubt my father needs my support to drink a glass of sulfur water." Helen smiled graciously and started to back away. Enzo stood behind her, his face not betraying any sort of merriment at this reply.

"Very well," Mother said without relinquishing her grip on my wrist as she pulled me toward the well. We neared the honorees at the front. "I know he can seem a bit old hat at times, but your father is always right," she said under her breath. A waiter handed Mother and me goblets of mineral water, and she took a long draw before addressing me again. "That Mr. Rossi will stop at nothing to attach himself to one of our girls. Thank heavens it won't be you." I nodded at Mr. and Mrs. Taft and tipped my crystal into theirs, feeling the weight of the tradition and requirement as I did, half shocked that Enzo hadn't followed me, that he hadn't insisted on disputing the comment he wasn't close enough to hear.

It was humid for White Sulphur. Even in the shade of one of the Greenbrier's many century-old oaks along the lawn, all of us were sweating. Edith leaned over the collection of our discarded hats, rumpling the white cotton picnic blanket that the Greenbrier's employees faithfully set out for us each afternoon, and reached for the pitcher of lemonade.

"I swear these costumes are a curse," Edith said, eyeing her black-and-white-striped cotton dress. Her skin was flushed despite the cool drink.

Anzonella laughed at her sister and dabbed her forehead with the end of her apricot silk sash. After the ceremonial imbibing, most of the guests had taken coaches down to the site of the Centennial horse show, including our families. We'd opted to stay, mainly because we'd all seen it before. For some reason all the betting men liked to see the place often, as though the way it looked in drought or rain or full sun or under clouds mattered tremendously to their fortunes.

"Perhaps tomorrow we should all appear in our chemises," I said, drawing the hem of my first layer of cotton away from the second.

"Women used to," Bolling said, leaning against one of two highly coveted wicker lawn chairs and closing her eyes to the canopy of gnarled tree branches. "Years ago, before the bath-house, women could simply recline right in the open river. I don't know what's happened to that practice, but I daresay it should return."

"Can you imagine? Just sitting out there nearly naked for the world to appraise?" Edith asked. "Hand me another sandwich, would you?"

I handed her a fried green tomato sandwich from the silver platter.

"I do enjoy a Russian bath, but I'm glad for the tubs and the walls," Bolling said.

"I think I'd like the wildness of bathing directly in the river,"

Anzonella said. The lawn was almost vacant today save a group of men my grandfather's age led by Thomas Marshall, Jerome Bonaparte, and Thomas Clay on the other side under a similarly large tree. Trails of cigar smoke filtered up to the treetops, and much coughing and grunting was to be heard. Soon our fathers would replace these men. It was the way it worked here at the Greenbrier, each generation assuming the previous one.

"Ask Helen to tell Mr. Dulaney that she'd like him to build a spa directly atop the river. You know she'll have anything she wishes from now on." I detected a slight edge to Bolling's voice.

"It absolutely cannot be a shack of old if they are to accommodate it though," I said, the idea of a frontiersman's outpost building amid the loveliness of the old cottages and the hotel utterly appalling. "It must be beautiful—white and green— soothing and bright at the same time. A place to relax and a place to rejuvenate—"

"And they should commission you to decorate it. Girls, you should see the Tuckermans' drawing room. Dorothy decided to change it a bit last night and—" Anzonella's attempt at my praise fell on deaf ears.

Bolling laughed, a short bark under her breath. "See? Everyone knows it's true. Helen will get whatever she wants just because her father has the gumption to put his name in the ring for president. What's wrong with our fathers? Our families are all just as fine."

She was now sitting erect, her eyes glaring as she spoke.

"Please tell me this isn't about that Mr. Rossi," Edith said. She rolled her eyes. I busied myself with pouring another glass of lemonade, hoping no one would address me about the topic.

"Of course it is," Anzonella said. "Bolling was clearly his

favorite until Miss Taft came flouncing onto the scene, and now, it seems, his attention has shifted."

I took a sip of my lemonade, trying to concentrate on the bite of the citrus and the sweetness of the sugar instead of the urge to stake my claim, to tell them all about what he'd told me, how he'd begged me last night. For as much as I doubted his feelings toward me, my own sentiments suggested affection could strike as deeply and quickly as he said. I wondered what it would be like to walk the piazzas arm in arm, to live wherever we wished, to see Europe not from the confines of American society but from the thrilling view of an auto racer's wife who could wander at will. But then again, perhaps Anzonella was right. Perhaps Bolling was his pet yesterday and I last night and now Helen today. Perhaps my suspicion had good reason.

"It's not that I want to marry him," Bolling said. She fiddled with the wide yellow ribbon bound around the crown of her head, accentuating her elaborate coiled coiffure. It was clear she'd tried this morning, that she'd had her maid switch up her normal braided low bun to draw attention to her long slim neck—one of Bolling's most noticeable beauty marks. "But I do want him. Is that wrong?"

"It is if Helen wants his hand," Edith said. "Surely you know you shouldn't confuse the poor man if it's marriage he's after."

"Of course that's what he's after!" I could feel my cheeks blush and immediately wished I had the self-control to omit myself from the conversation entirely. "He's here, isn't he? And he's paying quite close attention to all of us. Not to mention Enzo is Italian and here with an Italian diplomat. Doesn't anyone think it's odd that they're here? Especially with Austria-Hungary and Italy's relations in a delicate state." What was I doing? Was

I spreading my father's assumptions—the same I'd argued him on—because I agreed with him? Or was I mentioning them because I wanted my friends to keep their distance?

Anzonella swallowed a bite of sandwich. "Enzo, is it? And I don't think it's strange in the slightest. Last year, Mr. and Mrs. Von Stengel were here, as was Mr. Izvolsky, and no one so much as batted an eye," she said. "It's only because Mr. Vacchelli has come with a handsome nephew that there's any sort of speculation. I'm assuming you're echoing your father, Dorothy, are you not? I doubt you've suddenly taken interest in politics. Mine said something of the same, but I'll not believe anything unless it's proven."

I nodded and took a sip of my lemonade.

"Forget I said anything." I felt foolish.

"When do you suppose everyone will return from the race-track?" Edith asked, thankfully changing the subject.

"Now," Bolling said, reaching for her straw hat lined with silk gardenia flowers and trimmed with lace. Sure enough, I could hear the distant sound of wheels over cobblestones. We all fell silent, watching the line of black coaches congesting the circular drive. Footmen and nannies emerged from the front of the Greenbrier and opened the doors, then began helping men and women and children step down from the carriages. So far, I didn't see any of my contemporaries—Helen or Enzo included.

I felt eyes on my face and turned to find Anzonella looking at me. She pinned her hat to her head, then clutched my arm and pulled me close.

"Green looks horrible on you," she whispered. "Either own your feelings or squash them, but don't go round tarnishing reputations because you can't bear the discomfort. I shouldn't have to remind you of the dangers, but I shall. Jealousy is how it all began with Aunt Violet, and look at her now. She's stuck in a crumbling castle in Luxembourg with Prince Noah, who is now nearly ninety and quite frail, while Archie has lived a happily married life in Tuxedo these past fifteen years. Mother said her last letter sounded a bit like she was going mad. And all because she decided to marry Noah to spite Archie for passing her by. I daresay I imagine she'd trade her title for a chance to change her mind." Anzonella paused. "Which reminds me. Perhaps there's a way to save her I haven't thought of. In any case—"

"I'm not sure what you're implying, but even if jealousy turns my heart to stone someday, I promise you I'll never marry a man my grandfather's age," I said, my nose wrinkling in disgust. Violet's horrid match with Prince Noah had been the talk of Tuxedo for months, according to my parents, and I knew from her saying so that Anzonella had taken it especially hard. Violet, though not an aunt by blood, was Mrs. Kane's friend since birth and had been a regular fixture in the Kane house until Anzonella was five. She still talked about the stories she would tell and the forts she would build the children in the nursery. Violet had been Anzonella's heroine.

"Good afternoon, ladies." Warren appeared before us with Henry, both appearing to be in jovial spirits.

"Anzonella, Dorothy, care to join us for a stroll on Lovers' Lane?" Henry winked at Anzonella and she blushed and stood. She hadn't told me that their friendship sparked at the dance. I took Warren's hand and let him help me up. A walk on Lovers' Lane was a momentous occasion in our parents' time and sometimes still was. It meant that a couple was serious. If the walk progressed down one path, a proposal would be had, but if a stroll ended along another, the courtship was over. Warren and I had walked both sides together countless times, knowing neither end applied to us. It was fun nonetheless. We laughed at the nervousness of some and the overtures we overheard, especially if they were well-received. It was altogether embarrassing if a proposal was made and rejected.

I looped my arm through Warren's and we strolled alongside Anzonella and Henry. Henry was sweating, his mustache glistening with perspiration, despite the shade of his straw bowler, but Anzonella didn't seem to mind and leaned into him as they walked. In contrast I could feel the heat radiating through Warren's linen jacket and let my arm drop back to my side, holding on to him only with the grip of my fingers.

"Do you think you've bet wisely on the show, Warren? Today's exhibition made me think I'd better reconsider my vote," Henry said, nodding hello to a line of young children as they skipped from the cottages to the hotel lawn. Warren laughed and removed his hat for a moment to wave it in front of his face.

"What does it really matter?" I asked, finding everyone's fascination with a horse show rather funny when it would neither make nor break anyone's fortunes—except perhaps some of the nouveau riche with their impulse to make it seem that money didn't matter. How many shows had I attended in my life? Hundreds? Horses and guns and arrows and cards. Those were the tools of gentlemen's sport. Otherwise, the same men considered games trivial or improper. "It would be much more entertaining to see all of *you* run round the course like the horses. *That* would be something to bet on."

"They wouldn't make it around one side," Anzonella said, swinging our way for a moment. "Never mind that they would feel undignified. It's much more of an ego boost to place your chips on the right beast, dear Dorothy."

"I suppose," I said, knowing she was commenting on my walking with Warren while secretly holding a candle for Enzo. "However, one would have to care a great deal about the audience to forgo the rush of running the race themselves." I wondered, given the reassurance I needed, if I would have the strength to take my own advice.

"You can't include me in that assumption, ladies," Warren said, completely missing the meaning of our conversation. "I daresay I would triumph at a foot race. I have quite a bit of stamina. Father has me work on the rails themselves sometimes."

"I often lift pencils with ease and strike the piano quite robustly," Henry said, practically losing his breath as we walked up the small hill beyond Baltimore Row's smart line of white cottages.

Lovers' Lane wasn't marked. That was the beauty of it, in a way. Though everyone knew of it, it was still a bit of a secret to newcomers. Warren and I fell in line behind Anzonella and Henry, wandering into a narrow aisle between groves of rhododendrons. None of us spoke as we walked, our merriment lost to the beauty and wildness of this place we loved. The path widened, the manicured grass underfoot flanked by ferns and wild bergamot and phlox, and behind that a screen of rhododendrons and oak trees.

"Shall we go the way of the leap or the short way?" Warren asked. The leap route was the long one, snaking around the top of the ledge and then ending at a spectacular view of the Greenbrier Valley. It was the place that prompted engagements, and there was no wonder why. It was breathtaking, the perfect place to jump headfirst into a love cultivated in a place that wasn't entirely real. The Greenbrier was an illusion. But in the blurry haze of a summer romance, some forgot about that. Not that I'd actually lived it myself. I'd only had the two flirtations, Grover, and before him, Christopher, the year I turned sixteen. Christopher had been visiting Tuxedo Park from Boston and we got on well from the beginning—like Enzo and me. He had kissed me in the woods behind the Costers' house after a barbecue and I thought we would fall in love. But the spark died when someone more suitable, more beautiful appeared. I'd cried myself to sleep for weeks over his choosing Lydia, praying every night that I'd wake up shorter.

"Perhaps the leap today. It's gorgeous out, and I'm trying to avoid the fawning over the Tafts," I said.

"Oh, don't let it take the wind from your sails. Helen's your friend besides," Warren said. He grinned at the mention of her name and I wondered if he, too, had been charmed by her new status.

"She is," I said, letting him lead me up the channel, away from Anzonella and Henry, who had decided to take the other route. There was no one else here today, at least that we'd seen so far. I sighed. "It's just difficult, you know. And quite strange. Even my own father is—"

"Shh!" Warren silenced me.

"What?" I asked. I jerked around, expecting to see a fox or a snake, some sort of wildlife that would merit the need to remain quiet. Instead, my breath caught.

"Oh. Thank you," I said. Behind us a few yards, Enzo and Helen walked arm in arm. She was beaming up at him, the humidity or her affection flushing her cheeks. He glanced my way, not even flinching when our eyes met. My stomach lurched. I wanted to apologize. I wanted to tell him I meant nothing of what I'd said, but I knew I wouldn't. I'd only apologized a handful of times in my life, and on all of those occasions, I was pressed to do it. I also knew that my accusations could still be right, despite the way my soul withered every time I saw him with someone else.

"They're a handsome couple, aren't they?" Warren asked. I swallowed and nodded. "Mr. Taft talked with him the whole time we were visiting the track. He was quite interested in Enzo's racing and kept asking advice about who he should place his bet on. Perhaps he sees a bit of himself in Enzo, what with him being raised outside of society as well. If their rapport is any indication, Mr. Rossi will be Mr. Helen Taft by the end of the season."

"I doubt that," I started. I knew what I was going to say next. I was going to echo what I'd told the girls this afternoon, the rumor my father had started, the rumor I hated. "But I suppose I could be wrong. Love can happen that quickly." Enzo believed it could happen in a moment. The thought startled me. If he could fall in love with me in a night, he could fall in love with Helen within the span of a day.

"Yes, it can," Warren said quietly, breaking from my hand to pluck a sprig of Queen Anne's lace from the side of the path.

"Mr. Abercrombie, Dorothy. How do you do?" Helen asked. She waved a gloved hand at us, and I wondered how in the world she was able to keep them on in the heat.

"Good afternoon, Helen! I'm sorry I haven't been able to greet you yet. You've been so occupied," I said. I didn't like my tone. It sounded forced and she'd done nothing wrong. I hoped she couldn't hear it. Enzo didn't even look at us but kept his eyes trained on the path. Even his profile was a lovely sight, the picture of strong lines and determination.

"I know. I've barely gotten to catch up with any of you girls, but I hope to this evening," she said.

"I certainly hope you'll save a dance for me at the ball tomorrow, Miss Taft," Warren said, smiling politely.

"Of course I will," she said, and with a wink, she kept walking, her head crooked nearly into Enzo's chest. His hand moved up her arm, holding her closer, and at once I wanted to run to him, to tell him that if making me jealous was his goal, it was working and I'd had enough.

"I know it might sound crazy, Dorothy, but do you remember that first night last season?" Warren asked, disrupting my thoughts. "We'd danced I think our fourth waltz and then we took a break to get a glass of lemonade?" I nodded, scouring my memory for what came next, hoping the flower he'd picked wasn't for me. "That's when I saw her for the first time. She was wearing that white gown with the lace. She looked like a dream. I knew I loved her before I even heard her voice." He looked to the line of oaks on our other side, the side that in a matter of feet would give way to a vista, where we'd look down on the tiny town of White Sulphur and the home of the woman who'd lied and stolen his heart. If someone like Warren, someone so calculated and honorable, could love so quickly, surely Enzo's feelings for me could be true. I wanted to believe it, and yet the doubt wouldn't subside.

"Why don't you go to her?" I whispered. I turned and took both of his hands in mine. "Warren, I can feel your heartache. Surely you can forgive her. Surely she'd love you again."

He let me go and shook his head.

"My father won't allow it. He was outraged. He'll never get over it." Warren twirled the Queen Anne's lace in his hand as we walked.

"Are you?" I asked.

He looked at me, questioning.

"Over it? Have you forgiven her?" I clarified. "She's just a girl who wanted better. Can you blame her?" I said the words and suddenly realized how horrible I'd been. Even if Enzo did come here wanting to marry for advantage, was advantage all he was after? Eleanor had been keen to have love too. And if she'd found a man to love and a man to love her, what did it matter?

"I've forgiven her, Dorothy, but I'd lose my fortune if I married her. Father would likely disown me."

I couldn't help but laugh.

"*Your* father? He would never. He can be stern, but he loves you."

"Perhaps," Warren said, shrugging. "Even so, she could be married now. I'm not sure that I could bear it if she is."

"You must find out," I said. "There's no time to waste. We're only here for another few weeks and then you'll be gone for a year. Please, Warren."

He laughed.

"Since when have you become a romantic?"

His words stunned me. I'd never thought myself opposed to romance, but I knew he was right. Ever since Christopher hurt me, I'd been too proud, too reserved with men on purpose. It was only to defend myself from heartache, but in the process, I'd kept my distance from everyone. I had to find a way to let go of my fear, to open my heart, to risk rejection. Otherwise I'd become the warden of my own prison, an old maid living forever within the confines of Tuxedo Park or a woman locked in a loveless marriage.

"I'm not repulsed. Warren, I want it more than anything," I gushed without thinking. "I suppose I'm only scared."

"Well, well. She has a heart after all," he said. A grin tugged at the side of his mouth.

"Really? I really appear so unkind?"

"No," he said, nudging me. "Of course not." We walked a few more steps and he dropped the flower. "Would you mind if we turned around? I'm not certain I can laugh quite so easily at Enzo pouring his heart out to Miss Taft, if that's what he plans to do up the way. Perhaps it's time for me to go to town."

"I think it is." I dropped his arm and turned to follow him, catching one last glance of Helen and Enzo. As though he was aware of my every movement, he turned back and looked at me, his eyes catching mine before he shifted his attention back to my friend.

It was drizzling. It would have been a perfect night, really, except for the memory of tonight's dinner.

Warren had gone into town and didn't return to dine, and Enzo and Mr. Vacchelli had joined the Tafts' table. I'd barely touched my *aloyau* of beef and creamed turnips. My father and Mr. Abercrombie had been horrible dinner companions, the former swearing up and down that the Italians weren't to be trusted while the latter lamented his son's disappearance. I'd wanted to comment that Enzo and Helen and Warren were all well past the age of needing to be looked after, that they could choose to make mistakes, but I didn't. Instead, I'd turned my attention to the only conversation I could bear—the women gushing about the trappings of the Centennial Ball. Everyone, even Anzonella, seemed to be impressed with the little they'd seen being constructed in the ballroom—great statues of men on horseback, swags of flowers. It had all seemed the same to me, a replica of a traditional ball on a grander scale. It wasn't that I didn't love the Greenbrier—I did, deeply—but I'd felt peculiar at dinner, as though I wanted to tear all of it down, strip the grandeur and order from everything, and represent it like it was, a menagerie of different people silently desiring different things. If the Greenbrier's guests were colors, they'd be pinks and greens and blues and golds and reds in all sorts of patterns, though they all tried to fashion themselves a safe beige. The truth would be startling but beautiful.

The restlessness remained with me even after our evening tea and letter writing, after everyone else retired. I'd thought to sleep, but knew I'd only toss and turn, so I did the only thing I could: I escaped alone.

It was ghostly along the cottage rows. The lamps had been extinguished at ten o'clock, an hour ago. I could barely see the moon through the clouds wisping across the sky. I ran my hand over a row of low rhododendrons growing in a hedge along the front lawns of Baltimore Row, not minding that doing so soaked my gloves through. I didn't know what I was doing out here, really. All I knew was that I couldn't remain in the parlor, I couldn't bring myself to sleep, and walking usually helped me think.

The rain slowed, and I pushed the hood of my gray cape off my head and crossed in front of the springhouse to Georgia Row.

In the dim, I heard a howl. I stopped. I hadn't thought about foxes or wolves or any other sort of danger. I thought to go back but heard nothing more, so I turned down Wolf Row, the last row of cottages before the Greenbrier's groomed grounds gave way to woods.

Light was blazing in a window, the pane framing a man who looked just like my father. It couldn't be. I'd seen him come in with Mother and didn't see him emerge—but did I see him retire after all? I couldn't be sure. I crept closer, quickly recognizing that the cottage held not only my father but also a crush of men huddled around a table. I kept my distance, cloaked beneath the shadow of an old oak. I'd heard rumors of the Tiger, the infamous midnight gambling cottage, where, from as early as the late 1700s, presidents and senators and congressmen on both sides of the political coin apparently argued and decided our country's course round the whist table. I'd thought that tradition long since retired with my father's youth. Apparently, I was wrong.

My father turned slightly to address someone at his left. Even from here I could tell he was upset. His face was flushed, and he forcefully combed his fingers through his graying black hair. Everyone else was laughing. I prayed he hadn't been humiliated. Though typically mild-mannered, my father was proud, a man who couldn't be made wrong or the subject of a joke. If he believed he was either, tomorrow would be unfortunate for all of us. A wind blew over me, raining droplets from the trees and rustling the green and white buntings along the cottages' colonnades.

I kept my gaze on my father, hoping he'd not lose his composure. Unfortunately, I knew the way it felt when Tuckerman wits were worn ragged. It wasn't a slow fraying, but a singe. Mr.

Abercrombie appeared next to him, thrusting his fist playfully into my father's arm, and Father seemed to relax. Warren edged his way into the frame on the other side of my father, his hands bearing a glass, and in a matter of moments, my father had disappeared, lost to the allure of a bet.

When they were gone, when the pane framed only the comings and goings of gray heads, I realized I hadn't looked at Warren, not truly anyway. I hadn't seen whether he seemed contented or unhappy. Perhaps he hadn't seen Eleanor after all; perhaps he'd only needed time alone as I did. I started to go but was caught by a man walking past the window, a man whose profile set my heart skipping. At once I understood the underlying reason for my restlessness, why I'd ventured out, unperturbed by the chill and the rain: I'd hoped to see Enzo again. Alone. I wanted to talk to him, to remedy what I'd said, to know if I'd been passed over again—this time for Helen. And if he still felt for me, I needed to figure if I'd actually have the courage to leave everything, if love was strong enough to propel me toward freedom.

I huddled into my coat and turned away from the lighted window, determined to set my mind on something other than a man I couldn't will to emerge from the cabin. The conversation would likely be upsetting anyway. He'd clearly found favor in Helen Taft, and if he was indeed a man keen to marry solely for influence, I'd rather his attention be on someone else.

The Greenbrier loomed in front of me as I made my way back, one of its chimneys shadowing the moon. It would only take a bit of paint, a bit of color to make the cottages as magnificent as the hotel. I glanced at the bungalow next to me, one of the unoccupied bachelor lodgings. I could envision whitewashed wicker couches on the porch, the cushions covered in rose patterns or rhododendrons or the Greenbrier's signature green and white, the colonnades wreathed in roses to mimic the hotel. It would be beautiful, more romantic than it had ever been, an ideal place for a gentleman to entertain a lady. The little stoops would be the perfect setting for a private conversation or perhaps a proposal. I could hear the words spoken, the whispers, the feeling of a man's hand on my arm. I jolted and whirled around, narrowly refraining from screaming.

"Are you looking for me?"

Enzo stood behind me, a look of amusement on his face.

"No," I said, trying to catch my breath. "No. Of course not. I couldn't sleep. I went for a walk and then I saw . . ." I gestured behind him to the Tiger, hoping in the moment it took for him to turn around, I'd be able to gain my composure, to lie convincingly, but he didn't take his eyes from mine.

"Yes. That wretched place," he said. "I saw you from the window and thought that I couldn't let you walk the grounds alone this late at night."

I tried to gauge the tone of his voice.

"Why not?"

I cleared my throat, regretting the question. I was only fishing for the words I wanted to hear: that he had been looking for a reason to be near me. I pushed a tendril back from my forehead, knowing I looked akin to a wet rat. "It's only that I'm quite familiar with this place, you know."

"I needed an excuse to rid myself of the joy most find in gambling. It invites ruin and destroys destiny. Practical thievery. That, and the company of your father," he said.

I should have been offended at this, but I knew Father could be insufferable when he was sure of himself.

"Did you tell him why you were leaving?" I searched the darkness behind him for any sign of Father's approach. He'd lock me in the suite the moment he discovered I'd been traipsing around alone.

"Of course not," Enzo said. "I told my uncle. He wanted me to keep him in the whist game, but I couldn't bear it any longer. Your father kept glaring at me from the other side of the table, making comments about how I am a leech to his comrades."

Enzo paced past me.

I remained where I was, and he stopped when he didn't hear me following. He looked even more handsome in the hazy moonlight, his white shirt unbuttoned beneath his black jacket, and I felt the echo of his warmth, felt his hands on mine.

"I'm sorry," I said.

Enzo laughed under his breath.

"It's all right," he said. "I know where you get it from now. Your suspicion and harshness can hardly be helped."

Anger and jealousy flared. Helen Taft was timid and kind, but she was also smart and witty and beautiful. Of course he'd not continue to be transfixed by me once he'd made her acquaintance—if his sentiments had been sincere at all.

"Everyone else is as snide and suspecting as I am," I said. "The others just disguise it with confidence." I sighed. "I have my heart to consider."

I strode past him, but he caught my arm.

"And what are your considerations?" he asked, his eyes locked on mine.

I stared at him, hesitating. I didn't have the courage to tell him the truth—that I felt for him, that if he was lying about his feelings, it would crush me. Instead, I shrugged free of his grasp and left him on the path, trudging between the cottages and up the small hill to the entrance of Lovers' Lane. I couldn't go home yet, but I certainly couldn't linger on the promenade waiting for my father to tire of the games and discover me. My eyes blurred. I was always the woman who walked away, a woman too insecure, too afraid of being wounded to be honest and gracious, even if the man in front of her enraptured her. I wanted nothing more than to loosen my stays, to just breathe, to rid my mind of who I was.

I sank down on a rock covered in moss, looking into the darkness of the woods, where the pathway forked. Moisture seeped into my blush cotton skirt, chilling me, but I didn't mind. It was beautiful wilderness, and though I couldn't see the blooms, I could smell the jasmine and honeysuckle. I closed my eyes, willing my body to relax and my heart to slow, listening to the sounds of the wind rustling the leaves, promising more rain.

"Please don't leave me like that again. Do you truly believe it? What your father says about Uncle and me?"

I opened my eyes to find Enzo standing over me. He pushed his hair back from his face. His eyes were shaded. I could only see the shadow of his figure, and I was glad for it. I knew what I'd see if the moon was bright. Despite knowing him for only a few days, I'd seen the glint of hurt more times than I was proud of, and I couldn't bear it again lest I concede my heart to a man who might never really love me.

"I don't know," I said simply.

"I know last night. I know what you said, but I—"

"I was confused," I whispered. "I wanted to believe you, but then today, I realized that I'd been right. You and Helen. I saw the two of you all day."

"And you suppose I've suddenly decided to love her? That I'm courting Miss Taft for political gain?" He leaned down, his fingers braced on the bit of rock at my side. I could smell his cologne—lavender and leather—and the rye on his breath. I kept my gaze fixed over his shoulder.

"That seems the case," I said. "But I don't want to believe it. I want to believe you. Seeing you with Helen today was a torture."

Before I could finish explaining, his mouth was on mine, his fingers threading the hair at my nape. I thought to stop him, but couldn't, reaching for him instead, deepening the kiss. He leaned over me, cradling me with his other hand, and as my back met the cool rock, I stopped him.

"Enzo, I—"

"Dorothy, I'm sorry," he whispered, but he didn't move away. I didn't want him to. "I couldn't help it. This evening, when I saw you walking with Mr. Abercrombie . . . Miss Taft wants me to court her, and I know that will lead to her thinking I'll propose by the end of the season. Already I can see it, but if you . . ."

He drifted off and I stared at him, stunned, before I broke free of his arms and stood.

"Do you intend to? To court her?" The edge to my tone was unmistakable, and he stood where he was, his fists clenched at his sides. As if on cue, the rain began again, drizzling through the trees at a steady clip.

"No," he said simply.

"Then why would you walk with her? Why would you remain by her side all day long? It's unkind to feign affection, but perhaps you make a habit of it." I felt foolish. He was doing the same thing to me. A familiar pain gripped my chest; a familiar tension watered my eyes. Surely this wasn't happening again. I'd wanted so badly to be wrong about him.

"I wasn't pretending to enjoy her company," he said. "I do. And no. I don't feign affection, but I've given in to lust more times than I'm proud to admit." He took my hand and I let him, despite feeling like my heart was breaking. "Don't you understand? I can find others interesting; I can find them attractive, but you're different, Dorothy. I meant what I said last night. We're the same, you and I. It's you that I—"

"If you feel for me at all, you're a coward for turning to someone else so quickly. Last night I was scared. I was worried that the care of my heart was not safe with you. And you didn't come after me. Instead you let me believe you were angry and that your affections had transferred to Helen."

"I can't pretend I wasn't afflicted by what you said. I thought my confession unrequited. Still, I should have followed you. I should have told you that you're wrong, that you're the most striking, the most exquisite woman I've ever seen."

He engulfed me in his arms. Despite his words, I didn't move to embrace him. I couldn't.

"Even so, what are you doing? What do you want with me? What do you want with Helen?"

"I want you," he whispered, wiping the raindrops from my face.

"What will you tell Helen tomorrow?" I asked.

"What is there to tell? What should I say?"

"That you can't see her? That your affection lies elsewhere? I want you too. I want to believe you." I took a breath, afraid to say more but knowing I had to. I had to lay my heart bare or risk losing him. "Ever since I saw you, I've been dreaming of running away. I've been dreaming of going back to Italy with you."

I expected him to kiss me again, to rejoice with my words, but he only stared at me. I couldn't take his silence.

"Or perhaps you're not as certain about me as you say you are. Perhaps you want to string Helen along, just as you're doing to me. At least you'll enrapture one of us." One of us was a consolation, and I had a feeling it was me. He let go of me and held up his hands. Even in the dark I could see his face harden.

"I thought I was right about you. I know it's hard to believe, but from the moment I saw you, I had this feeling that you were the one, that you'd be mine." He heaved a breath.

I opened my mouth to reply but thought better of it. I wanted to tell him to forget what I'd just said, to tell him again that I wanted him, that I wanted love more than anything, but something held me back.

"You may feel for me, but if you won't trust me when I'm sincere about my affection for you, perhaps there's no way to convince you." He turned away and started down the path, not waiting for me to follow. "You claim to need surety? Marry your dear Mr. Abercrombie. Lord knows he'll never change."

Seven

OCTOBER 31, 1946

I clutched the rail and hoisted myself up the wrought-iron stairs to the hotel's north entrance. The pigeon's wings along the top of my felt hat took flight, and I reflexively clutched the brim.

"Careful, dear, there's a bit of ice," Lee whispered beside me, gently steadying me on the step.

"I'm meeting Mr. Bowman, Mr. Small, and Mr. Smith," I said. "Perhaps you should return to the cottage and begin drafting notes to the jobbers. Of course, they already know we're here, but they'll need a bit of timeline and—"

"I'd like to stay," he said. "It'll be easier that way to know what you're thinking, the requirements of each job. And, I don't particularly want to ask, but are they all essential? You know we've discussed that as it stands we only have around six months before we'll need to begin looking at cutting staff and talking about your other expenses—the company building, your apartments at the Hampshire and at Sutton. I know you want the best, but they're awfully—"

"Yes. I will not work with anyone else. The resort's budget will cover their cost. And as I've told you before, I will not fire anyone in my employ. If this ship goes down, I go down with it," I said, cutting him off before he could further vocalize his opinion on my jobbers' fees and the current state of my accounts. I knew how close I was to the *New York Times* declaring my company's demise if this project didn't go through. I could still see the headlines declaring bankruptcy upon bankruptcy after the market crash. Society loved nothing more than the failure of a shamed woman. But regardless of the cost, regardless of the risk, I would not skimp. My reputation and my company were at stake. The C&O had to be convinced that I'd done my best or the chance of pay and acclaim was all but lost.

"And if you'd like to stay, you may," I whispered, "but utter any talk of my finances and I will—"

"Let me get the door, Mrs. Draper!"

I heard the slam of a car door behind me and Tom came bounding up the stairs. We paused, and now, lingering in the looming shadow of the hotel, I was faced with the magnitude of the project once again. The Greenbrier, currently in the state of Ashford General Hospital, was as broken and worn as the soldiers who had called it home. The white paint was starting to dapple and peel along the porch, and several worn rocking chairs tipped back and forth in the autumn breeze. I was thankful we weren't at war anymore, that there was finally peace, for both the state of my mind and the state of my company.

Phil Small and George Smith stood in the middle of the

reception room, both writing feverishly in small leather-bound notepads. They stopped when they saw me.

"Good morning, Mrs. Draper," Mr. Small said, striding toward me as though he were a tall man. His last name suited him, and I didn't enjoy towering over anyone, especially men.

"How do you do?" I said pleasantly. "This is Mr. Lee Carter, my business manager."

I stepped around Mr. Small and Lee, my eyes straining to see to the other end, to the upper lobby proper that marked the conclusion of the long narrow room. It stretched nearly the length of the hotel with no end. Again, I found it awful. It had the feeling of one of those horrid dinner parties where the table was so long that you never had occasion to speak to the guests at the other end. There was absolutely no warmth about the place, no temptation to linger, though I suppose that was the point of a hospital. Lingering wasn't exactly a good thing.

"It's a Brobdingnagian monster of a bowling alley," I said.

My voice echoed through the place and then I heard a low laugh.

"It certainly is." I turned around to see Mr. Bowman standing in the doorway, his narrow-brimmed Stetson pulled down nearly to his eyes.

"What do you propose here?" Mr. Smith asked. "Structurally, of course." Mr. Smith was the architect, a man Mr. Young had put on the job because he was a friend. I hoped the friendship would last the project. If he didn't like the way I did things, he'd have to compromise or quit.

"Screens, walls, new plasterwork," I said. "It will all have to be redone." I could see it now, broken up into completely different spaces. Regardless of entrance, guests would be transfixed by the path they took. Like a nesting doll, the main floor of the Greenbrier would require surprise after surprise, beauty atop and beauty beneath.

Mr. Bowman cleared his throat.

"There's been a bit of concern, Mrs. Draper, that I suppose I should share."

"You're welcome to speak your mind, Mr. Bowman, but I'm not troubled by concern," I said, walking into the long room, past the ramshackle groupings of old settees and couches and chairs I'd seen yesterday. It was worse from this angle than it had been from the main entrance, though both were startling.

"There've been some whisperings that your work is too splashy for the Greenbrier," Mr. Bowman continued. "Perhaps you would consider neutralizing a bit?"

I stopped in my tracks and laughed. I liked the way it startled Mr. Small and Mr. Smith, Mr. Bowman too.

"Who is whispering? Certainly not Mr. Young, the head of this operation, who hired me intending to make a splash. I *know* the Greenbrier," I said evenly. I was all too familiar with the executives, those beneath the barons, the CEOs, the owners, who shared my circle. These men weren't in charge, they were told what to do, and they often pushed back to assure themselves that they had a voice, that they were important.

"The Greenbrier has been neutral and proper its whole life, even in the old hotel," I went on. "Gravy shades and stuffy designs attract boring people and simply do not match the future here, gentlemen. Being surrounded by color makes people happy, and I intend for the guests to have an awfully fun time while they're here. I'm sure you would all agree."

They looked at me blankly. It was an expression I'd grown quite accustomed to over the years.

"You'll just have to trust that I know what is best," I continued. "In fact, just last night I was visited by the ghost of our dear departed President Martin Van Buren and he confirmed my vision." I could feel a hush fall over the men. They would think I was either a quack or a genius. I didn't care which one. "The theme will be romance and rhododendron." I waved my hand about the room as though with a flick of my wrist I could transform it.

"Van Buren's ghost?" Mr. Small asked. I could feel Lee rolling his eyes.

"I forget that you don't know the history," I said. "He loved it here. His great-grandson was a friend of our family. The Greenbrier was a place where some of the greatest minds from across the nation could come together and just be. Much of our activity took place outdoors, among the rhododendrons and roses, and it was quite a place for romance too."

"I've read enough to know that it certainly was," Mr. Bowman said.

"And now it's gone. Replaced by this," Mr. Small said. "I'm surprised Van Buren still wants to haunt this place."

Something inside snapped. Yes, the Greenbrier was a hospital, but the Greenbrier's legacy was far from over. I remembered the way the cottages had looked the last time I was here. They were sagging, in desperate need of repair, and yet it seemed like no one minded in the slightest. The old Greenbrier was a phenomenon, luxury beyond the physical, a way of life. I would bring that magic back, wrapped in the trappings of a fine resort.

"All of the moldings will have to be repaired or redone entirely. The floorboards are too thin and the molding along the crown should be punched up and whitewashed. I want all the curtains removed and every bit of iron or metal taken out immediately. This furniture is worthless. Give it away," I said, gesturing to the random pieces sprinkled around the room. "Mr. Bowman, if there are any antiques of meaning or worth, or furniture of quality, bring it to my attention. Otherwise, I want this hotel scrubbed clean. I want a blank slate."

"I'll have Tom look through the furniture," he said.

"I imagine the wartime internments were easier to deal with," Mr. Smith whispered to Mr. Bowman. "Are you sure we shouldn't try someone else?" I whirled around and glared at him.

"Of course they were easier to deal with," I said. "They were prisoners. They didn't care what happened to this place." I wanted to tell him that the other designers wouldn't care either, but responding to the insinuation that I could be replaced would let on that I felt threatened, and that wouldn't do.

"You'd be surprised," Mr. Bowman said. "Either way. Just fix it, Mrs. Draper."

"Don't you suppose you should call it a day?" Her voice echoed through the room. I didn't need to turn to know who it was. Jean had been with me from nearly the beginning. We met the day Dan left. I could still remember her walking into the foyer clutching the bouquet of yellow lilies she'd had the unfortunate task of delivering as the errand girl to a bygone florist. Only hours earlier, Dan had sauntered into the same foyer after months away in Europe and told me he wanted a divorce. I'd wondered how the news got out so quickly. Jean had looked at me up on the ladder holding a sheet of chintz wallpaper in my hands, set the lilies down on the white lacquered calling table, and started to cry before fumbling to open the note attached to my flowers.

Thank God Father only dabbles in the market. We've lost much, but we're safe. Love, Roger.

She could barely make out the words. I had no idea what had transpired that morning beyond my own calamity. *"I don't know what my brother means by that, miss, but you're clearly upset,"* I'd said, hastening down the ladder to call for tea.

I remembered being thrilled to help brighten someone else's mood, elated that the focus was not on poor Dorothy Draper. *"Surely you know it. The stock market has crashed. Many are completely ruined,"* she'd wailed. Jean had taken the paper from my hands then and enveloped me in a hug, a hug I would never admit I desperately needed. *"Oh,"* I said. It was the only word I could muster. Every family I knew flashed through my mind then, like playing cards shuffled. How many of them had lost it all? Even a moment of wondering was too much for me. In an instant, I found myself bearing so much pain I couldn't carry it—Dan leaving, families I loved in shambles—so I did the only thing I knew how to do. I asked Jean to help me decorate.

We papered the entire foyer by the end of the day, and she came to work for me the next. Jean was the only one I trusted entirely—except for my lovely Texan and likely successor, Leon, who was running the New York operations in my absence—and for that reason I had her unofficially manage the rest of my staff.

"DD," Jean said, reaching me. "It's getting late. Don't you think it's time to retire?"

"Not until I get this right," I said. Jean and Glenn had come in on the two o'clock train. I'd sent Mr. Bowman and Lee to greet them. Tomorrow we would begin in earnest, putting pen to paper, drawing concrete plans, but tonight I wanted to be alone, to sit and imagine what this place would be.

Jean sighed and set down her enormous Josef handbag, settling her small frame on the lumpy striped couch across from mine. Mr. Bowman had been kind enough to call for Tom to kindle a fire, and I was especially thankful now that the sun and the moon had switched places and the room was dark.

I leaned over my sketchpad, squinting at the Chippendale trelliswork pattern I was imagining as a sort of screen between the ballroom and a separate sort of lounge. I couldn't see as well as I used to, but I wouldn't succumb to glasses. They were for the elderly, and I had at least a decade left before that.

"Glenn's already running with your romance-and-rhododendron sketch. Last I looked over his shoulder, he'd drawn a larger print of it he said could be used for carpets," Jean said.

"I'm glad," I said. "Glenn's the best."

I stopped my pencil and closed my eyes, envisioning the room—a white plaster mantel, gay chintz on a Caribbean-blue background for the curtains, carpets adorned with whatever masterpiece Glenn was drawing, and floor-to-ceiling white trellis screens with arched cutouts running the length of the room on both sides to give the wide space a bit of coziness. Beyond the screens, my signature black-and-white-checked marble floors would pick up and extend to the windows. I'd outfit that little space with something like white wicker furniture. One couldn't help but be merry in a room such as that, and merriment was priority at the Greenbrier. Happiness was an addiction, and occasions that drew it out were occasions remembered. The Greenbrier had to be the backdrop of the nation's joy.

"I'm so glad to be here," Jean said. "Betty and Ted have been at each other for a solid week, and it's unbearable to work beside them." Betty was my secretary and her husband, Ted, my procurement director. Though he tried to hide it, Ted had eyes for other men, which had caused quite a rift in his marriage.

"It's only William," I said. "Ted returned from the war enamored with him, while Betty was hoping to have her charming husband back."

"Oh. Then perhaps you shouldn't have hired him despite Ted's begging, knowing the way it might fluster Betty," Jean said. She adjusted her velvet pancake hat over her left eye and then fiddled with the white feather affixed to the top.

"You're probably right, but he's a talent and I cannot let talent go flouncing around lest he go to work for Elsie or, worse, Elisabeth." My nightmare was losing genius to Dan's new wife, also a designer. As horrid as the divorce had been, Dan's marrying a fellow designer ten years my junior was more dreadful. They'd been engaged on Christmas Eve. I found out after my annual Christmas sing-along. My parents were there, my children too, and Diana and George had been lamenting the older set attempting to dance the swing. *"What if they swing at the w—"* George had stopped midsentence, his face blanching. They'd had to tell me then that they all knew—even my parents—that Dan was to propose that night. And after the engagement was official, I could hear the whispers. *"Elisabeth is the lovelier version of*

Dorothy." "*Elisabeth is so kind and gentle.*" "*Dan's traded the old biddy for the youthful edition.*"

In a matter of months, we both had new names. Elisabeth was a Draper, and I had transformed the Architectural Clearing House into Dorothy Draper & Company complete with a sleek logo of two entwined Ds. There would never be any confusion over who was the eminent Mrs. Draper.

"Write Leon tomorrow and instruct him to ask William to work on orders for Schumacher from his home office until I send Ted out hunting all the pieces I'll need here," I said, refusing to let thoughts of Elisabeth and Dan meddle in my happiness. Schumacher. I needed more jobs like Schumacher fabrics and wallcoverings—steadier commissions that lasted years. Perhaps with enough of them I could sustain us and count the large jobs as a bonus.

"Very well," she said.

That settled, I plucked my pencil from my sketchpad and began to draw the rest of the room. The guests would sweep into what I'd call the trellis lobby from an elegant ballroom done up like a cameo. The walls in the ballroom would be coral, or perhaps rose, the ceiling a pure white with two thin ovals of delicate white rose plaster surrounding an enormous crystal chandelier— perhaps something similar to that lovely Czechoslovakian piece in Catherine the Great's winter palace. The windows must be arches, like the ballroom in the old hotel, adorned in three shades of pink satin. This ballroom could be no less romantic than the one that had been destroyed. The ballroom was the most important place, the place where romances and regrets and memories were born.

"That will help some I'm sure," Jean said. "And as for tonight,

Tom's bringing the cook over to prepare supper at our cottage in an hour. Turtle soup and grilled sole fillets. Would you like him to bring your supper here, or will you be joining us?" Tom had somehow managed to make the Top Notch Cottage—another residence added after my time—livable for my staff. It was only just up the hill from Hawley House, and I was incredibly thankful.

Jean lifted her handbag to her lap, her irritation at the way I was continuing to sketch very apparent. I didn't want to stop for dinner. I was inspired, sitting here in this empty space. But I knew she was right. If I didn't take a break to breathe, tomorrow would bring exhaustion and subsequently the Will-to-Be-Dreary. It always loved to sneak in when I was having quite a time.

I stared at the fire, listening to the pop of the logs and the subsequent spark of flame that followed. My life had been like that—a blaze broken by sprays of change.

"Or were you hoping to have your dinner brought to Hawley House?" she pressed again. "Lee is there now, and I suppose Tom could arrange a delivery there if—"

"I'll join you at the cottage," I said. "I'll need to update all of you on the vision, after all, and our tasks for tomorrow. There's much to be done. I hope you're all right being here for a while." As much as I hated to ask Jean to accompany me to the abandonment of her husband—a man who looked like a copy of Clark Gable—he couldn't take leave from his job and I couldn't take leave of her.

"Of course I'm all right being here. It's Ben's busy season anyway, and this place is lovely. Oh! Before I forget. I have quite a stack of letters for you." She rifled through her handbag. "A few are for Lee, but I figure you may want to give them to him yourself. They came in just this past week. I haven't seen so many since you did that *Learn to Live* correspondence course or started the *Good Housekeeping* column. It took everyone to write your replies. Even Glenn." She extracted a large stack of letters bound with a rubber band. Sometimes I was still shocked to see a rubber band. During the war, when rubber was rationed, we'd had to tie correspondence with yarn. She handed them to me. "And remember the letters from all of your fans when you were on the covers of *Life* and *Time*?"

"Yes. I was practically Bette Davis for a time," I joked, glancing at the return address on top. I didn't know the name.

"And likely as famous," Jean said.

I laughed. "I doubt anyone else would agree with you," I said.

"Claudette Colbert and Constance Bennett certainly would, and they're of that Hollywood set," she said, referencing the two stars who had hired me early in my career, in '34, to decorate a gorgeous hotel near California's Lake Arrowhead. They'd called, having heard of my work on the Gideon Putnam in Saratoga Springs and the Drake in Chicago, but the only thing I could recall about the day I received the commission was Penny's bucket of seashells, the roar of a roller coaster, and the faraway piping of "Let Me Call You Sweetheart" from the carousel. Nanny had planned to take her to Rye Playland and to the beach and I joined them. I rarely did. I could remember how grown-up she looked as she scoured the beach, and the excitement in her voice when she showed me the bucket full of clam and scallop shells. She seemed so free, something I'd never been at the beach as a girl. It had been all heavy maillot bathing costumes and maids waiting with robes to hide our figures at the foot of the waves.

"Is it nice to be back?" Jean asked, interrupting my memory. "I admit I've never seen any landscape quite so breathtaking."

"It is," I said. "It's warmth and melancholy. I spent almost every summer growing up here. At the time, I couldn't wait to arrive, and yet amid the romance and wonder, society could feel stifling. There were the same families always. Expectations bearing down from every angle." I paused. "My last summer here, I tasted the possibility of escape, and I knew then that no matter what, I wouldn't be another society matron. I couldn't."

"Did you fall in love here?" Jean asked. She was a romantic, always reading romance novels and fainting over the latest engagements announced in the *New York Times*—after she clipped the most interesting articles for my attention.

"Yes," I said simply, closing my sketchbook and putting the stack of letters in my bag. "Come. Let's not keep the rest waiting."

Eight

My head ached. I regretted the glass of wine I drank with dinner the night before. I'd shocked everyone when I said yes to the drink. My staff knew how rigorously I stayed away from alcohol. It depressed the spirit and made people sloppy, and I abhorred both of those things.

"You have letters."

Lee knocked on the doorframe belatedly and grinned at me. I pulled the lapels of my silk night robe around my neck, hiding the curve of my breasts. I'd let him into my bed last night—not that it was an uncommon occurrence—but I hadn't asked him to leave after. It was the wine, I knew it.

He handed me the letters and sat down on the foot of my bed.

"I don't understand what's going on," I said, slipping my finger under the seal of the first envelope. "Jean gave me an enormous stack of letters just yesterday and they weren't the normal sort."

"What do you mean?" he asked.

"You know I receive at least twenty each week from women simply asking for advice. They've read one of my books or they subscribe to *Good Housekeeping* and they want to know what to do about their grandmother-in-law's dreary buffet or if the theme they've chosen for their husband's thirtieth birthday party is a good one. These were all from new designers from all over the country, but primarily students from the Art Institute in Chicago, telling me they'd like to study under me. I don't have the foggiest idea why they think I take on apprentices. Clearly I don't have time for that. I barely have time to apprentice Leon, and he'll likely hold the reins to this company someday."

I opened the letter and sighed.

"Dear Mrs. Draper, I have admired your work for a decade. My grandfather lived in Hampshire House during the time you were renovating it. I watched as the dreariness and stuffiness were stripped away, and at once, when I stepped into my grandfather's building, I was no longer in New York but in a cheery English country estate," I read aloud. I stopped and folded the letter, shoving it into the envelope. "Did I say something in an interview? If I did, I don't recall it and I regret it."

I glanced at Lee.

"I—" he started and then stopped. "I don't know. Why don't you let me handle these? I'll collect them and we'll figure a way to reply later." He cleared his throat. "Perhaps they're only confused. You know Ms. de Wolfe has begun taking younger designers under her tutelage. I assume it would only bolster her business."

"I can't imagine how she'd find the time. I'd appreciate you managing these," I said, ignoring the mention of Elsie. She wasn't quite my competitor—she did homes—but I didn't care how anyone else managed their affairs and I mimicked no one. I flipped through the stack of letters, keeping one from Leon and one from my dear friend Eleanor Roosevelt, and handed Lee the rest. "Now, do you suppose you could ready and make sure Jean and Glenn are awake and prepared to get started? Remind Glenn to bring his new pencils along and make sure Jean has her tape measure. They're always forgetting the most important instruments."

Lee groaned and walked toward his room.

"Very well," he said. "But I cannot be responsible for Glenn and his insistence on primping. I'm only interested in your beauty, my love."

He disappeared, not looking back, but the term of endearment shocked me through. Though we had never discussed it, I thought it was clear that we weren't in love, that we would never be in love, that this affair was simply fulfilling the bit of romance we both needed until he found a wife and moved back to Tuxedo Park, or until I became too busy to entertain a lover at all. If he was falling for me, I would have to let him go.

"Good." It was a whisper of a thought, but it seemed to come from a place far away, from a memory. I laughed. It wasn't as if he'd show up here to find me. If Mr. Taft was right, he was dead. I'd inquired of him only a few times, once in a reply to Helen—she'd mentioned that she didn't know of his whereabouts—and another time to Mr. Taft at a dinner for Roosevelt a few weeks after Dan left, only months before Mr. Taft passed. I could still recall the look on Mr. Taft's face. I knew before he said anything that it was bad news, that Enzo was gone. A loyal man, Mr. Taft had wondered about Enzo after that last season, and he'd written to Mr. Vacchelli a few years later asking after him. Mr. Vacchelli said he'd purchased Enzo a ticket on the White Star line's

Republic to return to Italy in early 1909, and there was record of him boarding. The *Republic* sank after a collision with an Italian immigrant liner, and a riot ensued between the passengers being retrieved by three separate rescue ships. Somewhere in the commotion, he'd been lost. No one had noticed his absence until months later when the passenger lists were finally reconciled.

I could still feel my reaction, the way my gloved hands reflexively clenched, my throat constricted, my eyes blurred. I'd asked if his body had ever been recovered and Mr. Taft simply shook his head. *"No, my dear. The ocean is cruel and so is this world at times. I'm so sorry to hear about you and Dr. Draper too. I'm sure you're out of sorts. Do me a favor and go visit the Greenbrier again. I remember how you were there, how alive your heart seemed. I'm sure it would enliven anew the moment you arrived."* My mind clung to the fact that they had never recovered Enzo. In a way, I'd been glad for it. It had given me a sliver of hope, stopped the inclination of the mind to imagine the horror of his final moments swallowed in the sea. Instead, I decided that everyone was mistaken, that he was likely out there somewhere—not with me, but perhaps married with children and grandchildren, happy—that he'd disappeared on purpose.

I took a long breath then let it go slowly and glanced at the letters in my hand. Leon, of course, and Eleanor. She was always checking up on me. I opened Leon's first and quickly reviewed it to make sure all was well. He was meticulous, organized, and understood my designs completely. He mentioned something about the Metropolitan Museum of Art querying about the possibility of my designing a restaurant, but the project wouldn't be for several years yet. I'd hoped for something else, something soon. I never sought projects; they had always come to me. But perhaps I would have to change. I'd write something to that effect in my reply.

I put Leon's letter aside and opened Eleanor's.

Dearest DD,

I trust it's lovely there. I'm jealous, if you must know. Here I sit, staring out at the city street watching the rain puddle and the people scowl as they slosh through. Our cities are missing the unbridled beauty of the country. I can feel FDR here tonight—a rare occurrence as you know he was barely here when he was living—sitting next to me, begging me to remind you of how special the Greenbrier is to him—though I know how important it is to you as well. It's important to the country. We visited during the war, when the place was Ashford General Hospital. I knew going in that we'd return regardless—I don't think politicians are revolutionary enough to relocate their retreats after all these years—and I wondered how we could possibly find the Greenbrier lovely again. The memory of mutilated men is not a fond one, but then we returned home, and I started longing for it. How at peace I feel that you are at the helm of this project, dear DD. Rays of sunshine will paint the walls once again. I know you'll make sure of it.

I dined with Dan and Elisabeth last night. It pains me to even write the words, but you'll doubtless hear of it and rather than seem disloyal, I thought to tell you myself. The invitation came, and I thought it rude to decline.

I sighed. It was inevitable. Dan had been FDR's doctor, a friend since college, and I didn't have ownership over their friendship. But the thought of Eleanor—one of my oldest friends—enjoying the company of Dan's wife, my replacement, unnerved me. Then again, Eleanor and Elisabeth were nothing alike. Eleanor was much more like me—bullheaded, motivated, and always right.

However, in the end, I'm glad I accepted. Both of them started by praising you. They truly do believe you're wonderful. But then Elisabeth mentioned that she'd recently received a telegram from a Mr. Bowman of the C&O asking her to come down to the Greenbrier, that they needed her expertise on a project of national importance. I don't know what this could possibly mean—Elisabeth herself seemed quite shocked too—but I hope this letter reaches you before she does. She asked me to keep this quiet, but of course I'll break my promise for you. You know I'm on your side.

I'd better close. I'm late for a meeting with the Democrats, and though it seems they would like me to run for something or other—perhaps they realize I'm just as smart as my dear FDR—I will have to decline. I'm passionate about my human-rights post with the United Nations and don't feel inclined to leave it for the scrappiness of politics.

Make it splashy, DD. I will be terribly disappointed if you don't.

All my love,

E

I dropped the page. The walls seemed to close in and I began to feel dizzy. I remembered Phil Smith's comment about how difficult I was and suddenly knew why Mr. Bowman had called

Elisabeth. Society was right—she was a gentler soul, younger, a better mother, a better wife, an army veteran. She was a woman who had somehow avoided the scandal of her own divorce because of her slightly lower social rank, a woman who found a way to manage both her career and her home. Elisabeth was my superior at much, but she was not a better designer. She had won the hearts of my family, inadvertently stolen everything, and my work was all I had left. She would not have the Greenbrier too.

My tweed coat was too warm for the blazing fire in the Greenbrier's hearth. The heat was spreading up my neck. I could feel it and hoped my skin wasn't producing those unbecoming pink splotches. I wondered if it was the heat itself or the thought that I was about to be fired, replaced by Elisabeth, that caused my perspiration. All could be lost with a word from Mr. Young. In an instant, Dorothy Draper & Company could be no more, and I with it.

"This upper lobby will need to be open, but warm," I said, trying my best to keep up some sort of normalcy as though I didn't know Elisabeth could arrive at any moment. If I let on that I knew, it would seem I was desperate or threatened, and I wanted Mr. Bowman to take note of my professionalism, my vision, my celebrity, and contrast them with hers. If there was a chance I could convince him I was better, now was the time.

"We want to invite joy, invite people to sit and visit here," I said. My voice echoed over us. The echoing had to stop, and I knew my design would deaden it. No one wanted their conversations to be overheard, but the way this place had been laid out, you could hear someone whisper from one hundred yards away. "I did something similar with the Coty Salon in New York in '41. They wanted people to linger, naturally, to buy more. Here, you want guests to return every year or, hopefully, every season. People enjoy places that feel pleasant and surprising and comfortable. I plan to create intimate rooms, special spaces for conversations, and make sure my design is something to discuss when natural banter falters."

"Oh. I was to tell you. Mr. Young has asked that the main lobby remain on the first floor," Mr. Bowman said as though he hadn't heard a word. Regardless, I knew right away it was the right idea. The main lobby downstairs was a spillover place for reception and it made sense for it to stay there.

"Absolutely," I said, biting back the retort that Mr. Young had hired me to outfit this place and I should be the one to decide the placement of such things.

Glenn cleared his throat beside me, likely stunned at my agreeable answer to someone instructing me on the particulars of my job.

"What do you see?" Jean asked. She was poised across from me with paper and a pen, ready to take notes so that she and Glenn could measure everything later. After all the numbers were figured, Glenn would sketch plans so lovely you'd want to jump inside them.

"Tradition and innovation," I said. "Black Belgian and white Georgian checkered marble floors—situated diagonally, of course. Just like the Hampshire House. It's become my signature and people must know that they're walking into a Dorothy Draper design the moment they step through the doors. We'll need something for the middle of the room—a round table perhaps—and several different seating arrangements through-out to foster intimacy. Of course I like wingback armchairs in that cheery sort of red, nothing too deep or Christmassy, and kidney-shaped sofas in the resort's signature—romance and rho-dodendron. The curtains must be done in that particular fabric as well or perhaps our Fazenda Lily instead. The walls, a vibrant aqua sky." I paused. Glenn was sketching the room. I could hear the hurried strokes of his pencil and knew that he was placing the tables and couches and lamps and vases already. He was a great designer, someone I trusted with my vision because he'd wholeheartedly adopted it.

I looked around, imagining. The room would still seem huge, even with the separation of the green lobby and the trel-lis lobby and the ballroom. "I'd like to add columns here too. Nothing Grecian, just plain block, done in white, in two rows down the center of the room."

The doors opened, blasting a heavenly bit of cold air into the lobby and depositing an elderly couple at the foot of our gathering.

"Oh!" Glenn exclaimed, rising to his feet and setting his sketchpad on the scratched cherry tea table. "This is Mr. and Mrs. Mosley, DD. Tom told me to expect them this morning. Mrs. Mosley is rumored to be quite a hand with upholstery."

I froze at the name and then let my gaze fall on the man. Mosley wasn't exactly a common surname, but it wasn't unheard of either. It had to be a coincidence. He didn't look much like the Frank Mosley I knew once upon a time. Then again, I won-dered how readily anyone from my youth would recognize me if I wasn't who I was.

"I've done all of these," Mrs. Mosley said, waving her hand at the window trappings around us.

I nodded and tried to avoid staring at her husband.

"And all of the upholstering of the furniture throughout the hotel."

Her work wasn't badly done, I noted, looking at the way the pleats and billows lay just so, but I needed a professional.

"I didn't choose the fabric," she added. She leaned on a small cane. Her body was bowed, her back curved, but her eyes were focused like a hawk on me and her mouth was pinched as though she dared me to criticize.

"You're proposing to sew for me?" I asked. "I'll need upholstery work in every room of this hotel. The curtains will be done by Mr. Handman. He does them for all of my jobs." It was a daunting task for anyone, especially for a woman who looked to be as old as my eighty-year-old mother. Then again, if Mother were here, she would slap me for thinking her old at any juncture, and I had a feeling this woman was the same.

"I meant to tell you, DD," Lee said from somewhere behind me. "Mr. Handman telegrammed last night to say that he's running behind on other jobs and though he would be thrilled to work on your curtains, he can't guarantee he'll be finished by our deadline."

Panic shot through me. I didn't do well with surprises and I didn't enjoy working with new jobbers. The people I contracted were experts, the best in their fields, and they completed tasks on time. What if my only seamstress was Mrs. Mosley? I couldn't imagine she was swift.

"I know you're planning to outfit the whole hotel," Mrs. Mosley said. "I'll set up in here somewhere and work morning through night. It's my time to help the Greenbrier, just like Frank here did."

I swallowed hard. I was hearing things. I had to be.

"Did you work here?" I asked. My voice sounded pitched, strained. Even if he was the same man I'd known, I doubted he would remember me.

"For thirty-four years," he said. "Just like my father, David, before me. I retired in '42."

I could tell he wanted to say more, but he only shook his head and tucked his hand into his wife's. If he knew who I was, surely he would have greeted me as though we'd met before.

"I'm not planning to ransack the place," I said reflexively. Perhaps they'd only come to make sure I didn't ruin their beloved Greenbrier. Even though I always won over the decision makers, there were always naysayers—Mr. Rolla's contractor in Brazil, who loathed my use of plasterwork, and Mr. Jeffries, Mr. Coyle's underling at the Hampshire House, who continually proclaimed to anyone who would listen that chintz shouldn't be mixed with any other sort of pattern. I could feel everyone staring at me. But the older man laughed.

"I know, Miss Tuckerman. I know."

My face blanched. I could feel it. And then I forced myself to breathe. Frank Mosley had known the art of discretion years ago and I was certain he hadn't forgotten. He wouldn't bring it up. Not here.

"Excuse me? Her name is—" Lee piped in, sure I would breathe fire at being called the wrong name.

"I know who she is now, sir. But the last time I had the pleasure to serve her, she was Miss Tuckerman. You look just as beautiful as you did then," he said.

Only older men could get away with lies like that. I brushed my fingers across my short, permed hair done up with a parallel part. I looked old now. I even had an old woman's hairstyle—a wreath of tiny curls made dark with dye. My maid, Bella, left behind in New York, was the best, truly, and yet nothing even she could do could bring back the full ebony coiled in a young woman's coiffure. That woman was long gone.

"You're kind," I said. "And you seem just as handsomely merry as the last time I saw you. You gave me a silver horseshoe." It was the only memory I dared reference out loud.

"Ah, the Hunt Ball. One of the finest occasions I've ever seen here," he said.

"He talked about it for months after," his wife said.

"I'm surprised you remember me," Mr. Mosley said. The gleam in his eyes said otherwise, but I appreciated the act nonetheless.

"You Mosleys were a fixture here. Everyone knew and loved your father first, and consequently we all knew and loved you," I said. "And we'll have more occasions like the Hunt Ball. That's why I'm here. Just because the old hotel doesn't stand doesn't mean the Greenbrier cannot be restored to its original glory."

"I expect it'll be better," Lee said.

"Please have a seat," I said, gesturing to two lumpy armchairs cap-ending our matching couches. "We're just going over some of my preliminary ideas. I assume it would be best if you understood my vision, Mrs. Mosley."

"I'll be of service in whatever way you'd like, Mrs. Draper," she said, easing her way into the chair.

I tipped my head at her and turned my attention back to the group.

"Have any antique pieces been recovered from the cottages or from the rest of this place?" I asked Mr. Bowman. "It would help to know how much furniture I'll need Ted, my director of procurement, to locate—or Lee to order."

Glenn snorted.

"Truly, DD, I know Ted and I will be gathering everything regardless—and painting and staining. How often have you resorted to using Lee for anything other than—"

He stopped short. Lee's face burned. Mine did not.

I gestured to the blank space above the plain mahogany mantel. Everyone was watching me. I could feel their eyes. It was thrilling, the way they waited for me to say something. They thought I was a genius. A part of me was amazed at that. Growing up, I'd been deemed too creative, a terrible disappointment when it came to traditional studies. I wondered what Mr. Mosley thought, if he could see how far I'd come from wearing the heiress's mask.

"Above the mantel there, I'd like to see a large portrait, someone influential," I said.

"Martin Van Buren?" Lee asked. I could detect a bit of humor in his voice and ignored it.

I shook my head.

"Heavens, no," I said. "He would positively faint with horror. His family always made it very clear that he did not want any sort of hero legacy. I was thinking of someone a little more universally loved. Perhaps a George Washington. In particular, the Lansdowne portrait by Gilbert Stuart in 1796 comes to mind."

Mr. Bowman choked on his tea.

"Don't you suppose that painting alone would eat our entire budget, Mrs. Draper? I thought I read it appraised for nearly four million pounds twenty years ago when the Lansdowne property was sold."

I shrugged.

"I'd settle for one of the copies done by his daughter. Either way, Jean, write and have Leon or Ted obtain one for me, won't you?"

I heard Jean sigh. She was constantly pretending to be irritated with me, but she knew me inside and out. Plus, Leon had a plethora of connections in London, and Ted loved a good hunt.

"I hate to mention it again, Mrs. Draper, but surely even a copy of the Lansdowne portrait could cost millions and—"

"I understand, Mr. Bowman," I said, yet again having a tremendous time voicing politeness. Interjecting talk of money into creative planning was completely improper. "However, I have been hired to make this place a resort again," I continued. "And don't you suppose we should try for the very best pieces and adjust if needed? I don't think it would hurt to ask for more money either if it comes down to it. Mr. Young will try to get it for me."

"And if there's none left to retrieve?" Mr. Bowman's eyebrows rose. "You know I believe in you and understand your talent, but this resort cannot be finished in the lobby."

"How dare you." I nearly rose but stopped myself. I knew immediately that I shouldn't have started, but now that I had, I couldn't stop. A hush fell over my employees. "I am quite versed in luxury and in the importance of minutiae. The Greenbrier will be outfitted not only from ceiling to floor, but from staff costumes to soap wrappers, from napkins to hand towels. Mr. Young has assured me that I will have whatever I need for this project. He knows exactly what it takes to make a splash. If you suppose you know otherwise—and I have a feeling you may believe you do—please enlighten me."

Robert Young was a man who didn't balk at spending money. He knew it was required to attract those with more of it. He'd done it well on his own. He'd come from practically nothing to owning majority stock in the C&O and rising socially to the level of some of my peers. He wouldn't let me down.

"I did not sign on to create a value resort outfitted by an average decorator," I continued. "In order to make a large profit, one must choose to make an equally large investment. The Depression is long over." I breathed, thankful I'd stopped before going into a full tirade. "This place must be made into what it used to be. Before, it was the summer resort of the Vanderbilts and Astors and Du Ponts and Kanes and Abercrombies and—"

"The Italian Vacchellis and the Swiss Wrangles and—"

"I understand," Mr. Bowman said finally, but I barely heard him. Mr. Mosley was looking at me. I knew he'd interjected on purpose. He remembered. He remembered everything that last season.

"Today, I also want Bing Crosby, the Duke and Duchess of Windsor, Sam Snead, Lucille Ball, Cary Grant, Katharine Hepburn, Jimmy Stewart, in addition to all of the families that once graced these grounds. The Greenbrier is an escape, a place where they can walk the halls and play like they're nobodies because everyone is somebody."

"I admit we're on the same page in that," Mr. Bowman said.

"We don't do things halfway," Glenn said. "The whole place will be a glamorous splendor, the backdrop to American aristocracy."

"I look forward to seeing it," Mr. Bowman said.

"I'm confident the sketches for the lobby and the accompanying rooms will be drafted in a week or so, and then I'm sure

DD will set me to pasture while the others labor over the rest of this place," Glenn said, knowing full well he'd be getting no breaks. I laughed.

"Goodness, Glenn, I think you've forgotten you're a draft horse, not a thoroughbred. I'll need sketches for every bit of every lobby, the guest rooms, the dining room, the cottages, all the common rooms. Perhaps you'll have a few minutes roaming the pasture in a few months or so when we go to print on the fabrics."

"I assume this means you won't need me for a time yet?" Mrs. Mosley asked. I shook my head.

"No. Not until our fabric is in," I said. "The bulk of the work is to come. The work of outfitting is tireless, as my staff understands." A collective groan rose from my employees.

"We're well paid, thankfully," Glenn said, always the one to add something inappropriate.

"The last bits are thrilling for all of you," Jean said. "I'd know. I'm always the one looking in and you're all so absorbed every time. And then at the end, you're beaming. It makes it worth it." She was right. Though the end of a project nearly always sent me plunging into cardiac arrest, I was never more satisfied than when surveying a finished job well done.

I looked around at my staff. They were tired. It had been a long day, and though I could dream until next month without a minute's break because I knew how imperative it was that this resort be done quickly, they were not me.

"Let's retire," I said. "It's time for tea."

Everyone stood, and I walked over to greet the Mosleys formally.

"Thank you for coming," I said, clasping Mrs. Mosley's hand. "I'm thrilled to have found a local talent, someone who

understands the history of this place and the guests yet to come."
In truth, though her presence had at first felt like an intrusion,
I was glad to have her involved. The staff were vital, and they
needed to feel as I did—that they were a part of this place. That
sort of loyalty would translate to happy guests too. She nodded
and squeezed my hand back.

"And what of your history?" Mr. Mosley's voice came from
beside me. I wanted to disappear.

"Whatever do you mean?" I asked. He was grinning, a
sparkle in his eye. I didn't know why he seemed so jolly.

"You never married him," he said. My mouth went dry. The
last time I'd seen Mr. Mosley flashed in my mind—the confusion, the hurt, the unbridled love I'd felt echoed in my chest.

"Of course I didn't," I finally said, and turned to find Jean,
wondering which man he meant.

Snow threatened, but the cottage porch was the only place I
could stand to be. Through the windows, I could hear them
all toasting and laughing, but I didn't want any part of it. The
afternoon had been busy. I'd continued on with Jean after lunch,
wandering back and forth on the main floor, trying to envision
the three rooms I'd planned so far, but I'd been distracted. I
couldn't keep on pretending I didn't know that the C&O was
bringing Elisabeth in for a second opinion, and I thought the
secrecy unfair. I'd have Jean schedule a conference with Mr.
Bowman tomorrow to discuss it.

I pulled my mink closer around my neck and stopped the
rocking chair.

"Surely there's a place in town," Glenn said, already slurring. I could hear him clearly through the windows. Usually they tucked their drinking away, but here, there was nowhere else to go. Dinner had been at my cottage this time, a spread of baked steak and mushroom gravy and green beans and yeast rolls lining the chintz runner Jean had made sure to bring from our office in New York.

Lee laughed, throwing his head back. He never laughed that way. It was false, something he used to try to fit in with Glenn and Ted back home, but he'd never truly find camaraderie with them. Lee was a different sort, a man who loved numbers and thrived in the literal, a man who didn't fully understand the design world. For some reason, that attracted me.

"Have you seen the town?" Lee said. "It's a block at best. The hotel has a bar, but you can't even see it. It's hidden behind the reception, as though they didn't want anyone to know it was there." Of course he'd had a drink when we arrived, when I'd insisted on looking over the Greenbrier alone. I could feel irritation welling in my chest. Drinking had become a sport in itself as of late. It used to be that drinking only accompanied sport—sport and after-dinner cigars.

"Then that's where we shall go," Glenn said. I could see Jean rolling her eyes. The last thing she needed was a drunk Glenn. She'd wind up being his caretaker, and no one was more high maintenance than Glenn when he'd had too much.

"Do you think we could tell her we're playing games at Top Notch?" Lee asked.

I turned away quickly, hoping Lee wouldn't see I'd been listening. A breeze drifted over me and I let my head drop back against the wooden slats. I was still being whispered about, even as a woman of authority, as the boss of a grand company. I didn't like being lied to or left out. I couldn't imagine how I would feel if I was made to go back to Tuxedo Park. I had no doubt I'd become reclusive like that poor Huguette Clark, who locked herself away in her mother's mansion after her divorce to avoid hearing the gossip.

I stood, determined to set Lee straight, but then the gleam of moonlight on the springhouse caught my eye. Hebe, the goddess of youth. Years ago, I'd laughed at people taking the water and hoping for vitality. Now I understood. I wished one could turn back the clock—only so there was more time for living. I knew I wasn't at the end yet, but even so. There were still so many spaces that needed to be washed in happiness and color, so many things I would change to buy my business more time.

Entranced, I grasped the frigid whitewashed rail and pulled myself forward, down the porch and then down the steps. The chill was bone-deep as the wind picked up, whistling past the Greenbrier and through the cottages and into the valley of the lawn. The path was paved now, and I didn't like the noise. My short block heels clopped.

I could hear the water gurgling as I stepped into the springhouse. The pump was there, just as I remembered, and I reached for it, not at all minding the way the metal felt like ice through my gloves. I cranked, and water poured from the spout. Without thinking, I leaned over, letting it stream over my lips and down the front of my wool cape.

"You're mad."

I startled, whirled too quickly, and fell. I could feel the burn, the sting of an abrasion on my skin.

"Are you all right? Tell me you're all right!" Lee exclaimed, rushing to my side. I touched my stockings, felt the blood gathering on my shin, and quickly scooted my leg beneath me. It felt like a lightning shock when I did, and I whimpered. I coughed, hoping Lee hadn't detected the sound.

"I'm fine. You frightened me, that's all," I said.

"I'll call a doctor. Here, let me help you up." Lee reached for my arm and gently pulled.

"I don't need a doctor." I bit my lip, trying my hardest to stand alone. I would have to lean on him back to the cottage now, and that fact alone made me want to cry. "I was only testing the waters. It used to be a tradition here, you know, to take the waters."

"Let's go home," he said, and I let him take my hand.

NOVEMBER 2, 1946

I could see Tom's Packard pull around to the back entrance right below the northern parlor I occupied as she sashayed out of the lower floor and onto the drive. She was wearing a pink silk kimono-style top and a straight black velvet skirt finished with a velvet bow at the waist. As much as I wished she weren't, she was quite fashionable. Tom opened the car door for her, and she started to sweep into it, Lifton leather briefcase first. I knew the brand because Dan had gifted me the same one years ago when our friends, the Coyles, asked me to decorate the Carlyle lobby, my first commercial venture.

"Elisabeth!" I flung the glass door open, very aware that I'd unfortunately selected the most boring ensemble I had—a dark-gray wool suit with a box-pleated skirt and heavy hose to cover the bruise from last night's fall. *Thank goodness for the box pleats.*

She glanced at me, fixed a smile on her lips painted Revlon Raven Red, and darted up the stairs, holding her wool bowler adorned with pink silk roses onto her perfectly fixed chignon.

"I'm sorry to appear out of nowhere like this, Dorothy," she said, out of breath. Her gloved hands reached for mine. "I truly am."

I nodded. It was impossible to find Elisabeth insincere or rude. That irritated me.

"And I'll not be in your way whatsoever. I've been sworn to secrecy on this little project I'm doing, but I'll just say that I did not campaign to do it. I was approached by recommendation of General Eisenhower—you know how dear the Eisenhowers are to me given I've decorated their homes, and how integral General Eisenhower was in our victory—and I had to agree. I would have written you right away if I could have, but they asked me not to. I suppose they were hoping my presence wouldn't be known at all."

I stared at her, wondering what in the world she was going on about.

"You're not here to bid on my resort?"

She laughed.

"Heavens, no. You know I enjoy smaller spaces—houses, apartments, and the like. This is just a little place. Something I can't discuss. But, Dorothy, did you really think I would try to interfere with all of this?" She waved her hand around while keeping eye contact. It was quite uncomfortable. "Even if I could spare the time away from home, which I cannot and don't want to, a venture of this caliber is best left with you."

"Well, I appreciate your saying so." I was both utterly confused and relieved. "And it's lovely to see you. But if your project is not the Greenbrier, then why are you here? Last I checked, the C&O owns everything now, bought outright from the government, so Eisenhower or even *my* dear President Roosevelt shouldn't have a say to any of it."

Elisabeth's face flushed. She had such milky skin that her every emotion made itself known immediately. I wondered if she was lying, if somehow she'd learned that art.

"It's not *not* the Greenbrier," she stammered. She let go of my hands and sighed. "It's just a little place around here that I'm supposed to decorate for some . . . some people."

I recalled the Tiger cottage. It had been more than a gathering place for late-night gambling. I'd overheard enough conversation from my father over the years to know it was also a place for the decision makers of this country to meet without formality, a place where they could essentially hide. What if they were planning to reconstruct it and put Elisabeth at the helm of its outfitting? *Ridiculous.* I'd met all the presidents in my lifetime save Truman and had been very close to both the Tafts and the Roosevelts. If a project such as that was being done, surely they would extend the opportunity to me—especially given I was already here. I was practically one of them, after all.

"And you're sure you're not trying to win this resort from me?" I stared at her, watching her face for any sign she was lying. I didn't like asking the question again, as though I was desperate for this job, but in truth I was, and I needed to ensure that she wouldn't derail me. Beyond the hotel or possibly reviving the Tiger, I couldn't imagine what she was doing here.

"I did not put my hat in the ring," she said. Her eyes were wide and I could tell she was afraid I was going to ask her more questions, questions she'd have a hard time lying about. Her response didn't satisfy. Perhaps she hadn't bid on the project, but the C&O had gone to her, and though she insisted she didn't have the time to do the Greenbrier, I didn't entirely believe it. People always came up with excuses as to why something wouldn't work before seizing victory. It was security in case one drew the losing straw—and in Elisabeth's case it helped to defuse potential conflict, something she abhorred. If she took the hotel from me, I would hear it from Mr. Bowman or even possibly Dan, but never her.

"Very well," I said, though I wanted to keep pressing. "Now that I've caught you and your presence is known, would you like to stay on for tea? I could probably have the cook summoned."

"Oh, that sounds lovely, Dorothy, but Dan has me booked on the next train, so I'd better be going," she said, nearly sounding regretful. "Speaking of Dan, I have to say that I'm so sorry about Jean. It wasn't my idea, I swear it. I've been wanting to write you to that effect, but it felt disloyal to Dan."

I stared at her, having no idea what she was talking about.

"What do you mean? Jean is fine. She's just inside," I said.

Elisabeth's cheeks reddened once more.

"I meant about her salary," she whispered. "It was Dan's idea to stop paying it. He said it had been twenty-five years and he felt traitorous to me to continue to support your company when we did the same sort of thing. I told him how ridiculous it was, but he wouldn't be swayed. You know how he gets when he's set on something."

The news shocked me. This was the first I'd heard. Dan had begun paying Jean's salary before our divorce was final. It was a goodwill offering, a way I knew he was hoping to keep things amiable. I hadn't needed the money at the time—far from it—but I let him do it and I let him believe it made up for his leaving me.

"Oh," I said and laughed, attempting to appear lighthearted. "I appreciate it, but it's of no consequence. I can't even remember when he wrote to tell me."

"He called," she said. "I think it was in July, if that helps jog your memory. I cried. I thought it was so horrid. I just knew you'd think I was terrible and jealous."

"I don't think you're any of those things," I said, truly meaning it. I understood the way Dan operated. The moment he had an idea, there was no stopping him—he would spend weeks at the hospital researching, following a hunch, or sail off to Europe or China on a moment's notice in hopes of finding a cure for William Douglas's migraines or FDR's polio. This allowing space in his life for his wife's business development was new. When we were married, he'd barely acknowledged my career aspirations after his initial encouragement to start my company. He'd send a gift here or there—usually through a courier—but he'd been too involved in his studies, in his own profession, to notice otherwise. Even when I'd mention a feature in the *Times* or a new job won, he'd barely say a word. It was always a distracted *"Wonderful, dear"* while his gaze remained fixed to a medical journal. He seemed to be different with Elisabeth. Doting even.

"Thank you, but I'm sorry all the same. It was quite a bit of money if I recall," Elisabeth said, interrupting my memory. There was the talk of finances again. Beyond the fact that it was improper, the weight of another salary, a hefty one at that, landed hard on my shoulders. Who had Dan talked to? Since Jean was still receiving her salary, I had a feeling it was Lee. I wondered why he hadn't told me. Then again, July had been a hard month. We'd closed the books on both the Versailles and the Palacio Quitandinha, finally realizing we were never going to be paid.

"I'm just fine," I said, biting my tongue. A lesser woman would give in to fury and insult him, saying indecorously that Dan's contributing a portion of his paltry physician's salary was hardly needed, just like it wasn't needed when we were married, when his every whim was financed by Tuckerman pockets. Unfortunately, that wasn't true now.

A distant train whistle interrupted the silence.

"I'm thankful for that, Dorothy," she said. "I'm truly sorry. And I apologize for giving you such a start today."

"It's all right," I said, squashing the urge to ask her again about why she was really here, about her intentions with my hotel. "Safe travels," I said. "And always lovely to see you."

"You as well, dear," she said, seeming to be satisfied with my response. She let go of my hands and bounded down the steps to the waiting car.

"Say hi to Dan for me," I called as she waved, even though the thought of him made me want to hit something. How dare he pull Jean's funding—and without so much as talking to me personally. Perhaps Dan was behind Elisabeth's appearance here. Perhaps he'd encouraged her to compete with me, though if that was the case, I couldn't figure why. I would always win. I had to. I'd always be more famed, more loved for my work than both Dan and Elisabeth combined. Plus, I'd done nothing to anger him. I'd always kept my hurt, my disappointment, tucked behind a facade of amiability. I did this in part for the children, but mostly because letting on when one was wounded gave away the upper hand.

"I will!" Elisabeth shouted, and then Tom closed the door. That September day in 1912 flashed in my mind—the arbor of roses, the crush of my family and friends, Dan standing in a tuxedo waiting for me. Sometimes the disparity between our wedding day and now was striking. *Please tell the man I swore to love forever hello—the man I woke up to and told secrets to and had children with.* The longer I lived the more I realized life had the capability to make family strangers and strangers family.

I'd treated my leg with peroxide, but still the cut was ugly, the bruise hardly concealable when I was sitting down and my stockings stretched thin across my legs. Lee was staring at it. I could feel his gaze from across the room and returned his attention with a glare. I knew he meant well, but I didn't appreciate him regarding me like a china doll. Men didn't get the same sort of tenderness the moment their hair turned gray. They were deemed strong well into their seventies. It wasn't fair.

I walked around the small guest room, trying my best not to limp. The news that Elisabeth probably wasn't contending for my hotel had relieved me, energized me, and now I only had to make it to two more guest rooms. Two more, and half of the rooms on the hotel's second floor would have a vision. I stopped for a moment, watching the way the sunshine beamed on the far wall. One always needed to figure the sunshine into design. A color looked different in the light and in the dark, and it wouldn't do for a room to look gloomy or shabby for half of the day.

Jean yawned. I could hear the slight squeak as she closed her mouth. They all seemed exhausted this morning. Perhaps they'd gone to town after Lee put me to bed. I wished they would have included me. I always threw the merriest parties, but then, I was their boss. Sometimes I forgot that. I spent more time with them than anyone else, after all. I missed my friends in the city. Perhaps I should ask Eleanor or Mae Davie to come down. Then again, they had their lives and commitments too. Careers and frequent travel didn't allow for fast friends.

"I'm sorry to say there won't be time for a nap today," I said, turning to the doorway where my team was gathered. Lee's face reddened while Jean's countenance hardened.

They all nodded, even Glenn, whose smile stretched across his face like a Cheshire cat's. He knew he was in trouble and didn't at all care. That was part of his charm, the only bit of him that was like me—save the knack for design.

"This room will be yellow. Pale enough to avoid mustard in the evening, but vivid enough to be known as yellow instead of winter white. Perhaps pineapple."

Jean scribbled as I squinted at the two windows. The view was the entrance to the hotel, the long circular drive leading in from the train station. The guests here would be watching others coming and going. The room needed a tea table and sitting area for such sport.

"What was Elisabeth doing here?" Jean asked, still writing. I'd wondered how long it would take one of them to ask. To his credit, Lee had simply come close and whispered that we could talk about it later.

"I don't know," I said honestly, and decided to leave it at that. I would find out eventually. Jean scowled. I could tell she wanted to know more but wouldn't ask in front of Glenn and Lee.

"Glenn, please ask Mr. Bowman again about the quest for any usable furniture. Anything suitable can be painted and re-purposed," I said.

"Surely you're not going to paint the antiques, Mrs. Draper." Mr. Mosley's head appeared over Glenn's and Lee's shoulders. I wondered how long he'd been standing there. I laughed.

"Of course I am, Mr. Mosley. Not all of them, of course, just the dreary dark pieces—if there are any left to be had."

He pushed forward, and when he stood in front of my employees, he removed his old-fashioned bowler and crushed it to his chest.

"No wonder," he murmured to the stained carpeting before turning his attention back to me. "Mrs. Draper, Mr. Bowman is . . . he's concerned about your direction here. He'd planned to take you on a tour himself, but he's been called back to New York and asked me to step in. You need a reminder, Mrs. Draper."

"Of what?" I snapped, struck with the notion that Elisabeth truly could have become versed in lying, that perhaps I was to be replaced after all. A hush fell over the room. I could almost feel Jean holding her breath. I was finished with Mr. Bowman and his concerns.

"This is the Greenbrier," Mr. Mosley said without balking. "No one knows it better than me. This wild scheme of yours is not what we had in mind."

"We?" I asked. My question was rude, but really, what say did he have in my design? He didn't work for the C&O.

"The C&O has hired me to help monitor this project," he

said. "I've known the resort longer than almost anyone, after all."

"Perhaps, though in a—" I stopped short. I couldn't come right out and say that his experience was different, that he'd been an employee and I the esteemed guest. It was rude and I was upset. I always lashed out when I was feeling insecure. It had taken nearly a year's worth of therapy to unearth that little tidbit.

"No one will find the direction you're heading satisfactory," he said, his voice warbling as though he was about to shout.

"If that's so, then I quit." The blood drained from my face and I felt my body rush cold. I didn't mean it. I couldn't quit, couldn't let my company fail and watch my staffs' lives crumble with it.

To my surprise, Mr. Mosley just laughed. "That's the Miss Tuckerman I remember," he said.

I wondered how much he could actually recall of me. In all the years my family had frequented the Greenbrier, I'd never had a full conversation with him or his father before that last summer, our only interaction being friendly greetings at the front door or swift exchanges in the hallways.

"Please come with me anyway," he said. "At the end of our tour, if you still wish to go, you may, although it would sadden everyone."

"I hope you understand I was only speaking in jest. I'm not going anywhere, Mr. Mosley," I said. "But you've caught me in the middle of my work. And though I'd be happy to wander around with you, I must be frank: I'll not alter my designs. Mr. Young knew of my strategies before he hired me. In fact, he hired me because he and his wife are fans of my particular style."

"Yes, I know," he said. I could hear the sigh in his voice. "It's only that, well, you know the Greenbrier. And that's important. But you've not been familiar with the new hotel as I have, and I'd like to tell you what it was like those twenty-eight years before the internment and the hospital."

As much as I didn't want to admit it, he was right. I hadn't walked *these* halls as a guest. I didn't have memories in this place.

"Perhaps there will be some things you'll keep for the people who loved it during that time," he continued.

"Very well," I said. I thought of the old hotel. Though I'd often thought of the ways I'd alter it—and did make changes at times when being upset called for it—most of the others would be devastated to walk into a completely altered resort. The new Greenbrier held people's memories too. And though it would certainly look different from now on, Mr. Mosley was right: I needed to preserve some of the touches that guests cherished. The reopening of the resort—along with the lavish three-day party boasting every notable in the country—would be a reunion as well, and I wanted the Greenbrier's beloved to feel like they were coming home, no matter when they'd last visited.

"As for the rest of you, I've changed my mind. Go take a nap. It'll be a late night," I said.

I stepped through the crush of them in the doorway and took Mr. Mosley's extended arm.

Mr. Mosley was a slow walker. I had a feeling he'd meandered even in his younger years. I used to be annoyed by sloth. I'd even fired a few jobbers because they were so leisurely, but now the pace—only the walking pace—suited me.

"Most of the soldiers came through these doors."

Mr. Mosley breathed hard and caught himself on a small beam in front of the whitewashed double doors leading out to the Greenbrier's lawn. The lower north entry was horrid, much worse than the upper entry. The floors were a slate linoleum scratched with the memory of wheelchairs and wheeled gurneys and whatever else had been brought through the doors. The curtains were a shabby thin gray, allowing the fall light to cast an unnecessary spotlight on a mismatched pair of oak chairs and a metal table serving as a sitting area.

"I greeted them the same way I've greeted guests since your time, but it was hard, Mrs. Draper." He didn't look at me as he spoke, letting his eyes fall on the entry. "I've never seen such terror. And to think—thousands of miles from the action. I can't imagine what the medics at the front line would have seen."

"The stuff of nightmares," I murmured. I'd often dreamed of the war—likely because in my waking hours I ignored it—especially when I knew George and Ted were over there fighting. There was no way to fix war with color, but I'd tried. I'd never been so busy as I was during those years. I'd taken any job to distract me from the horror of the world, and it had mostly worked.

"Before, this entrance was one for guests coming in from sport—from a picnic on the green or a day at the links or a leisurely ride. It was a wonderful place to work, an easy place to be happy. All the politicians came in this way. Even in the war years," he said. "During the internment I worked here, too, and enjoyed simply being able to nod at the traitors instead of having to greet them with false warmth at the main entrance."

"The old hotel's porch faced the same way," I said. I remembered the wide porch, the way we'd often reclined on the stairs and watched the world go by. "We must figure a way to invite others like me to reminisce, to take in the view they remember. Perhaps we should arrange some comfortable chairs on the second-floor veranda, a little sitting area."

"Very well. So long as you don't paint the pillars pink. Let's go this way."

I balked, taken aback by the remembrance of another man saying nearly the same thing. That man had been poking fun at me, though, while this one was truly concerned that I'd turn his beloved home into a circus. He led me down one dreary corridor and then another until we were standing beside an indoor pool.

"Finally," I said. The pool was beautiful, fashioned in exquisite tilework with a wall of windows and a ceiling of glass. "This is beautiful." I could see it now—the ceiling would boast billowing white curtains while the pool deck would be outfitted in wicker and banana-leaf upholstery and ferns.

"I'm not trying to ruin this place," I said finally. "I want it to be magnificent, the way it was before, only better, more alluring to all the right people."

Mr. Mosley turned to me, a slight smile on his lips.

"And that's precisely the reason I wanted to speak with you in private," he said. "I'm not really concerned with your vision. In fact, I think it's just what this place needs—as does Mr. Bowman, deep down. But there's a matter I needed to discuss with you without your employees."

I nodded, biting back a retort.

"I know it seems peculiar, but for years I've been employed in a different capacity," he said. "I've been tasked with looking after a hidden suite reserved only for the use of the government. After

Wolf Row and the Tiger cottage were demolished, the meeting place was relocated here."

My breath caught. I was right. Suddenly, the candlelight beaming from the windows of the Tiger, all the men of the Greenbrier crushed into four rooms, the faces of nearly all the influencers I'd known flashed in my mind.

"It wasn't quite a secret. The Greenbrier has been a political hotbed since the Revolution," Mr. Mosley went on. "But it wasn't discussed openly, their meeting here. Oftentimes I wouldn't even know when they'd arrive. The suite always had to be ready."

"Of course," I said, feigning like I had known all along. "Eleanor Roosevelt wrote me just yesterday begging me to look after it. However—"

"Then you do know about it," he said, interrupting my near inquiry about Elisabeth's involvement. "I wasn't supposed to show it to you, but to be quite honest, Mrs. Draper, it pains me that your former husband's wife is doing the embellishments when I think it should be you. Don't get me wrong, she is a kind person and a woman of clear skill, but you have a deep history here and I don't quite see why they wouldn't have you do all of it. I want you to draw up your own plans so I can share them with the committee before the other Mrs. Draper gets started. Perhaps they'll reconsider. I may be fired for doing this, for going behind General Eisenhower's back—it was up to him to find someone to furnish it—but I plan to retire next year anyway."

"Thank you, Mr. Mosley," I said. Thinking of Elisabeth instead of me outfitting what were arguably the most important rooms at the Greenbrier made me horribly jealous. I would never admit it, of course, but it made me wonder if everyone in Washington, and perhaps beyond, thought Elisabeth was superior. I could feel the doubt creeping in, the urge to remember the whispers, the bad press, my failures. I had to have the whole thing, the suite included.

"Of course," he said.

"I don't quite understand why you have been so kind to me, but I appreciate it all the same," I said. I reached to shake his hand and he clutched mine.

"My whole life I've watched people," he said. "I've kept an eye on the wealthiest, the lowliest, the old and the young, and everyone in between. A long time ago, I decided that the worst thing to be was a society girl with dreams because society wouldn't allow both. That last summer you were here, I watched you, and even though you hadn't figured out your passion yet, I knew you had something boiling inside of you. I hated that for you because I knew you'd either fold, beaten into place by society's rules, or become a scandal."

"You're quite perceptive," I said, blinking back tears.

"I don't know that I am," he said. "It's true you're not Tuxedo Park anymore, but you're nowhere close to Bowery either. You're straddling both worlds and you've triumphed. I know it hasn't come without heartache, but . . ." He shrugged.

"I'm not sure that everyone would think I've triumphed," I said. I had no idea why I was allowing such vulnerability in front of Mr. Mosley. Then again, he'd seen a side of me few knew, another person, really.

"Perhaps not, but does it matter?"

I shook my head, but it did matter. The view of me from the gates of Tuxedo Park mattered much more than I would ever admit. Everyone was kind enough to my face for the sake of my parents. They had always been supportive in my adulthood when it was clear I was going to choose my own way, and some of our peers had even hired me, but the majority still couldn't understand or approve of an heiress who chose to dirty her hands in commerce.

"In any case, go ahead and take a look if you'd like," he said.

"I would," I said. "I don't know where it is."

"Oh, that's right," he said. "I forget you've never been inside this hotel. This way."

He led me around the edge of the pool, through the remains of a men's lounge, and toward a closet. The bathing towels were stacked tall on the racks. The stench of mildew and dust tickled my throat and I pinched my nose to keep from sneezing.

"Just here." He lifted the lowest rack and suddenly the wall stood open.

I didn't know what I was expecting, but this wasn't it. The suite was narrow and old, without a trace of political luxury.

"This is their gathering room," Mr. Mosley explained, laying a hand on the antique oak dining table in the center of the narrow room. There were only six chairs gathered around it, and at the far end, before a faux window, two wingbacks flanked the closed tweed curtains.

"How drab," I said. The walls were painted a dark hunter, completely void of any photographs or paintings or even maps. Men loved maps. "Last I knew, they enjoyed a little merriment when they met." I recalled the way the Tiger had looked from the outside, like a party. This appeared more like a shoddy boardroom.

Mr. Mosley chuckled.

"Oh. They do." He motioned me toward a closed door and opened it, revealing a carved mahogany desk adorned with stacks and stacks of papers.

"This is their fun?" I asked. "Avoiding filing?"

"No," he said, chuckling. "This is one of their employee's offices. He wasn't ordinarily this unorganized. He was made to leave in a hurry." Mr. Mosley grunted. I knew he wanted me to ask why this gentleman had been excommunicated, but I didn't. I didn't enjoy gossip. It was in poor taste. "But he was tasked with keeping all of this." He closed the door to reveal a portable bar filled with playing cards and decanters filled with different types of scotch and bourbon and cigars.

"You were right to show me. Something will have to be done with this. Our country's greatest minds cannot be holed up in a closet masquerading as a dungeon."

I glanced at the stacks of papers on the desk and noticed they were on the floor too. In this room, the only decoration to be seen was a small Westclox Big Ben alarm clock and a gold lamp boasting Hebe holding up a green bowl that housed the electric light.

"I do like the lamp," I said. "That's the only thing I'd permit to stay."

"It is appropriate, isn't it?" Mr. Mosley shuffled toward the desktop and plucked the lamp up. "After all of her time atop the springhouse, Hebe has become quite like family here at the Greenbrier. Dan was quite fond of this too."

"Everyone wishes for unending youth," I said. "I'm fond of it as well."

"Oh, I don't think that's what he was after," Mr. Mosley said. "We had many a talk about how we simply wanted to go back to our youth for a moment and choose differently. Then again, I might not have the missus if I did, and she's grown on me over the years."

I stared at him, sure he was going to laugh, but he didn't. At least he was honest. Dan had always sworn he'd fallen in love with me at first sight. That was a lie. I hadn't loved him at first either, but he was tall, successful, from a favorable pedigree— though far from that of Tuxedo Park—and easy on the eyes. By the time he proposed, I knew I loved him. The truth of that love was simple and honest. If Dan had said the same, expressing the true way his love for me had bloomed slowly, I would have been convinced of his feelings. Looking back now, in the wake of his leaving and remarriage, I didn't know if he'd ever really loved me.

"One thing is for sure. This room will not grow on me. I would propose to get rid of everything. This space needs to be patriotic, not dreary. I'm seeing wide stripes of red, white, and blue for the gathering room, with a slick white tile floor. Glenn and I could work together to create an upholstery pattern appropriate for the chairs and—"

"If our little scheme works, you can't tell Glenn," Mr. Mosley said, cutting me off. "No one can know about this place. It's a secret, a place they can go without any eyes, a place where they can hide. Do you know how important this drab office was during the last administration? FDR was here at least once monthly. He needed treatment, too, so he was—"

"I'm very aware of his needs, Mr. Mosley. My former husband was his physician."

"*Was* his physician," he echoed. "But in his later years, he often sought advice from the doctors here. It was convenient." Mr. Mosley was right. Dan had backed off after Frank improved, knowing his presence would only remind the man of how terrible he'd felt.

"In any case. Charles Edison, Francis Biddle, Henry Wallace,

Dr. Mary Bethune, J. P. Morgan, Raymond Moley—anyone of influence to him was here often. Truman has already written, eager to visit as well," he continued. "It's important to have a place away from Washington, a place to decompress and hide from the world. Some of the best fireside chats were recorded here."

"I understand the importance of discretion, but how would you expect me—or even Elisabeth—to complete it on my own?" I said. "Surely whoever is chosen will need assistance."

"In your case, you would order the needed trappings and feign that they're for a guest room. Mr. Bowman, myself, and the missus will help you arrange it."

I rolled my eyes. I could see it now, Mr. and Mrs. Mosley falling to their demise while hanging wallpaper.

"Surely Tom will be of assistance too?"

Mr. Mosley lifted a triumphant fist in the air. "Yes!" he said enthusiastically. "I'd forgotten about him, but he's good young blood and already aware of this place."

"And he would have all of this clutter removed for me?" I gestured to the office.

"Afraid not. Many of those papers are classified, and I'm sure we'll have instructions from the administration on what to do with them. For now, whoever is chosen will simply have to work around them," he said. "Now let's be going."

We stepped out of the suite, and once the door had been transformed back into the linen closet, he smiled at me. "Your country thanks you for your consideration to serve."

"My service?" I laughed out loud. "I'm being paid quite well, Mr. Mosley. I wouldn't say I'm serving anyone or anything. The C&O Railway is the charitable party."

"I don't mean your service to the resort," he said, extending his arm once more. "I mean your consideration regarding decorating this suite. You see, it's not just a meeting room. During the war, it was a place where they knew they could hide if something happened. It will always be a refuge for the administration. Even if the rest of the world is ruined, they'll be out of harm's way."

Nine

Ordinarily the Greenbrier's displays were fantastic, the presentation of our dinners to our teas to our lawn picnics arranged thoughtfully and beautifully on the same delicate china they'd used for as long as I could recall. But today's lemonade was an exception. The waiters had arranged the watermelon in two gargantuan bowls on a long oak table on the lawn below the hotel. They looked like two pig troughs, likely because all the effort had been directed to the horse show and the Hunt Ball. I leaned against the porch pillar, desperate to stay out of the sun that had slowly begun to wash our group in light and heat. I plucked a bit of damp coral mirage from my thighs.

"I don't care who I dance with, so long as Mr. Vanderbilt asks me at least once," Bolling said. Remembering Anzonella's friendship with Mike, she added, "Do you mind, Anzonella?"

We'd been talking about other things—tomorrow's race, the ball's decorations, the carts of flowers we'd seen rolling through the lobby, how something had been wrong with last night's scalloped potatoes. The turn of conversation was inevitable. The Hunt Ball was only a day away, after all. I glared at the table of watermelon, the impulse to overturn it jolting through my veins.

"Of course not, but Mike? Have you forgotten about Mr. Rossi so quickly?" Anzonella said, cooling herself with a lace-lined floral fan. I swallowed, focusing on the crystal pitchers of lemonade facing haphazardly in different directions, though nothing could keep me from recalling the way Enzo's lips had felt on mine, the way his body had pressed against me, and the way he'd responded to my self-consciousness with anger.

"I do hope you've completely blotted Mr. Rossi from your mind if you plan to set your sights on Mike," Anzonella continued, pushing back against the tufted emerald cushion.

The white wicker creaked as Helen, who was sitting next to her, turned away from the conversation. Her cheeks were flushed. She hated this talk of Enzo as much as I did, and I wondered what he'd told her. Had he kissed her too?

"Mike is a good man, you know, and he deserves—"

Bolling reached over from her chair, resting her hand on Anzonella's arm.

"Mr. Rossi was only a picture postcard, dear. I ran into Mr. Vanderbilt last night on the veranda after cards and we stayed up talking for nearly two hours before ending the evening at the piano with 'Cuddle Up a Little Closer, Lovey Mine.' Oh, how I should love to have an excuse to talk to him always. And the bonus would be you darlings, of course. I suppose I'd trade my Georgia for New York, so long as you're there, too, although . . ." She heaved a sigh. "I'm getting terribly ahead of myself." Bolling propped her feet on the railing, letting her hem of pale blue

Greek key lace dangle. No one else was about. The place was utterly silent and would be for fifteen more minutes—until the coaches arrived from the racecourse.

"We would accept you with open arms," Anzonella said, her icy demeanor warming with the knowledge that Mike wasn't Bolling's consolation. I didn't entirely believe it, but I knew Bolling enough to know that despite her thirst for attention, she was loyal and true, and if she chose Mike she'd look at no other.

"And what of you, Helen?" Anzonella asked.

"Me?" Helen shifted uncomfortably in her seat and began to twirl a gold basket-set ring of her mother's.

"No. The other Helen," Bolling snickered. Only three feet separated Helen and me, possibly less. Without her response, the question would swiftly fall to me, and in a matter of seconds, Anzonella would know there was something. She always did.

"I suppose I'd like a turn with anyone who asks," she said.

"Spoken like a president's daughter," Anzonella said, smiling. "But truly. You're among friends. Don't let manners mask the truth." She elbowed Helen lightly.

"Enzo, of course. I'd like to dance with Enzo and only Enzo."

Helen tried to pull her lips in to keep from smiling, but she couldn't. My chest tightened and I could feel my mind start to spin. At least I'd rejected him. At least I hadn't been foolish enough to think that a kiss—the second and best kiss I'd ever had—meant his words held truth.

"Why?" I couldn't help the question. It whispered from my lips as easily as a White Sulphur summer breeze, and I immediately regretted it. I was always too impulsive; I always needed to know, and the knowing almost never failed to ruin me.

"He's breathtaking," she said.

I looked at her, her slight figure, her doe eyes, her rosy complexion, and wondered how I'd ever thought, even for a second, that Enzo would truly choose me. Words were just words, and whatever had transpired between him and Helen was powerful enough to give her surety.

"And smart. And witty. I could see him standing beside me."

I nodded, willing her to stop, sure my face had paled.

"Oh, Helen. You don't mean it," Bolling said. "He's pretty, of course, but he's an *auto* driver. And there have been rumors that his father squandered his inheritance on gambling and had to take to mining. Father said Mr. Vacchelli mentioned that Mr. Rossi's grandfather was a decently prominent judge, and when he found out that one of his sons was bankrupt, he disowned him and made him change his last name."

"I don't care what he is or who he comes from, and neither does my father," Helen snapped, her command of character returning. "Unlike your fathers, mine didn't come from deep pockets. He understands that a man can make a name for himself if only he works hard and takes advantage of the connections he's given. He doesn't see Enzo as a risk to my future security as yours do. Instead, he sees his potential. Enzo is honest and worldly and incredibly smart. Did you know he speaks five languages? My father wants nothing more for me than a match with a man I love."

"And you suppose you love him already?" I asked. My mouth was dry, despite the fact that Enzo had practically told me he loved me and kissed me after. She shrugged.

"Love at first sight can't always be a myth."

"Has he said the same? That he loves you?" I looked away then, staring out at the lawn. Even the old men had departed to the track today. There'd be no distraction from an answer, no sudden interruption of Warren or the subject of our conversation or an asthmatic coughing fit from the group of the country's retired.

"I don't need him to," she said. "I simply—"

Anzonella stood, rattling the wicker settee and unsettling Helen's confession.

"There's the first coach," she said, gesturing to the empty drive and yanking my arm with the other. "Come, Dorothy, let's greet them." She pulled me down the steps, away from Bolling and Helen before they could reply that there was no such coach, her fingers digging into my arm.

"You don't need to drag me. I'll follow," I said, nearly out of breath. Anzonella eased up on my arm and slowed at the start of the drive, but I kept walking, figuring if I was already off the porch I may as well step a few feet out on the lawn and transform the watermelon into something less likely to attract livestock.

We stopped at the foot of the table and I shimmied a long white platter from beneath the bowls. I extracted each slice of watermelon with care, very aware that the pure white tablecloth simply wouldn't look the same with pink splotches. I heard Anzonella sigh beside me before transitioning to the other end to help with the second bowl.

"Are you going to tell me what that was about?" she asked finally. She didn't look at me as she deposited the fruit on the platter.

"No," I said, "but thank you for stopping me. I'm afraid I couldn't bear to hear her answer." I situated the platter of watermelon and quickly shoved the bowl under the table.

"You're going to have to do something, Dorothy." She shook

her head and lifted her hand to shade her eyes, I suppose to get a good look at me. "I know you take advice from no one, but for the sake of the rest of us, please take mine. I'll say it again—either forget him or love him."

"Ladies! Ladies!" A frantic male voice sounded behind us, and Anzonella's plea was cut short as two waiters hastened toward the table. "Do let us arrange the refreshments, and if it is not to your liking, simply let us know!" the elder said, his gray hair nearly sopping with perspiration and his green livery soaked through in spots as well.

"I was happy to do it," I said. "It was a joy, in fact. Arranging simply makes things pretty, and when things are pretty, you can't help but feel a bit more optimistic yourself." I smiled at the men and sauntered back toward the porch ahead of Anzonella, sure I could make everything make sense—I simply had to put everything in its order.

Ten

AUGUST 14, 1908

D on't touch it!" Mademoiselle swatted my hand from the gold-beaded strand of chiffon she'd woven into my coiffure as I stepped out the door. It had taken her nearly two hours to perfect my hair and I'd fidgeted the whole time.

Idle, all I could think about was Enzo at the horse show. It had been a sweltering affair, watching sixty-five horses parade around a mile loop for hours, and despite the way all of us had drooped like wilting flowers, Enzo only seemed to get handsomer, the sun darkening his already deep features. All of us girls had been seated together in the grandstand—I suppose one could call a ramshackle section of benches that—and after the men spent an hour smoking cigars and downing a glass of whiskey on ice and jeering at the poor horses, they broke away from our fathers and the old men and joined us. It had been lively, all of us talking and laughing together without the expectation of pairing up to dance or walk. Warren and Enzo had taken turns being the entertainer of sorts, mocking the announcer and gesturing wildly when a favorite horse faltered. I'd noticed, toward the end, the way Helen had leaned toward Enzo, the way she wanted him to settle on the bench beside her, but he hadn't. Instead, he'd looped his arm around Warren's shoulder, tossed his straw hat to me, and hooted and whooped when the day's cups were awarded. We'd even made eye contact several times, when societal traditions seemed too ridiculous to ignore. We were the only ones laughing when the jockey riding Mr. Bonaparte's horse, Sugar, mounted on the right instead of the customary left and Mr. Bonaparte slammed his cane down so hard on the rail that the end splintered off, or when Mr. Appleton tore the bowler from his head midway through the race and swore when he realized his jockey was wearing the wrong chintz stock tie. Perhaps the unpleasantness from last night could be remedied after all.

"Come along, Dorothy. We absolutely can't be late for the treadmill." Mother walked out of her room looking beautiful, almost Grecian in her ivory chiffon gown. Her look tonight was much softer than normal, and it suited her. Everyone would promenade around the ballroom for the Hunt Ball tonight, even the generations that had long since occupied the balcony and the sidelines.

"I'm so merry I'm almost all right with the fact that I lost so much money betting on the show today." Father smoothed his pink tuxedo jacket, the uniform required for the men tonight as the jockeys had all worn pink. His other hand clutched the gold-painted pole of the American flag.

"You look so handsome in blush," Mother said to him, her eyes glistening. I knew what she was thinking, or rather, remembering—falling in love with Father.

"Thank you," he said. "And you look radiant, as always." He turned to look at me and took my hands. "My dear. You're a vision." I'd chosen a Persian-blue fitted gown with sequined acanthus filigree detail and a long train. The fabric shimmered blue, gold, or gray depending on the light. Metallic lace, gold cord, and sky tulle adorned the bodice.

"Thank you," I said. I felt awkward about compliments, even when they came from Father. "You seemed like you were enjoying the race today. Do you suppose you'll be a horseman after all?" Though everyone in our circle was an equestrian to some degree, Tuckermans often rode only for leisure and watched races for the social aspect.

"Afraid not," he said. "But your Warren might. Did you see how enthusiastic he was at the show?" *Your Warren.* The narrow walls and carved moldings started to close in. I didn't want to lose my temper, but he had to stop pushing me, pushing us. "It might even be the two of you hosting a ball like this years from now."

I kept silent and followed them out of our room, hearing the hum of voices from the lobby below as we started toward the grand staircase.

"The Abercrombies do have quite a bit of land for racehorses if he prefers," Mother said. I stopped on the landing, feeling the heaviness of the gold sequins and beads as though the dress weighed fifty pounds.

"Stop," I snapped. "I don't know how often I have to remind you that Warren and I will not marry. We don't love—"

"It doesn't have to be about love," Father said, turning to face me. "He respects you and you him."

I tried to step around him, but he caught my arm. I was

aware of guests pushing past us and the crowd of people below us, but I didn't care.

"I've heard it will happen tonight," he said, "that he plans to propose."

I laughed out loud.

"Then you've heard incorrectly," I said. "Warren and I have an understanding."

Father kept his eyes on mine, unflinching, as though he knew something I didn't. The feeling unnerved me.

"Star, I'm begging you," he said. "He's a good man, an honest man, with the means to ensure your comfort, who would treat you the way you should be treated."

Mother was looking at me, too, her eyes misty.

"Your father and I were engaged on a night like this," she said. I looked to Father and back again to my mother, wondering what sort of delusion had befallen them both.

I pulled my arm away from Father's grasp and edged past him, hurrying down the stairs.

"Perhaps I'm promised to someone other than Warren," I called when I got to the bottom, before I had time to think about what I was saying. I heard Mother gasp, and I walked faster to dissolve into the crowd making their way to the ballroom. The crush made the short walk a long affair, and I could hear the whispers swirl. Some had undoubtedly heard my pronouncement.

"Oh! I love this song!" Mrs. Nicholson, an eighty-two-year-old former debutante of the Greenbrier, crowed beside me. Underneath the roar of chatting and laughing and whispering, I could barely make out a baritone voice singing a ballad. "It's called 'Sleeping, I Dreamed Love.' Mr. Nicholson sang it to me the night we met," she said, turning to her other side.

I heard Mr. Vacchelli reply, "Is that so? The song must have been quite popular the world over. In fact, I recall my grandmother singing it in Italian. She used it as a lullaby to my mother and my mother to me." I glanced at him, inadvertently meeting Enzo's gaze.

The crowd careened forward, eager to enter the ballroom, and Enzo pushed around his uncle and Mrs. Nicholson. I was very aware of his body pressed nearly against my back. His mouth quirked up at one side and his dark eyes were locked on mine. "Is it true? You're promised to someone other than the dashing Mr. Abercrombie?"

I took a deep breath, inhaling the sweet scent of cedar floating from the ballroom. Above the heads of the guests in front of me, I could see a bit of the splendor—swags and screens of evergreen and gigantic bouquets of blue, yellow, red, and white roses holding the swags to the chandeliers.

"I'm not—"

"You may have said it without thinking, but I can't help but believe you said it thinking of me, thinking of us." The last part came out in a whisper and he stopped moving. His hand brushed my arm and I turned to face him.

"What of Helen?" I asked.

"Darling Enzo." Helen materialized from the crush. She was dressed immaculately in a blush silk gown with a gold-threaded wheat motif. "It's nearly time for the treadmill, and we've been asked to occupy the second spot behind my parents."

He let me go at once, offering his arm to her in turn, not bothering to respond. I watched them go, feeling as though I'd been trampled, and then turned to look for Warren.

He was waiting for me beside the entrance to the drawing

room, our usual spot. Unlike my father, he looked terrible in pink. The color only intensified his ruddy complexion.

"Ready to do this again?" I asked him.

He placed his American flag under his arm and pushed a hand through his hair, barely nodding at me. His face was pale, and he offered his arm to me without so much as a reply. We walked into the drawing room to take our place, and suddenly his free hand clapped over the back of mine. I glanced at him, wondering what in the world he was doing, hearing my father's words echo in my mind. Surely Father was mistaken. Surely this gesture of affection was only because he'd made a visit to White Sulphur and had been disappointed. With the race and the hubbub, we'd had no time to speak. I gently pulled my hand away and walked beside him, through the mill of the guests trying to find their places and socialize at the same time. We were supposed to walk in behind my parents, and the moment I saw them standing next to the fireplace, I began to go that way. Warren stopped. His eyes searched the room blankly and when they found mine, stayed.

"What's gotten into you?" I whispered, forcing a smile at Anzonella, who was standing beneath the crystal chandelier with Henry. "Don't tell me you're nervous about jumping the hurdles. They're only a foot and a half, after all. They can't have our fathers tripping over them."

I laughed, hoping to coax the same merriment out of Warren. The idea for tonight's treadmill was ridiculous, after all. Who had ever heard of making adults appear like horses? Not everything should be themed, especially this way. A critic could absorb enough hilarity out of tonight to last a lifetime—if any critics were to be found. I glanced toward the doors to the ballroom, at

Enzo, who seemed to find this spectacle as ridiculous as I did. He kept pursing his lips in an effort to stop his laughing at Mr. Hunt showing Mr. Vacchelli how to step over the hurdles.

"Is he that captivating?" Warren said, his voice strangely gruff. I turned, feeling my cheeks redden. The urge to lie welled up, but I took a breath and nodded.

"Yes." I took Warren's arm the moment I said it and pulled him into place behind my parents. His father wouldn't have to walk the treadmill, seeing as how his wife was states away, but I knew he'd be waiting, watching us from the sidelines as though if he looked away for a moment, he'd miss seeing Warren sweep me into an embrace.

"Oh, how handsome you look, Warren," my mother said. "Can you imagine the loveliness of—"

Thankfully her words were cut short by the introductory notes of the national anthem, and the drawing room doors were flung open to reveal lush garlands and bouquets and two gargantuan papier-mâché horses bearing jockeys in pink flanking the elevated orchestra stand.

I watched Mr. and Mrs. Taft promenade into the room, whistles and applause raining atop "The Star-Spangled Banner" and atop Enzo and Helen as they sauntered in next. And then it was Mr. and Mrs. Thayer, waving their flags. The procession went quickly, though everything—the flag flapping, the cheering, Warren singing with a hitch in his voice—seemed muted. Nothing felt right.

"Gave proof through the night that our flag was still there," Warren sang under his breath. His eyes were teary. I'd never seen him cry.

"Are you all right?" I was well aware that we were next, that my parents were stepping out as I spoke, but I couldn't ignore whatever was happening with him.

"Yes, of course," he said, handing me the "reins" attached to his shoulders—black ribbons I was to hold as he stepped over the hurdles. He looked at me. "I've only just found the rest of my life, darling."

A lump in my throat choked me as he smiled and fixed his gaze on the rest of the room. He'd never called me darling except in jest. Warren waved his flag and grinned, but I could barely acknowledge the rest of the partygoers. When he finished the last hurdle and the son of Mr. David Mosley, one of the Greenbrier's most seasoned employees, handed us our favors—a silver horseshoe for me and a jockey cap for Warren—I broke away from him.

Enzo was on the other side of the room, his head bent down toward Helen's, but when he felt my gaze, he looked up and smiled. I grinned back, despite the same nagging doubt that he was only putting me on, hoping he'd make his way toward me as soon as he was able.

"He's to propose," Warren said. I hadn't realized he was still beside me, and wished with all my might he'd abandon me. "He told me today before the betting that Mr. Taft has given him a ring and asked him, if he loves his daughter, to propose in haste before they depart."

My breath caught. I could feel my heart pounding, creating the sensation that I should run across the ballroom and ask if it was true.

"That seems quite forward of Mr. Taft. And Enzo said he planned on it?" I could barely speak but forced the question from my lips. Less than an hour before, Enzo had insinuated that I should be promised to him. Was he truly so fickle?

"Some may think it a bit quick, but Taft and Rossi got on well from the start. Taft came from modest means the same as Rossi, and they share the same natural charisma. I'm sure Taft has his sights on grooming him into a political man." Warren shrugged. "I don't suppose Rossi said outright that he was going to propose, but the impression was clear enough." Warren touched my arm and I recoiled. "Does it upset you that terribly?" he asked.

I laughed loudly. I could pretend just as well as the rest of them.

"Of course not," I said. "Does it upset you that Anzonella is paired with Henry nearly all evening?" Almost everyone fancied Anzonella. She was beautiful. But she was also familiar, and so for almost everyone, Warren included, the novelty of winning her affection had waned.

"Why should it?" he asked.

"Exactly," I said. "Now, if you'll excuse me."

I pushed past a group of elderly couples still humming "The Star-Spangled Banner," a few of them trying, rather badly, to harmonize.

"The second dance?" Warren asked, and I nodded as I left him. Anzonella and Edith and Bolling were gathered in the middle of the room, their escorts nowhere to be found. A large silver horseshoe hung over their heads, in the center of the string of evergreen.

"Warren has cracked," I declared as soon as I was in earshot. They looked at me, their faces revealing not an inkling of surprise. Anzonella fussed with the pearl embroidery along her gray silk bodice and cleared her throat.

"I suppose he hasn't told you?" she asked. My nose wrinkled. She leaned in close. "I overheard Father telling Mother this afternoon that Mr. Abercrombie is ill. They don't think he'll live to see another season here."

I blinked at her, shocked. Everything I'd said, the way I'd tried to make him laugh, seemed cruel. He'd been mourning his father. Why hadn't he told me?

"When did they find out?" I asked. Mr. Abercrombie looked perfectly jolly. Even now he was tipping a glass of wine to his lips, his arm around my father's shoulders.

"I imagine after the show today. He went to see Dr. Moorman complaining of shortness of breath and dizziness, among other things," Edith said. Apparently, she'd overheard the same conversation.

"Ladies and gentlemen, it is my pleasure to welcome you to the Greenbrier's Centennial Hunt Ball. What a day, what a century!" The strings and brass silenced as their director, Carl Neumann, turned away from the instruments to face us. "To-night, we honor not only the history of the Greenbrier, but a century of the best waltz pieces in the world by the unparalleled Johann Strauss. I hope you'll enjoy the music and dance until you feel the need to kick off your shoes." With that he turned, and the ballroom came alive with men and women scurrying to pair up. I glanced around for Warren, hoping we'd find each other. I needed to talk to him, to comfort him. He was one of my oldest friends, after all.

"Dorothy." Enzo appeared in front of me and reached for my hand. "Will you dance with me?"

I clutched his hand in turn and nodded. He whirled me to the middle of the ballroom and then drew me against him, but I stepped back.

"I don't know that I should," I said.

His eyes narrowed and he held me tighter. "What does that mean?"

"There's a rumor spreading that you're going to propose," I whispered. His hand flattened against my back, and I closed my eyes to remember the way his touch felt. The opening notes of "Roses from the South" drifted over us.

"I am," he said, leaning in to my ear. "I'm a man who should be married, a man who wants love and children and steadiness, something I've never known." He led me confidently and without warning, spun me. I'd heard enough and tried to let go, but he wouldn't let me. "I grew up impoverished, never knowing if I was going to starve. I never questioned whether I was loved, but my life was a speculation at best. And then, racing . . . I'm everywhere. Rome, then Ireland, then Paris, then Ostend in Germany to train. It's exhausting, and I can't keep it up. I want a wife, a normal life, a fulfilling adventure." He took a breath. "I want that with you," he said. Goose bumps rose along my arms. "I thought I'd already told you."

"Why?" I asked, faltering as we moved. "We've argued, we've said unkind things." I recalled the ways I'd insulted him and wished so badly I could take it back.

"Ah, well. The way I see it, we were working things out. We were only testing each other, as we should. It seems our hearts barely acknowledged the words. Despite the misunderstandings, we remained drawn together by our want for something different, by our humor, by our affection for each other," he said. He dipped me, and I nearly stumbled. I didn't know how he could keep up the steps with our fate in the balance.

"Even so, you barely know me." It had been only weeks, and even though I thought I loved him immensely, I wondered if it would last. "Don't you suppose our swearing to marry after such a small amount of time would be a risk?"

"I race cars," he said. "I'm quite good at taking risks when I feel sure of the victory. We are perfect. We would make each other happy. And you love me, Dorothy. I love you."

"I love you too."

I tipped my face to his, wishing so badly we were in the dark on Lovers' Lane instead of in the middle of everyone.

"If I ask you, will you say yes?" His blue eyes were steady, unfaltering. Elation and panic struck through me. As much as I loved him and wanted to agree to marry him and let him take me away from the society I longed to escape, saying yes would mean saying goodbye to my family, to my friends, to everything I'd ever known. The moment I agreed, Father would surely disown me. The question held a tremendous amount of weight.

And then I remembered that only moments ago he'd been escorting Helen, and only hours before, he'd been holding her engagement ring. My mind snapped to the countless etiquette books we'd been forced to read as debutantes. *It is presumptuous for a gentleman to make a proposal to a young lady on too brief an acquaintance. Two months' time, at least, is necessary to ensure a gentleman's love and will prevent the worst—divorce, infidelity, poverty, scandal.* I recalled Alva Vanderbilt's visit to see Mother ten years back. I'd eavesdropped in the library while Alva detailed the way everyone had turned their back on her following her divorce, and how her whirlwind romance with Willie at the Greenbrier was to blame for it all. She had no idea he would turn out to be such a prolific womanizer.

"I want to," I said, "but before I do, I need to know you past this week, past this month. We would need that long to make plans and discuss where it is we would want to live, in any case. I want to see you in the light of the real world, without the glow of the Greenbrier, without the distraction of Helen and Warren and our families."

He looked away.

"Enzo," I said.

"You're unsure about how you feel," he said. "I told you before that my parents were engaged after two days. They're still mad about each other. From the time I was a boy, my mother told me to do the same, to find someone I was completely enamored with and to not delay. I found you, but it seems you haven't found me."

"I have found you. I love you," I whispered. "I only need a little time to say goodbye." I felt tears pooling in my eyes. I wanted to tell him about my parents, too, about how love didn't need to be rushed.

"I know and I understand, but this, the Greenbrier, this is it for me, *mio angelo*. I need to be married right away. Please say you will."

"Why?" I asked. "Why the Greenbrier? Why do you need to be married so quickly?"

Enzo's jaw clenched, but his stare didn't falter.

"The moment I stepped off the train, I knew I never wanted to go back to Villaputzu or even to Rome, to that life."

He still wasn't answering my question.

"I'd never been keen to settle, really, but I felt it suddenly, as though I was desperate to cling to the wonder of this place and never let it go. I knew this is where I belonged and then, when I saw you, I understood. I was supposed to feel this way because I was supposed to find you."

"You do know that none of us live here," I said. "My home is

Tuxedo Park, a place filled with large homes and larger people. We don't have to go back to your town or Rome. We could live in Scotland or California or Spain, wherever we decide feels like home. We can buy an a townhome in a city or a little villa in the country or both if we like."

He gripped my hand. "*You're* my home. Wherever you are. That moment I stepped off the train it was you I felt, I know it was."

"We'll be together always, if you'll only wait a little longer," I said. I thought of my parents, people who—regardless of their prodding in my relationships—deserved better than for me to promise myself so quickly to a man they didn't know, a man who would take me away from them forever. As much as I wanted to say yes, to go to the chapel tomorrow and swear that I'd love him forever, I couldn't yet, and I was right. "If you truly love me, you'll wait just a bit longer. Why do you feel so compelled to rush?"

"If you love *me*, you'll say yes right now." He lowered his voice as the music quieted, but his body pressed against mine, the urgency to hear the longed-for words occupying his whole being. A tear escaped my lids, sadness mingled with frustration, and he lifted his hand from my back and wiped it away with his thumb. "Please don't cry, *mio angelo*. There's no need when we can make each other so happy."

"I need two more months," I said. "I promise I'll love you every second of those months, but I need them to dream, to plan, to say goodbye. My grandmother Minturn, my mother's mother, is turning sixty-five at the beginning of October. She's my last living grandparent, and my entire family will be together for a big luncheon on the lawn. We could count it our farewell party. We could get married the day after."

"I can't," he said simply. His hand bridged along my shoulder blade and I felt his fingertips grazing my skin. "If you change your mind, Dorothy, I'll not recover. I'll be alone."

Under normal circumstances, I would've laughed. Enzo would never run the risk of dying a bachelor if he wanted to marry. He was much too handsome, too smart.

"Is my word not good enough?" Anger started to bubble in my chest. "You'll not trust me with your heart? Eight weeks, Enzo. That's all I'm asking. In the scheme of our whole lives, it's nothing."

He shook his head. I was vaguely aware of another waltz starting, and he swept me in his arms to keep up the pretense that we were having a merry time dancing.

"I can't. I haven't been entirely honest, and as afraid as I am that you'll think my affections feigned because of it, I must tell you the truth. You deserve to know."

He sighed.

"Last year, my best friend, Fede, died at an auto race in Stuttgart. His car was run off the path by another, and before I could help him, the auto burst into flames. From that moment, something shifted. My racing began to suffer, and I began to lose. With my losses in several races recently, Fiat has dissolved their endorsement and I no longer have cars to drive. The Lancia race was my last opportunity to win, to prove that I could still perform. To be honest, it couldn't have happened at a worse time."

He twirled me. "Five years ago, when I left Villaputzu and my parents to live with Uncle and race, I thought I'd never return, that all of the poverty and hardship was behind me forever, that I'd never smell the stink of a silver-mine village again. But three months ago, I received a troubling letter from my mother. For ten years, unbeknownst to her or me, my father had his pay and Mother's—she serves as a mill keeper—advanced with interest, and he squandered their money on dice games and drink, the same way he threw away his inheritance from my grandfather. Father was injured a couple of years ago in a rockfall that killed twenty-five men, and Mother said that the mine owners compensated him until he recovered. But recently, the mine was sold, and now the new owners are settling the books, calling up his debt. Eight million lire is due to the mine by the twentieth of September or my parents will be jailed for the term of their loan. My father is a failure at best, but he's barely able to walk, and my mother isn't in good health. A jail term would be a death pronouncement, and I can't have their lives on my hands. I promised Mother I would either pay their debt by the deadline or return and work the term in Father's place. At the time, I thought paying their debt an easy thing. I could accumulate that much with a few wins on the circuit, but now . . ."

He trailed off. I couldn't breathe. The dream I held moments ago was evaporating in my hand. He looked away, toward Mr. Vacchelli dancing with Mrs. Talbot. I hoped he was planning to tell me something else, something promising. Surely all his talk about finding a home in me wasn't a lie. Surely, even if he couldn't sweep me away to Italy, he still loved me. Surely he wasn't using me. Surely he wasn't just as Father had supposed from the beginning.

"I asked Uncle for the funds, but he has given Father billions of lire in the past. He believes Father deserves jail and has tried to convince me to break my promise. I won't. I can't. Despite his pleading with me, Uncle knows that. That's why he brought me here. I'm like the son he never had, and he wants to help me. I can't go back, Dorothy, and I can't take you back there either. I'm not suited to mining or to life in Villaputzu. Uncle believes there are singular opportunities here in America . . ." Enzo's voice faltered. I couldn't speak.

"He told me there's a way I can get out of returning." His gaze met mine. "My grandfather has left me an inheritance, the same as my father's. If we marry soon, I'll meet his terms in time to receive the money from my grandfather's trust and send it back home. Marriage may seem like a silly stipulation, but he wanted to ensure the family continued. In any case, I wouldn't have to go to the mines, my parents would be safe, and I would finally be free. I would need to obtain a position here—I'll be rendered penniless after I relinquish my inheritance—but Uncle says that unlike in Italy, where suitable posts are mostly closed to me, passed down from generation to generation or requiring a certificate won from an expensive university, America is a land of opportunity, a country full of prospects for men like me. I promise you I'll make my mark. I'll not let us—"

"And I'm your way out?" This story wasn't going to end the way I'd hoped. It was a horrible, wretched tale. He wasn't going to tell me our love was all that mattered. He needed something and thought I was the answer. I thought I might faint. My head spun and my skin pricked with goose bumps, but I swallowed hard and forced composure. "I'm your way to freedom?"

I realized the irony in my questions. I'd thought him *my* way out, when all the time, I'd been his. The difference was that my love wasn't dictated by a timetable. My want for freedom was my choice, and if it accompanied love, all the better. But I'd never force love for liberty, even if I faced a fate as harrowing as Enzo's.

As much as I wanted to free him, I would forever wonder if he loved me or if he'd only used me.

"I should have listened to my father. Do you even love me? Perhaps you're only feigning affection for me because you've heard my family has a greater fortune than Helen's. I have no say in my father's business affairs, and the possibility of him creating a post for you is unlikely at best." My tone was icy. I knew that, but his confession dug deep into my heart, unearthing the insecurities buried there.

Enzo's fingers clenched mine.

"No!" he said. "No. I do love you. You must believe it. You feel it as I do, don't you?" He waited but I said nothing. "Yes, I came here hoping to find a wife, but I never thought I'd find love. I suppose in a sense, you are my way out, but what does that matter if we love each other?" He cleared his throat. I pulled away from him, but he held me tighter. "If I was only after someone to unlock my chains, there's another willing, but in you . . . in you I have both love and freedom. You must take me at my word. If I could only extract my heart and hold it out for you to examine, you would see the truth, but as it is, I can only plead with you to trust me." I wanted to believe him. Even if the chance at Italy was gone, there were hundreds of other places we could go. I still loved him, and knew I'd agree if it meant his love forever. But I wasn't sure he truly loved me, not given what was at stake if I didn't say yes. "Dorothy, if we marry in the next month, I'll receive my inheritance, and my uncle has agreed to deliver it to Villaputzu. Please, I need the promise of your hand."

"Your desperation is palpable, and I can't blame you for it," I said. "As much as I wish I could soothe it, as much as I love you, I'll not change my mind. I won't have my marriage tainted by talk of deals and finances. My marriage will be about love and love only, and for you to assume that I would forfeit my ability to know the truth of your heart before swearing my life is both senseless and dismaying. Is two months so much to ask?"

"It is when the stipulations of your grandfather's trust hold your well-being," he said. "Without marriage, I'll be forced to return home to pay the debt myself.

"My uncle knows my affliction. He knows of my affection for you, but at the same time is urging me to be practical, to marry Helen quickly. She's pleasant, Dorothy, and she loves me. Her father has promised me a job in Washington, a translation position on his campaign."

"So that's what this is about," I snapped, horrified that he'd choose a profession and Helen over his supposed love for me. "This is why you're pressuring me to accept tonight. If I don't, you'll need to propose to Helen to secure the post. You're afraid you'll lose the offer and your chance at marriage and freedom. Does Helen know? I imagine not. She'd be terribly embarrassed."

He looked down at me, his eyes stony.

"She knows all about it," he said. "She knows I don't intend to return to Italy, and if I marry her, I'll need a position here. Her father knows that. He's practically handed her over to me, but I cannot accept until I know you won't take my hand."

"She knows about everything?" I asked, doubting it. "Even me?"

Enzo shook his head. "No," he whispered. "And she doesn't know about Fiat or my family. She only knows that I want to start a new life here."

The waltz was coming to a close, and regardless of my anger, I was aware that this could be the last time he held me, the last time I felt this way.

"I'll find work if you'll have me, if you'll say yes. But if you don't, I'll have to accept Mr. Taft and Helen. Please understand, Dorothy." I couldn't. As much as his eyes bored into mine, begging me to say yes, I didn't. I needed him to risk everything for our love. I wouldn't compromise my happiness.

"Enzo," I whispered. I let my head rest against his chest, feeling the rise and fall of his breath, well aware that my father and Helen were watching. Father would scold me later, but it didn't matter.

"Dorothy?" he asked, his voice strained.

"I love you. If you'll wait, I'll marry you. I will not change my mind. Even if knowing you must come in the form of letters from New York to Italy and back again, at least our love will be deeper than the thrill of a feeling. And when the time is right, when we do marry, I'm confident we'll find a way to settle the debt and find you a post. But if you cannot wait, our marriage would be founded on a transaction, not love, and our promises would be a lie."

"If I return to Italy, I won't be able to come back to you."

"Of course you could. I could book your passage back or I could come to you," I said, but he shook his head.

"I wish it were that simple," he whispered, "but I'm telling you the truth. This is my last chance. If I'm made to leave, I'll not be able to return. I know you believe we could find a way to pay what they owe, but I'm not sure I believe it. It would take much to win your father to our side. And even if you turned your back on his wishes and ran away after those months, do you suppose you would live with me there? I don't think you understand. My family doesn't live in any sort of splendor. Life there would mean living in a two-room hovel. We would struggle for food and medicine and money of any sort. I will not go back, and I would never allow you to follow me."

I opened my mouth to say that it wouldn't matter, that I'd live in a canvas tent if he would only wait, but I wondered if that was the truth. I'd never wanted for anything. How would I respond to poverty?

The song ended and we let each other go, our eyes heavy with the repercussions of our own reservations.

I withdrew to the refreshments after the fifth waltz, when Warren begged a break. After much prodding, he still hadn't admitted that his foul mood was a result of his father's ill health, and I was tired of trying to pry the news from him. He went to smoke a cigar on the patio, and I sought my own version of peace.

I twirled my spoon in my half-melted ice glass, watching the lemonade gradually absorb the shaved pieces. Was that what we all were? People with grand ideas who eventually dissolved into others' expectations? The orchestra was playing "Tales from the Vienna Wood" now, and the ballroom looked like a dream—the lush green forest decor made magical by the sparkle of the ladies' dresses. The scene reminded me of the lightning bugs flitting around the lawn at night, their glory sparking color on the beauty of the Greenbrier, even when the lamps had extinguished the sight of the grand old trees and the flowering rhododendrons and the handsome face of a man at the spring.

I watched Enzo now, his tall frame the picture of elegance as he danced with Helen. He had by far the greatest command of the waltz, especially in contrast to the other young men, Warren included. It was strange to think Enzo hadn't grown up among people like us. As if he could feel me, Enzo turned his face just slightly and met my eyes. We'd done this all night, neither of us able to forget our conversation, though it was impossible to continue.

"Miss Tuckerman." I startled, finding Mr. Vacchelli beside me. "How do you do?" He tipped a champagne flute to his lips while keeping his attention fixed on the dance floor instead of addressing me properly. Like his nephew, he'd been occupied all evening, but he by a variety of the Greenbrier's most illustrious widows.

"Well, thank you," I said, still twirling my spoon in the ice.

"May I have a word?" he asked, his voice going so quiet I could barely hear him over the music.

"Yes. Of course." I let the spoon go and set the crystal goblet on the tea table beside me. Mr. Vacchelli glanced behind him at the refreshment table, finding only Miss Stanley, a new debutante of sixteen, and Mr. Languire, a nearly ninety-year-old veteran of the Greenbrier.

"You're fond of Enzo," he said. It wasn't a question.

I felt my face burn, but laughed anyway. "Don't you suppose you're being a bit forward, Mr. Vacchelli?"

He merely shook his head. "Do you deny it? That you and my nephew have formed a bond of sorts?" His bushy eyebrows rose and he took another sip of his champagne before turning his attention back to the subject of our conversation, who was now dipping Helen. I looked at his hands, the way they cradled her back.

"No," I said simply. At least this statement wasn't one-sided, as though I were some sort of lioness prowling the Greenbrier looking to devour handsome foreigners.

"I would like you to withdraw your affection."

I looked at him as if he'd gone mad. How was such a thing done? Was it even possible? "Why? Do you understand who I am? Who my family is?" I snapped, immediately feeling pompous but unapologetic. I was an iron heiress. Did he not think me good enough for the nephew of a diplomat, a man who, left to his own merits, would be a bygone race car driver without fortune?

Mr. Vacchelli chuckled. "Of course I know. I very much respect your family, Miss Tuckerman, and of course, any other family would be overjoyed to find their son under your doting eye, but Enzo needs to settle."

"I don't—"

"He has a political mind, like mine, and Mr. Taft has generously offered him both his daughter's hand and a position in Washington, a post where his command of languages will be celebrated. This course is his destiny, Miss Tuckerman, and I will not see it squandered."

I turned to him, feeling a lump in my throat, trying to ignore the echo of my father's words of warning. Perhaps Father had been wrong about Enzo, but he'd been right about Mr. Vacchelli.

"I adore Washington—the lovely mall, the magical Potomac. I've been meaning to get out of New York for quite some time. I think we'll be happy there," I said. I forced a tight smile, watching Mr. Vacchelli's face pale.

"He's to wed Helen Taft," he said evenly.

"Perhaps I don't understand." I glared at him, fully aware of my impropriety. "You told Enzo you were bringing him here to find a wife, to help him escape his chains. Were you lying? Did you have it in mind to shackle him to a different sort of prison cell all along, a cell more agreeable to your interests?"

"Don't be ridiculous," he said. "Of course not. But I know my nephew. He will lead a happier, more fulfilled life on Helen's arm, serving Taft's administration. In any case, a match with you is impossible. Your father does not approve of a swift engagement and neither do you. Perhaps you love my nephew, but you feel this match is too hasty and you worry what will become of the two of you if the choice to marry is an incorrect one." I kept quiet, wanting to disagree with all my might but knowing he spoke truth.

"It is all horribly unfair," I said. "Don't you want to be sure of his happiness? Don't you want to be sure that the woman he marries is the woman he'll love not only at the Greenbrier, but everywhere life will take him? Only a bit more time is needed. I love him tremendously. Will you not consider giving his father the money so Enzo can choose the woman who holds his heart?"

Mr. Vacchelli shook his head.

"I cannot. Charity for my brother has bled my accounts nearly dry too many times. I have told Enzo to forget him, to let him lie in the filth he created. If he would only take my advice, nothing would stand in the way of your match. Of course he won't. His heart is much too soft. Enzo will marry in a month's time or return to Italy."

He smiled.

"And in any case, as I said before, he will be happiest with Helen serving his new country. Politics are in his blood. This match is everything I'd hoped."

"Precisely," I said. "It is everything *you* hoped. It seems to me that you'd enjoy a place in Washington yourself, seeing as how you've retired your post abroad." He stared at me and I swept the ice goblet from the table before tipping my head at him and taking my leave. "Good evening, Mr. Vacchelli."

Warren was smoking. He was leaning over the railing looking intently out at the side lawn and the cottages, though there was not much to look at from this angle. No one occupied the lighted walk and the cottages were dark. He twirled the nubby end of an extinguished cigar in his fingers while his other hand drew the ignited one to his lips. I'd never much liked the smell of cigars. The smoke was much too heavy. I didn't understand how men could sit together inhaling it in a closed room. At least tonight, the sweet star jasmine broke the stink of Warren's second, or perhaps fifth, cigar.

"I'm fine, Dorothy." He didn't turn around as he said it, and I wondered how he could possibly know it was me.

"Who's Dorothy?" I said, forcing my tone as high as it could go. He turned around and grinned, just barely.

"You're not here this season, Louise, so it would be impossible that your voice has implanted itself in the body of Dorothy Tuckerman." Warren almost laughed as he said it. Louise Ambrose, a debutante of the Greenbrier who had been introduced several years before me, had always spoken in a childlike manner. It had been baffling until we understood she used the voice to win sympathy from her father and subsequent beaus.

"I could see you in the reflection," Warren said, gesturing to the bank of windows to his left. He took another puff of his cigar and turned back to the darkness. I stood next to him, leaning over the white railing in turn.

"You're not fine," I said. "I'll remind you that it's quite all right to be upset about your father's illness." I placed my hand on

183

his jacketed arm. The silk was smooth under my fingers. "We're friends, Warren, and I love your father. I'm here for—"

"I've told you that's not it," he said. "You know I'm not a liar." He looked at me and then down at my hand on his arm. He abruptly dropped the spent cigar on the ground and placed his free hand over mine. I wanted to withdraw from this strange affection, but I couldn't, not when I knew he needed me.

"Dorothy, I—" The sweeping notes of the "Lagunen Waltz" filtered through the glass doors behind us; the last song of the evening. I turned without thinking, catching a glimpse of my parents' faces flushed in memories. "Go on," he said. "I know you'd like to dance."

"No," I said quickly, though of course he was right. I wanted to capture Enzo, to steal him away from Helen, even if I could only do it one last time. "I'm quite tired," I lied.

"Then would you walk with me? I just need to get away from here for a moment." He withdrew his hand, finally, but extended his arm instead. We wandered down the steps and around the side of the Greenbrier to the lawn. The great oaks looked even more ancient beneath the moon tonight. Nature was a marvel—the way the beauty of the oaks, the brown and green, stretched to mingle with the bright blue sky of day and the cobalt ink of night. Both were enchanting. In the sunlight, surrounded by the bright pink rhododendrons and the yellow daisies and the cream roses, I often wondered about God's mind, trying to figure how He'd arranged all the patterns and colors and textures perfectly.

"I'm going to miss it here," I said, half to myself. New York was glorious in the fall, Tuxedo Park awash in oranges and reds and yellows, but even in our gated community, things were busy and chaperoned. Here at the Greenbrier things were slow and lazy and full of possibility.

"There's something, Dorothy, we said we'd never do." Warren stopped and removed his top hat, running his hand through his hair. My heart quickened, and my father's words rang in my thoughts again.

"Then let's not. Come on. Let's go to the springhouse and see which one of us can drink the most water. Winner must fetch the other any refreshments they'd like for the remainder of our time." I tried to pull him down the hill, but he wouldn't budge.

"I need to say this, Dorothy, before I smoke all of the cigars at the Greenbrier."

I met his eyes. They were tired, glassy. Even so, I could feel his body trembling beneath my hand crooked round his arm. He glanced up to the hotel and then down the stretch of walk paralleling the cabins. We were alone.

"My father is ill. Very ill."

I swallowed and nodded. There was no escaping whatever he had to say. There was no one to interject, nowhere to run.

"When he told me of his ailment, he said that his dying wish was that I marry."

My breath caught. Fleetingly, I thought that now was the time I should escape to the woods, to a new life, but then I looked at Warren and knew I couldn't leave him so distressed.

"Warren, I'm sorry. I can't even imagine the pain of it all. Will you go to town and propose? It just occurred to me that you never told me what happened with Eleanor. Did you ever see her?" I was babbling. I was well aware, but if I stopped he'd start talking again, and if he aimed to propose to me, I'd decline.

"No. I didn't see her, and I didn't tell you because there's

nothing to tell. She's gone somewhere else. Her family is gone."
He shrugged as though the news didn't matter.

"You love her," I said. "Surely someone would know where she is. Did you ask anyone?"

Warren sighed and shook his head.

"Love isn't always supposed to last," he said. "We were ill suited. Ultimately that would've caught up to us, and anyway, regardless of my feelings or hers, I couldn't marry her. Not with Father so ill. News of my union to Eleanor would kill him."

I rolled my eyes.

"He loves you, Warren. He would only want you to be happy."

"Which is why . . ." Warren trailed off and adjusted the ends of his jacket before meeting my eyes. "I realized a few days ago he's been right all along. About my happiness, I mean."

"How so?" I asked. "Do you intend to take over your father's business after all?"

"I've always planned that," Warren said, laughing under his breath. "It's you I've been wrong about."

He dropped to one knee and his hand clutched mine. My stays were iron.

"Warren, please get up. This is nonsense. The grief of your father's illness is disrupting your sensibilities." My voice was almost hysterical, and I lowered it as best I could. "I love you, Warren, but not this way, and you don't love me. There's no passion and—"

"Hear me out," he said. He was pleading with me, and at once I was reminded of Enzo, the way he'd begged me to accept him. I wanted to, badly. Why was this happening? How was I to endure two proposals in one night, neither of which I could accept?

"The other night, Dorothy, when Father told me of his prognosis, I wept. I told him that his life wasn't supposed to end yet, that he had so much more to do, to see, and he stopped me. He said that he'd done everything already—that he'd had a wonderful career, that he'd raised a family, that he'd known the love of a woman. And then he asked me if I thought he and Mother were in love and happy. I said yes, and he told me something I never knew, that they'd married before they really loved each other, that they married for my grandparents. He sees himself and Mother in us, Dorothy. He sees the way we care for each other, the way we understand each other. He thinks we're starting to fall in love but can't see it, and I have to agree."

I blinked at him, feeling his fingers clutch harder around mine.

"You're upset," I said softly. I couldn't bring myself to say what I really felt—that his father was wrong and that, unlike Enzo or Warren, I wasn't willing to gamble forever on possibilities. An eagle called and was met with silence.

"I am," he whispered, "but I'm not out of my mind. I know what I'm doing. Dorothy Tuckerman, will you be my wife?" I breathed, trying to force calm, wracking my mind for the right words to say. In the end, I pulled him to his feet and placed my hands on his face.

"You're dear to me," I said. "One of my dearest friends. And if in time we both find ourselves in the throes of passion, with love our only true north, I will marry you without hesitation, but right now we don't. I can't." Warren removed my hands from his face and turned away. I walked beside him up the lawn, a lump in my throat.

"Warren! Dorothy!" I stopped, startled, whirling as Helen

Taft came bounding from the path behind the cabins. I raised my hand and a moment later saw Enzo emerge behind her, his gaze touching me then immediately shifting to Warren.

Helen reached us and leaned over to catch her breath, one hand on her heart, one hand extended toward us, her third finger boasting an enormous rectangular emerald flanked by two sizable diamonds.

"Do tell them, darling. I can't breathe," she said as Enzo came to a stop beside her. My stomach flipped and I stared at Enzo, my eyes pooling. This time he didn't look away.

"Helen and I are engaged to be married." The statement sounded distant and everything around me suddenly felt foreign, as though in a moment's time the Greenbrier had been transformed into a place I hated. I could hear Warren talking.

"Congratulations. And after only two weeks. Sometimes the best marriages are born of simply taking a chance."

Helen was laughing, a high-pitched tinkling.

"We're risking nothing really," she said, pitching herself into Enzo's arms. "We're mad about each other and that's all that matters." His hands closed around her waist, but his eyes didn't break from mine even when he planted a kiss on her head.

Without thought, I reached for Warren, seizing his hand. I tipped my head down, leaning in to his ear.

"I suppose you have a point," I whispered. "I've changed my mind. I'll take a chance on us." He leaned away from me, his eyebrows drawn. Reaching into his pocket, he withdrew a diamond-clustered rose-gold solitaire, pulled my hand between us, and discreetly slid the ring onto my finger.

"I know this has everything to do with him," he whispered

back. "But I don't care. You won't regret marrying me, Dorothy. I swear it."

I could feel Enzo's eyes on us. I grinned at Warren and turned to face Helen, whose face was the picture of merriment.

"We have some news as well," I said, lifting my new ring to the moonlight.

"Oh! Isn't this just marvelous?" Helen jumped up and down. "Don't you agree, darling?"

Enzo nodded, and she turned back to me, oblivious to the glint in his eyes. I felt Warren take my hand and looked away from Enzo, sickened by the mess he'd made.

As we reached the Greenbrier, we met the crowd, the parade of merry ball goers swallowing the four of us as we ascended the stairs to the lobby.

"It wasn't supposed to be this way." His voice came behind me, low enough that Warren and Helen couldn't hear it. I turned my head just slightly.

"This," I whispered. "This is your doing."

Eleven

DECEMBER 3, 1946

Darling. Darling, wake up." I opened my eyes to Lee. He was cradling me in his arms. "Are you all right? You fell out of bed."

I felt bruised, and my heart was still racing, my pulse rushing through my veins.

"Yes, of course. I just had a nightmare is all." Though it wasn't exactly a nightmare. It had been horrible and wonderful. We had been in the midst of a war, and bombs were dropping on the hotel. I'd been running through the halls, trying to find the suite for refuge, when Enzo had appeared out of nowhere.

"Tell me about it," Lee said. "It helps to talk about it."

"Another war." It sounded ridiculous, but I'd lived through two wars and I wasn't used to peace. Lee lowered me to the bed and kissed my forehead, finding his way beside me. His fingers stroked the damp hair away from my face.

"You're safe." Lee pressed against me and his mouth fell on

mine. I let him kiss me, let his hands dip into my silk gown. I closed my eyes as his mouth dropped down my neck to my collarbone. "I'm here," he whispered. "There's no separation between us, no room for war or fear. No dark secrets."

Secrets. At once, I was only vaguely aware of his touch, of the way my body rose up to meet his. I thought of the stacks of papers on the discarded desk. The men still thought they might have a reason to hide. Did the risk of war persist?

I stopped Lee, placing a hand on his chest.

"There's no need to try. I won't be able to go back to sleep." I sighed and sat up. My body ached from the fall, but I dared not tell Lee. He collapsed against the pillows beside me.

"Is it too much?" He almost whispered the question. I knew why. Ordinarily, I'd give him a verbal lashing for a sentiment like that, but I couldn't muster the strength. "It's a large resort, Dorothy, a massive undertaking for anyone. You're just coming off of the enormous Quitandinha project, too, and you must be tired. I understand the company needs this to survive, but, darling, you can't kill yourself to make sure the rest of us stay afloat. I think the stress is—"

"I'm used to pressure," I said. I sighed. "But I'm impatient too. I want all of it done immediately and done well so I can have the check in hand, but that can't be. And there's the matter of Elisabeth just showing up." I looked at him, hesitating to tell him the rest, to show him how I really felt, but he kissed my forehead and my resistance crumbled. "She's won everything," I whispered.

I remembered it clearly, the day I realized Elisabeth had stolen my children from me. George, Diana, Penny, and I had been having a rare picnic in Central Park, complete with the loveliest cucumber sandwiches and fresh orange juice and eclairs, celebrating that they were all home for a weekend together for the first time in eight years. In the distance, church bells rang out. *"Oh!"* Diana had said. *"It's one."* *"We must be going, Mother,"* George had said, hastening to put his half-finished sandwich back in my picnic basket. *"Elisabeth is taking us shopping for Easter ensembles,"* Penny had explained. *"I'm sorry to rush off."* She gave me a kiss on my head, and before I could beg them to stay, they were gone and I was left alone. I'd rationalized then that perhaps they were simply trying to balance the two of us, but the doubt seeped in—of course they preferred Elisabeth. I rarely saw them. I was always away on business. Elisabeth was naturally softer, more maternal than I'd ever been.

"She's won everything," I said again as my eyes blurred. "And I'm worried."

"She doesn't hold a candle to you," he said, tilting my chin to meet his gaze. "No one walks into one of her rooms and immediately says, 'Elisabeth Draper,' but when someone enters one of yours, Dorothy, they're transfixed, and they know. I've overheard Mother and countless other women speaking of your designs when they're in the mood for decorating. You're not just a designer, dear; you're a brand. They'll say things like, 'I bought that chintz upholstery because it reminded me of a Dorothy room'—a *Dorothy* room, and no one asks who. Think of how much you're adored even in . . ." He trailed off, immediately realizing his error. He'd meant to say even in Tuxedo Park, where my name was mostly synonymous with scandal and disappointment. Everyone might know my designs, but heaven forbid their daughters turn out like me.

"Thank you," I said simply. I didn't deserve him. Not really.

I took him for granted, saw him as a playboy when he truly cared for me.

"Just think of the opening," he said. "Keep your sights on that glorious day. Everyone of any importance will be chanting, 'All hail Dorothy Draper, the Queen of Decor.'"

I pursed my lips in the dark. Though I dared not let on, that day worried me too. What if I failed? I could see their veiled faces now—all the royals of the country pretending to love what I'd done and then gossiping about how horrid it was. The news would reach the rest of Tuxedo Park by the next day and they'd have a good laugh at my expense. *That's what happens when you neglect your husband by having a career,* they'd say, leaning into society's lies. *"You start to have all of these business notions and wind up making a fool of yourself."*

Thinking of Dan reminded me of what Elisabeth had said yesterday.

"Why didn't you tell me that Dan stopped paying Jean's salary? I would have been all right, you know," I said.

Lee sighed. "For a lot of reasons, but primarily because I didn't want it to hurt you, and I didn't want you to worry. Jean is paid a lot. Five thousand a year is more than most businessmen make."

"I am aware," I said. "But this is my company, Lee. I need to know if something is affecting the bottom line, especially in times like now when we're barely hanging on."

"It's not. Affecting the bottom line, I mean," he said. His cheeks reddened and he looked down.

"What do you mean?" I asked.

"I've been paying her," he said.

My stomach dropped. Anger coursed through me.

"Of course you know I don't live off of what you pay me," he went on. "My salary would be a feather in my cap, but my inheritance is how I survive—how we survive. So I've been paying her from my checks." He looked at me. "Please don't be upset, dear. You know it's nothing really. It's just money. I'd give you so much more if you'd let me." His voice softened at the last bit.

"Stop," I said, barely able to contain myself. I wanted to yell at him, but what good would that do? "Dan owed me. He owed me the loss of a marriage, the loss of my children, the loss of my reputation though I did nothing wrong. That salary was penance. He didn't do it because I needed it. I had my family's money, and when he left I secured jobs one after the other—Hampshire House and Arrowhead Springs and Coty Salon." I stopped and took a heaving breath. "But now I owe you. I don't like being beholden to anyone. You've been paying her since July, so you will take two thousand out of my account immediately."

Lee reached for my hand, but I pulled away.

"Please don't be angry," he said. "I only did it because—"

"I know you care for me," I said. "But you are also my business manager. I expect you to perform accordingly."

"I can't take it now," he said. "Pay me back after the resort is complete, after you get the rest of your commission."

I shook my head.

"It will deplete nearly a month's security," he said. "We'll be down to an operating budget of three, possibly four months. The new contract from Schumacher Fabric that Leon just sent over gives us possibly a bit more time, but if you take the two thousand out it'll be a wash at best." He paused. "And if for any reason you spend more than the C&O has budgeted for this project—which, you have to admit, could happen—the excess will absolutely send us into bankruptcy. Please, let's keep the two thousand in the accounts for now."

"Take it out or I'll have to let you go," I snapped. I knew how this would affect us, but I would rather be bankrupt on my own accord than saved by the pockets of Tuxedo Park.

"Very well," he said, rising from the foot of my bed.

"I'm going to the hotel," I said, forcing my body from beneath the blankets. I'd never get over my fury and fear if I didn't face it head-on, and the Will-to-Be-Dreary loved fear more than anything.

"Don't be ridiculous. It's three in the morning," Lee said. "There could be ice."

"I don't believe I was asking."

I dressed as hurriedly as I could, slinging open the armoire door and selecting whatever I saw first. The red velvet swing dress was hardly appropriate for a day's work, but I didn't care. I was the boss. I slipped it over my head and fumbled for my long ombre tweed jacket.

"I'll be ready in a moment," Lee said. I could hear the sigh in his voice and my irritation rose.

"I don't want you to come. In fact, I forbid it," I said to his shadow as he traipsed across the hall.

"And if you have another fall? If you can't find the switches for the lights? You cannot go alone," he called. I could hear the screech of his drawers opening and rolled my eyes.

"You can come over at seven. I'll not have you come along right now. It's my choice to risk calamity and you'll not stop me. I need to make haste on this job and you'll slow me down."

It was liberating to realize that here, in the quiet of White

Sulphur Springs, I could venture out alone in the middle of the night with the threat of ice my only concern. At home, I would be stuck in my apartment. I squinted at my hat rack, finally settling on a black felt turban with a wide, dramatic fan perched on top. I fitted it to my head and immediately felt warmer. The armoire mirror caught my reflection. In the dark, I looked more familiar to myself. The wrinkles and sagging skin dissipated in the dim, and the youthful girl I really was came back. In a few years, it would happen. I'd become elderly and unrecognizable—though precisely when this phenomenon occurred, no one knew.

Lee walked into my room. "I know you're angry with me, but I have to ask: You're not going over to confer with the departed, are you? I know you said you had a vision of Martin Van Buren, and of course, that happened when you were alone, so—"

I tipped my head back and laughed despite my irritation. "Of course not. I only know I can't waste any more time."

"You look beautiful," he said. He stepped forward to button my jacket. "I'm sorry I interfered. Please know I was only trying to help. And I have no doubt this project will be your most important work. Tomorrow the jobbers will be in from the city and you'll get to talking real plans. You'll feel better then." He paused. "I know you, DD."

"I suppose you're right. And I suppose you're forgiven as long as you never finance my company again."

"You have my word," he said. "Here." He leaned over to retrieve my leather document case from atop the dressing table and handed it to me.

I hadn't figured how cold it would be. I tucked the key back into my pocket and ran my hands along the wall, hoping to find a switch. Finally, I found them—the hideous circular metal Bakelite switches that were always installed in industrial quarters and hospitals—and flipped them on. The light beamed over me, startling in the early morning dark. I'd chosen the north entrance, hoping that the narrow situation of the parlor would feel cozier as I worked, but the channel of a room stretched in front of me endlessly—past the ballroom, past the gargantuan lobby, past the mess halls. The original architect, Frederick Julius Sterner, was supposedly a genius, but he should have consulted me first.

I stared into the darkness, freshly aware that I was alone. Anytime I'd thought of ghosts here, I'd been thinking of my family's old contemporaries, people I knew whose haunting would be more welcome than frightening. But now I realized there were others. Soldiers whose stories were told here, in this very hotel, and likely a few prisoners of war too. Other people from those times would visit, people who needed to know warmth in a place that had felt foreign or cold. And though I couldn't pretend to feel pity for the conquered in our most recent war, I softened toward the children interned here, children who had never had anything to do with the state of their parents' loyalties.

I shook my head and walked to the fireplace, kneeling next to the hearth. I stacked wood for a fire, trying to ignore the enormous, clunky mahogany mantel. It would have to be fixed—perhaps with a delicate marble floral-and-vines piece from one of the dismantled manor homes in England. I made a mental note to have Leon wire a note to Mr. Southton, a London man with a fine eye, to see if he could come up with something quickly.

There were old newspapers beneath the firewood rack. I tore a page off of the *New York Times* and crumpled it. I'd been interviewed for countless magazines and newspapers over the years, once for a feature piece in the *Times* called "The Pleasure of Decorating." I'd been promoting my book *Decorating Is Fun!* At the time, I'd been thrilled at the prospect of being interviewed, by being seen as the housewife's greatest helper in achieving the home of her dreams. Four months later, the article embarrassed me like no other. I'd been speaking to a group of acquaintances at a tea, guiding one of them through color choices and furniture selections, when one of them had angrily interrupted.

"Enough! I know you claim that nine out of ten women are convinced that decorating their homes can be fun, and perhaps I'm the one of ten, but we're entering a *war*, Mrs. Draper, a *war*. I don't care if my wallpaper is peeling and my floors are scratched and my bedding is moth-eaten. My husband might be going, and he might never come back, and no amount of decorating is going to make me feel better about that."

I was flabbergasted. I tried to explain, to tell her that I'd been through a war already—and a depression and a divorce—and keeping my mind occupied with bright colors and the excitement of a new room was the only thing that kept me going, but it was no use. The woman stormed out and the others followed. It was one of the most humiliating experiences of my life, and it took me a few days to get over it. But I knew I was right. Women left behind in wartime needed projects and cheer. The same woman wrote to me a few weeks later, apologizing and asking me to call on her personally and give her some tips.

The flame caught, and I pushed away from the fire. I didn't bother to get up and find a suitable chair. It was much too cold to stray away. Instead, I grasped my notepad and closed my eyes. I thought of my friends coming back to this resort, the celebrities gazing upon its glory for the first time, the soldiers returning to confront the horror of what they'd experienced here.

Pale shell-pink walls, emerald-green carpets. A pink-and-white bedspread on a gleaming white four-poster. Armchairs with our rhododendron print. A thick glass serving table outfitted with a silver tea service.

Blazing orange-peach walls, billowing white curtains. A bench just below the bed upholstered with an orange-peach cushion. Against the wall, a sitting area with striped hunter and white chairs. Large lamps with chunky hunter bases.

Walls papered in roses and rhododendrons. Two twin beds painted ruby red. Two matching ornate china urns on either side of an antique marble-topped dresser. White porcelain sconces.

Each room was a new canvas, a new project, a new dream. Soon I'd filled a notebook with ideas. I barely noticed the sun peeking over the mountains in the distance, washing the lawn in blush gold, or the fact that my fire had been reduced to embers. I'd planned at least fifty rooms tonight. Combined with the others I'd already completed, only thirty or so remained— more than enough direction for my team to get started sketching the final rooms.

I stood, no longer afraid of the stretch of emptiness before me. My muscles ached from sitting, so did my bones, but I started walking anyway, clutching my notebook under my arm. The stretch of hall between the north lobby and the ballroom needed to be regal, something that told even those on a virgin visit how important the Greenbrier was to the world. I didn't use dark wall colors often but thought a dusky shade suited here, perhaps a hunter-green wall with rows of busts. I'd done something similar, a Roman theme of sorts, with the Carlyle Hotel lobby, and it had been well received. Here it would be Henry Clay and Martin Van Buren, Henry Taft and FDR and Teddy Roosevelt. I thought of the treadmill of old, how we'd lined up to enter the ball-room. Perhaps the tradition could be reinstated, and the line of bachelors and bachelorettes could gather here, reminded of their responsibility to be the country's next generation of great minds.

I blinked, and I could see it—the line of black tuxedos and flowing silk gowns in front of me, the closed glass doors that would open to reveal the ballroom and the orchestra, the floral garlands, and the critical eyes. I could feel Warren beside me, the familiarity of his presence. How strange it was that a man who'd been so much a part of my life had so suddenly ceased to exist in it. I didn't know if he ever thought of me. I doubted it. But for so long we'd been a support to each other and then we lost touch and never spoke again. Mother and Mrs. Abercrombie wrote sometimes. Ten years ago, Warren was married with six children, an investment man after the company was sold. Perhaps I'd try to locate his address for the opening. Then again, it would be strange. We hadn't spoken in so long, and our last conversation had been unpleasant.

My eyes blurred. The emotion caught me off guard. I hadn't expected to cry; if I had, I would have stopped it. I cleared my throat and blinked, composing myself. I imagined the hush that would come over the ballroom the moment the first guests passed through the hall and beheld it. I needed them to feel the same sense of romance and allure that I always had. The same sense of belonging too.

My stomach growled so loudly it echoed. Lee would bring

food when he woke. He always did. Again, I felt guilty. He needed a younger girl, someone who would adore him and have his babies, someone who would let him take care of her, but he wouldn't go even if I asked him to. He was stubborn that way. I suppose that's why I liked him so much.

I kept walking. I knew I should stop and dream, but my mind conjured what it did when it wished, and I wasn't inspired to go over the lobbies at the moment. I gripped the cold polished walnut rail and walked down the stairs to the reception. I recalled the way we'd been treated upon arrival in my youth— carried by coach from the train station to the front doors, greeted by men and women in sharp white liveries while our trunks were whisked to our rooms and unpacked before we stepped foot in our suite or cottage. I still didn't know how they'd arranged that, but by today's standards of hospitality it was magic.

I thought of the old Tiger cottage, of the diplomats and senators and presidents and former presidents crammed between its walls, the pipe and cigar smoke clouding the windows. They had the whole resort at their disposal, and yet they'd settled for a ramshackle old cottage to be their meeting spot, something far enough from the hotel that the newcomers wouldn't suspect. It was as if they'd grown tired of opulence and for once wished to be treated like an unimportant citizen of the country they governed. The tiny closet space beside the pool was no different.

I started down the hall toward it. Mr. Mosley was right to tell me about it, to let me in. I couldn't imagine anyone else having the insight to decorate a space like that one. I understood politicians. I understood important people. I was descended from generations of them. My blood was here before the *Mayflower*, after all.

Making my way into the linen closet, I lifted the towel rack and pushed the door open. The room was dark as pitch and I again found myself searching for a switch. The lights were easy to find this time, and I flipped them on. The room was clean, the slate blank enough for me to see what I'd do. My eyes shifted from the table to the closed door of the office. That desk would have to go sooner rather than later. That room would be repurposed into a little fainting room of sorts, with oversize chairs and couches. The men would need a place to relax after long meetings.

I opened the office door and sighed at the neat stacks of paper still heaped on the desktop. There were, thankfully, no knickknacks muddling the space save a crumpled rhododendron pressed in glass tucked between the piles. I stared at the blossom for a moment, feeling my heart soften with memories as I studied the perfectly preserved pink-red and deep green. It was no wonder the rhododendron beat the honeysuckle and wild rose to become the state flower of West Virginia. Just a glance had the power to transport one back to the magic of a summer memory in the mountains. I set the blossom down.

The closest stack of papers looked to be translated meeting minutes. The first was in Spanish. I knew enough to read that the visiting diplomat was the former prime minister of Spain, Manuel Garcia Prieto, but couldn't make out the rest.

The second stack was in English, and I plucked the page off the top.

January 12, 1942
    Activities observed as dictated by Mr.
Roy Sibert:

```
7:22 AM: Fremd Von Lengle asked to send
    a correspondence to his daughter in
    Stuttgart. His request was granted
    pending a reading of said correspondence
    by General Larson.
9:00 AM: A company of Italians gathered
    in the lobby to play cards. Their
    conversation was monitored closely
    by staff and will be detailed in an
    accompanying report attached to this list
    of activities.
```

The lights went out. I gasped and dropped the paper, sure my fate had been sealed. I would die in this secret room in the Greenbrier without anyone to find me.

I pressed against the wall to steady myself. I listened for a commotion but heard nothing. Perhaps ice had caused a power line to fall. That happened sometimes in the city. I took a breath, comprehending the true cause of my fear. I'd been in my apartment at Sutton Place after the divorce, the first night I'd ever been alone. Penny was with Dan, and Diana and George were off at school. *The Dodge Victory Hour* was playing on my radio, and I'd finally sat down to enjoy a dinner of peaches and cream when I heard the shouting. It grew louder as I waited, seeming to end up across the street from me. I'd just transformed Sutton Place from tenement housing, and as such, similar properties surrounded it. I heard the pop of a pistol and then the electric went out. The shouting continued—something about the cost of rent—and I remained frozen in my chair, helpless. I didn't have the fences of Tuxedo Park or the security of a man's fists to protect me if the mob burst through my door. Even in the moment I realized how silly that was—they weren't after me—but all night I remained in the armchair, unable to sleep and praying for morning to arrive swiftly.

I fumbled for my notebook. Nothing horrible had happened that night and nothing terrible was about to occur now. I found the edge of my notebook, grabbed it, and started for the door. As pleasant as it had been to dream in the secret suite alone, I'd designed it in my mind at the first visit and would draw it elsewhere. If I was to be trapped inside the hotel, this was not the place.

I stopped for a moment beside the pool. The electric was buzzing again. I heard the current rattle, then the lights flicked to life again. Above, the ceiling of glass displayed a touch of pink in the otherwise black sky. The color reflected on the water, making it look wonderfully like the pink champagne my dearest friend Mae Davie and I often used to toast at our Friday luncheons when I was in the city. I grinned and let myself yawn. This was confirmation: God loved color, and using it abundantly was only right. The Bible never talked about the beauty of blacks and browns and beiges—only golds and royal purples and sparkling whites. If any naive uppers from the C&O disagreed with my plans for their dear resort, I would simply remind them of this fact. They may attempt to dispute me, but they would certainly stop when it came to the Creator.

Hurried footsteps echoed in the corridor beyond me, and then Lee appeared. His white shirt was rumpled beneath his overcoat, his hair a fright, but at least he'd had the foresight to find a good pair of pressed pants.

"Thank goodness," he breathed when he saw me.

"Is something the matter?" I asked.

"I don't know. I mean, I don't think so, but when the electric went out, I came over right away. When I saw the fire dwindled and you nowhere to be found, I couldn't help but think something terrible had happened. I've been through the whole hotel." He took a breath. "What are you doing down here?" He eyed the water then me. "Thinking of going for a swim?" His lips turned up.

I laughed.

"Of course. Can't you tell I'm in my swimming costume?" After the fright, I was glad for the humor.

"I suppose I could be convinced to join you. The others haven't woken, and Tom's occupied with arranging the Cinquinnis' arrival at ten thirty. Someone from Linker and Wexler will be here on the two o'clock, and Buck on the five. Mr. Handman swore he'd be down as soon as he can, but this timeline is making me nervous."

"I'll write him right away," I said. No one would be allowed to slow my progress. I couldn't afford to wait.

It was hard to believe it was time to begin the construction phase already.

"So?" he asked again.

I glanced at Lee. He started to edge out of his overcoat. Surely he was joking.

"I can't swim," I lied, laughing, though it could be the truth. I hadn't been for a swim in years.

"Very well, Mrs. Draper," he said. "I had a feeling you wouldn't agree to jump in with me—as much as you want to."

He winked, and I took his hand. "You know me well."

"Glenn and Jean will be in the ballroom shortly. I woke

them assuming you'd need to brief them on your visions for the remaining guest rooms before the others arrive." He paused. "I also want to say again that I'm so sorry that I overstepped with Jean. My intentions were pure, I promise."

"I know," I said.

He let go of my hand and extended his arm. "Shall I escort you to the ball, my lady? You don't suppose the others will suspect anything, do you?" I balked as he tucked my hand into the crook of his arm. Twice in one morning I'd been reminded of Warren. I hoped it didn't mean he was away from his family in South Carolina and floating about at the Greenbrier. Furthermore, I hoped it didn't mean he was still holding on to me after all this time.

"You seem at peace here. Besides the nightmares, of course," Lee commented as we walked through the dark corridor of abandoned shops to the first-floor reception. Books, record covers, and large posters of the mountain views were still displayed in the windows. Newspapers—likely from the war—and magazines were lined up behind them, all collecting dust.

I sighed. "I know," I said. "Besides bankruptcy looming, it's the most settled I've been in some time." It felt right, being here. "You're young, Lee, so perhaps you won't understand just yet, but I was only eighteen the last time I was here. My parents were still lively, and my heart was still innocent. Well, until—"

"You want to remember and forget. I know what you mean," Lee said, saving me the trouble of explaining myself.

I was surprised by Lee. He'd grown up in Tuxedo Park across the street from the Lorillards in a Bruce Pope–designed shingle house, the son of one of J. P. Morgan's partners and the most proper society woman I'd ever met. I'd never asked about his romantic entanglements. That was outside of our unspoken agreement. He never asked me about Dan, or anyone else for that matter. It was easier that way. I'd always assumed he'd had a few infatuations, but he was likely permitted to court only a few select girls. Now, thinking it over, I understood. He'd had his heart broken, shattered. Why else, after working for me only six months, would he have fallen into my bed?

"Have you ever been in love?" I asked.

Lee chuckled.

"Besides with you?"

"You're not in love with me," I said.

He stopped in his tracks, right at the edge of the steps. "Why would you say that?"

Our eyes met, and I shook my head. "I'm nearly as old as your mother," I said. "I'm a distraction, not the love of your life."

He looked down at his feet. Perhaps he thought this was a test. I didn't mean it to be.

"I don't want you to love me, Lee. It's all right if you don't. We both need something from each other right now."

"I didn't at first," he said. "But you're . . . I just do." He kept his gaze down. When I didn't respond quickly, he cleared his throat. "And yes. I've been in love before. When I came back from the war, she was married."

I squeezed his hand, feeling the reverberation of heartbreak in my chest. I wondered who she was, if I knew of her, but I didn't ask.

"I'm sorry," I said.

It all made sense now. He'd been so eager to prove himself at the beginning, to stay hours beyond closing at the office, to spend time listening to my rants when he didn't have to, to risk kissing me when it could have meant his termination.

"It's behind me. And you're ahead," he said, forcing a grin. "Now let's hear about the exquisite genius you've concocted in this notebook."

Twelve

DECEMBER 3, 1946

I could hear Bing Crosby before I saw the record player. "Sweet
Leilani." Though I didn't much care for the song or the Hawaiian
sentiments—I was mostly a city girl who didn't like bathing suits
or hot sand or the sting of salt water, even in Newport—the
music was a nice break from the silence.

They were chattering. Planning, I hoped, rather than gossiping about last night's outing to the Avlon's barroom. They'd tried
to keep it quiet, but Glenn was never one for whispers. When
Lee and I departed their cottage for ours, I told him to go with
them, but he seemed shocked and then confused.

"No, of course not. I don't want to stay up all night imbibing."

He was lying, but I conceded. They always lied around me
anyway, and I simply lacked the energy to scold them all the
time.

We turned the corner and I felt tears rise at the sight in the upper lobby. Bella was standing beside the player behind Glenn and Jean, poised with notepads and pens.

"I didn't know she was coming," I said.

Bella was my maid, but also my friend. As I'd struggled to do up my hair and dress myself this last month, I realized how much I relied on her. Before she worked for me, she'd been a sort of lady's maid to my actress sister-in-law, Ruth, always making her look glamorous. Because of my arrangement with Lee I hadn't asked her to come, but now that she was here, I was thrilled.

"I thought to surprise you," Lee said. "I hope you don't mind. It seemed like you could use her here. She does up buttons and brushes hair much better than I do."

"You were right to send for her. But what of you?" I whispered as we neared the room.

"Bella has been situated with Jean and Glenn. She'll come at approximately seven each morning and depart after undressing you at night," he said. "I've assured them that I am only staying with you for your protection."

I sighed. Though I gave Lee little credit, he really was a wonderful business manager.

"Mrs. Draper!" Bella was the first to rush to my side. "Magnificent, it is!" I smiled, quite unsure what she was talking about. Bella was a Scot and sometimes it seemed her sentences were confused—at least to my ears. "The resort!" she said, squeezing my hand enthusiastically. She looked radiant for having just stepped off the rail.

"You haven't seen the room on the far end," Glenn said, chuckling as he spoke. "The officers played darts against the mural." I was glad for the dismemberment of the mural. I found it hideous.

"Two points for Stonewall Jackson's horse!" Lee shouted.

"Yes, it's lovely indeed. But this resort, Mrs. Draper! It will be a masterpiece." Her voice floated over us and I heard Glenn cough. He knew how much I despised open talk of a work being finished before it was.

"Yes. But right now, I'm afraid it's still a hospital," I said.

Lee pulled a chair out at the head of the table, and I sat down and opened my notebook.

"Good of you to be here so early," I said, biting back a quip about the headaches they must be nursing. I couldn't always be their mother. "Now, I've worked all night and there are instructions to be made. I've worked up new room designs. I've made several suggestions here in my book, and we'll go over them floor to ceiling to knob so you can see to it that they're done right."

Glenn's hand shot up in the air as though he were a school pupil. "Mr. Bowman came by early this morning inquiring about ordering wall paints. Is it too early?"

I looked at Jean and waited. Surely she knew the answer, but she kept her head down, scribbling something in her notebook. I answered for her.

"Of course it's not," I said. "We'll have to order more, but since we'll be finished with all of the concept sketching in short order, we should absolutely begin with the rooms along this corridor. The colors are here in this book as well. Oh! The Cinquinni brothers will be in on the next train. They'll need a tour and instruction. Jean, I trust you'll retrieve them and execute the tour? Glenn, I'll ask you to talk to them about vision, as you have always seen what I do."

Lee fidgeted beside me. Although no business manager ever

did tasks like the rest, he felt out of place without an assignment, as though he was only useful as my lover.

"Lee, please work with Glenn and wire Ted to begin to run the numbers on all of our needed supplies. When that's finished and initial orders are placed, wire Mr. Bowman and Mr. Young with the invoice," I said. "Also, if you wouldn't mind terribly, please check in with Leon and see how he's faring in general, running the place in my stead."

"Yes, ma'am," he quipped. "And if I begin to notice we're over budget I'll let you know."

"Yes. Do," I said. "So we can tell C&O we need more." I said the last bit mostly to avoid letting on that Lee was referencing our company's budget.

"But it is a budget, Mrs. Draper," Jean said. "Mr. Bowman was awfully firm."

I shook my head.

"That's true, dear, but they understand that it takes an investment to gain returns. It will be just fine."

Silence filled the room as it always did when my staff knew there was no point in arguing with me.

"Oh. I'll need you to tell Leon to wire Mr. Southton, Lee. I need a mantel for the north entrance parlor and likely a rug, preferably an antique Aubusson."

"Anything else? You know it'll take a month at best to get anything over here, and I don't want you to miss your window," he said, pulling out a chair next to Jean and sitting down. He always sat next to Jean. I half wondered if he found her attractive. She was a very good-looking woman, after all, though thankfully married to a man equally gorgeous. As Lee addressed me, I noticed Jean pull a large stack of letters from her bag and press it into his hand. I'd ask about it later. I was somewhat popular with my fans, but not enough to merit that much correspondence.

"A landscape," I said, remembering. "I need one for either side of the fireplace in the north parlor, but I'm unsure I need something like that shipped from England. In fact, could someone wire Ted and ask him to scout something American? This is the Greenbrier, after all. I'd also like a Franz Bueb piece for over the mantel in the trellis lobby, something black and white that will contrast nicely with the colors."

In the distance, beyond the "Chattanooga Choo Choo" playing low, I could hear a door open and several men shouting. It sounded like they were moving something into my hotel.

"Mrs. Draper, we've found some antiques," Mr. Mosley called from what would be the trellis lobby. At once I wished for an office door.

"Very well. Set them out of the way and I will review them when we've finished meeting," I said.

"I'll have them placed in the north parlor and I'll wait for you there," he said. "I know the history of each piece."

"Good. In fact, separate the pieces by insignificant and important if you can. I don't feel compelled to keep things simply because they're old. If they fit, they do. If they don't, I'll set them out on the street."

"For whom to carry away?" Glenn asked, his eyebrows raised. "This isn't New York, where trash or treasure seem to be whisked from the road by the masses so long as it's free, and I doubt any homeless of White Sulphur Springs would find bulky furniture helpful to their plight."

Jean choked on her coffee and even Bella chortled.

"Don't be ridiculous," I said. "We'll set them out for the train.

The discarded pieces can go back to New York for auction—that is, if they're of any worth."

After three hours of meetings, the staff departed for their luncheon and Mr. Mosley arrived with a foil-wrapped egg-salad sandwich for me.

"Lee told me you wouldn't leave for lunch," he said, handing it over.

"Perhaps I would have today. I've been working since three in the morning," I said, looking over the antiques. Tables and rocking chairs and mirrors and oil lamps and armchairs crowded the north lobby. At first glance at least half of it would have to be scrapped.

"Three in the morning? Surely not, Mrs. Draper," he said, but I tipped my head at the fireplace. I'd burned nearly the whole stack of wood and only three skinny charred logs remained.

"Here?" Mr. Mosley asked. He removed his hat and pressed it to his chest. "I'm honored to have you here," he said. "But this sort of dedication isn't necessary."

"Ordinarily, I sleep until seven," I said. "I had a dream and was awake anyway."

"Of course, this would be entirely up to you, Mrs. Draper, but as I was wandering up this way just now, I began to think— what about adding an English boxwood garden with a brick path just outside here?"

Mr. Mosley gestured out the window.

"Brick?" I asked, barely stopping myself from yawning. I could use a strong coffee. "That would be lovely, I think. So long as the material is authentic. It cannot be modern manufactured brick."

"I know some gentlemen who have several old estates at risk of collapsing. I suppose I could write them," Mr. Mosley said. "It could be an opportunity for them to contribute a piece of their history to their beloved Greenbrier."

"Who?"

"Oh. I forget you may know them. The Martins, Jeffersons—Olmstead has fallen to Martha's side, not Thomas Senior's. Of course, they're loyal to the other spring."

The Homestead and the Greenbrier had been competitive for as long as they'd both existed. Some were loyal to one; some were loyal to both. My father hadn't ever thought it important to visit Hot Springs. I think West Virginia was quite Southern enough for a pure-blooded Yankee. "And the Abercrombies." He met my eyes and I shook my head.

"Surely not the Abercrombies. Of course, I knew they'd sold off parcels of land, but I thought they retained their home."

Then again, if the Martins and Jeffersons could both have estates in disarray, the lesser-known Abercrombies could certainly.

"I'm sorry," I said, lifting my hand to my chest as though doing so could steady my heart. "The Abercrombies were especially close to our family."

"And to you, if I recall," Mr. Mosley said. I was tempted to ask him right then and there why my courtships were a fascination. All the belles had them, after all, and I'd long since been married, made a mother, and divorced.

"Yes," I said finally. "For a time, Warren and I were . . ." I tried to channel my mother. In recent years, after Father's death, she'd become so bold. She believed women were about to be liberated, and she embraced all that meant wholeheartedly, throwing decorum out the window. Somehow, I'd only been able to go so far. I could entertain lovers and own my own business privately, but open discussion of my love life continued to be off-limits.

"Have you spoken to him since?" Mr. Mosley asked, not minding my sensitivity on the matter. "Perhaps you could ask him on behalf of the Greenbrier, of course?"

I tipped my head back and laughed.

"I haven't spoken to Warren in years, Mr. Mosley, but if you would like to go on the hunt, I'd support that," I said, regaining my earlier professionalism. "I always understood the Abercrombie estate to be quite a place." I turned toward the antiques, pretending to appraise a hideous water-stained English hunting print. "And if you find enough brick to make the walk a definite addition, please let me know so I can send for my landscape architect. He's all the way in Long Island and will need advance warning of my employ."

I plucked the print from its presentation place on a table and set it behind me on the floor.

"This is the pile to be given away or dispatched to New York auction houses," I said, moving on to an old intricate mantel that would look quite nice painted white. Perhaps for the trellis lobby.

Mr. Mosley gasped.

"Not that print! It once hung in the Colonnade cottage. And that mantel there was pulled from one of the oldest homes in this county."

"I can use the mantel, but the print will go. I never noticed it, though we occupied that cottage every summer except my last, which proves it's unremarkable," I said.

"That's right. Your family was in the set of rooms right above the porch during the Centennial," Mr. Mosley said. "I trust you'll know this painting then." He walked around an old table and I stopped him.

"I could use this too," I said, running my hands along the simple cherry table. The black marble top was cracked, but I could fix that.

"Wonderful!" Mr. Mosley said. "You know, the last time I saw that table, the men were using it for cooking. The army men, I mean. Young and I had come back to tour the place for the C&O and—"

"How were they using it for cooking?" I asked. There was no range, no heating element.

"I suppose I should say they were fixing sandwiches atop it," he said as he leaned down, searching for something in the conglomeration of decor behind the table. "And strangely enough, I love this table because of it. It was a bit of normalcy, you know, after their being confined to wheelchairs. Seeing them arranging their lunch was a sign they'd get better."

"Very well," I said. "It's saved."

I started to tell him where it should be moved, when he righted. I gasped. He gripped a gilded frame housing the Jasper Francis Cropsey landscape I'd moved from the hall to our sitting room all those years ago.

"This was in your suite," he said. "Perhaps you know it?"

"Yes," I said quietly. "I do."

Thirteen

AUGUST 14, 1908

I didn't know how I could bear the remaining weeks of the season. I closed the carved cherry door to my bedroom and fumbled with the silk buttons down my back. Trying to undo them myself was futile. I'd have to wait for Mademoiselle to finish settling Roger.

The new diamond ring on my finger caught my eye. I had barely looked at it. It was lovely, a brilliant solitaire encircled by rose-gold filigree and finished with a perimeter halo of diamonds, but I couldn't bear its weight. I pulled it off and set it on the nightstand next to the small crystal vase displaying two red roses. The Greenbrier's staff always made sure we all had fresh flowers every morning. Normally, I thought the gesture an unnecessary but lovely touch. Tonight, the red reminded me of blood, how it boiled with anger and burned with passion and made a mess of love—if love was even a consideration.

Warren had tried to kiss me only moments ago, forcing me

to duck around his face and give him an awkward embrace at the door to our suite. I was afraid he would try again, but instead he pulled away, his countenance a clear picture that he understood, that he'd not try to kiss me for some time yet, that just because I wore his ring didn't mean my feelings had changed.

A picture of Helen and Enzo kissing wormed its way into my mind—his hands on her waist, her fingers in his hair, the warmth of his mouth pressing against hers. I wanted to think that I was the only one to know that feeling, to know him that way, but there was no question—he'd not do as I had. He would play the part of the doting fiancé because he was. Perhaps he loved me, but he certainly didn't abhor the prospect of Helen. He'd even admitted it.

I plucked the crystal vase from the table, crossed to the window, pushed the pane up, and tossed the roses out. I watched them fall, absorbed by the boxwood bushes below. I didn't want to be reminded of this night for one more minute. I closed the pane and whirled, realizing that in my fury I'd become light-headed. This was my life now. My eyes landed on the four-poster bed, the old, historic type I was sure occupied many of the bedrooms in the Abercrombies' Southern home. I'd have to sleep in one of them with Warren, be intimate with Warren. The thought made my stomach turn. Would he be happy with that? Surely he'd thought about it before he proposed—or had he? Perhaps he'd settle for a friendly sort of marriage instead, one in which I remained in my own quarters and he in his, one in which we never touched each other besides a friendly hug or an affectionate kiss on the cheek.

I wanted to rip the brocade bedspread from the mattress and pitch the hundred-year-old cherry dressing table out the window with the roses. My life was in shambles.

I looked in the mirror. My black hair had come loose a bit, and wisps gathered around my face. My left eye always looked sleepier than the other. My mother's eyes were like this, and it gave her a beautiful, mysterious look, even now. And my nose. My nose started a bit too high and was too straight. No wonder he hadn't wanted to wait for me. No wonder he'd chosen a position and another woman over me. I wasn't nearly beautiful enough to be put on a pedestal above well-being, even if he did love me. *His* ambitions, *his* freedoms were more important, and Helen wasn't a horrible consolation. I let my hand drift over the beading on my bodice. I'd dressed hoping he'd be stunned by my ensemble, that he'd sweep me off the dance floor and out into the night, kissing me all the way to Lovers' Lane. Instead, we'd both gripped tightly to our own stubbornness, to the rigid manner in which our individual freedoms would be won, neither one of us willing to risk imprisonment—even if it meant love. I wondered how our decisions would serve us later, if we would dream of each other forever and wish we would've chosen differently.

The writing desk in the corner beckoned me. Its stationery drawer was slightly ajar. I sat down on the red velvet stool. My hands shook as I gripped a pencil and withdrew a piece of paper, as if he'd see what I was about to write. He wouldn't, but this was the only way. I had to surrender my feelings to something, and this unfortunate piece of the Greenbrier's stationery had drawn the shortest straw.

Dearest Enzo,

I could barely write his name. I felt pressure build in my eyes and blinked it away.

I loved you. I love you. How terrible you've been and yet how much I long for things to be different. I'll never forgive you for proposing to her. I meant what I said. This mess, all of it, is your fault.

I pounded my fist on the desktop, furious at my inability to stop the tears. One drizzled down my cheek and onto the paper, watering the lead.

Two months. That's all I asked and yet you said you couldn't. Two months against the span of perhaps forty years, and we would both be free. Even if you had to go back for a while, I told you we would figure a way to pay the debt. After, we could go anywhere. We could start over somewhere. Will your post love you? Will you ever truly love Helen? I can't bear the thought of the two of you. Even tonight, the moment I saw her, the moment you appeared, my heart was crushed. I wanted to wake up. I was sure I was wrong. You moved so quickly. And then I had to do the same. I couldn't allow you to wound me without wounding you. I saw your eyes. I was glad for your pain. I was glad because it mirrored mine.

I hope your marriage fails. How desperately I hope you'll despair for me. But in the same breath, I know I won't take you later regardless. How could I? I'll not be made a consolation. It would be altogether embarrassing, and as much as I don't love Warren, I couldn't leave him for you, not after both of us are married.

I'll spend my years hoping to forget you and the way I love you. I'll never forgive you for refusing to wait for me. I'll never forgive myself for refusing to accept you.

A knock at my door disturbed my writing. I folded the paper and stuck it in the secretary drawer. It wasn't like he'd see it anyway. Nothing I said would matter. Our fate was set.

Mother breezed into my room. "Darling! I'm so thrilled for you! When you said you were otherwise promised, you gave me quite a fright, but I'm glad to know you were only teasing." Her gaze caught the discarded ring on the nightstand. I wiped any trace of tears from my eyes before she looked at me.

"At least someone's thrilled," I mumbled, looking down at my hands.

"Doesn't it fit?" she asked.

I looked up at her, shocked she'd disregarded my clear unhappiness. She was never this way. She had always been sympathetic. Even if the whole world was against me, she was always for me—until now.

"It does," I said.

"We looked everywhere for you—Father, Mr. Abercrombie, and me. Wherever did you go? We had champagne brought in after the ball concluded. Poor Warren just kept saying he thought you'd already retired."

I laughed under my breath.

"He *knew* I'd retired. He walked me back to the suite."

"Aren't you happy, darling?"

Mother sank down onto the bed. I could see her reflection in the mirror, her kind eyes hooded with concern.

"You know how I feel about Warren, Mother," I said.

"Then why did you agree?" she asked. "I know the two of you are mostly comrades now, but in time you'll—"

"It seemed inevitable," I said quickly. I would never admit the truth. That part was worse than accepting Warren, knowing I'd only done it to spite a man I loved. It dawned on me that I was exactly like Anzonella's poor aunt Violet. "I don't know. I'm sure you're happy, though, and Father as well, and poor, dear, doomed Mr. Abercrombie." I stopped, knowing if I didn't, I'd completely snap, and I wouldn't recover easily.

I stood and paced toward the door before she could answer. "Where's Father?"

"Down in the barroom, of course," she said. "But, Dorothy, get some rest. Surely you'll see more clearly in the morn—"

I flung the door open before she could say any more, paced down the hall and out into the hallway. My fingers clenched. I didn't know what I was going to say to Father, but my pairing with Warren was as much his fault as it was my jealousy, and I needed someone else to blame.

I couldn't see who was inside, but I could smell the cigar smoke. It choked me as I sauntered down the drab hall toward the bar room. From here, I couldn't see anything except a thick carved mahogany door. It was supposed to be that way, hidden, so women couldn't easily observe how many nips of bourbon their husbands enjoyed. I thought it was silly. Where was our neat little club away from the men?

The barroom was located on the bottom floor of the hotel, tucked to the end of the east wing. There were no windows from the inside into the room, but as I approached, I realized the door was slightly ajar. I leaned closer, easily spotting my father, Mr. Abercrombie, Mr. Taft, Mr. Phinizy, and Mr. Kane gathered next to the ancient polished cherry bar marked by years of glass rings and plate scratches. The crystal tumblers and liquor bottles glistened behind the bar in front of a gilded mirror, and I watched as the barkeep extracted one of the long necks and poured five shots of what looked like bourbon.

Mr. Kane reached over, clapping the barkeep on the back. My father was laughing at something, the butt of a cigar pinched in his teeth.

"I'd like to offer a toast," Mr. Kane said loudly, upsetting the hum of the room. It silenced and I watched as a group of silver-haired men in the corner stood. "To my friends, Tuckerman and Abercrombie. To the news that two of the mightiest families in our great country will finally be joined. Goodness, you deserve this after all these years."

"Hear! Hear!" Mr. Abercrombie said. "Son, come on—"

Before I could stop myself, I pushed the door open and paced across the small room toward my father, only vaguely aware of Warren emerging from the opposite side.

"Star, what—" My father lunged toward me, doubtless stunned at my appearance, but I edged away from him and plucked one of the filled glasses from the bar. Holding it high, I pasted on a wide smile and surveyed the room, my gaze faltering on Enzo, who sat on a stool in the corner. I kept my eyes on him, satisfied by the way he didn't balk.

"What are you doing?" Father murmured, edging in front of me, but I lowered the glass and whirled away, freeing myself once more.

"Offering a toast," I said loudly, raising the nip of bourbon again.

"To sacrifice," I said, glaring at Enzo. "To the sacrifice of Warren's happiness and my own for the sake of all of you."

Without thinking, I tipped the glass to my lips and swallowed the liquid. I coughed, nearly vomiting at the taste. I was opposed to liquor. It brought people to their deaths, and no wonder why. Father took me by the shoulders and forced me out of the room.

"Dorothy, what has come over you?" His voice was stern, his breath heavy with the reek of the alcohol I'd just tasted. "You've embarrassed us, embarrassed Abercrombie, and most certainly Warren. Your behavior is unacceptable and you'll apologize immediately . . . tomorrow morning," he said, no doubt thinking my second appearance in the barroom a worse possibility than leaving the men with my crassness.

"Don't scold my fiancée too much, Mr. Tuckerman." Warren appeared behind my father. He'd been drinking heavily. His hair was disheveled and his eyes were glassy. He leaned in the doorway and smiled at me. "It's not her fault. I felt the same way only a few nights ago, until I realized that happiness might not be exactly what I thought. She and I will be just fine."

I stared at him, wondering if he comprehended anything he said. He wasn't happy either. He assumed we'd be happy later. But this wasn't his fault. It was mine. I was too jealous, too hasty. Why hadn't Enzo come after me? Did he still not understand that all of this was his doing, the result of his hasty proposal to Helen?

"She's not your wife yet," Father said, snatching my wrist. "Apologize to Warren."

I took a breath and looked at my fiancé, a man who stirred no passion in my heart, but who had been my friend for almost a decade.

"I didn't intend to embarrass you," I said, absolutely opposed to apologizing for pronouncing the truth. Apologies were for regret, and I didn't often find myself in that place.

"Darling," he said, stepping toward me. "You didn't."

"Stop," I said before he could reach me. I edged away from my father. "Stop acting like this, like you love me."

His eyebrows scrunched. Over his shoulder, I could see Enzo leaning over the bar, his black hair falling in his eyes.

"Dorothy, you know—" Warren started.

"This is an arrangement," I said. "It's not a love story for either of us. And though I suppose I'm willing to go along with it, don't pretend that it's something it's not."

"You know I've loved you for a long time," he said.

My father was smiling, nodding at this supposed confession.

"We've loved each other always," I said. "As friends. I can't discuss this further. I'm tired." I turned and paced down the hall, praying Warren wouldn't follow. How much effort it must take for him to pretend he was enthralled with me. He was a better person than I to feign love, to concede the course of his life for his father's happiness.

"Sleep will do you well," Warren called. "Tomorrow will be a better day."

Fourteen

AUGUST 15, 1908

"Miss Dorothy." Mademoiselle woke me, prodding my shoulder with her index finger. I heard the clack of the silver tray, no doubt holding the same thing it did every morning—grapefruit juice and coffee. Light streamed over me and as I raised my head, I caught sight of the diamond on my dressing table. I'd hoped it was a nightmare.

"Yes?" I sat up, sweeping my braid over my shoulder.

"You have a visitor. Miss Helen."

She smiled but lowered her voice to tell me this news, as though she somehow understood that Helen's visit wasn't entirely welcome.

"Have I overslept?" I asked, hoping the answer was yes, that I wouldn't have to go down for formal breakfast, that I wouldn't have to face Warren and Enzo and Father and Mr. Abercrombie and Mr. Vacchelli and everyone else who heard of the double engagements last night.

"No. Of course not," Mademoiselle said, smoothing her linen morning dress. "Have you ever been late in your life?" Her eyebrows rose. "You have not because I have taught you how important timeliness is. Now get up. Let's dress so that you may greet your guest."

She walked over to my armoire and I collapsed against the pillows. It would take great theatrics to entertain Helen. It wasn't her fault, but I couldn't bear the thought of being alone with her, not at this point. Surely she knew how I felt about Enzo.

"Come along, Miss Dorothy," Mademoiselle said, pursing her lips and holding up my corset and a gown much too cheery for today—Chantilly lace with blush ribbon interwoven through the skirt and finished with a large bow in the back.

"I'd prefer black," I said, taking a sip of my juice before discarding my nightshirt and stepping into my corset. Mademoiselle sniffed and ignored my muttering, disagreeing by tightening my laces with vigor.

"Mr. Warren is a nice man," she said. "He'll make a fine husband."

I glared at her as she pulled the gown over my head.

"If you're so keen, why don't you take my place?" I asked.

She stopped buttoning my dress and our eyes met in the mirror.

"Do you think he'd have me?" Her lips lifted in a smile and we laughed. Mademoiselle rarely made light of anything, but she knew exactly when to do it. "Would you like your hair at your nape today? The style looks just lovely on you and—"

"No," I said. "No. I'm not married yet, and I like looking a bit whimsical." I sat on the red upholstered dressing stool, and

Mademoiselle took my braid down and coiled my hair atop my head.

When she finished, I sighed.

"Do you suppose she's still here?" I asked.

Mademoiselle smiled.

"I'm afraid so. She asked for tea and your mother came in just then. They're likely conversing about wedding plans."

I stood and made my way to the door.

"Thank you, Mademoiselle," I said.

I stepped into the hall, wishing I could avoid this meeting, but Mademoiselle was right. Mother and Helen were sitting on the settee, both sipping tea and laughing.

"Sorry to keep you waiting, Helen, I—"

"That's all right," she said. She turned from the settee, her face flushed, likely with the knowledge that the handsomest man I'd ever seen was going to be her husband. I wanted to tell her everything I knew—why Enzo needed to marry, that he was using their marriage to escape from a miner's life—but I could tell in her face that it wouldn't matter. Even if I did, she would defend him. She would understand his logic. She would assume he loved her anyway. Her beauty would convince her of that. She was a better woman than I, a woman who had inherited her father's impulsive sympathy.

"I only came by to ask what time you'd like to picnic, but I'm stunned, Dorothy. Your mother tells me you redesigned this room on a whim?"

I shrugged, wondering what she meant by a picnic.

"I suppose I did. It needed a little brightening."

"Dorothy is always reconfiguring and redesigning. She has quite an eye for it," Mother said.

"I daresay. Warren is a lucky man. Your home will be positively beautiful."

I forced a grin.

"You know," she went on, "my aunt Lucy has been talking about needing a decorator with a keen eye for her new ladies' golf room at her club. She's quite serious about the sport. She's in Providence, and I know it might not work with our weddings and with your moving south, but I'll mention your talent. If it suits, perhaps that decorator could be you?"

Helen looked at me, waiting for an answer. My fingers tingled at the prospect of being asked to decorate at such a time when I might otherwise find my pillows soaked through with tears nightly. It would be a perfect distraction. Men's golf rooms were dank little places filled with dark ornate mahogany lockers in which to store clubs, chairs of the same finish that swiveled but were otherwise horribly uncomfortable, and walls washed the color of ash or cream soup. A ladies' golf room would be bright, colorful, a vibrant sort of lounge with concessions made for sport—a citron four-paneled mirrored screen for changing, perhaps, and lockers lacquered a shiny white, and comfortable armchairs upholstered in chintz.

Mother cleared her throat. "That is so kind of you to think of her, Helen, but of course she'll be completely occupied with wedding planning, not to mention moving five states away and having her own home settled to her liking," she said.

I swallowed and nodded. Hearing my fate vocalized this way compounded the horror of my new arrangement.

"Yes, Mother's right," I said, finding my voice. "But it sounds like tremendous fun. If she finds herself delayed and can wait, I would love the opportunity."

"I know it was quite an abrupt thought, but this room is just lovely," Helen said. "In any case, as I said, I've only come by to ask what time you'd like to picnic? It seems the men have arranged a get-together."

I thought I saw a glimmer of something in her eyes, but then it was gone, replaced by the joy of her smile. Perhaps she'd put them up to it. Perhaps she knew good and well about my feelings for Enzo and intended to punish me by forcing me to endure a meal in their company.

"Oh," I said. "Whyever would Enzo and Warren do that?"

If the meal had, in fact, been planned by the men, the arrangement was peculiar and cruel. They both knew the state of my heart.

Helen laughed.

"I know. Men organizing anything is a shock. But it wasn't Enzo and Warren's idea. It was old Mr. Bonaparte and his peers' doing. Apparently, they've decided to arrange these sorts of things for the newly engaged. They have it in their heads to root couples' friendships at the Greenbrier, I suppose as a way to solidify our fondness for the place—as if getting engaged here weren't enough. Enzo and Warren attempted to explain that we are already peers, but they wouldn't be swayed."

"Well, as lovely as that sounds, I'm sure we're all going to be quite busy today, what with the second race and all. In fact, I don't suppose it'll be done by lunchtime, so perhaps we'll free ourselves from the arrangement after all," I said, leaning over and pouring myself a cup of tea.

"There's always time for a picnic," Mother said. She was pushing me, disagreeing in a polite way, but I wasn't going to concede. I laughed.

"If Warren weren't the betting type, perhaps you'd be right," I said, lifting the cup to my lips. The steam smelled wonderful, of bergamot and lavender, and for a moment, I was calm.

"Actually, it's my understanding they are planning an evening picnic . . . after the races," Helen said. "At the overlook on Lovers' Leap. They've already spoken to the Greenbrier's chef about preparing the meal and have left the time up to us. I know it seems like a bit of an imposition, but I think it's awfully romantic, don't you, Dorothy?"

I grinned at her, feeling terrible that she'd been made my enemy this season. Any other summer, under any other circumstance, I would have been thrilled to enjoy a picnic in Helen's company. She was one of my oldest friends, after all, and before this fiasco with men, I'd been nearly as fast with her as I was with Bolling and Anzonella.

"I do," I said. It wasn't Helen's fault she'd been wedged between Enzo and me; it was his. "Perhaps we should have them bring the dinner around seven?"

"The four of you will have the most memorable time," Mother said, discarding her teacup on the table. "Do you suppose we should head down for breakfast?"

"We'll have a merry dinner indeed," I said, extending a hand to Helen. She took it and smiled.

"I'm thrilled, Dorothy," she whispered, leaning her head against my shoulder as we followed Mother out of the door. "To know we've both found love." I kept silent because she was right. We'd both found love—with the same man.

Lovers' Leap was unoccupied except for the four of us. General Watts had taken the horse show with ten blue ribbons, as everyone expected, and the heat and the length of the day had left everyone exhausted.

Enzo spread the blanket out on the narrow green space between the hedge of rhododendrons and the rocks along the ledge of the overlook. He plucked his straw hat from his head and tossed it on the patchwork quilt, meeting my eyes as he did. We'd spoken around each other all day, able to restrict our conversation to pleasantries in the midst of a group of twenty-five or so, but I'd caught his gaze more than once. I knew he wanted to talk to me, to explain his proposal to Helen despite my admitting I loved him an hour before. I had no interest in engaging him at all. I didn't want to hear it.

"Isn't this lovely?" Helen looped her arm around Enzo's and immediately recoiled. His black hair was damp with sweat and his white shirt was nearly translucent beneath his linen jacket.

"You're positively soaked," she said, sinking onto the blanket. "Are you sure you're all right? I've never known someone to sweat so." Helen Taft was one of those women who only glistened in the heat. Her yellow dress rippled in the mountain breeze and her cheeks were only cherub-rosy. In contrast, my lace dress clung to my limbs, and the wisps of hair that hours ago were made to look whimsical now lay plastered against my temples.

"Surely you saw Dr. Moorman at the show today. He was literally dripping. If he's not concerned, I don't think I should be," Enzo said, chuckling as he folded his tall frame on the blanket next to Helen.

"I'm only relieved to know you're not to be a miner. I imagine you'd dissolve altogether belowground." Helen laughed, but Enzo looked away. He'd told her everything, and like I'd suspected, she wasn't bothered in the slightest. Perhaps there was something wrong with me. Perhaps all of this was my fault. Even so, I wasn't Helen. I wanted a bit of surety, and that wasn't too much to ask. I glanced at Enzo, noticing his eyes still fixed on the ground. Was he embarrassed?

"I nearly thought I'd melt on my way up here myself," I said, hoping everyone would forget the mention of the mines. "The hike was quite difficult. Especially after a day in the sun."

Warren took my arm and helped me down. I situated my skirt as best I could and kept my eyes on the overlook, at the deep green valley untouched by the Greenbrier or anyone else. Sometimes I could see herds of deer traipsing to the forest on the other side, and hawks and eagles swooping from their perches to snatch a meal. They went where they pleased, roaming freely. We could all do the same if we chose to. But time after time we returned to civilization, to the fences and rules and gates. Perhaps some enjoyed being hemmed in. I, on the other hand, was a mouse who longed for a wide-open field but couldn't resist the cheese on a trap.

"I know this is supposed to be a merry occasion—toasting to our upcoming nuptials—but I can't say I'm much in a celebrating mood after losing so much money," Warren said beside me. He set the picnic basket down with a sigh and unbuttoned the lid, removing a crystal pitcher of lemonade and four glasses before he set out the trays of chicken salad sandwiches and tiny bowls of ambrosia. The Greenbrier's picnics were always delicious, but I wasn't at all hungry. I'd endured hours of congratulations from everyone during the show, and now, among only three others, I couldn't bear to pretend any longer.

"I tried to caution you against betting at all. It's the sort of game that renders only a few victors," Enzo said, his lips barely lifting. Surely all of this gambling reminded him of his father's fate.

"I know it," Warren sighed. "Ah, well. I suppose I'll throw less in the pot next time."

"Did you see Father's face, Dorothy?" Helen asked. "Your father and mine were standing together at the end, and when it was clear Father should have taken your father's advice regarding his bet, he nearly cried."

Father had tried to talk Mr. Taft into taking odds on the favorite, but Mr. Taft, always one for an underdog, decided to try for another. He'd bet heavily on Mr. Thornton Lewis's horse, likely because Mr. Lewis had been kind enough to transform his land for the show. I glanced at Enzo, his fingers clasped with Helen's, and thought perhaps Mr. Taft's charity had gone too far. Without Mr. Taft's offer of a post and his daughter's hand, perhaps Enzo and I wouldn't be in this awful tangle of misery.

"I did," I said, laughing and forcing myself back to the conversation. "Sometimes it's best to go with the majority, to align with tradition."

Enzo looked up sharply, and Warren's hand wrapped around mine. Both had thought I'd been talking about them.

"Then again, the excitement of risk can be worth it," Helen said, pouring herself a glass of lemonade. She poured me a glass as well and handed it across the quilt. The sun was setting slowly, the magical hours of evening summer washing everything in gold. Would I have occasion to be up here again? Probably not this season. My heart ached with missing the Greenbrier already, missing the wild beauty and the unchaperoned picnic and the tension of misunderstood love—even if at the same time it was something I hated.

"That's certainly true," Enzo said. He smiled, though his eyes harbored melancholy.

"You're all crazy," Warren said. "I don't have any fondness for betting on something I can't control and then subsequently losing what I've worked so hard for."

Helen coughed. "You mean what your father has worked so hard for. Let's not pretend we've worked a day in our lives," she said, reaching for a china plate and a sandwich.

"Speak for yourself," Warren said, grinning. "I've worked quite a few days along the rails at Father's bidding."

"I think I'd like to work," I said, "when I figure what it is I want to do. It would be nice to be in charge of a task, to feel a sense of accomplishment."

"Of course she doesn't mean going into business formally," Helen interjected swiftly, doubtless thinking if she did not, the men would consider me improper. Professions were for women who needed wealth, whose fathers or husbands couldn't provide the luxury required by a woman of fine lineage. As unlikely and unfathomable as it was that I'd ever become a businesswoman, I thought professions sounded exciting.

"But she's certainly talented enough to be a resource within our set," Helen continued. "You both should see the Tuckermans' sitting room here. She's reworked it, and it's beautiful. I must admit I tried to convince her to do my aunt Lucy's ladies' golf room before her mother reminded me that she'll be too occupied with wedding planning and decorating her new home to do it."

Warren chuckled and turned to me.

"Your mother is right, darling. You'll have plenty of work to do. The estate is large, and my parents won't mind what you do with the trappings. And then, of course, there will be our children and social engagements. I suppose if you're set on working with your hands, there's always more than enough to do in the gardens." His fingers drifted along my arm as he said it, and I edged away. It was still too peculiar, this shift in his affection. Children with Warren sounded all right, so long as I didn't have to be a part of creating them.

"Somehow, I doubt that decorating the Abercrombie estate, or overseeing children or parties or weeding, will satisfy the exotic Miss Tuckerman," Enzo said. "She's much more suited to upsetting convention. I agree with Helen. When she's finished at her own home, I imagine she'll set her sights on her friends' rooms and walls, talking them into letting her paint them pink or—what was it? Sky or sunflower?"

I laughed. I thought of our first conversation, the first time he'd made me smile, and wished we could go back and start over.

"Dorothy, a wall painter? Don't be ridiculous." Helen flicked Enzo on the arm with her index finger and laughed. "She would hire someone to do that bit. That's hardly a job for a woman."

"I think I'd like to paint walls," I said. "I'm much better with walls than people."

At that moment, a hawk took flight, soaring into the sky from its perch in an old oak beside us. I stood and wandered toward the ledge, ignoring Warren asking where I was going. Soon the raptor was below us, circling the valley, floating on the air.

"I'm envious." I glanced at Enzo suddenly beside me. His hands were wedged in his pockets and his gaze was fixed on the hawk. "It's so free," he said. Another hawk began circling beside the first, going around and around, searching and searching.

"No, it's not," I said. "Not now, at least. It's hungry."

Enzo pushed a hand through his hair.

"Dorothy, I don't like this," he whispered. "It's not right. You with him."

I kept quiet, watching the hawks. I'd already told him it was his fault, and it was. He could wait for me. He could come back from Italy or I could go to him there. There was nothing else to say.

"When I saw you last night," he continued, "I remembered the night you met me by the spring. When I walked out of the woods and saw you, Helen disappeared. All I wanted to do was take you in my arms and kiss you. Please, Dorothy. Reconsider. We can be happy."

"The food is glorious. Come on, you two," Helen called.

"I can't talk to you here," I whispered. I glanced at him and felt my reservations start to melt. I couldn't stand it.

"Will you meet me tonight? By the spring? There's so much I want to say," he said.

"I can't," I said. "Unless you've changed your mind."

We looked at each other for a moment, both hoping the other would bend. Enzo shook his head.

"My hands are tied."

Fifteen

DECEMBER 11, 1946

I stood outside smoking a cigarette and dreaming of the solitude of a walk in the woods just beyond. Everyone was here today, and I needed respite from the constant company. All the commotion was making me nervous. Typically, it made me excited—the sign of a project coming together—and I loathed that I couldn't really enjoy the process this time. This was my largest commission to date, my *chef d'oeuvre*, yet at the moment, I was chained to haste.

Tony Cinquinni, one of my plaster men, was yelling at his brother, Lou. I could hear his shouts, muffled by the distance and the door. The painters were in the main lobby trying their best to find the correct sky shade, though every bit of paint they'd chosen was wrong. Sky wasn't ocean or blue-violet or baby powder with a touch of color.

"Oh rats!" Mrs. Mosley's voice startled me. She was sewing—quite inappropriately—in the north parlor instead of in the vacant reception room I'd suggested. *"The light there is too dim for these old eyes,"* she'd said. Mr. Handman was easily her age, and he and his staff worked in a Brooklyn basement proficiently.

"It will all be perfect," I said to myself. The phrase had become my mantra, the only thing besides my cigarettes that was able to calm my nerves as of late. I pulled my fur coat tighter around my neck and exhaled, watching the smoke cloud when it met the frigid air. It looked like snow today, but that was all right. I'd never seen the Greenbrier cloaked in white, and I knew it would be lovely. Even so, I closed my eyes to the view and imagined a spring reopening: the Easter green of the mountains and the pink rhododendrons, lines of horse-drawn coaches bustling back and forth from the station—the coaches *must* be horse-drawn—the doormen rushing out to greet the guests as if welcoming them home. In my daydream, the doormen were in kelly green, a close match to the new grass on the lawn, but deep enough that the liveries would seem crisp, the color a pop to the touches of white in the costume as well. And the head doorman, the man standing at the entrance, should have a bit of distinction. I thought of the smart uniforms I'd seen in Europe. You could spot them from nearly a mile away if you squinted—the dots of crimson and kelly green standing outside every hotel.

I let my mind wander, imagining a young man taking my hand and leading me out of my coach to the open front door of the Greenbrier. I could hear Mozart from the grand piano in the lobby. It had to be Mozart or perhaps Strauss. None of today's crooning. Everyone must immediately understand that they were entering a piece of history.

"Are you feeling all right, Mrs. Draper?" I heard Jean's voice and nodded, thankful it was her instead of Glenn coming to issue another statement about the incompetency of the painters.

"Yes. Just trying to tell myself it will all come together. It will, won't it?"

"It always does," she said. Her words calmed me, though she didn't have any idea about my actual worries, which included that paying Lee back for his unwanted generosity cost me a month's worth of operating income. I thought of Dan, how he must have thought me extraordinarily tolerant not to respond to his withdrawing her salary. Even if the call had come directly to me, I would have acted as though it didn't matter. From the moment he left, I promised myself I would never allow him to believe he had the upper hand in any part of my life. Nothing he did would have the power to affect me in the slightest. I had emerged from his leaving stronger, more famous. In my observation, nothing made divorced men more wonderfully perplexed than when the women they left triumphed instead of cowered.

I extracted my cigarette case and extended it to her. She clicked the silver clasp open and located a matchbox in her pocket. My breath caught. It was an old box from the Palácio Quitandinha. The outside was done in my palm leaf motif I called Brazilliance. I quickly snatched it from her hand and replaced it with my usual Radium brand. Somehow utilizing anything with the Palácio Quitandinha name seemed like eliciting a curse, as though lighting one match would cause this project to go up in flame the same way.

"Those matches are too old," I said.

"I suppose they are," she said wistfully, as though she thought I had wonderful memories of Brazil.

"And you're right that it does work out most of the time," I said, correcting her earlier statement a bit. "I suppose that should be enough confidence for me."

"Remember the day we met? The day I helped you paper your foyer?" She took a drag and grinned. "I'm not sure I ever told you this—there were so many other horrid things to not talk about, you know? But the florist let me go right before I showed up at your house. They had invested over half of their livelihood in the market and couldn't afford to keep me on. When you hired me that day, you gave me hope." She looped her arm through mine. "And even though you've had setbacks, Mrs. Draper, everything seems to work out when you're involved."

"I'm terribly glad the florists were investors," I said. "Not that I'm happy for their hardship, of course, but I'm glad to have you." Jean didn't know about Brazil and the Versailles restaurant both going belly up, and I wanted to keep it that way.

I finished my cigarette and snuffed it out on a worn crystal ashtray.

"When you have a moment today, I'll need you to write up a letter about costumes," I said.

"Costumes?" she asked. "What sort? Santa Claus would be festive this time of year." Jean giggled and extinguished her own cigarette.

"Don't mention it to Glenn. He'll volunteer," I said. "I was thinking of costumes of another sort. I'll need the letter to be sent to Mr. Bowman. Tell him I'll need his staff to come to a training. Afterward, they'll not only be doormen or coach drivers or maids, but characters in a play. The guests must feel like they're in a dream, that they've stepped back in time, and uniforms and manners are an essential part."

"Of course," she said. Jean looked optimistic today, wearing a smart yellow suit instead of the drab grays most of us had been wearing for weeks. Her hair was done up in a beautiful chignon.

"Don't you look lovely," I said. She smiled and smoothed the front of her jacket.

"Thank you," she said. "I work for a smart-looking woman and can't dress as though the Will-to-Be-Dreary is my guide."

"You absolutely cannot," I said. "You're working on The Greenbrier, after all."

Something crashed, an earsplitting sound that tore at the eardrums and set senses to flight.

"What was—"

A collective shout was heard from the ballroom followed by a litany of Italian curse words. I practically ran inside, pushing my way past Mrs. Mosley, who barely looked up.

The ballroom was covered in plaster. Large pieces of white cameo lay jagged on the wood floor. The Cinquinni brothers stood in the midst of it, coated from head to toe in powder.

"The ceiling has fallen," Lou said, gesturing upward. He was shorter than I, and thinner too. I turned to Tony. He had his hands on his hips, appraising the bare ceiling. The only evidence of the plasterwork were security wires hanging here and there.

"Clean it up," Tony said, instructing Lou. Tony was rotund and quite tall, towering over his brother in both age and authority. "It's either your fault it fell, or it's the construct of the ceiling, but I have to think it's the former. Look at the wire on my side and then yours. Unbelievable."

I looked as he spoke and noticed he was right. There were only a few on Lou's side.

"I'm only missing a couple," Lou spat, thrusting his hand at the ceiling.

"I apologize, Mrs. Draper. So long as the problem isn't with the hotel's joists or trusses, we will start over and it will be perfect," Tony said.

"I know it will," I said, not bothering to reassure them. They were grown men after all and quite versed in licking their own wounds, but as I looked at the ceiling of plaster in pieces on the floor, I wondered how much the plasterwork would eat into our budget if it was done over, fell again, and the hotel's structure was to blame for the ceiling's crumbling. The Cinquinnis would certainly require full payment each time it was constructed. Too many mistakes like this and it would be a reprise of the Palácio Quitandinha. My company wouldn't have a chance. I felt the weight of the matchbox in my pocket. I would have to throw it away immediately. Perhaps even looking at it had set us on a path to catastrophe.

"There will be more wires," Lou said, finally calming. "It will be so strong this time that if a hurricane sweeps the whole hotel, the ceiling will remain intact."

I nodded and glanced out the window. Father had deemed Dan and me able to withstand any storm, unsinkable. I told him that sentiment hadn't boded well for the *Titanic*, but he'd only waved me off. Mother wasn't that way. It wasn't that she hadn't wanted me with Dan—she had—but she'd seen me in love once before, and as much as I loved Dan, she recognized it was different. Real love, first love, was maddening. In the years after that last summer here, I'd gone over it time and time again. My heart had wholly belonged to him, never fully to anyone else. Perhaps I should have fought for him. Perhaps we would have made it last forever despite everything else against us. But he'd walked away. Just like Dan had. Neither came back for me.

"There you are. We've found it." Glenn waltzed into the room outfitted in his holiday red and green tweed. I couldn't help but imagine him in a Santa Claus costume and chuckled under my breath.

"Found what?" I asked.

"The blue," he said. "I'll show you."

He held out his arm and I took it. Beyond the ballroom, the white latticework was being installed by an army of local men. They lifted a large floor-to-ceiling piece into place on the east side of the room while Mr. Smith barked orders at them. I hadn't seen him since the second day on the job—he'd simply been sent architectural plans and asked to sign off on them—but I hadn't forgotten his comparing my amiability to the Axis diplomats. Noticing me passing through, he tipped his head.

"I was mistaken," he shouted over the grumbling of his men. "We make quite a team, Mrs. Draper."

"That we do, Mr. Smith," I said. "As long as you continue to sign off on all of my designs."

"So far you haven't violated any of my rules," he said, grinning.

"That's unfortunate," I said, "because inevitably I will, and you'll be forced to break them for me."

At that, Mr. Smith laughed out loud.

"Afraid not. We can't have the ceiling collapsing on the guests for the sake of design."

"I suppose you're right," I said. "That would be horrid. All my work swallowed up in calamity."

"Stop flirting," Glenn whispered, yanking me forward.

"I'm not," I said, finally catching up to the conversation, though of course Glenn knew better.

The moment we stepped into the main lobby I gasped.

"Yes!" The blue was perfect. The exact shade of a White Sulphur Springs sky in summertime. "I'm thrilled. Exactly what I had in mind."

"I know," he said.

"Thank you, Glenn," I said. He always liked when I pointed out the occasions he read my mind, which was quite often. Glenn grinned and ran a gentle hand along his perfectly coiffed hair. It was a good thing he'd never been made to go overseas during the war. He would have rather had his head blown off than have his hair fashioned to the shape of a helmet.

A flash of metal caught my eye. A tall, skinny fellow was holding a ladder at the far end of the room, right before the lobby gave way to the dining room, while a young man atop it fixed a hideous thin copper wire to the perimeter molding.

"What is this?" I paced across the room, but the men gave me no mind. "Excuse me!" I said firmly when I reached them. The man scaling the ladder turned to look at me, still holding the wire in place.

"Yes, ma'am?"

I blinked. He should have been in the movies. He looked like a mix of Cary Grant and Jimmy Stewart. Even so, he was interfering.

"What do you suppose you're doing?" I asked.

I stood straight, doing my best to command respect. He clearly didn't know who I was. It was a peculiar feeling when everyone else indulged your every whim.

"Installing the fire alarm, ma'am," he said, nodding to the ceiling. Ma'am again. Southerners and their manners. I knew it was a measure of respect in the South, but ma'am always made me feel old. "The copper reads the temperature, see, and when it reaches—"

"Take it down," I said.

"What?" The man holding the ladder finally found his voice.

"Take it down. It won't do with the decor."

The young man laughed.

"Fire won't likely do well with it either," he said. "Anyway, I can't take it down. It's required if the hotel is going to open."

Glenn and Jean came rushing to my side. Glenn's heavy cologne engulfed me in a cloud before they arrived.

"We'll paint it white and no one will ever notice," Glenn said hastily.

"There's nothing else to be done about it, DD," Jean said.

"What's your name?" I asked the young man. "I'll check this so-called rule, and if it's not the case, you'll come back to remove it."

"Ed Ballard," he said, reaching down for another measure of copper.

I heard the lobby doors crash open but kept my gaze on the man refusing to take down the unsightly wire.

"Dorothy." Jean abruptly grabbed my arm.

"What is it?" I snapped, disentangling myself from her grip.

"Elisabeth," she whispered. Surely not. I turned in time to see Elisabeth sweep into the foyer and descend the steps to the lower floor, toward the pool and the suite. She caught my eye and lifted her gloved hand in a small wave before disappearing. Despite all the goings-on, evidence of my vision being made reality, I felt hollow. I had just given Mr. Mosley my proposal, and he promised to get it to General Eisenhower while we broke for Christmas. It had seemed almost a sure thing, my winning the suite, but now I was faced with the truth: our efforts had been too late, in vain. I'd lost. Visions of newspaper headlines flashed in my mind—*Divorced Heiress Goes Bankrupt, Elisabeth Draper Takes Up Decorating the Greenbrier Hotel.* I shook my head. I was not finished yet. Far from it. And I would not allow the Will-to-Be-Dreary to dig me an early grave.

"What is she doing here?" Jean went on. "Again."

"Oh," I said, trying to appear calm. "She's just helping me with a little something." It was better to seem to be in the know, in control. I could tell Jean wanted to ask more, but she didn't press me further.

"Enough about her. Have you seen the Washington yet?" Glenn asked, taking my arm. He led me away from the horrific sight of the wires and Elisabeth toward the fireplace, where a large painting covered in brown paper was propped against the mantel.

"The Lansdowne?" I could hear the trembling in my voice. If we'd procured the Lansdowne, I could rest at Christmas. I could rest knowing at least the lobby was a work of art, a place of wonder, and the rest would be in place in short order.

"Not quite," he said. "But close. A copy done by Stuart's daughter, Jane. Ted worked tirelessly to find it. There's only one. It's still a very expensive, very exclusive work."

I peeled the paper back slowly, unveiling the painting brushstroke by brushstroke. Glenn was right. It was still a masterpiece, a piece of American history, and I knew that when Eisenhower passed through this room, he'd immediately realize his error in selecting Elisabeth for the suite. I wasn't only a decorator. My family's roots ran so deep in American soil that I'd been cloaked in patriotism since birth, raised as American royalty. I knew how to find items that meant something to this country.

"When this wall is painted, hang this immediately. Right over the fireplace," I said. I could see it now, the glint of the firelight on the black mantel and the colonial-era gilded frame. For a moment I closed my eyes and imagined teatime at the Greenbrier. There must be high tea. The maids would serve steaming coffee and tea and small cookies and meringues and petits fours. Guests would sit on couches in front of this fireplace and sip and chat and look at Washington. In a way, we were alike, Washington and I. He was the first president; I was the first professional interior decorator. When people thought of this country, they thought of him. Perhaps when guests thought of this place, they would look around at my masterpiece and think of me too.

"Before Christmas," I said. "This painting must be up before then."

Sixteen

JANUARY 16, 1947

The Washington was up. I stood freezing in the lobby, burrowing as best I could in my mink. Tom had just started a fire, and the lovely new black marble mantel glistened along with the gilded frame atop it just as I'd hoped. Everything was coming along beautifully. The local workers and Mr. Smith had kept up until the morning of the twenty-fourth, and the dedication was obvious. Every room was painted. The partitions had been installed to my exact specifications. Even the floors were perfect. I stepped toward the fireplace just to hear the click of my Naturalizers on my signature black-and-white checkerboard floors.

"I'm sorry it's so cold, darling," Lee whispered. I was shocked they hadn't solved the heat problem by now. With Tom gone to ignite the fireplaces throughout the hotel, Lee looped his arms around my waist and pulled me against his chest.

Christmas had been strange this year. Lee was absent,

spending almost all our time off with his parents while I procured every small contract I could find to tide us over a few more
months. A week before Christmas, he'd asked me to join his
family, but I refused. I was too old to be a giggling sweetheart
intent on making a good impression on my beau's parents, especially given I was much closer to their ages and didn't plan on
making an honest man of their son. Plus, I didn't need to give
the Tuxedo Park tongues another reason to wag about me. That
happened enough already. So I'd visited Mother on Christmas
Day without telling him. I thought it would be a pleasant afternoon, just Mother and me—the children were with Dan—and
glasses of eggnog and trays of molasses cookies and fruitcake, but
the moment I passed through the Tuxedo gates, a melancholy
I hadn't experienced in nearly forty years settled in my spirit. I
hadn't bargained on how it would feel to visit Tuxedo Park after
being at the Greenbrier. At once, the memories of the last time
I'd made the trip descended on me like a vast storm. I'd recalled
the way my shoulders bowed as the carriage careened into our
drive, as though I were about to be returned to my prison cell; I'd
felt the hollow emptiness of my nineteen-year-old soul and the
swollen bulge of my eyelids over eyes that couldn't stop welling
with tears. For all of Christmas Day I tried to rid myself of the
memories, but couldn't, and when Mother asked me to spend the
night, the thought of staying in my childhood bedroom, a room
I was a few months away from occupying again if things didn't
turn around, made me nauseous.

"I missed you," Lee said.

I honestly believed at one point during the holiday that he'd
finally decided to leave me. I felt a bit sad about it, but figured
he'd had enough. I couldn't blame him. Then again, I hadn't

seen the rest of my staff much either, though they had grudgingly come to my twentieth annual Christmas sing-along and lunch on the twenty-first. They'd pretended to enjoy it. So did Penny, who had come in from Ohio for the occasion, knowing I'd need some help. Though Mother always hosted with me and was as vibrant as could be at eighty, it was difficult for her to lift furniture and hoist serving platters. It had been good to see my daughter—George and Diana, too, though they'd come only briefly—for an afternoon tea and gifts. They promptly left, taking my grand-children, who loved me, over to Dan and Elisabeth's for the remainder of their holiday. Christmas was always a reminder that society thought I'd chosen the wrong course, but what else was I supposed to do when Dan left? Nanny and the boarding schools had the children, Dan had Elisabeth, and I had the Architectural Clearing House, soon to be Dorothy Draper & Company.

"I missed you too," I said to Lee, though what I really meant was I'd missed this place. The moment I stepped off the train, I'd felt relief. Here, I could leave the last thirty-eight years in New York behind. Here, I was appreciated for my work. Here, people loved me, and as strange as it seemed, I felt the love I'd left here thirty-eight years ago. I craved that feeling, even the heartbreak.

Lee turned me around.

"I know you went to see your mother at Christmas. There's no way you would have left her alone. So why didn't you come over?"

"You know why," I said.

"No. I don't," he said. "I told you my parents don't know. They only know you're my boss. I wouldn't have taken you in my arms, though I would have wanted to. And if you would have let me, I would have told them everything. To hell with what anyone else thinks, Dorothy. At what point do we decide to let them talk, to let everyone think what they will, and live anyway?"

I took a breath. He was from a different generation—or perhaps he was simply wiser. Either way, as much as I wanted to ignore the whispers about me, I couldn't—not entirely anyway— and I'd given up the futile efforts to expunge myself of caring. As much as I'd once thought otherwise, a part of me would always want to be accepted.

"I was busy," I said finally. "I was only in Tuxedo for the afternoon and then I had to get back. You know how urgently I've needed to solidify new business dealings."

I sat down on the couch in front of the fireplace, hoping he'd be satisfied with my answer. Only then did I see the upholstery. The rhododendron print was perfect. The huge burst of red-pink flowers and hunter leaves popped against the mint background. The stitching was tight, the seams nonexistent. Mrs. Mosley had been a find after all, especially since Mr. Handman was still quite delayed.

"I know. And I know part of that was my doing. I shouldn't have paid Jean's salary. But I could have helped you over Christmas. Not to mention, I've come up with several ideas that will ensure Dorothy Draper & Company is around for centuries, if you'll only let me tell you." Lee paused. I wanted to remind him of what happened the last time he overstepped, but I refrained for the sake of peacekeeping. "But I can't believe you were too busy to see me. Perhaps you didn't *want* to. It was Christmas, Dorothy, and—"

My staff interrupted. Jean tipped her head at Lee. She was wearing a knitted tilt hat embellished with pearls, and it looked lovely on her. I watched Lee, sure he would at least blush at the sight of her, sure he still noticed the beauty in women his age, but he barely lifted his hand.

"Does the upholstery suit, Mrs. Draper?" Mrs. Mosley situated herself in the oversize armchair facing the fireplace.

"It's perfect, Mrs. Mosley. Well done," I said.

Her husband patted her shoulder. "Before we begin, Mrs. Draper, I wondered if you would have a few moments later to walk the halls with me? I have a question about the larger Greenbrier staff that I think could be addressed absent this group," Mr. Mosley said.

I met his eyes and smiled. It had been so kind of him to try to win Eisenhower to my side. I knew he was only going to tell me that Elisabeth had won the suite. At least it wouldn't be a shock. I'd only seen her in passing over Christmas and she seemed in jovial spirits. Of course, she had no reason to be in a poor mood—she had the love of her son, Seth, my children, my husband, her clients, and now the confidence of the country.

"Of course," I said, and stood. "Everything is coming along so nicely," I said to the others. "Stay the course. My focus for the coming weeks will be the smalls—the china, the hand towels, the soaps. Glenn, I'll need your print revised for some of those, of course, and will seek you out as—"

"Mr. Young's wife, Mrs. Anita Young, will be here tomorrow." The lobby door smacked shut and Mr. Bowman appeared, shaking his head as he said the words. "And Mr. Abercrombie has written that he'll send the bricks for the garden."

"Warren?" I asked before I could stop myself.

"Yes. Warren the third," Mr. Bowman said. "The elder is deceased."

I knew that. He'd been ill the last season, but hearing

Warren's name after all these years was surreal. I wanted to ask if he knew the request came from me, from my staff, but I refrained. I hadn't wanted to write to him, so his reply was none of my business.

"That is wonderful news!" I said. "About the bricks, I mean."

"It is," he said. "And I've invited him to the opening as a thank-you."

I heard Mr. Mosley draw a sharp breath and turned to find him staring at me. Even now my mind whirred with the implications of our meeting again. What would he be like? I prayed he was happy.

"But, again, I must say: Mrs. Young will be here tomorrow. She's an interesting bird, Mrs. Draper, and I must warn you ahead of time that she will try to interfere. Bob even mentioned it himself in his telegram," Mr. Bowman said.

I rolled my eyes. "Let her try."

It was too cold to be outside. Nevertheless, Mr. Mosley and I made our way to the first floor by veranda so no one would follow. The metal railing was freezing, even through my kid leather gloves. He leaned to open the door to the channel of closed shops inside the north entrance.

"I'd like you to see what's been done with the suite. It's a part of the hotel, after all, and I was the one who involved you at all, so—"

"I don't need to see it," I said, interrupting him. I'd thought we were simply going somewhere private so he could tell me I'd lost the suite. My skin prickled. I didn't want to pretend to fawn over

Elisabeth's design or try to find something kind to say if I honestly loathed it. "I saw Elisabeth slip down here right before we broke for Christmas. I know it's her design that was chosen, and rightly so. She's worked to win the Eisenhowers, and good for her."

"It turned out well, Mrs. Draper," Mr. Mosley said. "It's lovelier than I thought it would be. Won't you please just humor me and take a look?"

I walked behind him, fuming inside. I didn't want to be a good sport about this. I'd had to work to be a gracious runner-up over the years, and it still took an incredible amount of effort. The suite was going to be awful; it *had* to be awful.

We slowly made our way around the pool and to the men's lounge and finally to the closet. He pushed the bar up and the door opened.

I stared, waiting to find myself so filled with jealous rage that I acted out and threw something, but I couldn't speak. The suite was outfitted in *my* designs, in *my* vision.

"I'm sorry to have taken care of this without telling you, but Eisenhower sent the wire over the holiday and we didn't want to bother you. Mr. Bowman, Tom, the missus, and I had some time over the break. No one was around to need us, so we spent our time in here. I only thought it would be easier for you," he said. "And, I'll admit, I wanted to surprise you too."

"What about Elisabeth?" I asked when I finally found my voice.

"Eisenhower agreed that your ideas better suited the space, so he promised Elisabeth a few rooms in the White House should he ever become president—and believe me, he intends to," Mr. Mosley said with a chuckle. "I imagine she was pleased with that deal."

The wide stripes of red, white, and blue looked magnificent, just as I'd dreamed. The white tile encouraged the room to glow. Bishop-sleeve draperies of red with gold tassels were perfect, making it seem like there were actually windows beyond them.

"Did Mrs. Mosley do these?" I asked. He shook his head.

"She could have, but I know how particular you are. I spoke to Mr. Handman and he was thrilled to comply."

"Mr. Handman? He's still so behind on the curtains for the hotel."

Mr. Mosley shrugged.

"I suppose he knows that and wants to make it up to you."

The idea that Mr. Handman was working day and night on my curtains gave me such joy. His delay had been a worry.

"Perhaps," I said.

The large antique table still occupied the majority of the room, but with the proper furnishings, it would look fit for presidents and their circles. One of the walls boasted a large map of the Greenbrier in the early 1800s, framed in gold filigree, while another held portraits of the presidents from Washington to Lincoln.

"When you mentioned portraits, we thought to have all, but then decided you might not want to set a precedent that we display everyone. These portraits were already on the wall at the President's Cottage. We decided to repurpose them. Unless, of course, they won't do."

Mr. Mosley fidgeted with his cufflinks and scuffed his shoes on the floor.

"I want to be critical, but it's just as I imagined," I said.

"And in here, we've cleared the desk for secretarial correspondence. I thought to get rid of it, but I assumed it would be needed—"

"It is," I said. "But trinkets are not." I plucked the crumpled rhododendron pressed in glass from its spot next to the Hebe lamp I'd approved. Despite my words, I turned the rhododendron over in my hand.

"If I may, Mrs. Draper?" He leaned against the desk and looked at the ornament in my hands. "The man who owned this worked here for thirty-three years. This was one of his dearest possessions, and every government official who's ever been here absolutely adored him. They would want the room to give tribute to his service somehow."

"Are you sure? He must be some man for you to beg to preserve something so inconsequential." I held up the crushed flower. Mr. Mosley smiled.

"It wasn't insignificant to him. Sometimes I'd come in and he'd be staring at it. I knew it was a memory, but he never would tell me."

"What happened to him? I'm sorry for your loss," I said.

"Oh. I'm sure he's alive," he said. "As I mentioned, he was forced out, in a way. Not by any of us. Still, it's a shame. He'd been here for years, first appointed by Taft during his presidency, I believe. I suppose they were peers."

"Taft always did take to good people," I said.

After all this time, it was still hard to think of Mr. Taft without thinking of Enzo. If Mr. Taft hadn't come here on tour, if Enzo hadn't proposed to Helen, what would have become of us? Perhaps he wouldn't have boarded the *Republic*. Perhaps he would have been safe, alive. After I heard the news, I wondered if his drowning had been my fault, if our marriage could have saved him. But it was ridiculous to wonder now. Whatever might have happened was ancient history.

"And to the Greenbrier," Mr. Mosley said. "I think Taft was here more than any other president."

Though I didn't ordinarily concede anything, I did this time. I set the sprig of rhododendron back on the desk.

"Thank you. No one else will see this suite. Only those who knew this man," he said. I sensed a bit of emotion in his voice and found his eyes watery. "The manner in which he was dismissed was unfair. We all thought so."

"What was the reason?" I asked.

I wasn't sympathetic to much. People who only cheated once were still cheats; people who stole once were thieves. Business worked differently. Forgiveness was always due but employment was not.

"I can't say," he said. "But I can tell you that he did nothing wrong, that he loved this place, and that he did more for this country than some presidents."

I glanced at the lamp and the flower and was convinced I was right in letting them remain. A patriot. I could concede for a patriot and the thoughtful Mr. Mosley.

"Why didn't you ever come back after the Centennial?" he asked. He wasn't asking flippantly. The question seemed personal, as though he'd taken offense at my abandonment. I shrugged.

"Most of us didn't. We came of age in that season, married, moved here or there, and had our own families. Then the wars came and between them, the Depression, and I don't know. None of us vacationed as grandly anymore." I grinned and then forced a laugh, praying it would lighten the mood. "But all that dreariness is over and a new age of luxury is upon us. Perhaps now our children will understand our manners and expectations and the importance of a fine vacation."

Mine, especially Diana and George, fought convention tooth and nail as I had, but in time they appreciated certain things bought by our privileged lives.

"I pray they do. Thank you again for letting us keep these things," he said, gesturing to the desktop.

"Of course," I said. "I hope viewing them keeps this special fellow in everyone's memories."

Seventeen

AUGUST 20, 1908

The tea had grown cold, but that didn't matter. No one wanted to retire. Even Mother, who usually turned in after dessert, was still here, reclining across from me on a green velvet settee. The men were smoking in the room across the hall. I could smell the acrid bite of it when someone opened the door to come or go. Normally, it was just a brief tea in the Rose Room after dinner, but tonight, after the excitement of the ball and the horse show had passed and departure loomed, no one was keen to rush off.

"Do you suppose this will be anyone's last season?" Anzonella asked. She fiddled with the enormous purple feather affixed to her straw hat. She'd held it on her lap the whole time, as if in need of something to busy her hands. She hadn't spoken to me since she'd heard of my engagement. Even at the horse show she'd huddled next to Bolling, mustering only head nods and shakes when I attempted conversation.

"Only those poor souls whose bodies simply cannot hold

on for another year," Mrs. Kane said. "I can't possibly imagine that anyone would miss summer at the Greenbrier. Not for the world."

"I do hope we'll be able to attend next year," Helen said. I couldn't see her. She was behind me somewhere, likely seated next to her mother on twin armchairs in the corner beside the door. I perched on the edge of a tufted damask couch next to Edith and Bolling and Anzonella, my view the empty fireplace that gaped like a toothless open mouth below the enormous mahogany mantel. I plucked the delicate china cup off the tea table and drank the last sip of my cold tea.

"Your Enzo seems to love it here," Mrs. Phinizy said, her voice coming from the piano bench in the same corner as the Tafts. "Surely he'd do everything in his power to make it."

I felt my stomach clench. How awful. I'd have to face him year after year. I'd have to see a pregnant Helen, knowing she carried his child. It was almost enough to tell Warren I didn't want to return. But I loved the Greenbrier, possibly more than I loved Enzo, and if I was going to be tortured by his poor match, he would have to be tortured by mine. It was only fair.

"What of you, Dorothy?" Anzonella's gaze fell on mine. She was smiling, but her eyes were glaring.

"I—"

She started laughing before I could say more. Everyone stared at her, no one understanding the humor.

"Never mind," she said when she caught her breath. "I forgot. I suppose I should just ask your dear, darling Warren. It's his wishes that truly matter. Isn't that right?"

My face burned. I could feel the blood coursing through my veins, the urge to overturn the tea table nearly impossible to keep in check. She was my best friend. How could she say such a thing? Then again, we'd hardly had occasion to talk about the how and why of my engagement. I'd been engaged one night, and the next day, when I'd tried to explain, she'd ignored me.

"Anzonella!" Mrs. Kane scolded.

"What a ridiculous comment," Mother said.

"No," I said simply, answering her question and meeting her gaze.

"It's all right." Bolling placed her hand on Anzonella's leg. "Soon enough, you'll have someone to think about the future with. I'm sure he'll ask," she whispered, low enough that only the group of us could hear. I felt my forehead wrinkle. Surely Anzonella wasn't jealous of my engagement. She'd never seemed to worry about marriage, always knowing it would come sooner or later.

Anzonella shifted, looking at Bolling as if she'd gone mad. "I don't want a proposal. At least not right now. I only think it's silly that people make life-altering commitments when they're hurt, commitments that might keep them from actual happiness."

"I think I'll write a letter," Mrs. Kane said, rising and pacing toward a small desk beside the fireplace that held a stack of the Greenbrier's stationery. "Everyone should do the same. A little silence would do us well."

I forced a yawn and stood. "It's been a lovely evening, ladies, but it's time I retire."

"I'll come with you," Mother said, rising from the sofa. "The men will be up late talking about what's to be done following that string of bank robberies in Springfield, and I don't suspect your father will be an exception." According to the front page of the *New York Times*, a horrific skirmish in Illinois had left several injured and a few dead. I didn't know the particulars. I avoided news of tragedy as often as I could.

Bolling snorted. "They act as though they're in Washington, as if they're actually able to change things from a smoking room in White Sulphur Springs."

Mrs. Kane's eyebrows rose. "Surely you know they can. And will. You're a Phinizy, Bolling. You know that this group, our men, have tremendous power. The Greenbrier has been Washington's ears since the 1700s. That's half the reason coming here every year is so necessary. Without our gathering, the country would be positively in shambles."

I skirted the back of the sofa, nodding quickly at Helen and Mrs. Taft before I departed, Mother on my heels. I knew plenty about the Greenbrier's influence, how from Henry Clay and President Van Buren's time to today, our gathering each year dictated the following twelve months of governance. Clearly, other countries understood this. That's why Mr. Vacchelli and Enzo were here, after all, despite their insistence otherwise, and why the Swedish ministers had visited last season.

"Are you well, my sweet?" Mother looped her arm through mine as we made our way down the dim hallway lined with old-fashioned oil lamps. The Greenbrier extinguished almost all the electric lamps at night.

"Positively elated," I said, clearly lying. I gripped the carved cherry railing and hoisted myself up the stairs to the landing and our suite. I was exhausted. I'd had to wear a false smile all day and nothing had ever tired me so.

"I know you don't love Warren," she whispered, looking around as though he would materialize. "But I know you will. You love him as a friend already, and that foundation is—"

"You've already said that. I don't want to discuss my fiancé," I said. The ring on my left hand felt too tight, and I had a strong urge to pry it off immediately lest it become stuck.

"Very well," Mother said, withdrawing her arm from mine and unlocking the door to our suite with a scowl on her face. "But someday you're going to explode if you don't discuss it. And I'd rather that not happen after you've had children."

"Children? That's assuming I ever find myself attracted to Warren," I said. I caught the closing door with my hand and out of the corner of my eye saw Father in the sitting room. I didn't want to discuss Warren with him either. Perhaps if I idled in the hallway for a moment longer, Mother would talk him into retiring. "I'll be there in a moment."

Mother sighed and nodded, plucking the pins from her hair as she walked toward her bedroom.

The door shut. I sat down on the floor and let my head drop back against the wall, shutting my eyes.

"Miss Tuckerman!"

I startled, finding one of the bellmen standing over me. He was panting and sweat trickled down his face beneath his straw bowler.

He caught his breath. "I'm Frank Mosley, Mr. David Mosley's son. Sorry to give you such a fright." David Mosley was the Greenbrier's most seasoned bellman, going on thirty seasons. "Mr. Rossi insisted that I was to deliver this letter to you tonight, discreetly, without delay," he whispered, looking around. "When I found that you'd retired from the Rose Room, I ran as quickly as I could." He reached into his smart green jacket and extracted a small envelope, handmade from a piece of the Greenbrier's stationery. "When I delivered your letter to him this evening, he opened it right away. He must have been eager to hear from you."

I felt my face pale.

"What letter?"

"The one your mademoiselle gave me," he said. "It was in the stack with your parents' correspondence."

I was going to be sick. I took a deep breath. Why had she sent my letter? I hadn't even put it in an envelope; I hadn't set it out on my letter rack.

"Will you take it, Miss Tuckerman?"

Only then did I realize he'd been holding Enzo's letter out to me.

"Yes. Yes, of course," I said, taking it.

"If you wish to respond without the whole of the Greenbrier whispering, you can find me by the main entry door most hours of the day. Shake my hand, slip the note in my palm, and I will figure a quiet way to arrange for him to receive your reply," Mr. Mosley said. "I don't mean to say that the other staff gossip, but most do. I consider it poor taste."

"Thank you," I said.

He tipped his hat and turned to go. When I was alone again, I opened the note.

I wish I hadn't read your letter. I don't feel pity for you. Since the beginning you've known of my captivation with you, and still you've kept me at arm's length. Though not directly, I asked you to be my wife and you hesitated. On occasion, love does not have time to delay. It doesn't have the luxury to think things over. It simply clings to hope and jumps, trusting that the entwining of two souls so uniquely and clearly intended for each other will certainly survive any turbulence or testing. I wish you were as sure of me as I of you; I wish you were willing. I wish that you trusted my love for you, and that my need to marry, my uncle's meddling, didn't matter. I wish our match could be won easily, and that it didn't require such tremendous sacrifice—a yielding that neither of us feels able to grant. It is impossible.

As for you, I don't wish you ill. I have made my choices and you have made yours, after all. I hope you find love with Warren. I hope you have happiness you've never known. I'll never forget you. I'll never try to. I've never felt longing like I have when thinking of you. I've never felt the need to be so near to someone, even though I know you'll break my heart. I won't feel that with Helen. She's steady. She's smart and sure like her father, and I'll be that for her as well, but I'll never forget the rush of you. I'm sure I'll long for it always. You're wild and bold, a rhododendron in the midst of greenhouse roses, and I pray that you aren't ever tamed. I'll never see those magnificent blossoms without seeing your face.

Change your mind. I had to say it.

I stared at the letter afterward, feeling as though I'd been gutted. On the edge of the paper, he'd drawn a sprig of rhododendron. I ran my hand over the drawing, wondering if I was being ridiculous. Perhaps he was right. Perhaps I should run to him, tell him I'd marry him tomorrow. Then again, I could say the same of his willingness to wait two months as he said of my lack of impulse.

"Dorothy? Whatever are you doing out there?" Mother called

from behind the door. I heard the latch click open and quickly crumpled the letter in my palm before she could see.

"Just thinking," I said, following her back into the sitting room. Thankfully, my father had retired.

"Come in. We can sit and stitch and I won't say a word." She reached for my discarded stitching below the white makeshift tablecloth covering the tea table. I was an awful hand at sewing because I didn't care.

"I'm going to go to my room and draw awhile," I said. She stood in the darkness, watching me. She wanted me to come close, to confide in her, but I couldn't. That was the hardest part. Even my mother wouldn't understand.

I opened the door and shuffled to the windows, catching the sliver of a crescent moon and the cool mountain breeze as I lifted the pane. Neither of us would compromise. Our fate was sealed. I swept the brown damask curtains back to look at the grounds below. The lawn was vacant. I wanted to depart down to the lobby and out into the wild, but I stopped myself. I'd be looking for him, and what would I say if I found him? We'd kiss, I'd feel his arms around me, his body pressed to mine, and nothing would change. I closed my eyes. Even the memory tortured me.

I gripped the windowsill and breathed deep, finally opening my eyes. I startled, my gaze falling on his. He was standing in the middle of the lawn now, washed in moonlight, his face tipped up toward mine. He pulled his hand from his pocket and lifted it to me and I did the same. Then he walked toward the cottages without looking back.

Eighteen

AUGUST 26, 1908

It was drizzling, and a foggy haze eclipsed the view of the mountains out of my window. Mademoiselle pulled at my hair, twirling the bulk of it up into several figure eights and affixing the bunch to my head with a dainty silver flower pin.

"How did you come across my letter, and why did you have it sent to Mr. Rossi?" I asked, watching her face in the mirror. "I didn't put it in an envelope, and I didn't place it in my letter rack. I didn't intend for him to see it."

"I'm so sorry," Mademoiselle mumbled, her lips pinched to pins. Her face reddened. "Your mother was out of stamps and envelopes, and I thought to borrow some from you when I came across the note." She situated more pins into my hair and then patted my shoulder. "You didn't have any envelopes either, so I assumed you wanted to send the letter but hadn't a way." She paused and I could feel her unease. "Did the letter cause trouble for you? You may have me fired if you would like."

Mademoiselle hadn't made a mistake in all the years she'd been with us, and I could tell my question about her misstep had rattled her. Her hands shook as they finished my hair.

"Of course I won't have you let go. Despite the shock of knowing he read my letter, I'm glad for it. I doubt I would have had an occasion to tell him what I wanted to say otherwise. Did you read it?"

I wouldn't blame her if she had—it had been quite a salacious letter, after all—but I didn't want her telling Mother about my personal correspondence.

Mademoiselle shook her head and reached for more pins, then looked at me in the mirror.

"I did not, but I wasn't surprised to read his name. I see the way your eyes sparkle when you speak of him and the way your eyes dull when you speak of Mr. Abercrombie. I thought perhaps this wasn't the first letter. Please excuse me for assuming you wished to send it."

"You didn't tell Mother about it, did you?"

"Absolutely not. Speaking of your mother, do you suppose she will attend the luncheon as well? I've already situated her coiffure but failed to ask where she was going." Mademoiselle always knew when to change the subject.

"Of course," I said. "Her aversion to rain is not so great that she'd miss an engagement. You know that."

Mrs. Alexander was hosting a farewell brunch this morning in her cottage, as she did every year before returning to Virginia a week earlier than the rest of us. She always spent an exorbitant amount on veils of yellow and pink roses to drape along the white railings of her cottage. I wondered how the flowers were faring in the weather and hoped they looked perfect. Mrs. Alexander was a lady of the highest degree, and if anyone deserved perfection, she did.

My door burst open and my little brother came flying through, still in his nightshirt. His hair was disheveled and he wore a milk mustache from breakfast. He'd grown so quickly.

"Dorothy!" he said, folding at the waist when he reached me. "Your friend Miss Kane is here. She's at the door." He flung a hand behind him, and I placed my palm on his back.

"Which one?" I asked, doubting it was Anzonella, especially after last night.

"Miss Anzonella."

Mademoiselle slid a final pin along my scalp and I glanced in the mirror. I'd chosen an ensemble fashioned from silver-gray lace and goldenrod crochet, a soft summer dress that in a few weeks would be replaced by heavy silks and velvets. I pinched my cheeks and lips, watching them both bloom pink as Mademoiselle and Roger disappeared out my bedroom door. I looked too pale this morning. Perhaps silver wasn't my color. Then again, it didn't matter anymore. It wouldn't surprise Enzo that I looked pained, and anyway, I was engaged, on the course to finding myself an elderly matriarch.

I stood and leaned over, eyeing the slight crystal vase boasting one cabbage rose. I'd started drawing it last night to occupy my mind, but I was overcome by the need to write another letter and had turned the page over and poured my fury and pain onto the paper. I'd been cruel but honest. I would not allow Enzo to rise above me, to claim that he was the wounded one, that he loved me more than I loved him. He was just as selfish, and I'd made that pointedly clear.

The door swung open and Anzonella appeared. She avoided my eyes, twirling the point of her white silk parasol on the floor beside her. "I don't know what's kept you, but our mothers have already departed, as have my sisters, and it's rude to be late. You know how Mrs. Alexander dislikes it when we sneak in at the last moment." She finally lifted her face to mine and smiled. "And if Mrs. Phinizy eats the last of the grits again, I'll blame you for at least a year." I wanted to ignore Anzonella the way she had me, but something inside wouldn't let me. I needed her.

I laughed under my breath and swept my thin white cloak off the end of my bed.

"I'm happy to hurry, so long as you promise to sit on the opposite side of the room from the Tafts," I said.

Anzonella's face sobered and she fiddled with the Brussels lace along her yellow bodice.

"Very well. But you should know I haven't come to discuss your entanglements. The whole idea of you and Warren disgusts me." She sighed and met my eyes. "You love Enzo and he clearly loves you, yet you're willing to ruin both of your lives—and Warren's and Helen's too."

I swallowed, unsure I could say anything without crying, and I didn't want to cry in front of anyone, even Anzonella.

I whirled and, pretending to smooth the base of my quilt, swept the letter out from its hiding place under my mattress and into my palm. He would be waiting for a response; I was sure of it. Even in the midst of today's shooting games and tennis matches, even though he'd be expected to join the men on the lawn after retiring from sport to discuss politics, he'd wonder if Mr. Mosley would meet him with a reply. Perhaps this time he'd see that he'd been wrong to insist on right now, that it made sense to wait for love.

"I don't plan to utter a word about it," I said, forcing a grin. I looped my arm through Anzonella's, always acutely aware of my great height next to her tiny frame. "But you should know that it all happened so quickly, that I needed you."

The rain had mostly stopped by the time we stepped out of the hotel. Still, it was foggy and our dresses of silver and yellow and royal blue stood out like the sun.

Mr. Mosley stood in his cheery green at the foot of the stairs to the walk. Our eyes met and he extended his hand to me.

"Good day, ladies. Miss Tuckerman," he said.

"Hello," I said as my friends echoed his greeting. I shook his hand, and in an instant the letter was gone. For a moment, my nerves began to swim. I thought to go back, to retrieve my note in case it somehow found itself in the wrong place, but I had a feeling this wasn't the first time Mr. Mosley had been entrusted with secrets.

"What a shame," Bolling said, gesturing toward the lawn. The ribbon pole, erected for the children's fancy ball this evening, had been put up prematurely, and now the silk strips of green and white drooped like the wilted rhododendrons bowing around the perimeter of the lawn.

Bolling looped her arms through mine and Anzonella's, poaching some of the protection from our parasols as the trees dripped overhead. A group of older women were in front of us, their posture similarly girlish despite their silver hair and matronly fashion. The Greenbrier did that to people, reminded them of their youth, polished off the tarnish of winters and unfulfilled dreams.

"That will be us in forty years," Bolling said, taking note of the same women.

"I hope so," Anzonella said.

I stepped over a puddle and grinned at the way Bolling stepped directly into it, muddying her kid leather boots without notice. As much as I longed to break free from society and its fences, I would miss my friends. Even so, I could feel Warren's ring under my glove. It was slightly too tight anyway, but the constant reminder of a future I didn't want didn't soften the constriction.

"Good morning, ladies!" Henry and his father leaned over the railing of their cottage porch, the latter raising a cup of coffee to us as we passed.

"Hello!" Bolling and I said in tandem, though I noticed Anzonella kept quiet.

"What a parade of beauty," his father called, looking to us and then behind us. Beauty. There was too much of it here—too many beautiful women and handsome men, too much beautiful vegetation and scenery and cool air. It muddled common sense and flooded it with romance. The springhouse was just below us. I could feel its pull and let my eyes wander to where I'd let Enzo first hold me. Did I actually love him? Would I love him the same wandering the rigid roads of Tuxedo Park? Would I want him as badly if I'd met him in a New York City ballroom? Would I find him as enchanting if he was one of us, a society man promising the life I'd always lived? Or was I a victim of the Greenbrier's intoxication as well?

"I don't know why he bothers to address us," Anzonella muttered. "Unless he's decided to try his wooing on you, Bolling." As much as she refused to admit it, Anzonella clearly wanted Henry to propose and was sore about him taking so long.

Bolling laughed. "It won't work. I know I've been quiet about it, but I'm still very taken with Mr. Vanderbilt."

"I'm so glad to hear it!" I said, thrilled to find a topic I could be enthusiastic about. "Do you suppose he'll propose? Anz, can you imagine our fortune if Bolling moved to the city? We'd see each other all the time."

Anzonella looked around Bolling to me.

"*I* would be thrilled. I imagine you'll be in South Carolina by then, though. Don't you think?"

I'd forgotten. Just for a moment.

"No. No, I don't think," I said.

"Whyever not? Surely Warren will be in the business of Southern Rail. It's his family's work," Anzonella said.

I stopped.

"You're right. I don't want to marry him. Is that what you wanted to hear?" I snapped the words under my breath and immediately looked around, sure I'd find Mr. Abercrombie or Warren himself directly behind me.

"Don't worry," Bolling said. "They're all at the Dry Creek Battlefield Memorial this morning. The men took the horses out right before we departed."

"Why did you say yes?" Anzonella asked. "Tell us the truth, Dorothy."

"You know it already," I said. I didn't need to say it aloud.

"To spite another man. Do you suppose I should accept Mr. Jones's countless proposals because Henry and I can't be? Should I throw my life away to hurt Henry?" Mr. Jones was a forty-five-year-old balding bachelor who came to the Greenbrier each year to flirt with young women. Years ago, he'd attached to Anzonella, much to the chagrin of Mr. Kane and Anzonella as well. Thankfully, he was absent this year, but he still wrote letters to her from his Kansas ranch.

Bolling's eyes were wide, going from Anzonella to me and back again. She had no idea what was transpiring, and I didn't either. I didn't know that Henry and Anzonella had parted ways.

"Why?" I asked. "What happened?"

"Nothing," Anzonella said softly. "Nothing yet. But he told me last night that when Carrie Astor returns from her European tour, he's planning to propose. He said that if it hadn't all been planned long ago, he'd have chosen me. I wouldn't have believed him at all except that he cried. He told me he loved me but that he didn't have a choice. He already asked Mr. Astor. It's funny. I didn't know I was planning on marrying him until I found out it couldn't be. He's been a friend to all of us, and our falling in love was simply an accident."

"He has a choice," Bolling said. "He should write to Mr. Astor and say he was wrong, whatever the consequences may be. What kind of man cowers under a mistake?"

"A man who values reputation over love," I said.

"It's his decision, regardless," Anzonella said, lifting her chin. "I refuse to be responsible for his suffering. Which is more than can be said of you, Dorothy."

"Enzo chose Helen," I said, my voice like ice. I was tired of being made the villain.

"No, he didn't," she said. "Unless he's lied to me about the way you rejected him and then accepted Warren's proposal. I found him on the porch the morning after it all. He was devastated and confided in me because he knows you and I are fast friends. I'll never understand how you could be so careless with the feelings of a man you love."

Bolling was aghast. "He proposed to you too? Why did you—"

"He said I had to accept him now. He wouldn't wait for me, even for two months," I said.

"And why should he?" Anzonella said. "Either you love him or you don't."

"You don't know everything," I said. She looked at me, waiting for me to elaborate, but I couldn't. As much as I wanted to, I couldn't talk about his needing to marry, about his family, and I shouldn't have to. Anzonella should always take my side.

"It doesn't matter. If you—"

"I've known him for a matter of weeks," I said, cutting her off. "We barely know each other. He's the nephew of an Italian diplomat who is now engaged to the next First Daughter. And you're accusing me of being too cautious? Are you sure you aren't simply projecting your disappointment on me? You've known Henry for years. Of course you would say yes in a moment. That's why I said yes to Warren. I could sense his unhappiness, his need for me. So it's true, in part, that I accepted because I don't want Enzo to be happy, because I want him to realize his mistake. But I also accepted because Warren is my friend." That part was mostly a lie and she knew it.

"You're not being a good friend," Anzonella said finally. It had started to rain again, and the water trickled down the edges of our parasols and onto our skirts. "And you're breaking two hearts in the process."

"Girls! Girls! I've been calling for you!" Mrs. Alexander flew down the steps of her cottage and raced toward us. "The brunch has started, and I'm afraid that you'll miss the loveliness of it all for the dreariness of this rain."

I turned away from Anzonella and hastened after Mrs. Alexander and Bolling. Even in the weather, the swags affixed to Mrs. Anderson's railings and trellis were lovely, the roses wearing the raindrops with grace.

The cottage was full of tables dressed in lace tablecloths and the Greenbrier's delicate china and vases of roses and our mothers and grandmothers and sisters and aunts dressed in similar fineries.

I took my seat next to Edith, barely able to smile at Helen across the table. She didn't return the gesture. Either way, Anzonella was right. I would break two hearts. I could spare Enzo's and mine, but in exchange crush Warren's and Helen's, or I could live with the repercussions of the path I'd chosen in jealousy and anger.

"I'm having one of my Worth ensembles sent down for the ball," Anzonella was saying to Helen, lifting the china teacup to her lips. There was one more fine affair, the Century Ball, and then the season would be over.

Edith asked me, "Do you suppose you'll all attend the staff baseball game tomorrow? If it doesn't rain?" The Greenbrier scheduled so much at the end of the season, and tonight's children's ball would precede tomorrow's baseball game followed by the last Sunday evening concert, the ladies' bridge party, and the Century Ball.

"If I were a betting sort, I'd choose the culinary staff for the win," I said, reaching for a lemon tea cookie. "They're on their feet much more often than the office staff and—"

"Why don't you?" Anzonella said. "Bet, I mean. Your fiancé is arranging my father's money for the wager, and I'm certain he'd take Mr. Tuckerman's, too, if your father would be willing to part with any for you."

She smiled, and I would have been certain she'd forgiven me if not for her eyes. Her glare cut me through.

"Enzo is of the impression that the office staff will make off with the cup," Helen said. Her cheeks flushed as they did every time she said his name. "They're much slighter than the culinary group, and with his racing background, he assumes they'll be quicker so long as they can hit the ball."

"So it's Warren against Enzo," Bolling said, her eyes twinkling. "Interesting. Whatever does the trophy look like? A gold star?"

I kicked Bolling under the table and she winced. Almost everyone knew Father's nickname for me.

"I believe it's a baseball diamond with a little man in uniform set atop it," Helen said. She met my eyes and I wondered if she knew of Enzo and me as well. Surely not. If she did, I highly doubted she'd go along with the engagement. Helen Taft was a woman of strength, a woman who commanded her future with thought and foresight. Then again, perhaps she saw our romance and thought only that Enzo and I were nothing but a spark, an infatuation that would drown in a moment.

"I do hope it's a good match," she continued, pausing to take a sip of her tea. "Father made some grumblings about leaving early, and I want to inhale every last joyful breath of this place if we're made to leave in a day or two."

My breath caught. A day or two. Would Enzo go with them?
Bolling patted Helen's back.

"I know we're not supposed to speak of such things," she
said, her voice low. "But I saw the *Times*. Has your father been at
all worried?"

Helen took a small bite of tea cake and set it down on the
plate.

"I don't know what you mean," she said, but she kept her gaze
down, away from Bolling's stare, and I understood she was lying.
Whatever news had made the front page was indeed a point of
contention.

"Austria-Hungary and Italy," Bolling whispered. "The tension
between countries is rising, and favor is not on your intended's side. They'll need an ally if conflict were to ensue, and it's
rumored they'll come to us."

I knew I should turn away, take up conversation with
Anzonella and Edith, but I couldn't.

"Enzo isn't involved in such things," Helen said finally. "He
loves the art of language, and he loves sport, but he truly has no
interest in politics at all."

"But his uncle would like him to." I said it before I could
stop myself, forgetting that I had been the only one privy to that
conversation.

"He's hardly a puppet," Anzonella said, chiming in. "He's
a man of nearly twenty-five years, a man who's made his living racing autos. He doesn't seem keen to follow in his uncle's
footsteps."

She was wrong, but everyone else thought she was right.
Perhaps he didn't want to become a renowned member of the
American political class, but he'd be made one regardless. He'd

gladly become a ventriloquist's doll, so long as it meant he didn't have to return to Italy.

"I'm sorry I brought it up," Bolling said. "I only hoped the news hadn't made trouble for you."

"Thank you, Bolling. It hasn't. Father and I know and trust who he is, though I was quite surprised to find that a friend of mine is concerned about his motives regarding me."

Helen turned to look me. I could feel my face pale and immediately plucked my teacup from the table to hide my horror behind a calculated sip.

"Enzo and Dorothy have a most remarkable friendship," she said.

The table silenced. I wished Anzonella or Bolling would say something. They knew how terrible this was, but they didn't speak. I laughed.

"I wouldn't call it remarkable," I said. "We've taken a few turns around the dance floor, but that rarely signals a true bond."

I could feel Anzonella's eyes on my face and wished she would stop this, but I knew she wouldn't. She wanted me to crack, to tell the truth, but I couldn't. Especially not here.

"He told me you don't believe him to be sincere about anything," she said, disregarding my attempt at squashing her statement. "He was withdrawn last night, nearly sulking, and I asked him why. When it was clear he was disturbed by your assumptions, I honestly couldn't figure the reason, so I asked. He told me that you two have exchanged words on several occasions, words that have made him question his honor."

Words? I swallowed, praying someone would say something. I was almost certain his melancholy was a result of my letter, but what had he told her? Surely not that we were in love, that she was his steady consolation prize.

"Words, you say?" Edith asked. "And when was this, Dorothy? At the Hunt Ball? I noticed the two of you looking rather forlorn while you were dancing."

"We were only discussing our futures," I said. "Everyone does that. And if we seemed disoriented, perhaps it was because we were separated from our matches."

Bolling coughed.

"Are you sure that's all?" Helen asked. "His future seems quite bright. Why would he think his integrity is in peril if the only things discussed were our marriages?"

"I don't know," I said simply. "Perhaps you should ask him."

Helen heaved a sigh and smoothed her napkin across her lap.

"Forgive me for accusing you," she said. "It's only that I find engagements tiring. Don't you, Dorothy? It will be perfect the moment we say 'I do' and all is settled."

I nodded, unable to say more. Our fates were tangled like a thin gold chain. They would never settle unless they were broken and restored.

Nineteen

JANUARY 17, 1947

The letter taunted me, the envelope seeming to glare from my dressing table. Bella unclipped my rollers and attempted to fluff the short curls, pinning them to my head in little loops. Beneath my hat, my hair always looked fuller, as though I were hiding a swirl of thick black in the crown. Bella worked wonders.

"You're upset this morning, Mrs. D," Bella said through lips holding all of my pins.

"It's the damn unions." I clapped my hand over my mouth the moment I said it. Proper women didn't curse to make their point. Bella laughed.

"And what do they have to say? I pity them. Going up against Dorothy Draper."

I tipped my chin up and nodded. Bella was right. They'd regret it. They'd change their mind.

Lee looked in, his dimples deepening when our eyes met in the mirror. Just as quickly he was gone, walking down the hall

283

to his room, but before he disappeared, I caught sight of his red sport coat. The shade was unmistakable, a McIntosh apple red reserved for the members of Tuxedo Park. He'd never worn it before—at least not in front of me—and at once I was taken back to my wedding day. I was standing at the back of my parents' piazza holding my father's arm, watching the fog misting over Tuxedo Lake, the altar abloom with hydrangeas and roses, the ladies' gowns in golds and midnight blues, and the men—save Dan—united in their red. I remembered hearing the whispers even then, the same whispers I'd heard the night we met. *"He's a doctor like his father,"* as though that fact alone made his dressing differently acceptable. I recalled wondering at that moment how much my loving him had to do with his social standing, which allowed him to linger just outside of Tuxedo Park. We never laughed, but he was kind and handsome and had no desire whatsoever to live within the confines of the Tuxedo gates. But Lee did. I'd ignored that fact on purpose. Did he think he could return with me? Did he think I would embrace it? The thoughts were silly.

"Mrs. Draper? Are you all right? What did the letter say?" Bella asked again.

"They've refused to require my new uniforms. It's an atrocity. The vision won't be the same without the housekeepers and coachmen and doormen dressed in finery. It will throw the whole thing off."

I winced as Bella pushed a pin across my scalp. My skin was much more delicate than it once was. When I was a young woman, Mademoiselle had made my hair to hold batting and feathers and ribbons and more pins in one evening than I wore in a month now.

"What will you do?" Bella asked.

"I don't know. First, I'll take it up with Mr. Bowman—or rather Mr. Tuohy, I suppose. I'm so sad Mr. Bowman's leaving." I truly was. He understood the Greenbrier, and he seemed to understand me. I hadn't heard of this Tuohy fellow, but he needed to get on board.

"And if they don't understand the urgency, I'll have to petition the unions themselves, and they won't want that. I've been known to cause quite a stir," I said.

I thought of my early days in business, when no one in permits or government or decorating knew who I was. That had been hard. I'd had to rely on my parents' name, my married name in some circles, and when that didn't work, I'd had to use Eleanor's. The name Roosevelt always made a union man perk up. But now, at least in New York, I sensed my presence was dreaded in almost any office of law or regulation. I rarely asked permission first. It had never been my style.

"I've always loved this beret." Bella fetched my electric-blue hat from the rack and fixed it to my head. It was new this season, and I especially enjoyed the way the straw glass embellishments sparkled like ice. Winter often slid into the doldrums category, but I couldn't live that way. Every day had to be a celebration. I was living my dream, after all.

"DD?" Lee appeared in the doorway. I tried my best to ignore his coat. "Tom's come by to tell me that Mrs. Young has arrived and requests an audience with you this afternoon for tea in the hotel."

I laughed. Beyond commissioning me for the job, the C&O's CEO, Robert Young, hadn't set foot in the hotel. He clearly hadn't known to tell his wife that it was less than luxurious at the moment.

"Has she been inside the hotel yet? Perhaps she should first. I don't prefer my tea with plaster dust and paint fumes," I said.

"I thought to inquire the same, but Tom said that she insists on a proper tea in the middle of the lobby with three attendants," Lee said.

"Oh. Very well."

Either she thought I wanted finery or she was one of *those* women. I hoped for the former. Some of my greatest friends were *those* women—always wandering around with an air of importance, scrutinizing every breath of those around them—and though I understood their need for control and prominence, I'd resigned my residential work because of them. They simply weren't ready to hand their homes entirely to me, and I wasn't willing to compromise my design for them. For a time I had been thrilled to reinvent my friends' residences—until Mrs. Winchell's outburst. The Winchells were a fine family, but she was unable to fully relinquish her love of beige and thought to raise her voice about it. She'd been the worst, but in the end, both Winchells had loved my design.

Businessmen were much easier to handle. They didn't give a fig about decorating so long as people liked it in the end. I hoped the tea was nothing more than Mrs. Young's desire to meet me. I was famous, after all. Perhaps she only wanted my advice for her home.

"Don't patronize me, Glenn." I swatted his arm and snatched the dull gravy-brown towel from his hand, then thrust a ruby one toward him. "The towels must be as elegant as the rooms."

"I only thought the rhododendrons would pop on a neutral color," he said.

He looked ill today, but perhaps it was the horrid bathroom light or the color of his suit. The blue bordered on pastel, and no one looked good in those. Behind him, I watched one of the White Sulphur Springs men carefully place a gorgeous lamp with a shiny black base on an antique side table painted white. Even the guest rooms would be masterpieces. I smiled, remembering the first time I'd been noticed for decorating. It had been here, at the Greenbrier—though of course no one back then, save one, had ever thought I should decorate for a living. Only women without station or a providing husband did that.

The insecurities washed in. Most of the time, I'd trained myself to believe that everyone thought me a celebrity. I wasn't working in a factory. I was a business owner, after all. But on the other side of the coin, I was a divorcée, working. What did Mr. Bowman say behind my back? What about Mrs. Young? Did they pity me? I knew almost all of old society did. My employees didn't. They lived and breathed design as I did, but what of the rest? What of the people in the middle and the new money? What would people say if I was bankrupt as well? Everyone would pity me then.

"The towels will be ruby, and the rhododendron will be beautiful on the bottom," I said, only responding so Glenn wouldn't notice my quiet.

"You're right, of course," Glenn said, bracing himself on a new porcelain claw-foot bathtub. I nodded and started to walk out, but Glenn caught my arm.

"You're going to go down in history for this project, dear DD. People will never forget you. You'll be a bigger name than Elsie or Jean-Michel or anyone after you. To think that you could have wasted away simply decorating and redecorating your houses. Thank goodness Dorothy Tuckerman wasn't satisfied with homemaking."

I swallowed, stunned at the sentiment. Enzo had said something similar at our picnic long ago, but I'd thought nothing of it then. Decorating wasn't even a profession in 1908, and society women with particular skills offered them free to their friends.

"Thank you, Glenn," I said. Lee sauntered into the room with a fresh haircut. The almost-curls around his ears were gone. So was his Tuxedo Park sport coat.

"Did you decide on a soap?" he asked from the doorway.

"Yes," I said. "I think I'm going to go with lavender. Rose is too feminine and pine too seasonal."

"Are you going to marry him? If not, may I?" Glenn whispered behind me. I shook my head.

"I don't know what you're talking about," I whispered back. "But I'll never marry again."

Glenn snorted, and in the mirror in my periphery, I could see him shaking his head. I knew how obvious it was that Lee and I were more than business associates, but it was none of my staff's business, and a proper woman never acknowledged her conquests.

"I completely agree with the lavender," Lee said, finally reaching us. He was wearing a holly-green wool suit that made his eyes beam green. "Relaxing and luxurious. I'm amazed at you, Mrs. Draper." He took my hand, lifted it to his lips, and kissed it. No one did that anymore. Nowadays it was no issue to kiss a woman on the cheek, even if you'd only just met.

"It's no doubt she's a star," Glenn said. I looked at him sharply. Today he'd echoed both Enzo and my father. Father had been the first and last person to call me Star.

"Absolutely no doubt," Lee said, keeping hold of my hand. "And now I've come to escort our star to the lobby. Mrs. Young has arrived and is already seated for tea." He met my eyes, gritted his teeth, and then leaned in to whisper in my ear. "I must warn you. She's already been talking to Mr. Smith about a certain curve in the staircase from the upper lobby to the lower. Mr. Smith said he couldn't do it, and she's threatened to fire him. She said something about requiring grandeur for the Duchess of Windsor's entrance at the opening."

I rolled my eyes, though the idea of Mrs. Young possessing the power to fire anyone was quite startling. I'd have to finesse my disagreement.

"Perhaps to her, Wallis is some sort of foreign royalty, but to the rest of us, she's just Wallis Simpson of the Baltimore set," I said. "Not to mention, we'll not be holding court in the lower lobby or anywhere else for that matter. This isn't England. If she wants an entrance, it'll be best suited for the ballroom. I'll talk her into something like that."

"Mrs. Draper, is the lamp placement to your liking?" The man I'd spied earlier stood on the other side of the whitewashed four-poster bed next to one of two matching lamps.

"Yes. Thank you, sir," I said. "If you have any other questions, direct them to Glenn. I'll be back to sweep the hall later today."

"Very well," he said, tipping his head.

"Now let's go," I said to Lee with a sigh. "I do hate to waste time with this woman, but I suppose I have to, don't I?"

"You don't have to do anything, my darling," he said, leading me into the hallway.

"I know," I said. "But Mr. Young is the reason I'm here, so I suppose I could extend a bit of hospitality to his wife, as long as you interrupt me after a half hour or so. I can't be too generous with my time."

"You're right," he said, his voice low. "Every moment lost will affect us. Dorothy, I've been putting it off because I don't want to upset you, but we need to sit down and talk at some point very soon." He clasped his hand over the back of mine curled around his arm. We started down the stairs.

I could feel the tightness in my shoulders pinch. The worry was taking a toll.

"Yes," I said. "But right now, please let me focus on my work. All of this talk of calamity is dampening my spirit."

"Of course," he said. "Let's discuss it later."

"The cakes must be warm for Mrs. Draper. *Warm.*" The high-pitched voice echoed down the corridor, past the green lobby, through the trellis, and into the ballroom. As Lee and I walked, workers tipped their heads and regarded me with a sort of caution, as though they'd just felt the tremors of an earthquake and knew I was wandering toward the epicenter.

"No more than twenty minutes," I said as we neared the lobby. "As my business manager, I need you to insist that my time is better spent elsewhere."

"Longer than twenty minutes and the tea and the cakes would be cold anyway. Heaven forbid," Lee said.

Mrs. Young was microscopic, smaller than even her husband, who was barely taller than five and a half feet, with a hat twice her size. The fabric resembled a yellow accordion and was situated in two layers of fans that dipped over her face and ended in two channels down the back of her gray silk dress. The staff had brought in furniture to suit her—a dainty mahogany tea table with equally dainty chairs. I didn't know where the set had come from, but it didn't match and would be discarded immediately after our tea—discarded or perhaps reassigned to whatever suite the Youngs would occupy.

"Mrs. Draper!" Mrs. Young extended her arms to me but didn't bother to rise. She only flexed her fingers in and out like a toddler eager for a bit of candy. The gesture looked strange on a woman my age. I forced a smile, and when I finally reached her, I sat down without leaning my much larger body against hers for a strange sort of embrace.

"Lovely to meet you, Mrs. Young. I trust you had a nice ride down?" My voice no longer echoed, and I was tickled by the way the lobby was shaping up. It was perfect and beautiful, just as I'd imagined.

I fluffed my white linen napkin and set it on my lap, then reached for the white china teapot, but Mrs. Young shooed my hand away and snapped over her shoulder for a man I'd never seen who stood beside the door. He hastened to her side, poured the tea, and immediately returned to his post. I lifted the tea to my lips, inhaling the bergamot and vanilla.

"The travel wasn't bad, though there've been rumors you're to outfit a private car for us. Is that so? It would make the train much more bearable."

I choked on the tea and coughed.

"I'm decorating this entire hotel, Mrs. Young," I said.

"I know. But I'm sure you'll have a teensy bit of time for the C&O executives. We're in the car an awful lot, and it's quite dated and uncomfortable."

I didn't like the insinuation that I owed the company more work than the massive amount I was putting into their resort. Other designers might gladly do all sorts of favors for a job this size, but I wasn't one of them.

"When I've finished the resort, I'm certain I'd be amiable, so long as we can settle on the terms."

"Very well. I'll have Robert work with you to figure a way to factor it into this project. After all, I was the one to encourage him to insist the C&O provide such a vast amount of funds, and I've been the one to pat his head when he frets and says things like, 'The budget is already met, darling.'" She sat back and sighed. I felt my heart sink. We had exceeded the budget? This was news to me, and likely to Lee as well. Last I checked we were right on the mark, and Mr. Tuohy hadn't said otherwise. My mind began to race with the dreaded what-ifs. What if they couldn't afford to finish the project? What if the hotel never opened? Perhaps I shouldn't have insisted on importing that mantel from England or acquiring the Lansdowne copy for the lobby.

"This is lovely, Dorothy. May I call you Dorothy?"

I nodded, forcing myself out of worry. I'd sort this out with Lee later.

"You know I was the one to tell Robert that we must have you decorate. You're famous, you know, and so well connected."

"Well, thank you, though I—"

I tried to be gracious, to dissuade talk of my pedigree and

sway among my class, but some people didn't understand my dislike for that sort of chatter.

"No need to deny it. You're the best. In any case, there are a few little tiny things I've noticed are a bit . . . wrong." She pursed her lips. "For instance, I noticed the staircase to the lower lobby—"

"I don't intend to be ungrateful or rude, Mrs. Young," I said gently, "but my work is far from finished, and furthermore, it is mine. I've been hired to outfit this fine resort, and when I am finished it will be the most breathtaking resort in the country. However, I don't make a practice of adjusting my designs to fit anyone else's preferences. Even in home decorating. I apologize if my stance is hard, but this is my work. I hope you understand."

I took a breath and prayed she wouldn't explode. Even if Mrs. Young turned out to be another Mrs. Winchell, she'd eventually come around. I was sure of it.

"I want a new staircase. One fit for the duchess," Mrs. Young said, looking away from me and adjusting her countenance to something so smug I would have left immediately, had it not meant my termination.

"I'm confident that Wallis will be just as impressed by the current situation," I said.

Mrs. Young gasped and put a hand to her heart.

"I certainly hope you'll address her properly when you greet her, and the duke too."

"Oh, it'll be fine, Mrs. Young," I said. "I've spoken to her often enough to regard her informally."

My tea mate's eyes flickered with something I couldn't recognize, then she sat up straight and dabbed the edges of her lips with her napkin.

"I forget, you know, that you and my dear friend have been cut from the same cloth," she said softly.

So this was the reason for her visit. She'd intended to show dominance, to establish she was just as important as I or her husband or any of the stars who would attend the opening party. I saw it often in women who had come from nothing. With the right husband and riches, they felt they had to prove something to fit into the upper class. I hated the way society made women feel inferior in so many ways.

"Not exactly the same cloth," I said. "I'm quite a few years older than she. And she's from Baltimore—a world away from where I grew up."

"Tuxedo Park," she said, taking a bite of a tea cake. "I remember now."

"Please don't hold it against me," I said, hoping to remedy the strange turn of tone in our conversation. "I ended up fleeing by marriage, if that makes it any better."

I took a sip of my tea, wishing it were still hot.

"I'm so sorry about you and Dr. Draper," she said as though he'd announced his leaving yesterday.

The urge to laugh out loud was so strong I pinched my arm under the table to stop it.

"I did have occasion to meet the new Mrs. Draper and your daughter Penny up in New York once, at a play, I believe." She said it quickly, as if confessing something, as if she needed me to know she'd met Elisabeth. "Elisabeth seemed quite kind at least. I'm sure it's nice to have an amiable relationship. Especially when, well, you didn't want to be married in the first place. I'm still sorry the two of you didn't work things out."

The familiar anger sparked, and a knot jammed my throat,

but I didn't bother to correct her. I could tell in her tone she hadn't meant to be rude. She was only stating the presumed facts of my marriage, what everyone else thought about my part in it.

"It's quite all right," I said when I found my voice. "It's been nearly twenty years, and to be honest, I don't believe I could have handled two marriages."

Mrs. Young's eyes widened.

"The second to my job, Mrs. Young," I explained. "Now, tell me why this staircase is so important to you." Truthfully, I wasn't attached to the current staircase and would entertain her idea if it was a good one. I'd also do about anything to turn the conversation away from my disastrous marriage.

"Well, my great-grandfather was British. When I was young, I had occasion to see Buckingham Palace once, and I loved the curve of the main staircase. It was so grand," she said. "When Robert told me the duke and duchess would attend the opening, it just seemed there should be something royal here. This could be their palace of sorts, you know? Since they've been so ostracized by his family."

I nodded and added another lump of sugar to my cold tea.

"I understand why you'd want to do something for them," I said. "Let me talk to Mr. Smith and see what I can do. Perhaps we can have a suite designated specifically for their use as well. There's a little building attached to the main hotel through a corridor just beyond the dining room. General Eisenhower used it as a sort of conference space during the war. It's two stories and quite private. We were planning to fashion it into a presidential suite anyway, and thinking of it, I'm realizing I've already planned to use colors and patterns I know Wallis prefers—pinks and pale greens and orchids. It would be perfect. If for some reason the spiral staircase won't work architecturally in the main hotel, we could have one fashioned to bridge the stories in the suite. I've planned on a curved stair there anyway, so altering it won't incur additional cost."

Mrs. Young brightened. "Oh! Thank you! I have no doubt something so special will make them feel extraordinarily welcome." She turned around in her chair to face the entry. "And I meant to say earlier—what an unusual and lovely chandelier."

She gestured to the white birdcage fixture hanging sentinel over the landing where the upper and lower lobbies diverged.

"There must be points of interest everywhere," I said. "How else will people possibly find the topics necessary to converse?"

It seemed strange that talking points had to be provided, but they did. People lost all but a tiny ounce of childlike wonder as they grew to adulthood, and unless something extraordinary caught their eye, the conversation would turn to the weather or sport or, heaven forbid, professions. In my parents' day, that sort of talk would have been highly inappropriate, but somehow the wars had softened the social rules. It was both a blessing and a curse in my opinion.

"It's a shame, but I suppose you're right. And you're planning to outfit all the employees in darling little costumes, I hear?"

"Yes," I said, though of course if the unions didn't cooperate, I had no idea.

"Oh! How exciting!" Mrs. Young clapped.

At just the right moment, Lee appeared looking frantic. I hoped it was all a charade.

"DD, Mrs. Draper, come quick. The bricks have arrived, and before Mr. Alexander arrives on the three o'clock from Long Island, do open them. There's a note, and apparently you're the only one permitted to read it."

Twenty

I looped my arm through Lee's as we walked toward the reception entrance, where the bricks had been deposited.

"What do you mean I'm the only one permitted to read a note? They're only bricks. Have them moved to the north side where the blasted boxwood garden and path will reside, and leave them for Mr. Alexander to worry about," I said.

Lee stopped.

"Before we go to the bricks—I don't want you to think I was eavesdropping, but I was working on a bit of accounting in the dining room and heard Mrs. Young say something about us going over the C&O's resources." He ran a hand across his face and shook his head. "The bottom line is that it's not true. They budgeted $4.2 million for the design work, and we are right at that number. However—and I didn't even feel compelled to mention this, as it's not going to be an issue—but Mr. Mosley's boxwood garden was not a thought shared and approved through

297

Mr. Young and his board. So the eight hundred to complete the wall project falls outside of the C&O's plan. I told Mr. Young that it was adopted on the recommendation of a longtime Greenbrier employee and politely told him to find the money, which he agreed to do."

Although the issue had been handled and it wasn't going to affect my bottom line, this was my nightmare. The Palácio Quitandinha trouble had started the same way. I'd been paid only half of my commission when the particulars of my agreement with the hotel's owner, Joaquim Rolla, began to unravel—primarily because he was going bankrupt. Gambling had just been outlawed in Brazil and his pockets were filled with income from games. By the end of the project, I'd lost nearly forty thousand dollars.

"Please tell me this isn't happening again," I said. "And Mrs. Young made mention of me doing a railcar for the C&O as well, also under the resort budget. I—" Lee clutched my hand.

"I'll get Mr. Young to tell his wife that you'd be happy to work on the railcar after the resort is finished. I know you're worried, but this is not Brazil, and so far the C&O has been a perfect client," he said. I wanted to trust him, to accept his words as truth, but he couldn't see the future. "They will uphold their end of the bargain. I'm sure of it. But, Dorothy, I can't keep pretending. Can you sit a moment?"

My mouth went dry. I followed him into a small room next to the entrance. He sat in a wingback chair, and I took the matching one beside.

"What is it?" I whispered. "Just say it."

He extracted his notebook from his briefcase and sighed. The moment he opened it, I knew. Red numbers riddled the page, interspersed with far fewer black ones.

"We have two more pay periods covered and nothing more. Rent for the office is not included in that. I thought we would have something come through. I thought we would be done by then, but, my dear, as marvelous as you are, as hard as you're working, we won't be finished in a month's time."

I swallowed hard and fisted my hands to keep from crying. I knew we were here, at this place, with my finances, but hearing it spoken so bluntly was difficult. I started thinking of Jean and Glenn and Leon and Ted and Betty and all of the people in my employ. I couldn't do this to them. I had to do something drastic.

"Call Cole Morrison. Have him list my apartment. People have been clamoring to buy it for years, and we'll get at least $150,000 for it."

Lee reached over and placed his hand on my leg. "We can't sell your home," he said softly.

"Yes, we can," I said. "And we will."

He nodded. "Very well," he said. "And where will you live? You know that we could—"

"In my office if I must," I said, stopping him before he suggested that we could marry, that his family's riches could save me from calamity.

He reached into his briefcase again and extracted two stacks of letters. He set them on his lap.

"I was waiting for the right time to discuss this with you, but now might be it." Lee sucked in a breath. "I mentioned before that other designers are taking on apprentices."

"Lee," I said. "My company is failing. When would I have occasion to train an apprentice?"

"Please hear me first," he said. "What I mean is that you could alter your business a bit. You would train designers in your way, for as long as you think it would take them to understand your vision. Then you would hire them out to do certain jobs under your name. You would create a dozen Dorothy Drapers. It would allow you to grow your business exponentially. You wouldn't have to be so selective with projects. You could take them all on and reap the benefits. You wouldn't have to do it all. You could relax. This company would thrive for centuries."

My skin prickled and I could feel my cheeks redden.

"And what would I do?" I snapped. "Become a figurehead? No one is Dorothy Draper but me. There could never be *one* more, let alone dozens. I am one of a kind, and no one can do what I do, save perhaps Leon, decades from now, after he's learned all he can from me. When I am old and decrepit, I will train someone up, I will choose my one successor with care, likely Leon, but that will be my choice. While I am living, I will be the only one in charge of my projects. I don't want to accept any opportunity that comes my way. It would cheapen my brand. We are not the five-and-dime of decorating, Lee."

"All of these people want to work with you." He patted the top of the letters as though he hadn't heard me. "I mentioned it to a friend at the Chicago Art Institute, and I suppose he thought we were definitely taking apprentices, because these letters started coming. Listen to this one." Lee opened the envelope of the first letter. "'I am obsessed with color, with the way it transports and transforms,'" he read.

I ripped the paper from his hand. I crumpled it up and dropped it on the ground. I was acting like a five-year-old, but I didn't care.

"You had the opportunity to be honest with me. I seemed miffed when I got the first of these letters, and you said you would take care of it. You should have told me right then that some imbecile had taken your careless, harebrained remarks as fact." I took a breath.

"I was afraid you'd react this way," Lee said. "I couldn't tell you because every time I try to help or have an idea—and this is a good one—you take offense to it. I only want to see this company last forever. I want to save it like you do. But right now, it's failing. I love you. I don't want you to fall, and I know if this company goes under, you'll go under with it. Please consider this. Please take care of yourself."

"Having an office full of other designers would be nearly as horrid as bankruptcy," I said. "I enjoy my work the way I do it."

"They would all answer to you," Lee said. "Think of it logically, DD. You would have help on projects like this."

I shook my head. My heart felt pierced through. How could he do this to me? I thought he knew me.

"Mrs. Draper, would you care to hurry?" Jean burst through the doors and proceeded to echo what Lee had already told me—that I needed to read the letter attached to the bricks before we could make any progress. My mind whirred. My company was a few weeks from bankruptcy, and Lee was out of his mind. Even so, this job wouldn't fail.

"Call Cole Morrison right now," I said, turning to Lee. "I want my apartment sold as swiftly and for as much money as possible. When we're paid at the end of this job, I'll buy another."

"Very well," Lee whispered. His hand brushed mine, but I pulled it away. "And I'll wire my friend at the art institute and tell him he misunderstood." He stood and hastened up the staircase and out of sight. I watched him for a moment and then resigned myself to forget everything he'd said. Regardless of the numbers,

I knew something for sure: if this project wasn't completed, and completed well, I would be finished.

"What do you think the note says, Jean?" I asked, forcing myself to smile. "Perhaps the Abercrombies had their silver encased in each block, or perhaps there is some stipulation for how they should be arranged to highlight the majesty of Southern clay."

Jean only laughed. I'd never told her, but outside of my lifelong friends, she was my best companion—warm, understanding, motivated. I know she didn't think of me that way. I was her boss, her work friend at best, but I was lucky to have her all the same.

"I'm betting that the note has something to do with the rumor going around that the bricks are from an old suitor of yours. Is that right?" she asked as we stepped outside.

It was a sunny day, cloudless but frigid nonetheless. I huddled in my mink coat, pulling the collar toward my chin. Jean didn't seem to mind the chill even though her gray wool dress was cut to the knees with butterfly sleeves. Jean had always been confident inside and out. I envied that.

"No," I said finally. "Not quite. Though we were briefly engaged."

Jean whirled on me, stopping me.

"I had no idea," she said. "When? Here? Were you in love?"

The questions were too personal, and ordinarily I would have refused to answer, but Warren had sent his estate's bricks and the least I could do was be honest.

"Here, a long time ago. And no, we weren't in love, though everyone wanted us to be."

"So Dan wasn't your father's first choice?" she asked.

I laughed. "Heavens, no. The Drapers are a respectable family, but Father wanted someone more like us, someone more apt to sparkle. Warren was certainly that sort or, I should say, his father was. All the old families of the Greenbrier were just like ours. It was nearly incest, the way we all married each other."

I could barely recall Warren's face. It was startling to realize, but I could only remember his smile and the smart manner of his dress and the way he made me feel at peace.

"He was, is still, I suppose, the quintessential gentleman. He's of old, old New York stock as well, migrated to South Carolina after the Civil War to rebuild the Southern rails. His family has come to the Greenbrier since Van Buren's presidency."

"I just can't imagine you living on a Southern estate." Jean laughed as we approached the crates of bricks all covered with a white tarp. On the far side of the tarp was a note, a small square of linen-colored paper.

"Of course I can't either," I said.

My name was on the front of the envelope. I hadn't seen his handwriting since the last season, but I would have known it anywhere. I opened the flap, aware that my hands were shaking.

Dearest Dorothy,

I thought I'd never see you again. Isn't it strange? When we left that September, I was sure it would be just like every other year. I felt certain we'd see each other in July and begin our silly charade all over again. But Father died, and your father remained in France on business too long to make it that next season, and Anzonella and Henry and Bolling and all the rest married and splintered off and we never returned.

Use these bricks wisely. They're all we have left of the

family estate, but I'm happy to give them to you and to the Greenbrier. A part of my heart is still there. It always will be.

I hope to see them, and you, under the wide blue sky with the birds singing and rhododendron blooming and star jasmine sweetening the air for the gay grand opening.

You've always been one to go beyond all expectation. The hotel will be beautiful. I'm proud to know you.

Your old friend,

Warren

I wiped the corners of my eyes. "You can have the bricks taken around now, and when Mr. Alexander arrives, set him to work," I said. Jean looked at me strangely and withdrew a handkerchief from her purse. "It's all right." I shooed the linen away, knowing that if I began to cry I wouldn't stop. "We're both alive and all is well. It's only that it's been years, and at one point in time, he was one of my greatest friends."

I wandered the halls alone. The dining room was shaping up to be lovely. The white Corinthian columns were stately, forming a perfect channel through the enormous room. The matching green and white blown-glass chandeliers situated down the center were spectacular. Soon the round-top tables would come, dressed in crisp white tablecloths, and the chairs would be slip-covered to match, with the rhododendron design embroidered on the back. Right before opening we would place palm fronds in large colorful urns. This room looked almost exactly like the old hotel's dining room—with my improvements, of course. Enzo and Warren would have a good laugh about that. That is, if they remembered the conversation we'd had the night Enzo arrived.

"Good day, Mrs. Draper!" A group of employees hustled past me toward the dining room carrying small paintings and mirrors and hammers and nails. I didn't have the slightest idea where they were heading or what they were doing, but I knew Jean had them occupied with my orders.

"It's a beautiful morning," I said. "Thank you for your work." I sighed. It was time for me to go. I didn't want to. I wanted to stay here until the opening, or possibly forever, but I couldn't. Lee was right about one thing: I needed more projects. We had inquiries from a few linen companies in England and a restaurant in New York and a museum, too, but as much as Leon tried in my stead, I needed to pop on a phone call or visit a site to win those contracts. I'd dreamed until my dream for the Greenbrier was perfect. My team knew what I wanted, and they would execute, as they did on every project. If I stayed, Dorothy Draper & Company would likely go bankrupt and the Greenbrier would never be finished. I would nitpick until I was convinced the whole vision should be scrapped.

Glenn was in the Hall of Presidents talking to Tony Cinquinni about an embellishment below the plaster bust of Jefferson.

"It's time for me to go home, Glenn," I said. The words came out in a sigh.

Beyond us, the windows in the north parlor displayed a cloudless blue sky and the gleam of sun on the lush green grass, obstructed only by the shadow of four-hundred-year-old trees on the lawn. It was easy to recall my father and Bolling's father and Anzonella's father and all the prominent men of the Greenbrier sitting under the largest one, and us girls sitting under another. I could still taste the bite of the fresh lemonade and smell the sweet cigar smoke floating over from the old men's gathering.

"I thought you would stay to the end for this one," Glenn said. I was surprised, actually, that no one had mentioned the length of my stay. Ordinarily I left a site right after I was done strategizing, letting my employees execute the design while I looked over sketches and dictated trappings from afar.

I could see compassion in his eyes and wondered why. He didn't know about my connection here. No one did, really, except perhaps Mr. Mosley.

"This isn't just a project for me," I said. "You know that with each project I aim for the heart. But this time the heart has been mine. So many people I loved were once here. Most of them won't see it. Some of them are gone. Regardless, I want them to be proud of what I've done. I want everyone who walks through the doors to be entranced, to understand how important this place is."

"You don't have to go," he said. Tony Cinquinni stood in the corner, pretending to survey Jefferson's bust. "This is your company, after all."

"I must," I said, though I was thankful that Glenn at least understood who was at the helm of this ship.

"Very well. We will make sure it's perfect," he said. "And I can tell you with honesty, DD, this place has already made an impact on me. Thank you for believing in me all of those years ago."

He said the last bit quietly. I patted his arm. After all this time, my staff had become my family.

"You are absolutely integral to this company, Glenn," I said. "It wouldn't be the same without you."

"The matchbooks are here!" Jean's singsong voice came from nowhere, and then she rounded the wall of elevators holding a matchbook over her head as though it were a Monet. She deposited the tiny square in my hand. The ruby was perfectly deep, and the rhododendron blossom popped against the background.

"Wonderful," I said, handing the matches to Glenn. "Look how lovely. From now on, I'll depend on you to ensure that the washcloths, towels, soaps are all to my specifications, along with the upholstery, of course. And, Jean, I need you to telegram Mr. Smith and tell him we'll need a spiral staircase in the presidential suite instead of the curved stair we planned."

Jean nodded, extracted her notebook from her bag, and scrawled my instructions into it.

"Telegram me when he confirms. I'm leaving in two days and there's a chance he won't be back to us before then."

"I'll say it again—you don't have to go," Glenn said.

"I know, but in truth, I do. Leon is swimming in inquiries for other projects, and though he does quite a job fielding them, Leon can't ask them to wait forever."

Glenn coughed. "Of course not. Not to mention, Leon's accent alone is enough to shock them."

I rolled my eyes. "Leon being Southern is actually quite a good thing. Southern gentility is very similar to British refinement. They don't rush, they don't push. They simply float the advice out there and hope it is taken."

Jean laughed and even Mr. Cinquinni chuckled.

"The opposite of the Dorothy Draper way," Jean said.

"Southern gentility combined with a little boldness could be very similar to my manner, actually," I argued. "And Leon's learning more and more about closing a deal, but until he's grasped it fully and integrated it with his want to be liked, he won't have realized his full potential."

"We'll hate to see you go, but we'll make you proud here," Jean said. Glenn looked down at the matchbox and ran his fingers across the design.

"I know you will," I said. "You always do."

Twenty-One

AUGUST 26, 1908

I ambled up the stairs to the lobby fisting two enormous bouquets of rhododendron, phlox, and Queen Anne's lace. We didn't need flowers. The staff had already set fresh sunflowers in our rooms, but wandering Lovers' Lane alone, I'd needed something to occupy my mind besides Enzo and Helen and Warren.

The lobby was quiet, thankfully. I started up the stairs to our suite and then turned around. Mother would be there and I didn't want to converse with anyone.

I nodded at Mr. Mosley and his father standing beside reception and walked toward the ballroom. I wondered if he'd had occasion to deliver my letter yet.

A crowd of maids were readying for the children's ball. They were gathered around buckets of pink and white roses, shoving them into tiny crystal vases much too small for a table display.

"We could make a dainty swag," one of the women said. "But I'm not sure we'll have enough roses to stretch it across the ballroom."

"What about rose wreaths for the girls?" I asked.

The women startled, all turning to face me at once.

"It's none of my business, really. It's only that little girls love to wear crowns of roses—at least I did when I was young."

The ball was about the children, after all. This wasn't the Hunt or the Century. It didn't need to be washed in romance, only elegance and a bit of fun.

"And the doorways can be flanked with big urns filled with ferns and wildflowers," I said.

I walked toward them, appraising my bouquets as I went. They would be just as lovely on display as roses. No one spoke. They all just stared at me.

"I'm sorry for meddling," I said, smiling, hoping to break the silence with friendliness. "Don't mind me."

I started to turn away but felt a little tap on my shoulder.

"Thank you." A young girl no older than I blushed and rubbed her fingers, bloodied from trimming the roses.

"Can I help you?" I asked, setting my bouquets down on the plain oak table next to the buckets of roses. "That is, if it's not too much of an imposition? I don't have much to do, and I'd love to help make this place special for the children. Not that you all don't already make everything gorgeous. My goodness, the Hunt Ball was magnificent."

"It's one of our favorite tasks," an elderly woman said, wiping her hands on her black apron. "But quite honestly, miss, we're missing six dozen roses. We'd planned on a screen of flowers, a fairy-tale tableau to go on either side of the stage, but that plan can't be."

"That sounds lovely," I said. "But I'm certain whatever you decide to do will be perfect. The children only want to dress up and dance and feel the magic of this place, after all."

The young girl stepped around me, appraising my heap of wildflowers.

"I think you might be on to something, miss," she said.

"Dorothy, please," I said.

"We have plenty of wire to assemble rose crowns," the elderly woman said, sidestepping five silent comrades to take her place beside the younger girl. "I imagine they *would* be thrilled by the prospect. It would be as if they were real princesses."

One of the women coughed. "They are," she said quietly, clapping her hand over her mouth the moment she realized she'd said it in front of me.

"I do imagine it's quite the same, except for the title of course," I said. "If you're all truly keen to do it, I'd love to help. I used to make my own crowns all the time when I was a child and bored at home. Most of my contemporaries were off at school when I was young, and . . ."

I stopped, realizing I was babbling.

"Please tell me what to do, Miss—" I looked from the young girl to the older woman.

"Ruth," the girl said.

"Beatriz," said the other.

"We'll need to trim them," Ruth said. She gestured to the buckets, all holding long stems.

I swept an armchair out from the table and sat down in front of the roses.

"I'll trim," I said, removing my gloves.

"But your hands," said Beatriz. "You'll not want to ruin them for dancing."

"Nonsense," I said. "If a man can't stand a few scabs, he'll not be able to handle me. I fear I'm pricklier than the roses."

The women laughed and settled in chairs around me, some grasping wire, some ribbon, some wildflowers.

"A prickly princess?" Ruth asked, her eyes twinkling. "I'm afraid I'll grow to love you."

Hours went by. I'd never felt so fulfilled. Before I knew it, dozens of finished crowns lined the end of the table.

"That's the tea bell," Beatriz said. "Do you need to go?" She looked at me and I shook my head.

"No. I can't say I'd enjoy the company, and—"

"You're in your element." A voice boomed across the room, the depth of it disturbing the tinkling of our chatter. I turned, watching Ruth's cheeks blush. He had that effect on everyone.

"I suppose I am," I said, sweeping a wisp of hair back from my face. He was standing in the middle of the ballroom alone, his linen jacket slung across one shoulder, his boots muddied from the Dry Creek Battlefield.

"I'm glad," he said. He wasn't happy with me. He didn't smile but tipped his head and kept on walking. "Good day, ladies."

"Good day, Mr. Rossi," they said in unison. Unless they'd been bluffing, no one had known *my* name, and I'd been coming for ten seasons.

They wanted to ask. I could feel their eyes as I clipped another rose, snipping the stem and then the thorns, but I didn't look up. I couldn't explain him and me, not to myself or to them. All I knew was that for the last few hours I hadn't thought of

Enzo or Warren or Helen. I'd felt purpose and joy instead of hopelessness and heartache.

Warren closed his eyes and rubbed his temples.

"What is it?" I asked.

"Today was awful," he muttered.

We were standing on the porch, watching the children process across the lawn, up the stairs, and through the lobby for their ball, dressed like their parents in tuxedos and glittering gowns. The girls would receive their crowns when they entered the ballroom, greeted otherwise by the Greenbrier's glorious wildflowers and the orchestra playing nursery tunes.

I could hear the notes of "Lavender's Blue" from here and hummed along.

I'd run into Warren by accident, retreating to the porch to avoid company after dinner, only to find him unaccompanied as well.

"The start of mine wasn't so lovely either," I said, not bothering to ask about his own misadventures. "But this afternoon I helped the maids decorate for the ball, and I have to say, it was the most heavenly experience."

"Perhaps I should have stayed back to help you," Warren said. "We were at Dry Creek, standing on the battlefield, having just listened to Mr. Gold's moving memorial to his grandfather's sacrifice for the Union army, when my father confronted Mr. Vacchelli. And then your father joined him and then Mr. Kane and then Mr. Phinizy and Mr. Bonaparte and the rest. They had been going round and round about the *Times* article, about what Italy plans to do if Austria-Hungary declares war. Everyone agreed that Italy must consider the response of the rest of the world, when Mr. Vacchelli asked about our alignment with England. It wasn't even an offensive question, but our fathers pounced on him. And then Mr. Taft took his side and Enzo as well, and I was left to mediate." Warren sighed. "It was awful. At one point I began to yell, but no one heard me. So I signaled a demonstrator to fire the cannon. It was the only way to stop them."

"I'm sorry," I said. I hadn't seen Enzo since he appeared in the ballroom. He hadn't seemed cheery then, but of course, there was no reason he should be, regardless of the happenings at Dry Creek. I wondered where he was, my mind immediately conjuring his most likely position—next to Helen, watching the children process in, her fingers perched on his tuxedoed arm.

Warren reached for my hand, but I pretended that I didn't notice and escaped his touch by fiddling with my hair pins.

"This season has been exhausting," he said. "As much as I love the Greenbrier, I can't wait to return home, to start planning our wedding and our future." I felt him edge closer but didn't turn to face him. We still hadn't kissed, and although he'd not likely sweep me into his arms in front of the hotel in broad daylight, I couldn't risk it. I didn't want to feel the press of his lips against mine, the tenderness without the passion.

"Warren, I—"

"Darlings, do come join us. You'll have plenty of time alone later."

Mother appeared on the porch, one hand gripping the open door to the lobby. I swallowed, half relieved at her interruption.

I'd almost been honest. I'd almost said it, that I didn't want to marry him, that he deserved better than my resignation. But now wasn't the time.

Warren sighed. "Very well."

He extended the crook of his arm to me and I took it. I edged closer as we neared the ballroom, hoping Enzo would see.

"They're dear, all the children," Mother said as we stepped inside.

Instead of searching for Enzo's gaze, I was struck by the simple loveliness of the room. The little girls looked like angels as they stepped alongside the boys, making the old Circassian Circle dance much more elegant than usual.

"Would you care for a lemonade, Miss Tuckerman?" Ruth appeared beside me, holding a tray of crystal goblets. I elbowed her lightly and swept a glass from the platter.

"I'm Dorothy to you," I said. "And look how lovely you've made this place."

The wildflower bouquets were wispy and whimsical, a magical backdrop to the children.

"This was all your imagining," she said, winking as she walked away. "The crowns are precious."

"You told me you helped, but you thought of all this?" Warren asked.

"I suppose I did. I wanted the children to have a good time," I said, holding my scabby fingers up for Warren to see. He grasped my hand, kissing the nicks.

"All better?" he asked. "Wear gloves next time. Your skin is too lovely to bear scars."

Mother laughed. "Dorothy's been making crowns since she

was a baby. Remember when we were building the second house? Mademoiselle lost sight of you and found you later making a wreath of poison ivy leaves."

"It's fortunate I wasn't very allergic. Only a small rash on my hands," I said.

"I want to say thank you, Abercrombie." Enzo appeared behind Warren's shoulder. Across the room, Helen was watching us, so I kept my eyes fixed on the children. "You were kind to attempt to thwart that unbecoming argument."

"It was nothing," Warren said.

"Dorothy, you look lovely this evening, as always," Enzo said. I'd never worn this gown before—a pale pink satin with a white mousseline tunic and sleeves embroidered with crystals and stones. I'd wanted to look softer this evening, less Amazonian and more fairy-like. I couldn't change my height, but the right colors could change everything. Something about my afternoon adventures had calmed me, given me purpose, and I wanted my dress to reflect that.

Enzo stepped around Warren and took my hand. His eyes met mine and I was startled to find a small piece of paper in my palm. He leaned into me, his body pressed against mine, just for a moment.

"Please," he whispered and then released me, leaving me to Warren and Mother and their questioning stares.

Twenty-Two

AUGUST 26, 1908

Meet me tonight.

That's all the note said. I unfolded the small piece of paper and looked at his writing again. I didn't know if I would go. If he had changed his mind, he would have said so, and I knew that whatever he wanted to say would only hurt me. Not only that, but he would kiss me. I'd let him.

I collapsed on my bed, wishing I were wearing my nightshirt instead of my ball gown. Everyone else had retired an hour ago. Mademoiselle had come to undress me, but I told her I would do it myself, that I was in the middle of writing a letter and wasn't ready yet. She looked at me as if she knew I was up to something but didn't argue. It would be a challenge to unhook all the tiny buttons down my back. Perhaps I'd simply sleep in my corset.

I twisted the engagement ring off my finger and laid it on the table beside me. What if tonight was the last night I'd ever have the chance to feel love? The thought startled me. What if I went through with marrying Warren? Or what if I never found another love like Enzo's?

Though I didn't know for sure, I assumed he'd be waiting by the springhouse. Unless he'd already tired of waiting for me. I stood, my heart hammering under my stays. He had to be there. He couldn't have left, not already.

I crept down the hall and out the door, making sure the latch didn't click. Frank Mosley and an older gentleman were in the lobby, busily dusting and polishing the tables.

"I'm afraid I've left my great-grandmother's hat pin on the lawn," I said, as though they cared where I was going.

"Do you need help?" Mr. Mosley asked, his hand stilling on a tabletop. "It's quite dark out there, miss."

"No," I said. "I know exactly where I left it."

His gaze lingered on mine as if he knew I lied. Perhaps another night I would have found any presumed knowledge disconcerting enough to turn back.

"I'm almost certain it will be there in the morning, ma'am," the other man said. "There aren't any thieves around here."

I laughed.

"I know that. It's only that I'll want it for my breakfast costume and don't want to send my poor mademoiselle down too early. Good night."

Before they could follow, I wandered out into the dark. I balled my hands into fists and breathed deep, trying to settle my nerves. What if he only wanted to tell me that he didn't love me anymore, that we had to stop this charade? It would only be right if he did. He was marrying Helen, after all, but the thought of us alone filled me with hope. I couldn't bear it if he wouldn't kiss me.

I turned from the drive onto the path to the springhouse, the rock giving way to dirt. I couldn't see him. The moon beamed through the columns, but I didn't see a figure. Perhaps he was behind one of the columns, or perhaps he'd abandoned hope that I'd meet him.

As I neared, I could hear the spring rushing beneath the well, the recent rain prompting the streams to overflow. I sighed and stepped beneath the dome, beneath Hebe perched above me. What I would give to stay young always, to have all the time in the world to find love. Instead, the years had sneaked up on me, rushing me, pushing me to concede my fate to convenience.

"I thought you wouldn't come." I whirled around to find Enzo lying on the bench behind me. He was cloaked in shadows, his hands cradling his head. He sat up and then stood.

"I—"

"Come here," he said, his voice low. I stepped toward him and he swept me into his arms. For a moment, sensibility crossed my mind, and then it was too late. His lips were on mine, soft and gentle. His body pressed against me, the strength of his arms, the smell of lavender and sweet jasmine rendering me helpless to resist him. I pulled him closer, my hands wrapping around his neck, his kiss deepening. Everything around us fell away—the cottages, the people, the hotel, Helen and Warren, and we were alone, the wild beauty of the Greenbrier our only companion. His kiss descended my neck and my breath caught, my body dissolving beneath his touch.

"Enzo," I whispered, but he only pulled me down on the

bench, down into the shadows where not even the moon could see us. He took my hands and pulled them to his chest, to the place where his heart drummed under my hand.

"Touch me, please," he said. He stopped kissing me and watched my hands instead, the way they drifted across his chest. How much I wanted to unbutton his shirt, to feel his warmth against me, but then his arms wrapped around me once more. His hands clasped my hips and his mouth found mine.

I gasped and closed my eyes as his lips found my ear. I wanted nothing more than to keep going, to let this fire of want flame wildly. But I knew he hadn't changed his mind. I hadn't changed mine.

"Enzo." I flattened my hand against his chest and sat up. His heartbeat was still there, skipping beneath my fingers.

"Please don't," he whispered. "Don't push me away. Not tonight."

Even in the darkness I could see his melancholy.

"I'll never push you away. Never. Leave Helen. Find a position. Wait for me."

He looked down. The hands that moments ago gripped my waist now lay in his lap. "I'm leaving tomorrow."

"What?" Surely I'd heard wrong.

"I'm leaving tomorrow," he repeated. "With the Tafts. I have to."

I recoiled, standing. "You don't have to," I said.

"You know that I do. Mr. Taft wants to introduce me to their family before the wedding and to everyone at my post before he goes out on campaign again."

He tried to take my hand, but I edged away.

"It's not fair, Enzo. If you cared for me at all, you should have left me alone. You should have stopped this after you made your decision," I said.

"*You* made this decision too," he said. It was the same argument, the same thing we'd gone back and forth about for nearly a month. "And you know well enough that I cannot stop myself from wanting you. You can't stop yourself either."

"We're never going to agree," I said, not bothering to address the truth of his last statement. Arguing wouldn't solve anything, and if tonight was our final time together, I couldn't bear to ruin it.

"I love you," he said. "I always will."

"I love you too," I whispered. "And I don't know that I'll ever love again."

He took my hand and squeezed.

"Tomorrow, when we leave, my heart will still be here. It will always be here. I'll remember this," he said, his thumb grazing my cheek, "and I'll remember that first time I saw you and the way you looked in the ballroom today. You looked so contented, so happy."

"For a moment, I'd forgotten about what's happening to us," I said. "The heartache was gone, dissolved into purpose."

"Perhaps purpose is the only way to move forward. I shall try it," he said. "And I don't know exactly what it is, Dorothy, but I can feel it. There's something inside of you meant for greatness. You're too beautiful, too passionate to lead an ordinary life, and you should thank God for that."

He saw something in me—what it was, I didn't know, but I allowed it to sink in, to make me feel valued and beautiful instead of peculiar.

"I know you'll live a life of influence," I said, touching his arm. "You'll affect everyone you meet. But always know I'm missing you. I'll miss you forever." Tears welled in my eyes, and I could see the same in his.

"You're my true love, *mio angelo*, my Dorothy," he said, pulling me against his chest. I remained for a moment, wishing I could stay forever.

"I don't think there's anything more to say," I said finally.

I cleared my throat, hoping to lift the weight of the moment, but nothing could.

"If I can figure another direction, I'll come for you," he said. "I'll find you."

He kissed me once more. I tried to hold on, to remember every movement of his lips, to remember the way he felt against me, and when he drew away, I sighed.

"I'm not going to marry Warren," I said. It was the first time I'd said it aloud and it felt good. "I won't be hard to find."

"Thank God," Enzo breathed.

"It's not of consequence anyway," I said, forcefully ignoring my anger to revel in this final moment.

"Oh, but it is," Enzo said. "Beyond my jealousy, beyond my own selfishness, if I could regard you rationally, Dorothy, you should never marry for anything but love."

"Neither should you," I whispered.

"I know." Enzo kissed my forehead. "I shouldn't. And yet I must."

I pulled away slightly, meeting his eyes.

"Don't. Please," I said. "Find another way and then find me."

He cupped my face in his hands, kissed me once more on the lips, and smiled.

"I'll try everything," he said. "And then I'll come looking for the house with the pink walls."

Twenty-Three

JANUARY 19, 1947

"I'll miss this," Lee said.

I was looking out the railcar window, listening to the train whistle blow for the third time. Our car had been moved from the visitor's track this morning and hooked to the first train to the city.

From here I could barely see the hotel, only a bit of white through the trees. It had been a melancholy morning. I knew my team was fully capable of finishing what I started, and yet it seemed wrong to leave.

"When I woke and didn't see you in your room, I thought perhaps you'd left without me," Lee said, startling my thoughts. He reached for my hand. His fingers drifted over my knuckles. As angry as I was with him as his boss, as his lover I knew that his heart was in the right place, that he only wanted to help.

"I needed to go for a walk. I know you don't understand, but I had to say farewell for now."

"You suppose I'm not enraptured with this place, but I am," he said. "We've been in a cloud of magic for months, and I'm sad to emerge from it."

"I am too," I said. I'd woken early and strolled down the lawn to the springhouse and then beyond, to the foot of the hills I used to walk as a girl. I daydreamed as I had then, about simply staying, leaving my responsibilities behind to live a life of freedom, but in that moment, I remembered I was no longer tethered to anything but the dream I'd concocted. I would never give up design. It was too much fun. I only worried I was on the brink of losing everything I'd worked for, worried that I wouldn't be able to pull my company out of trouble, and I absolutely wouldn't allow Lee or anyone else to bail me out. It wouldn't be fair to ask that of Lee anyway. I knew how he felt about me now—and how I felt in turn. It weighed on my spirit.

I turned to Lee abruptly, resigned to say what I'd decided this morning. I could see the cloud of steam from the smokestacks floating by in my periphery and thought about distracting myself again, but I couldn't.

"I have to let you go." The words came out in a whisper. He blinked at me, shocked, as though he hadn't heard correctly, but then he nodded.

"I understand. And it's a price I'll gladly pay for us. Let me find another job first, if you wouldn't mind. I know our being involved is inappropriate in the context of business, and I suppose I was naive to think we could keep it successfully hidden from the rest. Plus, I know you're not crazy about my ideas when it comes to the company."

I squeezed his hand. He wasn't making this easy. "I'm sure they already know, my dear. But that's not what I mean. I can't let this go on, you and me. You're still young. You deserve marriage, children, a happy life, a boss who values your loyalty and your innovative ideas. Some of that I simply can't give you, and the rest I don't want."

"Oh," he said. "I suppose I misunderstood. That's why you . . . that's why last night."

His eyes filled with tears, but he sniffed and focused out the window, blinking the moisture away and then clearing the rest with a swipe of his hand. He'd spoken of the possibilities of our return last night, insinuating that perhaps when my apartment sold, I could move in with him or we could find a home elsewhere, a home I knew he would love to be in Tuxedo Park. I'd kissed him instead of discussing it further, and then stopped things before I made a gesture of romance that would seem cruel now.

"I don't want to hurt you," I said.

The sentiments were an echo, and I was horrified at how often I'd been in this position since my divorce.

"You're the love of my life," he said. It was an impulsive declaration. "Who is the love of yours? Dan? Another lover? Or have you ever truly loved anyone?"

He withdrew his hand and stared at me. His misery had turned so quickly to anger. I recognized his emotion, the raw desperation to claw the heart from the one you loved and hold it forever. It was only bitterness and sensibility that made me doubt the truth of his love for me. Being at the Greenbrier had made it clear that the man I'd thought was the love of my life long before I was Lee's age still held me.

"I loved Dan. I love you. I didn't love the others. But when I was young, before Dan, I gave my heart away, and I'm afraid

I never fully got it back," I said. "I don't know why. Perhaps it was the mystery of him or the way he held me. Perhaps it was his confidence or the way he laughed when I was sure I was right."

"He was here, wasn't he?" Lee asked.

"Yes," I said. "It'll soon be forty years. I didn't even know him very long."

Lee's jaw pulsed as though he was about to rise from his seat, traipse back to the Greenbrier, and conjure Enzo.

I looked at my reflection in the window and fiddled with my hat to distract my attention from our conversation. It was one of my favorites, a bonnet cap with a halo brim boasting an Egyptian geometric pattern. I liked to imagine I looked like Cleopatra in it. I usually felt powerful when I wore it—this morning being an exception.

Lee sighed and shrugged, settling back against the tufted chintz cushion. I always liked the way he looked sitting down. He appeared folded, and one always knew that a man like that would tower when he stood.

"I suppose there's nothing I can do. I can't punch him. I can't shake your heart from his grasp and snatch it for my own."

I leaned over and placed a hand on his leg.

"I'll only pray that you're wrong, Lee. That I'm not truly the love of your life. Surely someone else will eclipse me—a beautiful young girl with ambition to match your own, someone who will thrill you and make you wonder how you ever could have entertained anyone else."

Lee laughed.

"You never got over him," he said. "What makes you suppose I'll resign my love for you?"

"He was my match. He was the only one who ever challenged

me, who ever dared to disagree with me and offend me, and yet made me want to be better. He was unconventional, not at all the sort my parents wanted me to settle for, and I think I loved him more for that."

Bella was getting out of the coach now, lugging my trunk. She would be glad to get home, to have all my affairs at her fingertips instead of strewn about a foreign cottage.

"And he was my age," I said. "He was the handsomest man I'd ever seen. Regardless of your feelings for me, you must admit you find women your own age more attractive."

"You're beautiful, Dorothy," he whispered, aware that Bella was right behind us, slowly boarding the car. "And if living amiably without a declaration before a pastor is the sort of relationship you want, I'll do it. If living in the shadow of another man is what I must do, I'll do it. If keeping my ideas to myself and working for free will allow me to be near you, I'll do it. I just can't bear to part from you."

I shook my head.

"I would welcome that if you were an older man with a wife gone or divorced, with half a life lived, but you're not. Please try for me. Please go out into the world and find love."

"Good morning, Mrs. Draper, Mr. Carter," Bella said, settling on the red velvet couch against the opposite window. "It will be good to be home."

"That it will," I said, stealing one more look at the hotel. As much as I dreaded leaving, it would feel good to be back in my office. It was the only way to win my company back from the clutches of peril.

"It seems I have no say in the matter," Lee whispered, undistracted by the turn in conversation.

"I'm sorry," I said.

The final whistle rang out. I heard the conductor yelling and the railmen shouting back, and then the wheels started rolling. Slowly at first, as though the train itself were as reluctant to go as I.

Twenty-Four

APRIL 3, 1948

New York winters were things to be survived, and I'd barely lasted this time. At each snow—and there'd been a lot of it—I'd threatened to board the train and go south, to poke my nose into the affairs of the resort, but every time Leon stopped me. "The opening day has been set. Surely you don't want to have to tell Mr. Young to push it back again."

He was right, of course. Mr. Young was an impatient man. Like me, he'd wanted the resort done faster, potentially in the fall of '47, and when that wasn't to be, he was uncharacteristically snide. I'd asked him, in that moment, if he wanted the Greenbrier to look like a Travelodge or the luxury resort it was.

My return to New York last year had brought me several new jobs—decorating Fefe's Monte Carlo nightclub, outfitting perfume packaging for Dorothy Gray, styling canvas awnings for Canvas Products of Missouri, among others—and though my apartment still hadn't sold, the fees were enough to allow me to take my time on the Greenbrier. This was fortunate, as it wasn't close to perfection by Mr. Young's planned opening season. There was no way our publicity man, Ben Sonnenberg, could spin a half-done resort into a masterpiece, even if he was the best. Mr. Young conceded, thankfully.

"White Sulphur Springs is the next stop, Mrs. Draper." An older man in a tailored C&O uniform breezed into my car. I tipped my head.

"Thank you."

Of course, I already knew where we were. There was a turn a half hour back, and from there the landscape changed from rocky peaks to rolling green hills. I'd memorized the way as a young girl and still felt the anticipation of imminent arrival at the Greenbrier.

"Will we be staying at Hawley House again?" Bella asked. I felt sorry for Bella. It had been difficult readying for the trip this time, and I had been in a mood. I always was before an opening.

"Yes," I said, taking a sip of my tea, now cold from sitting on the white lacquered antique table in front of me. I could feel the flutters, the nerves building. It wasn't only because I hoped the hotel was perfect. This time, I would step off the train only a few days before the opening, a few days before the critical eyes of everyone who was anyone—at least the famous sort who thrived on attention—landed on my work. As uncouth as my father had thought fame, I suppose I was dependent upon it. I needed praise.

The world out the window slowed. The new kelly-green leaves dipped and swayed in the breeze, the forest screening outsiders from the retreat. A few wild Bradford pears dappled the green, their sprays of white blossoms a reminder of the not-too-distant winter. Over a year had passed and I still missed Lee. It hadn't come easy to leave him. But just yesterday I'd seen him in the society pages on the arm of a banker's daughter. The girl was of some relation to the Prices. It had hurt at first, but then I'd noticed his smile. He wasn't faking. He was happy.

"We're here!" Bella seemed to sing the words. She was just as opposed to being cooped up as I was, and here, without the city concrete stamping out every bit of wild, we could breathe again.

The train came to a halt with the screech of the brakes and the wail of the whistle. I gasped. Sitting atop the perfect 1899 Studebaker carriage was a man wearing my driver's uniform. Glenn had written to say the employees were willing to wear them, that they actually preferred them to the drab beige they'd been wearing. They'd made a wise choice. The young man's tailored kelly-green jacket and pants were lined with cords of bright white. He looked like a picture. It all did.

I stood and breezed off the train before anyone could help me. I took a breath and found the air sweet. When I was young I heard Mother ask one of the bellmen what caused the mountain perfume. He'd shrugged and said he supposed it was only the phlox and wild roses and mint and honeysuckle. How easily country folk took it for granted. Back home, it was only the stink of exhaust and the slight tinge of garbage rotting somewhere.

"You look very smart, young man," I said.

I tipped back my wide-brimmed straw hat, outfitted with a large pink rose fascinator, to meet his eyes. Eye contact made people feel important, and he certainly was.

"You're the first impression the guests will have of the Greenbrier, and they will be blown away."

His cheeks blushed beneath his cap and he smiled. "Thank you, Mrs. Draper," he said. "If you think I look smart, you should see the hotel."

I unsnapped my envelope bag, extracted a crisp five-dollar bill, and handed it to him. His eyes widened. It was a lot of money, more than I should spend on a tip, really. I thought of the ten fives in my bag and my new business manager's stern warning. *"You could not have wrapped this project at a better time, Mrs. Draper. We could only keep it steady for the next four months without the last payment you're due from the C&O. Please, I beg you. Until you receive the check, keep spending to a minimum. Even your own. I'm factoring in your personal funds here too."* Mr. Weatherly was a retired partner from Ernst & Ernst who didn't bother to soften his concern for my company's welfare as Lee had. Mr. Weatherly's comments had kept me up many nights, but at least he hadn't advised me to eliminate any of my dear staff or started to prepare chapter 7 paperwork.

"Your coach awaits, Mrs. Draper." Another young man appeared, swiftly flicking the gold handle to open the door. The French goatskin interior had been treated, and the white leather looked nearly new. I decided to forget about the state of my pocketbook. What could I do about it anyway besides wait for Mr. Young to hand me the check?

"How lovely," I said. Bella's hand gripped mine and tightened. She only reached for people when her awe was completely beyond expression, and the only thing she could do to keep from squealing was to squeeze someone's hand.

I cranked the carriage window down, despite the slight nip in the air, and situated my skirt over my legs. Eleanor had surprised me by gifting me fourteen new dresses just for the occasion of the opening, each one a signature Dior. This one was quite young for me—a petrol-blue polka-dot two-piece with a razor-edge collar—and although at times I felt silly wearing something so girlish, it made me happy, and for that, feeling silly was worth it. Especially when the only people greeting me at the hotel were my employees. But in only two days—ten days before the duke and duchess and Bing and the Du Ponts and the Vanderbilts and the Kennedys would arrive—Mr. Young and a cadre of the C&O's business customers would arrive for an early tour, and I'd have to put the polka dots away and transform into the esteemed Dorothy Draper.

The coach rocked along the drive, past the small white gatehouse. I was holding my breath. If it wasn't perfect, if Glenn and Jean had deceived me, I would either scream or faint. The cottages came into view first—South Carolina row to our right—and then, straight ahead, the Greenbrier stole the show. The Bradford pears were in full bloom, and beneath them lay a blanket of pink tulips with flawless green stems. A brick path here in the front, made of Warren's bricks left over from the north entrance's boxwood garden, edged the natural beauty. Would I see him? I'd forgotten that he'd been invited too. I caught my reflection in the gilded trim. Would he still recognize his oldest friend? Would he still think me beautiful? I shook my head and nearly laughed out loud. What did it matter? My greatest hope was that this resort, my masterpiece, would outshine everyone. Even the Duke and Duchess of Windsor.

"Stop!" I yelled, and the driver yanked the reins. Just there, on the side of the hotel, were brown hoses. They stood out like a mud smudge on a Charles Frederick Worth ensemble.

"Is everything all right, Mrs. Draper?" The coachman hastened to my door. I shook my head and pointed.

"Those hoses. They're brown," I said as if he'd transformed into Ted, the man who'd failed to order the right color. At once my elation faded. If they couldn't get the hoses right, what else had they missed? "They must be green."

"Very well," he said. "Just a few more moments and your team will greet you. I'm certain they'll accommodate your request." I couldn't help but smile. His manners were impeccable, a perfect hotel man.

The coach continued and then stopped under the portico. The sun swept in through the four wide arches, and the moment the toe of my Naturalizer hit the drive, Glenn was by my side.

"A mint julep?" He extended a glass tumbler to me. Generous sprigs of mint protruded from the glass. I thought to refuse it but then complied, taking a sip to calm my nerves. "The barkeep told me the drink was invented here. Why didn't you mention it?"

I shrugged. I hadn't any clue. Then again, I'd never gone down to the barroom as a young woman except for once.

"The hoses are brown," I said.

"I know," Glenn said. "The green hoses are in on the two o'clock. Ted sent a wire this morning. We've made you proud, DD. I promise."

He extended his arm and I took it. Jean was waiting around the side of the coach. She was weary. They both were. I could see the bags under Jean's eyes and the way Glenn's shoulders slumped just slightly, but both wore smiles. This was the greeting made when they knew all was perfect, and it settled me.

The Greenbrier had been transformed. It was lovelier than the Plaza and the Breakers and the Drake. For the first time all afternoon, I was alone. The sunshine shone through the skylights and then through the billowy white linen canopy over the pool. The large palms and the white wicker furniture along the wide deck, the pink rhododendron blooms in large white vases, the shell walls, the brass and crystal chandeliers—it was perfect.

I could imagine the praise already. I could hear the gasps and the excited chatter—even from the same set that often enjoyed smudging my name. *Life* and the *Times* and the *Tribune* were all going to be here. They'd do features on the party, but the focus would be on my designs. I just knew it.

"It's remarkable, Mrs. Draper." Mr. Mosley emerged through the glass doors from the shops. The soda counter was already up and running, serving delicious sandwiches on my casual plates made specifically for the occasion. "The moment you walk into this hotel, you know it's a Draper design. It's unmistakable and lovely. I've only seen one other designer make a recognizable brand of his work, and that's Frank Lloyd Wright."

"Thank you," I said. "It's exactly how I envisioned it."

"Wonderful. Well, here we go. Let's take a look at the suite for your final approval," he whispered, looking around to make sure no one was about.

I started to follow him toward the linen closet and into the secret suite but stopped.

"Mr. Mosley. This is a bit unrelated, but perhaps you would know who to take this up with—there's an unsightly green slime on the springhouse. I walked the grounds a few hours ago and caught sight of it." That was the only thing I could think to complain about besides the brown hoses. I was supremely impressed.

"I'll take it up with Tuohy," Mr. Mosley said. "One of the men can scrub it tomorrow."

He pushed the rack up and the door clicked open.

"Of course, I wanted to make sure the suite is still to your liking, Mrs. Draper, but there's another reason I brought you here."

The door closed behind me and I felt trapped. I quickly glanced around, thankful that my opinion hadn't changed. The bishop-sleeve draperies, the white tile, the wide red, white, and blue upholstery, the massive antique table, and the gilded frame boasting the old map of the Greenbrier all still sang of patriotism.

"What is that?" I asked. I hoped the matter wasn't about money.

"I found something," he said, disappearing into the office. "We were going through one last time, making sure your designs in the cottages were done correctly, when I saw these in a closet full of his things at Bridgers' old place in Paradise Row. I know it'll touch you to have them again after all these years."

I circled the table and stepped into the office, my heart pounding. Enzo had stayed in that exact cottage during our final season. Of course, Mr. Mosley had known more about us than most, though he was always discreet.

"What is it?"

I hoped he wouldn't see my flushed cheeks in the dim room. His back was to me as he appraised the vacant wall behind the desk.

"They're not here," he said, only slightly turning. "I told Tom to put them in the desk so they wouldn't get lost in the fever of tidying for the opening."

"What are you looking for?" I asked again.

"I'm afraid I can't simply tell you. It has to be a surprise," he said.

"I've never enjoyed surprises."

"Even so." He faced me, his eyes lingering on the dried rhododendron blossom arranged beneath the Hebe lamp.

"At least tell me whose items I'm receiving," I said. "You said they belonged to someone."

"Yes," he said. "They were his." He gestured to the desk. "He lived in that cottage during his employ."

I sighed. "I see that this man, whoever he was, meant quite a lot to you and to others. But what I don't understand is why he would have been in possession of something that meant anything to me. I don't intend to be unkind."

He shook his head and laughed under his breath.

"You're not," he said. "When the old hotel was demolished, we were allowed to take some things we found as our own."

"Oh. I see."

Mr. Mosley was looking at me, his mouth opening and shutting as though he wanted to say something but wasn't sure he should.

"Have you ever made a promise and regretted it later?" he asked.

"Yes." I laughed. "Well, not really. I was thinking of my marriage vows just now and I suppose I was always willing to stand by Dan forever. I wasn't the one who left. But we did have the children and—"

"That's not the sort of promise I'm talking about. I agreed to keep quiet for a friend, and now I don't know that that's the best course," he said.

"Are you in danger?" I touched Mr. Mosley's arm, concerned.

His face brightened at that and he shook his head. "No. No, of course not. It's only that I wonder if his secrecy was wise."

"I don't think we should ever reveal a secret that isn't ours unless it's a matter of life and death," I said.

He nodded and flipped the lamp off. "Thank you," he said. "I suppose you're right."

Twenty-Five

AUGUST 27, 1908

I watched them go away with the rest, disappearing up the drive to the station where the Tafts' car was being hitched to the train. The crowd on the porch fell silent. The small American flags stopped waving, the well-wishers stopped hollering, and my father and his friends finished their out-of-tune rendition of "Hail to the Chief."

I'd kept my gaze on Enzo as they readied the coach. He'd looked at me several times, forcing a smile, his eyes blurred with melancholy. I wondered when I'd see him again. It wasn't a matter of if. We were too close now, too connected to the same set to think this time was the last. We were both stuck, though perhaps to him this was freedom.

"Well, there's still fun to be had." Warren appeared beside me, setting one of the American flags on the white railing. "I'm meeting the boys for tennis, but after could we take a walk?"

I didn't look at him. Instead, I kept my eyes trained on the drive. There was a chance, after all. A small one, but still. He could come back to me. He could come to his senses and abandon the train.

The sky was pure blue today, the sun shining uninhibited on the trees that cast the loveliest dappled shadows on the lawn. Days like these could be miraculous.

"Dorothy," Warren said gently. I saw his hand out of the corner of my eye, watched as it reached for my fingers gripped to the rail. He tried to pry me away, to take my hand, but I only clung tighter to the wood. "He's not coming back."

I finally let go and drew a breath. It filled my lungs, the sweetness of the Greenbrier restoring my strength as I turned to face him.

"I'll always love you," I whispered. "You're one of my greatest friends, but I'm not going to marry you, Warren. I can't." I pulled the ring from my finger and watched shock strike his face as I pressed it into his palm. It pained me and I walked away, pushing through the crowd toward the lobby. I couldn't bear to hear his response. I couldn't answer his questions or listen to him make his case. It wasn't fair. I was being cruel, I knew that, but there was no other way. Later, he'd ask and I'd answer. Later, I'd have the strength to argue with my father. But now, with a lover gone and an engagement severed, I wanted to be alone.

"Miss Tuckerman." Mr. Mosley stopped me as I walked into the lobby. "How do you do?" He extended his hand and I shook it, feeling the hard edges of a letter being tucked into my palm. Tears blurred my eyes. "I'm sorry you're so sad. I followed you out last night to make sure you were safe, and I saw," he whispered. "I didn't intend to spy, but I saw. Forgive me." Ordinarily, I would have been beside myself to realize we'd been found out, but I suppose I didn't have the energy now. I nodded.

"It's quite all right. It's over now," I said and turned away, starting up the stairs to my room.

The hall was quiet, and I stopped in front of the doorway. I knew if I entered, I'd find my brother and Mademoiselle, and I didn't want to converse with them either. I opened my hand and blinked at the envelope, at the roses and rhododendrons sketched across the whole of it. He'd done this last night. He hadn't been able to sleep either. I ran my fingers across the pencil lines, imagining his face gripped in concentration as he drew. I opened the seal. My hands shook as the letter came free of the envelope.

You were right all along. I am a selfish man. I'll break my own heart today. It will shatter the moment the train lurches from this place, the moment I leave you. I'm inclined to hope, so through all of this I've told myself I'll see you again. But in what capacity? We love each other. From the time of the ancients, love has been proclaimed as the most glorious, and yet I've turned away from it. Perhaps something is wrong with me. If I can, I'll come for you, but what if I can't? You'll forget me. You'll fall in love with someone else. You'll be happy without me. That is how it should go. I'm tortured by that thought, but I have given you up. I have abandoned love for security. I have abandoned love for money. I have abandoned love for a vocation. I don't know if it will make me whole. I imagine it won't. But if I shut off the light of love, if I let that cavern fill with ambition, I might be happy. At the very least, I'll be free.

I didn't read the rest. Tears dripped down my face and I didn't bother to wipe them away as I folded the note and put it back in the envelope.

Freedom? I stepped into our suite, acutely feeling the magnitude of expectation and manners and love. He said he'd be free, but I was beginning to believe there was no such thing as freedom. He would never be free. I would never be free. But perhaps, in spite of ourselves, we could both be happy.

Twenty-Six

APRIL 15, 1948

I paced in front of the windows. The sun wasn't up yet, but the moonglow was still bright enough to leave a trail of light on the polished wood floor. I wanted a cup of coffee. I needed the jolt to transform the unease into excitement but didn't dare wake Bella for something so trivial. I also wanted Lee, the comfort of a man's love.

Out of the corner of my eye, I saw the enormous bouquet of pink roses in a crystal vase on the tea table, a gift from Lee. The children—Diana, George, and Penny—and Mother had sent flowers, too, tulips and peonies, and Leon as well, a menagerie of spring blooms. Hawley House smelled like heaven.

I thought to go to Lee's bouquet and read the card again. He wished me well, it said. He knew everyone would be awe-struck. At once I thought perhaps I should have married him. I did love him. But that would have been selfish. I'd let him go and he'd found someone quickly. And when this was all over, if all proclaimed my work genius—Sam Snead and Judy Garland and my New York contemporaries, and the Floyds and the Du Ponts from the South who had only seen my designs on a smaller scale—I would realize that my need for a man was a passing want, a need to be told I was wonderful. All the men after Dan had been boosts for my confidence, after all, lovers who flocked to my every whim. Even Dan, when we were first married, was doting. There had only ever been one exception to that rule.

"What do you think?" I whispered, as though Enzo could hear me wherever he was. I could almost hear him laughing. I thought that was exactly how he'd react to my designs. Even in my imagination, I didn't mind it. He would only laugh because he'd known who I was long before the rest. I was the queen of any castle I occupied, I played by no one's rules, and I despised beige.

I pulled my blush silk robe over my chest and stepped into the stream of moonlight, closing my eyes. With the light behind my lids, I could envision daybreak. The first train, the eight o'clock, would stop at the station. The train men would unload the trunks and then the Duke and Duchess of Windsor. I wondered if the duke would be so shocked he'd say something uncouth. That was my greatest worry. He was used to all those drab English manors, after all. But then again, he'd renounced his throne. He was a bit of a renegade himself. I was counting on that. After this, I would be forever pegged as a genius or as silly.

"Mrs. Draper? I thought that was you."

I startled and turned around to find Bella yawning, her shadowed figure emerging into light as she cleared the hall from Lee's former bedroom.

"I can't sleep," I said.

"It's a big day for you," she said, heading for the kitchen.

"Curls and the yellow feathered hat for today? I was thinking a pompadour for tonight."

"Yes. That'll do. For today, the kelly-green Dior lampshade dress, the one with the dog-leash belt, and the navy crepe for tonight." I said it so casually, like I'd only chosen the ensemble today.

"Of course. I pressed both last night and will do it again this morning."

I could hear her jamming together the metal percolator pieces. She needed a jolt as much as I did. I wondered if Jean was up yet. I'd asked her—ordered her, really—to be at the entrance the moment the duke and duchess arrived. They were on the same train as the Youngs and their closest friends: Prince and Princess Hohenlohe, Lady Hartington, the Kennedys, the Dukes, Bing Crosby, and William Hearst. It wouldn't do for me to greet them. I wasn't a bellman, and I didn't want to hear words of praise if they weren't authentic. No one would know who Jean was, and she was a lithe, unobtrusive presence. She could wander in the periphery unnoticed and report back to me.

"Here." Bella set two china coffee cups and saucers on the dining table and beckoned me to sit. I complied, appraising the cup as I lifted it to my lips. It was a fine piece, kelly green on the outside and white on the inside. The rhododendron blossom was lovely and crisp against the white.

The coffee was strong. So strong I would have liked to cut it with a bit of cream. The sun was coming up now. You had to really look to see it, but the edge of the mountains boasted a sliver of gold-pink. As if on cue, the grandfather clock in the living room tolled the Westminster chime.

"Now," Bella said, "Leon sent a wire down yesterday and wanted me to remind you that you have *Life* at noon in the main lobby, followed by the *Times* at two thirty in the dining room. The staff will serve tea." She rose to retrieve another cup.

"Thank you," I said. "What would we do without Leon?"

"Mrs. Draper," Bella started, pausing in the doorway. Then she shook her head and flipped her hand at me as though she'd misspoken, disappearing into the kitchen.

"What is it?"

"It's only . . . do you want to write Mr. Carter a note? For the flowers?" she called.

"Oh." Bella was my maid, but at times she also handled my thank-yous and my social correspondence. "Perhaps you should do it this time. Simply say that I think they're lovely and I wish him all the best." A personal note from me seemed too much.

"Don't you miss him?" Bella asked, setting her full cup down. She was always such a romantic. Affairs did that to people, and she'd been having an affair with a married man for going on eight years. To my knowledge, she'd never had a real, honest-to-goodness relationship, and the longings and heartaches were all she'd ever known.

"Sometimes," I said. "But it was time."

"And if he was your true love?"

I let the question diffuse in the room.

"I know you hardly have time," Bella said hastily, trying to cover up the deeply personal question. "The magnitude of your work wouldn't allow it, I'm sure." She gestured in the direction of the Greenbrier and then took a small sip of coffee. "I apologize for overstepping."

"You're right, Bella. I'm desperately in love with my work," I said simply. It was the truth. In my adult life, it had been the only thing that gave me the same sort of rush, the only thing that stood to challenge me. And now, given the choice of true romance or design, I was apt to choose the latter.

"Forgive me for saying so, Mrs. Draper, but you should have both," Bella said.

"Perhaps most people should," I said. "But if society's whispers are even a bit true, I'm no good as a wife. The mark I'll leave on the world is the mark of color. I love design and it loves me back."

"It certainly does, but if I could be so bold, I think you're wrong about your marriage. You were a decent wife, but he wasn't good to you," she said.

I took a breath, feeling calm wash over me. Hardly anyone affirmed me this way.

"Let's get dressed," Bella said when I didn't respond. "It's nearly time."

"Dorothy!"

Jean was shouting. The front door struck the wall with a bang that shook the cottage. I stood quickly. I glanced at the letter I was pretending to write and said a quick prayer that the news was good. Jean never addressed me by my first name.

"Yes?" I met her in the sitting room, and as she grasped my hand, I noticed she was shaking.

"It's all they're talking about. You should have heard them, DD. The moment they walked in, they were stunned. Bing immediately said something like, 'One certainly can't be dreary in here,' and started whistling a tune. Everyone else simply stopped talking and moseyed about the lobby, wide-eyed. After receiving his coffee from Mrs. Oliver in her lovely lace costume, Mr.

Hearst removed a pad of paper from his bag and began taking notes. Mr. Hearst himself! Can you imagine? I could tell this pleased the Youngs immensely. They kept squeezing each other's hands and giggling." Jean took a breath and I followed, noticing the tension in my shoulders fading, giving way to confidence. "And the duchess practically fainted when she saw her quarters—I went up with the maids, she likely thought I was one. She went on and on about her room, how she knew you'd done it just for her. 'Well, this is a departure,' she said, 'and I know dear Dorothy's done this just for me. She understands, David. I told you she did. She's one of us.' That's exactly how she put it."

"I'm thrilled," I said. "So long as she tells that to everyone. As much as I've thought the fuss over Wallis silly, she does have the power to influence, and I'm happy she's impressed."

"There's quite a bit of hubbub up there," Jean said, gesturing to the hotel. "I know there's a group heading off to ride the mountain on horseback in an hour or so, and then some of the men are going to the links. Oh, and I heard there's a dance clinic being offered this afternoon, right before your lecture."

"It's a wonder people even notice the decor," I said. It was a shame, really. I'd envisioned people wandering the halls in awe, taking in every detail I'd worked so hard to dream up. But I had thought the same with all my projects, and beyond a few people particularly interested in design, my work was only a merry backdrop to their fun.

Jean laughed. "Perhaps they'd wander through an Albert Hadley or Jean-Michel Frank or Elsie de Wolfe without thought, but a Dorothy Draper? No. That's not possible. Didn't you hear me when I said your designs were the first thing they noticed?"

I grinned. "I pay you well, Jean," I said.

"Ms. de Wolfe might pay better," she said. "But I believe in *your* work. Just watch. Your designs will be remembered."

I stood behind the podium in the trellis lobby, perfectly calm. Jean was right, I told myself, needing the confidence. I was more heralded than any of the designers before me and any who would follow. The room was packed with reporters and photographers and a smattering of guests jammed among them. I wondered if the room would be as crowded if President Truman himself were here. I'd been at conferences where a room this size was only modestly full for Frank Roosevelt.

"Are you ready?" Mr. Young whispered. I took a step away from him—he was too short to be photographed next to me—and nodded.

"Of course."

I'd already given this talk once before, earlier in the week, to the small group of C&O investors Mr. Young was keen to woo, and they simply nodded and smiled at me. Of course, they hadn't known a thing about decorating. These people—the crews from *Harper's* and *Time* and the *Chicago Tribune* and *Vogue* and *Town & Country*—knew fashion and design. They would have questions. The idea excited me. My publicist, Ben Sonnenberg, always told me to make it sensational, to say something shocking during these press events. As if it wasn't my natural inclination to say what I wanted, instead of what I should.

Mr. Young took the microphone. "Ladies and gentlemen of the press, Mrs. Draper has spent the last year and a half here at the Greenbrier, and her attention to detail is obvious. She has transformed a hospital back into the glamorous social mecca the Greenbrier has always been since the days of Henry Clay. So, without further ado, here she is, the inimitable Mrs. Dorothy Draper."

I tipped my head at Mr. Young as the room erupted with applause and hoped he'd sit down rather than linger next to me. Thankfully, he quickly took a seat flanking the fireplace behind me. Seated, one could only guess at his height compared to mine.

"Thank you all for coming to celebrate the opening of this special little place," I began. "Some of you may not know that the Greenbrier isn't simply a project to me, it's a home. I was raised on summers here. Every summer but one, we stayed in the Colonnade cottage up the hill just there." I gestured to my right. "Back then, this Greenbrier hotel didn't exist. Only the cottages and the old hotel, a rather plain sort of structure. It was here, during my summers, that I came to know the spirit of the place."

I took a breath and focused on what I wanted to say.

"When I was asked to decorate, I knew immediately that the theme would be that spirit—romance and rhododendron."

I remembered my vivid dream that first night in Hawley House, how clearly I'd seen Enzo and recalled the beauty of the roses and rhododendron on the envelopes of his letters. I swallowed the memory and continued.

"But unlike others, I don't decorate safely or to command a sense of importance with the most expensive trimmings." There were a few laughs at that. "I decorate for feeling. There was a time, long ago, when I sat in the dining room of the old Greenbrier hotel and felt positively strangled by tradition. The spirit didn't match the decoration. Everything felt old and formal, the trappings done the way they were just because that's the way they'd always been. It felt dusty and stale, and the Greenbrier is not dusty and stale. These West Virginia hills are beautiful and wild, a place far removed from the constraints of city social schedules and presumptions. The Greenbrier is a place for rejuvenation, reinvention, and romance."

I grasped the small crystal glass of water on the podium and took a small drink, very aware of the photographer's bulbs blinking just as I did.

"Every room here is different. Not one guest room is the same. When I first arrived, I admit I was shocked by the clinical feel of the place. This lobby was one gargantuan room from the main entrance to the north entrance. In all honesty, the easiest thing to do would've been to put in a bowling alley and call it a day."

Someone cackled.

"And though, perhaps, the openness was required for a crush of stretchers and wheelchairs and emergency beds, it stifled the intimacy. I wanted to create nooks here and there, little places where one could find comfort regardless of her mood."

A hand shot up. It was one of the *Hearst* columnists. I recognized his round wire glasses and handlebar mustache. Didn't he know it was rude to interrupt? Didn't he know there was a designated time for questions? I pursed my lips and stopped to tip my head at him.

"Yes?"

"Is it true that that mantel behind you is a 1700s colonial piece that you embellished and painted *white*?"

I laughed out loud and then thought of Ben Sonnenberg.

"It's an 1801. Old wood is simply old wood, and I liked the ornament of it."

Some laughed, some scowled. It was perfect.

"One of your employees procured the piece from one of the

area's oldest homes," the old columnist jockeyed. "Isn't anything sacred?"

I looked him square in the eye. My statement would make a bigger impact that way.

"Whose home would that be?" I asked. "I certainly don't know the family's name. Did they do a lick of good for the people of West Virginia? Were they honorable or a complete disgrace? It makes a difference. If a piece comes from a place of no importance—I'm including personal importance here—then there's no reason to preserve it."

"Yet you write with pride at the desk of your great-great-grandfather," someone said from the back of the room.

"I do. Oliver Wolcott was a signer of the Declaration of Independence. Regardless, it's a piece important to me and to my heritage, so it will remain as it was. Furthermore, if an antique is simply functional as it is, and if it works with my scheme, I won't alter it."

"She reworked an old antique table the army used for food service in the north lobby," Mr. Young said behind me. "She kept the mahogany and simply added a marble top. It's lovely." I didn't turn but could sense the tension in his voice. Though my design had been well heralded by his friends, if the press didn't appreciate it, the rest of the country would think the Greenbrier was a flop, that he'd failed.

"I, for one, am in awe of your genius, Mrs. Draper." A man with a thinning gray hairline and a smart blue suit smiled at me. His cheeks reddened when our eyes met, and I was glad for it. This was something I could use. I could finally get back to what I wanted to say.

"My thanks, sir. I grew up between Tuxedo Park and New

York City—our family had homes in both places—and at a young age I began to realize something: people are more cheerful when the room is cheerful. People are more comfortable when they're not worried about knocking over fifteenth-century Chinese urns and smudging antique upholstery. There's a way to make something beautifully classy while still encouraging comfort and function and fun. That was my goal here at the Greenbrier, and I hope you will all settle in, that you'll make a home here. I'm certain that after you've breathed the mountain air and wandered the bright halls and had your fun out of doors and danced until your feet give out, you'll love this place as much as I do."

"You forgot to mention the bricks."

I noticed a door shutting at the back of the room, and the source of the voice appeared as the other reporters stood aside for me to address him. My breath caught, and when I could finally breathe again, I smiled. Warren looked just the same—older, but I would have recognized him anywhere. His hair still had the look of blond, though it was mostly white. He'd remained trim, without the bit of flab above his belt like most men his age, and his beige linen suit was flatteringly fitted.

"Yes," I said, hoping no one else could detect my voice shaking. "So that no one dare accuse me of ruining all antique sentiment, the bricks for the lovely brick walk are from an old South Carolina estate, owned by the Abercrombies, a longtime family of the Greenbrier. I hope that when you walk along, you'll remember that you're walking on history."

"Just a comment, Mrs. Draper." A woman, the only one in the room, raised her hand. "The moment I stepped off the train, I thought I was in a motion picture. In fact, I still think I might be. Every detail from the antique carriage to the smart uniforms to the beautiful room designs to the crimson hand towels to the ceremony of so many important people gathered in one place . . . it's all perfect."

"Thank you," I said. I couldn't seem to think of any other sentiments. Warren's presence had shaken my focus. "Generally my mantra is that if it looks right, it's right. That's served me well for twenty years."

I felt Mr. Young beside me and again stepped away.

"This concludes the press conference, folks. Off with you to enjoy the day. Tea will be served at four in the upper lobby."

He turned to me. "Dorothy, this is absolutely lovely," Mr. Young said. "I knew you were the right fit." He shook my hand, and when he did, I felt a small square of folded paper. I wrapped my hand around the check and held it tight, feeling, silly as it was, that I could jump for joy. One hundred thousand dollars, the rest of my fee. The company was safe; we were all going to be okay.

"It was truly my pleasure," I said.

Some of the press began to congregate at my side, eager for more answers, but I simply turned the other way. I'd said all I wanted. Now it was their turn to record the thrill of the guests. It was one thing for the designer herself to laud her work, but it meant so much more when the likes of Bing gushed.

"Twenty years? Only twenty?" Warren appeared beside Mr. Young and extended his hand to me. I ignored it and hugged him instead, aware of how familiar I was being, how I still had to bend down into his shoulder. He even smelled the same. "I'd say you've lived that mantra your entire life."

I watched Warren and his wife meander off the dance floor arm in arm. Her head was crooked against his neck, a similar stance to the one I used to take, but hers was different. Our comfort had been made by friendship, theirs by love. That knowledge alone was enough to confirm I'd been right to break our engagement. After all these years, after raising six children, she was still in love with him.

That's why she hadn't minded at all when he asked me to walk the treadmill again—a tradition I'd had no idea they were bringing back—leaving her alone in the crowd of mostly press and unattached elderly. *"Who would have thought we'd do this again, Dorothy?"* he'd asked as he'd offered his arm. I could see he wanted to say more. He felt sorry for me. Despite my fame, he knew I'd been abandoned, and though I hid it, it still hurt. We hadn't spoken in forty years, but he still knew me.

"It's a shame, Warren," I'd said at the end of the line, when I let go of his arm. *"If you were a woman we'd still be fast friends. I wish we hadn't lost touch."*

"I don't think that's true. Not really. The old place, those summers, seem far away. The people all seem far away too. It was another world."

He looked around then and so did I, at all the guests, at all the people with the right last names. We were supposed to know all of them, and though I suppose we did, this was a younger generation. The Kanes—Edith's daughter and her husband—were gathered at the end of the line beside the Van Pelts, who were visiting the Greenbrier for the first time. The Du Ponts, Vanderbilts, Astors, Phippses, Hardys, and Floyds were all here, honoring the tradition of the previous generation. Some of the elderly came out to pay tribute, though a few stood in the shadows scowling, likely cursing this new flashy hotel, wishing that the shabby old Greenbrier were still standing to separate the true lovers of this place from the people who'd only come to be seen. Of course, it was for the latter purpose that everyone had come in the first place, from the days of President Van Buren to the days of President Taft.

I stood alone now. Warren had retrieved me for a final dance to Judy Garland and Bing singing "Mine," but before that, I was occupied by acquaintances and strangers alike. I suppose I was—behind the duke and duchess and perhaps the Youngs—the belle of the ball. I could see one of the Du Pont men looking at me, pushing through the crowd on the other side of the dance floor. He looked glamorous. Everyone did in the light of my crystal chandelier, which washed the gowns and suits and crimson-and-rose draperies in a glittering gold.

"Dorothy." I felt someone brush my arm and turned to find Nora Thayer draped in a gray Grecian gown. Despite the success of the evening, I immediately felt hollow. Nora was one of Mother's younger friends from Tuxedo Park, a woman Mother had completely stopped conversing with after she continued to smudge my name in the community on account of my divorce and then my status as a businesswoman. *I wish she would stop telling people she grew up here. She is a disgrace, and we don't want anyone thinking we accept that sort.* I'd overheard Nora's sentiments myself once in the Tuxedo Club dining room and I'd never forgotten. She wasn't supposed to be here.

"Can I help you, Mrs. Thayer?" I never understood how I immediately lost my backbone when confronted with Tuxedo Park. I was overwhelmingly thankful for Mr. Young's check, relieved that I wouldn't have to return to the neighborhood in shame.

"I want to apologize," she said, pinching my elbow and

drawing me close. "I was horrible to you for years, mainly because I was scared. My daughter, Daniella, was so ambitious, so rebellious, and she always talked about you. I wanted grandchildren." She shrugged and then shook her head. "I know that doesn't make any sense, but it's why I campaigned against you for so long. A few months ago, we received the invitation to come here. When I saw your name on the invitation as the designer of this beautiful resort, I felt ashamed. I was wrong. My daughter is married now, with two children, but she's also a journalist. I'm proud of her and I'm proud of you. We all are."

Mrs. Thayer lifted her hand to reveal a single gold oak leaf pin, the symbol of membership in the Tuxedo Club. I'd never had one of my own. When I was old enough to be granted membership, I hadn't wanted it, and then in the midst of the divorce and my company's takeoff, I knew without doubt I wouldn't have been welcomed. Despite myself, my eyes filled. "Before we departed, I called a meeting of the members—your mother included—and I spoke about what I'd done and then the remarkable work you've done," she said. "I asked if the club would consider extending you an honorary membership, and they wholeheartedly agreed. We're lucky to have you, Dorothy. Even if we've hurt you too much and you'll not have us."

I lifted the gold pin from her hand and fastened it over my heart. The little whisper of doubt, the one that always told me I was an embarrassment, a disgrace, a failure, silenced.

"Everyone does things they're not proud of," I said as graciously as I could. "Life is about learning, Mrs. Thayer. It's about striving toward color and leaving the past in gray. I am thrilled and honored to accept the pin." I felt a lump in my throat but swallowed it down. I didn't want her to know how long and how deeply their judgment had affected me, and how meaningful it was to hear the words, *"I was wrong."*

"We'll look forward to your visits," she said. "I've taken up too much of your time. Have a wonderful evening, dear." She smiled and walked away. I watched her go, my fingers floating along the oak leaf pin, the same one my parents wore.

Meyer Davis struck up the next number, and from the first note, my arms prickled with goose bumps, despite the way my heavy kelly-green satin ball gown embroidered with crystal rosettes made me perspire. "The Blue Danube" was a popular waltz, arguably the most popular, but hearing it here, at the Greenbrier, was different. The pin, the song. All of it was too much.

I turned away from the stage, and my eyes filled with tears. I was surprised by it. I hadn't anticipated the emotion, especially during the celebration of my masterpiece. Crying wouldn't do. Especially now, especially here. I hastened out of the ballroom and through the hall of presidents to the north lobby. No one would be there, especially with all the excitement elsewhere, and I could be alone.

I stopped in the middle of the room and looked out at the night. Sentimentality engulfed me. This was the view I remembered. This was the view I'd seen the last time I'd danced "The Blue Danube." And I'd made this room softer than the others for that reason, because from this position I could remember bygone days on the lawn, bygone days at the old hotel.

A new age had dawned. New legacies would be made here, and they'd be made under the watchful eye of my designs. More than anyone else, I would be remembered here.

I straightened and smiled. I turned to the mirror above the

fireplace, hoping to ensure that my mascara hadn't run during my little touch with emotion. I ran my index finger beneath my eye to clear the bit of black, and the door to the veranda clicked open.

"Good evening," Mr. Mosley said. "This is quite a celebration. I'm proud of you."

"Thank you," I said. He looked sharp in his crimson bellman's suit. Though he was still officially retired, I'd had one made for him for the occasion. "Thank you for believing in me."

He nodded. "I always have." He walked toward me. "Do you have a moment? I have something for you."

"Of course," I said.

He smiled and withdrew a carved walnut letter box from behind his back.

"This is what I was looking for in the suite that day," Mr. Mosley said. He handed the box to me and I took it.

"I appreciate the thought, and the box is clearly a work of art, but I don't recognize it," I said. I turned it over in my hand. It was ornate, with a beveled oval glass window and a foliate scroll carving. Father had one like it once, but not this exact one.

"Open it," Mr. Mosley said.

I unlatched the small compartment, but the door wouldn't budge. I yanked harder, nearly dropping the letter box, and letters tumbled out, falling to the floor at my feet. Everything seemed to still and I could hear my heartbeat. The paper was yellowed, but his sketches on the back of the envelopes were still vivid, our handwriting also still clear. I placed the letter box on the tea table and leaned down to pick them up, feeling the tears rushing into my eyes again. There was the first one I wrote, the hateful, horrible, jealousy-infused scrawl, and his equally fiery reply.

"I thought I told you to burn these," I whispered. I'd asked

Mr. Mosley to get rid of Enzo's letters for me the day we left. I couldn't bear to burn them myself, but I couldn't bear to keep them either.

"I planned to," he said. "I honestly forgot for a few weeks. I'd stashed them in my desk drawer at my house, intending to set them ablaze that night, but I became quite busy with shutting everything up for the season, and then . . ." He trailed off.

My fingers hesitated on the last one, the one I'd received after he left me. But there was another. The paper wasn't aged like our others. It was white, the Greenbrier's emblem stamped on the envelope. I turned it over, sure the letter didn't belong, but my name was written on the front in a familiar hand, the same rhododendron blossom sketched below it. Everything fell away and I sat down on the tufted sofa, only vaguely aware of Bing's distant hollering about the raffle to win a diamond cigarette case.

I started to slide my finger under the seal when Mr. Mosley touched my arm.

"I tried to tell you," he said. "I wasn't supposed to tell you. In fact, I'm not supposed to tell you now, but, Mrs. Draper, I think you deserve to know."

"Know what?" I barely got out the words. Mr. Mosley sighed.

"Mr. Rossi worked here for years. After his engagement dissolved, Taft hired him on here, to serve as an interpreter for the government, and paid his parents' debt anonymously so Mr. Rossi felt he could remain. It was a classified post that required he keep many secrets, that required he let his uncle believe he'd been lost at sea, a position he held under the guise of working as an interpreter for foreign hotel guests."

I blinked. Taft had lied to me to protect Enzo's clandestine position.

"At first, some were skeptical. They thought he might be a spy, but Taft insisted he wasn't. He proved himself trustworthy." He sobered. "But when the second war came, he . . ."

I had a distinct urge to rise from my seat and shake Mr. Mosley. "Is he dead?" I asked bluntly.

"Oh no. I don't think so." He looked at the letter in my hand and then met my eyes. "I found the letter box in his old quarters. He lived in that cottage in Paradise Row. I gave him his letters back when I realized I still had them. I figured they were his and he could do with them what he wished." Mr. Mosley shook his head. "I want you to know I've never read them—then or now. Only saw the name on the envelope. Then we got the news you were coming." He lowered his voice. "I'm sworn to secrecy on this matter," he said. "I promised I'd not say anything about what transpired, which is why I've been giving you hints this whole time, hoping you'd catch on yourself."

"And when I didn't, you found it fitting to give me the letter box and encourage me to open it on my own."

"I figured that wouldn't be an overt breach of confidence," he said, grinning. "In truth, it's a miracle they're still here. I'm sure if he knew the exact time he was going, he would have taken them along. As it was, he wasn't able to pack his own things." He cleared his throat. "I'm afraid I've already said too much. Good evening, Mrs. Draper. I'll not break my promise, but I imagine that letter will tell you all you need to know."

He left, and I hesitated. Clearly Enzo had never expected me to find the letter. Even so, the temptation was too great. I tore what remained of the seal and extracted the page. It was dated July 6, 1942. It looked as if it had been written yesterday. Compared to the others, I suppose it had. Tears threatened when

I saw his handwriting and my name at the top, but I sniffed and blinked them away.

Dearest Dorothy,

It is quite futile, I'm afraid, that I'm writing you a letter. I know you'll never see it, but I suppose that's all right by me. I simply need to talk to someone, and since I'm afraid my situation has made my journey a solitary one, you're the only one I can tell. I've loved you all this time. I can say that clearly, knowing I'm in no danger of being found out.

I swallowed, willing my heart to slow.

I've kept track of you through the years in the papers. When you got engaged, Taft allowed me leave to find you, so long as I didn't mention my post. I got all the way to the gates of Tuxedo Park. I was asked who I was visiting and when I said your name, the attendant brightened. He said that you had just been engaged and were the happiest he'd ever seen you, that he'd known you your whole life. I didn't want to let you go, but I remembered how much we'd hurt each other before and I couldn't bear to ruin your life. So I left. And I've regretted it since.

When I read of your divorce, I silently rejoiced. I asked FDR permission to write to you, to tell you where I was and that I still hadn't stopped loving you. I thought perhaps he would be obliging because he knew you—I know your husband was his attending physician for a time—and perhaps he was and you didn't want to see me, but most of the time I think I know better. After all these years, I think you would find me if you could. I think you would have at least written back. And then there are times when I think you received my letter and decided to let us lie. It's unrealistic to think we could have a life together. People tend not to change, and I am always reminded that I decided long ago to follow ambition instead of love. I think I've made a mistake in that, but it seems that perhaps you've done the same thing and found it was the right choice. I'm not surprised at your success. And to think—you've made a living painting walls pink. I admit I am surprised at that.

A week ago, Justice Jackson appeared in my office. That in itself wasn't strange. The cabinet, or a few members here or there, often meet in the suite, but from the moment he got there, I knew something was amiss. He refused scotch—he never does—and paced despite repeated requests that he sit. Finally, he told me that despite my thirty-three years of service, in which I've kept every national secret, including the secrecy of my post, I'm to be interned with the enemy Italians at the Greenbrier and shipped back to Italy spontaneously, whenever passage is approved. It could be days or months.

I could barely breathe. He wasn't dead. He'd loved me all this time. At once, it came back to me, Mr. Taft's urging me to visit the Greenbrier after I'd asked after Enzo. He'd said something about being sure my heart would be healed anew if I went. He'd been trying to tell me.

I told him I was no longer an Italian citizen, that I'd sworn my allegiance to my country on June 10, 1909, and that the record would be at the Lewisburg Courthouse, but he shook his head and simply barked, *"There's no record."* I told him that was impossible, but he would not budge. *"It's not that I don't believe you,"* he said, *"but the court seems to have traded many of their records for new paper over the years. Without a record of your citizenship, we cannot keep you. You understand it's a risk."* I wish you'd been with me in that moment. It was my weakest. I argued him. I told him that I never would have been hired originally by Taft if I wasn't trustworthy. I'd served as translator, as interpreter for six presidents. Just writing that makes me wonder if I should be so wounded. After all, I've had a good run of things. After it was clear Helen and I were ill-matched, Taft still showed me incredible kindness. He knew how skilled I was with languages and how dedicated I was to promises—in fact, I was the one who fought Helen to remain engaged solely because I'd sworn to her.

I didn't enjoy the mention of Helen. I could still see their arms around each other. The sting of his intentions if I didn't accept him right away still felt like a barb in my heart. I'd tried to forget the way I felt when I heard of their engagement, but that sort of hurt never fully goes away. I wondered if she'd known where he was all along. Given Mr. Taft's sense of patriotism and the way he took his oath to office seriously, I doubted it, and yet it gnawed at me all the same.

For love, proposing to Helen was a foolish idea. If love was all I was after, I would have waited for you my whole life if that's what it took. But, knowing her, knowing President Taft, did award me a life of purpose. I suppose that is really all I wanted. I'm rambling on, but does it really matter? This isn't a real letter, and I'm not writing to you, really, my dearest Dorothy. Do you know your kisses are still with me? I can still feel them on my mouth. I loved you with a fire that nearly eclipsed all my senses, and I think you loved me the same. People don't kiss like that unless their souls are already dancing.

I ran my hands over his words, remembering. Even in the most passionate moments between Dan and me, even with all my lovers, even Lee, none compared to the intoxication of Enzo.

When I think of that, I think maybe I've wasted time. I wonder if I should have resigned my post the moment I found out about your divorce. Would you have given up your company in New York to live here with me? Perhaps. I doubt it. To everyone else here, I'm simply a translator for foreign guests, and that's what I would have had to tell you too. It would hardly be a post worthy of the famed Dorothy Tuckerman Draper.

It's all too late now. I'm to be sent back to Italy at age fifty-five. My parents and my uncle are dead. I don't know what I'll do or where I'll go. Will anyone hire me? I hope so. I want to say that I know I'll return, but that's unlikely. Thirty-three years of allegiance eclipsed by the absence of my name on a ledger. I should have filed with a federal court, but I was working here. I never thought something this horrible could happen. It's unbelievable. Regardless of my best intentions, I'm a prisoner now, a man lumped in with the likes of men who support the abhorrent Nazis. Your father was right all those years ago. Being with me would only end in ruin.

I hope you're safe up there, Dorothy. I hope despite your divorce, you're happy. I hope your children are as fiery and lovely as their mother. I hope you have known, deep down, that I've never stopped loving you, just as I know you've never stopped loving me.

Yours,

Enzo

I folded the note, a mix of anger and melancholy bubbling in my chest. Two rooms over, Meyer Davis was playing one of his old hits, "Look What You've Done to Me," and it seemed quite appropriate given the way I was feeling. Frank Roosevelt had never given me Enzo's letter, and he'd declined to come to his rescue, to prevent his being sent away. Frank had been a better man than to send another to do his dirty work. I was incensed by the way Enzo had been treated. I wondered how much of it had to do with me. Letting on that he was in love with the former wife of one of Frank's good friends likely hadn't won Enzo to his side, but surely Frank had known that Dan had left *me*. Then again, perhaps Frank's sending Justice Jackson truly wasn't personal. The country had been in the middle of a war, and he likely wasn't able to leave Washington. I still couldn't understand why he hadn't given me the letter. The only thing I could think was that he'd wanted Dan and me to reconcile. Eleanor and Frank had been our dearest friends, after all, and it was never quite the same after our divorce.

I closed my eyes and clutched the paper in my hand. Enzo had been alone, without anyone. The thought crushed me. How I wished, even for those few days, that I'd been with him. I suppose I had been, really. He'd had someone to write, someone to love.

He still loved me. I'd wondered for so long, and now that it was confirmed, an urgency to find him welled inside of me. Perhaps someone knew where he was.

And then what? We would marry, and I would leave my company behind to become a wife again? It would be a more difficult road than I wanted to imagine. Reality struck my mind, and I opened my eyes to the room. It was lovely, truly, the design soothing even at this hour.

If I'd come here and found him, if he'd been here when I arrived, it would have been fate. But he was gone, and I didn't know if he'd ever return. Suddenly, all the feelings I'd felt over the years—the heartache, the yearning—intensified. I took a deep breath to settle. I would try to find him. We could try to figure a life if I did.

But even if I never saw him again, at the end of things, I'd been the love of his life and he'd been mine. I closed my eyes to remember the first time I saw him. I could feel the air shift as all the women stared. He had disrupted dinner. He'd been that handsome. I had no doubt he still was.

I folded the notes carefully and placed them back in the letter box. The love of our lives wasn't each other. I shook my head at the thought, then realized it was the truth. He knew I couldn't abandon my company. It was the same reason he'd chosen secrecy and living at the Greenbrier over pursuing me. This place, this job, had been his life. Once again, fury overtook me, and I felt my face burn. He couldn't remain in exile. I wouldn't allow it. Then again, I wondered if he'd even want to return to the United States after he'd been treated this way.

"Excuse me, Mrs. Draper."

I looked up to see James Lane Barnes, editor of *Decorative*

Furnisher, a man I knew only because Jean read the magazine religiously and had encouraged him to interview me upon the opening of Arrowhead Springs.

"I didn't obtain an appointment, but I was hoping to catch you for a private word."

"Of course," I said, straightening.

"This hotel is magnificent. Even more spectacular than Arrowhead Springs—if you'll allow me to speak candidly. Word of this will spread to Washington, California, Europe," he said.

His mention of Washington made me think of Truman.

Surely Truman would know about Enzo. I would write him personally. If that didn't work, I'd have Eleanor deliver another letter and another until he did something. In the meantime, I'd write to the mayor of Villaputzu. It was a small enough town. If Enzo had returned there, surely they would know it.

"I hope I didn't offend you, Mrs. Draper," he said. "It's just that I enjoy a good party, and this is the best I've been to in my whole life. You've done a remarkable job."

I smiled. "No offense taken whatsoever," I said. "Thank you."

"Now, about that blockbuster quote," he said, almost apologetically.

He thought it was a chore, but this was what I lived for. In the distance, I could hear laughter and shouts as the duke took to the stage with Meyer Davis. I saw the ghosts, the long-gone faces of those I'd known before who had loved this place. They were smiling. The Greenbrier's spirit would live on. These were memories that would go down in history books, memories made within walls clothed by me. This whole place had been made on my vision, on my dream. Despite Enzo, despite Dan, despite the Depression or the wars, I'd made it.

"I saw an apparition the first night," I said, leaning in to Mr. Barnes, who immediately sat down and tilted toward me, his pencil scribbling in a small notebook he'd extracted from his tuxedo pocket. "At first it gave me quite a fright, until I noticed it was only Van Buren."

"Martin Van Buren, the former president?" Mr. Barnes whispered, almost speechless. Ghost stories weren't often well received. Ben Sonnenberg would positively love me for this.

"One and the same. He looked me square in the eye and said, 'Romance and rhododendron must be the theme.'"

Mr. Barnes's eyes widened, and the thrill engulfed me. At once, I understood Enzo, I understood Dan, because I was one of them. Where love left one desperate and uncertain, ambition empowered and strengthened.

"Did you ever think as a young girl that you'd be sitting here talking of seeing the famed President Van Buren, surrounded by halls and halls and rooms and rooms boasting your designs, and celebrities doing the same?"

He looked at me as though the magnitude of what I'd accomplished had only just dawned on him.

"Of course," I lied. "How else does one become Dorothy Draper?"

Epilogue

NOVEMBER 18, 1961

P erhaps we should use pomegranate for the drapes?"

I glanced over at the young man, Carleton, our new design assistant, and set down the piece of crystal I was holding. Leon, being occupied, had sent him to the Greenbrier with me this time—I was to decorate a room fit for white-glove dinners and corporate meetings alike—and I had to admit I enjoyed his company. Possibly better than Leon's.

"Pomegranate you say?" I asked.

I eyed the glass doors fashioned like windows that led out into a wide hallway. A tall man with ebony hair in a tailored blue suit wandered past and my hands reflexively grasped the gold top of my cane as though I was about to go after him.

"It would echo the look found in the cameo ballroom, but only slightly, only enough to give a nod to the ballroom's elegance and mimic the same timelessness here," Carleton said, but I barely heard him.

I forced my eyes away from the man in the hall who looked like Enzo and turned to glance at the mirrored double doors on the opposite side of the room where the drapes would reside. I realized my error as I saw my reflection in the glass. I was a seventy-year-old woman now, and Enzo wouldn't look like the young man I remembered. It was getting more difficult to understand that recently. I couldn't figure why. All I knew was that every time I came by the Greenbrier to wander the halls and touch up, I looked for him. I'd hoped, since the night I came across his letter, that fate would reunite us, at least for a moment. But it seemed as time went on that it simply wasn't to be. Perhaps it was best. Perhaps the magic would be gone, and God knew that if we saw each other again it would only dampen the fantasy we'd both hung on to all these years. Despite Truman's best efforts and my own, we'd never found him. Not even a trace. Truman swore Enzo was hiding, that he was so hurt by his treatment that he didn't want to be sought out. Recently, I'd started to believe he was right.

"I don't recall a pomegranate print, but I suppose . . ."

I started to give myself away, to say that I'd been forgetting about everything as of late, but stopped just in time. No one in my employ should know that. It would only discount my authority.

"I thought perhaps I could draw something up," Carleton said. He *did* have a natural knack for art. I'd seen his sketches back in New York, and they were impressive. "Pomegranate in color, of course, but also an embroidery overlay of the fruit on the material."

"I like it," I said, plucking another crystal sample from the tall table in front of me. I turned it over in my hand and then pinched the top of it, holding it up to the light. The crystal had to be just so. The Greenbrier was willing to pay $120,000 for the four chandeliers I was proposing, and they had to be worth every penny.

"I wonder what it's like to dance here at the Greenbrier in your brilliant cameo ballroom. There's such a sense of romance. It must be awfully easy to fall in love."

I glanced at him, but his attention was on his sketchbook. He was a handsome young man with high, chiseled cheekbones and a commanding presence. Even now, on a typical workday, he wore a fine-fitting Christian Dior tweed suit, with a brilliant kelly-green silk scarf fashioned like a tie. He had ingenuity—that was clear even in his choice of dress. And had he lived earlier, had God chosen to place him at the Greenbrier in 1908, he would have fit in perfectly.

"It is," I said. "It's quite easy to fall in love with this place."

I sighed. I was getting softer in my older age. I entertained talk of feelings and whimsy now, where even a year ago I would have steered the conversation back to the room at hand.

"It's magical," he said. "Every time I've had the opportunity to visit, I feel the history and the excitement and the future yet to come. I'm glad to be here, Mrs. Draper. I feel quite at home."

I glanced out the glass doors, past the hall, and through the windows to the lawn. From here I couldn't see the debris left over from the new construction—an enormous addition they were calling the West Virginia Wing. Most of the leaves had fallen by now, and the view of the mountains through the trees was spectacular. Just down the hill to the left was Hawley House. It seemed like yesterday.

Leon had always respected the Greenbrier because I loved

it, because it was my pet project, but I wasn't sure that he felt the same way I did. I needed someone who felt this place in their heart, who would dream of it when they were away. Though Carleton had only just become acquainted with the Greenbrier, he spoke of it as I did.

"I have a favor to ask," I said.

Carleton looked up and nodded. "Anything. I'm sorry about the Parisian sconces. They should have been in by now," he said.

I shook my head, unconcerned. We'd secured sconces—delicate gilded pieces adorned with musical instruments—for the walls between the mirrored doors from a fallen Parisian manor home, but European timeliness was different than ours. It was something I'd learned to live with.

"It's all right," I said. "But that's not what I wanted to discuss."

He closed his sketchbook, waiting.

"I want you to be involved with all of our projects here at the Greenbrier."

Carleton smiled, his face brightening.

"I know that you were once a teacher and a Spanish major too. I forgive you for that," I said.

He chuckled. "Thank you."

"But you were born to do this, to design. Especially here," I said. "You're not afraid of color and you're not afraid of bucking convention."

"That, I'm not," he said, tucking his sketchbook under his arm.

"It's not only that," I said. "I . . ." I knew what I wanted to say, but hesitated. It sounded too much like a farewell address, and I wasn't ready to let go quite yet. Regardless, something was amiss with me. I knew it deep in my soul, and I couldn't risk the Greenbrier withering without me.

"It's going to sound rather absurd, but this place is the love of my life. At first I thought it was because I'd met my first love here, and later I thought my affection a result of the fame it won me, but now I realize that the Greenbrier is my heart. It's where memories, love, ambition, success all merge."

My recollections flipped swiftly through my mind like photo frames. I cleared my throat and readjusted my tone to reflect the businesswoman I was instead of the pleading puddle I was becoming. "You're the only one who has ever articulated any feeling for it."

"You have my word that I'll treasure it, Mrs. Draper. I'll watch over it for you."

To anyone else the conversation would sound silly, as though the Greenbrier was my child and I was asking him to adopt. Well, in truth, it was.

"Good," I said simply. I turned my back on him to pluck another crystal sample from the tabletop. "It'll be this one, the Swiss."

"I was only thinking," Carleton said, taking the sample from my hand, "perhaps we should consider a permanent office here down the road. You know, to more easily keep an eye on things."

I nodded and kept quiet, lest the emotion give way to tears.

"We'll have a home here," he continued. "That way we'll ensure that not a smidge of Dorothy Draper will ever be erased from these walls."

"Yes," I said. "Yes. That'll do."

I wiped my eyes and grasped another crystal to distract myself from crying. I held it toward the natural light coming in from the glass doors, and then my fingers fumbled, the dropped glass pinging as it hit the others. A man was standing there, in the hall, looking at me. My world stopped. Despite the wrinkles, despite the age, I could see the square set of his jaw, the crystal-blue eyes, the smile that made my heart race. I was vaguely aware of Carleton rushing to my side, but then the door opened. The man's eyes filled with tears and he dropped his leather briefcase.

"*Mio angelo*," he breathed.

I blinked, sure I was seeing things again. But then I walked toward him. I was trembling. If he turned out to be an apparition, so be it.

"Enzo?" I reached to touch his face and his hand curled hard around mine. My throat tightened, and before I could stop myself, I started to sob. I felt the warmth of his tears on my fingers and mine on my cheeks. "What are you doing here? Where have you been? I had them look everywhere."

He drew me against him, and I let my head drop to his chest. For a moment, I was young again, standing in the springhouse, asking him to stay.

"President Kennedy's men found me in a small town in Ireland and begged me to come back. They said they needed me immediately. I didn't want to come, but something drew me here. I didn't know it was you. I didn't know I'd find you." His fingers brushed my hair, my ears, and then stilled as he held me. "I'm so proud of you. I've loved you for my whole life as much as I did that summer, Dorothy." He wanted to say more, I could tell, but emotion choked his voice.

"It's been fifty-three years. I've never stopped loving you, Enzo. I've never stopped." I lifted my head to look at him. He was still breathtakingly handsome. I could feel my heart pounding, my hands shaking, and then his lips found mine. I held on to him, deepening the kiss, sure that I would never let him go. At once, all of the heartache, all of the failures, all of the disappointments fell away, dissolving in the moment. None of it mattered anymore. Nothing mattered but this.

"Forgive me," he whispered against my mouth. "I should have waited."

Author's Note

Hi, dear readers!

First of all, I want to say that if you are like me and are sometimes tempted to read notes like this ahead of the story, resist! This note contains lots of spoilers.

If you're reading because you've come to the end of the story, thank you so much for going on this journey with me. I hope you've fallen in love with The Greenbrier and Dorothy Draper. They are a fabulous, beautiful pair.

Now for the stuff you'd like to know.

West Virginia runs deep in my blood. My family has lived there for nine generations, and though I didn't actually grow up in the state, it's my second home. I spent every Christmas until 2019 in Charleston, my family has owned a home at Flat Top Lake near Beckley for five generations, and I'm a graduate of Marshall University—Go, Herd! I am absolutely in love with West Virginia. In my opinion, it is by far the most beautiful state in the nation.

I grew up hearing stories of past generations' visits to the Greenbrier and have countless treasured memories there myself.

Four years ago, while visiting with my family, I was sitting in the famed Victorian Writing Room watching my children write letters, listening to my grandpa recount his summer home from Duke University installing a fire-alarm system in the hotel, when I decided I wanted to write a book set there. From that point on, I read everything I could find about the resort's nearly two-hundred-and-fifty-year history—books, newspaper archives, and magazine articles—and bugged the fabulous Greenbrier historian, Dr. Robert Conte, when I wanted to know more.

One of my favorite things about the Greenbrier has always been Dorothy Draper's designs. The bright, playful colors set the stage for fun and laughter and joy—everything one hopes for when thinking back on fond memories. As I researched, I started to discover how intrinsically linked the legacies of Dorothy Draper and the Greenbrier were. In many ways, though they were both already famed in their own right, Dorothy Draper made the Greenbrier a crown jewel, and the Greenbrier made Dorothy Draper immortal. It was a love story I couldn't resist telling, though it would, in some ways, be a challenge. In the novel, both Dorothy and the Greenbrier serve as main characters. I tried to be as accurate to their histories as I could while still telling a compelling story.

From the Greenbrier's inception, it has been a place for "royals" to congregate, the sort that includes presidents and congressmen and princes and princesses and industrialists and celebrities. At the turn of the twentieth century, that set included Gilded Age barons and their families, families like Dorothy's. I wondered one day early in research if perhaps she'd visited the resort as a young woman. I thought if she had, it would serve to explain the way I'd always sensed that the Greenbrier was more than a project to her. It was her pet; it was personal. I emailed Dr. Conte to inquire about Dorothy visiting early in her life, and he kindly asked Mr. Carleton Varney, who replied that it was possible but he wasn't sure. The prospect spurred my imagination. I began to wonder if perhaps something that occurred at the Greenbrier could have ignited the possibility of Dorothy's later empire—that perhaps her innate skills manifested and were noticed during that visit, or that perhaps a love she had as a young woman, a love who saw something great in her, had propelled her to build her legacy.

One of the many interesting things about Dorothy Draper's life is that business wasn't at all a likely future for her. It was almost unheard of to go from heiress to CEO because it was seen as improper, almost disgraceful, at the time. I have always thought that something monumental must have occurred to make this leap possible, and the 1908 section of the book was born out of this thought. In truth, Dorothy's shift from socialite to mogul was likely a result of her parents' influence and her natural talent. Her parents were some of the original house flippers—that is, if your houses were Gilded Age mansions and you did the designing and selling for fun and not for the money. The Tuckermans built and outfitted three homes in Tuxedo Park—a cottage and two mansions—and Dorothy herself engaged in the same sort of activity in New York City after her marriage to Dan. I suppose that's truly where people began to notice her ingenuity—especially in her Upside-Down House project. Her peers wanted a piece of her genius, so they asked to buy her homes. Later, in the early 1930s, she switched to doing commercial projects, where there were generally fewer noses in her work.

Despite the 1908 section being based on conjecture with regard to Dorothy's character, the 1908 season itself is as accurate as I could make it with regard to the history of the Greenbrier. A woman from Louisville, Kentucky, Miss Aubin McDowell, published a booklet about the Centennial season detailing all of the day-to-day activities and names of guests. The particulars listed in the booklet were used to frame the story. Enzo and Warren are both fictional characters, though men like them would have been found at the Greenbrier that season. I fashioned Enzo's character in particular after the foreign diplomats who vacationed at the Greenbrier, the Greenbrier's important and storied political past, as well as the rumor that Dorothy had a relationship with a race car driver at one point. The Tafts were actual guests at the resort during that season, as were the Phinizys and others, though of course I manufactured some attachments and romances between the guests. The Kanes, like the Tuckermans, may have visited at some point but were not listed in the booklet as attending in the 1908 season. I included the Kanes primarily because they were the Tuckermans' neighbors in Tuxedo Park, and their attendance would allow for many references to their home, grounding the reader in Dorothy's "real life."

In the 1946 section, I tried to stay as close to Dorothy's actual schedule, decorating process, and life circumstances at the time as I could, though I am absolutely certain I did not get it all right. For instance, the bird cage chandelier Mrs. Young points out during the tea was actually created by Dorothy for a later project, the cafe at the Metropolitan Museum of Art. Some particulars, and certainly process depth, got swept up in the forward movement of the story. The actual decorating process for a resort this substantial could be a book in itself—and is! See below for my further reading recommendations. I made some concessions to the timeline for the sake of the narrative. For instance, Dorothy's first visit to view the abandoned Greenbrier was in December, and our story begins in October.

Lee is fictional, based on various love affairs Dorothy had after her divorce. The idea that her company was teetering on bankruptcy was also exaggerated for the story, though it's known that she was sometimes slighted by employers and had to dip into her own personal funds at times.

The most notable piece of fiction in the forties section of the story is the secret presidential meeting space. Throughout its history, the resort has been an important gathering location for political happenings, and I wanted to nod to the future construction of the congressional bunker. Mr. Mosley, though a fictional character, is named for the legendary Greenbrier ambassador Frank Mosley, who began working at the Greenbrier in 1958. The grand reopening party was as accurate as I could make it, based on true events from the actual party, including a list of the many celebrities who crowded the halls.

The epilogue serves of course to reunite Dorothy and Enzo, but also to nod to the inimitable Carleton Varney, Dorothy Draper's protégé and current president of Dorothy Draper & Company, who has decorated the Greenbrier for the last sixty-one years. As much as one can't think of the Greenbrier without thinking of Dorothy Draper, one also can't think of the Greenbrier without thinking of Carleton Varney. A true Greenbrier love story wouldn't be complete without the three of them together somehow. I read somewhere that his first decorating venture at the Greenbrier was the Crystal Ballroom, so of course I had to set the epilogue there.

I believe that any work of historical fiction sets out to immerse the reader in an era they will never be able to experience in their own lives, to let them travel back in order to really feel the time and the place and the people. My ultimate goal with this story was for readers to grasp the spirit of Dorothy Draper and the Greenbrier, and to know them in a new, personal way.

Recommended Further Reading

Conte, Robert. *The History of the Greenbrier.* Missoula, MT: Pictorial Histories Publishing Co., 1989.

Draper, Dorothy. *Decorating Is Fun!* Garden City, NY: Doubleday, Doran & Company, Inc., 1939.

Draper, Dorothy. *Entertaining Is Fun!* Garden City, NY: Doubleday, Doran & Company, Inc., 1941.

Olcott, William. *The Greenbrier Heritage.* Philadelphia: Arndt, Preston, Chapin, Lamb & Keen, Inc., 1976.

Varney, Carleton. *In the Pink: Dorothy Draper, America's Most Fabulous Decorator.* New York: Pointed Leaf Press, 2012.

Varney, Carleton. *The Draper Touch–Deluxe Edition: The High Life and High Style of Dorothy Draper.* Palm Beach: Shannongrove Press, 2022.

Varney, Carleton. *Romance and Rhododendrons.* New York: Shannongrove Press, 2020.

Acknowledgments

First and always, I will praise God for the gift of creativity and the love of storytelling. He's the best storyteller I know, and I'm forever thankful that His hand is guiding my real-life story.

Thanks to my parents, Lynn and Fred, for always encouraging me—even when I wanted to sell my *Titanic* magazine door-to-door—and listening to me explain my story ideas with interest—even when they're still super jumbled and don't really make sense. Thanks for teaching me how to live a joy-filled, colorful life, and thanks for always being up for matching me in our Dorothy Draper leggings, Mom!

Thanks to my Wilkerson/Ballard family for the memories of our annual trips to the Greenbrier. I love you, Jed, Hannah, Reece, Gran, Gramps (I miss you!), Momma Sandra, Daddy Tom (I miss you too!), Uncle Jim, Uncle John, Aunt Cindy, Bill, Samantha, Jamie, Jancis, and Porter. Can't wait to play the penny slots and fall over on ice skates with all of you again this year!

To my Callaway family—Beth, Josh, Mady, Elise, Dianna, Johnny, and Jeremy—thanks for the support and the laughs and the memories mostly set in the West Virginia hills.

ACKNOWLEDGMENTS

Thanks to Maggie for being the best friend who ever lived, even when I make you wander along the side of a mountain looking for a long-gone path and bore you with historical details on our girls' weekends.

To my Authors Out of Carolina friends—Marybeth Whalen, Kim Wright, and Erika Montgomery—thank you for being there. I'm so thankful to walk this crazy publishing path alongside you.

Thanks to Cheyenne Campbell, Sarah Henning, Kimberly Brock, and Meredith Jaeger for the encouragement and the friendship and my favorite books.

To my Marshall BFFs, my Avondale girls, and my Park Crossing forever friends, thank you for the laughs and the smiles and the prayers and the gift of true friends to walk beside.

Thank you to my church family at Avondale Presbyterian Church. I'm so blessed to be a part of a community that loves like Jesus.

Thanks to Dr. Robert Conte for letting me bug you with endless emails and questions about the Greenbrier. This book wouldn't have been possible without you.

To the team at Carleton Varney / Dorothy Draper & Company—thank you for the inspiration and for keeping everyone smiling with your designs.

Thanks to my agent, Kate McKean, for your unwavering support, keen eye, and belief in this story. Thankful for you!

To my editors, Amanda Bostic and Kimberly Carlton—from the moment we spoke, I knew we were kindred spirits. Thank you for making this story come to life.

Thank you to the phenomenally talented team at Harper Muse—Margaret Kercher, Kerri Potts, Nekasha Pratt, Erin

Healy, Becky Monds, Laura Wheeler, Jodi Hughes, Caitlin Halstead, Savannah Summers, LaChelle Washington, and Patrick Aprea—I am so fortunate to find my book in such amazing hands.

Thanks to the many independent bookstores, bookstagrammers, book clubbers, bloggers, and readers who have championed my stories. Your support is so incredibly important. Please know how much I love and appreciate you!

Finally, and *so* importantly, *thank you* to my little family: John, Alevia, and John, I love you more than you will ever know. Thanks for painting my life in color.

Discussion Questions

1. *The Grand Design*'s earlier timeline is set in 1908, at the end of the Gilded Age, a time period I love because social boundaries and norms were on the cusp of great change. What did you enjoy about this period? What do you dislike about this period?
2. Like all of us, Dorothy had to fight deeply seeded insecurities throughout her life and was ultimately able to (mostly) rise above them. What surprised you most about her struggles and triumphs? Can you associate with her journey?
3. *The Grand Design* has a large cast of principal and supporting characters. Who did you most connect with and why?
4. How does The Greenbrier serve as both a character and a metaphor for Dorothy's life?
5. Even in the 1940s portion of the story, female business owners were rare and divorce was almost always considered the woman's fault. Why were these views

common during this time in history? Do you think these issues have been settled, or do you think they're still prevalent today?

6. The true connection between Dorothy and Enzo started because of their mutual desire to shake the shackles of their pasts and win freedom. Do you believe they both ultimately achieved what they were looking for? Why or why not?

7. Societal expectations always seem to follow Dorothy like a shadow. Discuss the influence of these expectations on her decisions. Have peers or societal pressures ever affected the decisions you've made? Have you ever decided to go against the grain or walk a different path than what was expected of you? What was the outcome?

8. The structure of the book—alternating between past and present—is used to create tension. In what ways does the past interfere with the present?

9. Dorothy's relationship with The Greenbrier is deep and important. Do you have a place like this? If so, what has made it so special to you?

10. Dorothy's love interests—Enzo, Warren, and Lee—are very different yet she finds honorable characteristics in each. If you were to go on a date with one of them, who would you choose and why?

11. Later in life, Dorothy finds that her closest family isn't necessarily her actual family or even her friends, but her employees—the family she chose herself. Have you ever found family with people who aren't related to you? If so, what made these relationships vital to

you, and why do you think they were important to Dorothy?

12. If you could attend one event detailed in the book, which would you choose and why?

13. The story is told against the backdrop of several important historical events—the Gilded Age, the World Wars, and the Depression. How do these events impact the characters? Could this story have been set in another time?

14. Share a favorite quote from the book. Why did this quote stand out to you?

15. If you could read this same story from another person's point of view, who's would you choose?

About the Author

Photo by Laura J. Meier Photography

Joy Callaway is the author of *The Fifth Avenue Artists Society*, *Secret Sisters*, and *The Grand Design*. She holds a BA in journalism and public relations from Marshall University and an MMC from the University of South Carolina. She resides in Charlotte, North Carolina, with her husband, John, and her children, Alevia and John.

joycallaway.com
Instagram: @joywcal
Facebook: @JoyCallawayAuthor